I0784871

A WITCH IS BORN

THE ADVENTURES OF CASSANDRA RHO

- BOOK ONE -

PHILLIP MARTIN

A WITCH IS BORN
THE ADVENTURES OF CASSANDRA RHO
BOOK ONE

Map art prepared by Shaun Carroll.
Cover design by Teddi Black Design.
Formatting by Author Cultivation.

Second Edition

This is a work of fiction. All of the characters, names, incidents, organizations, and dialogue in this novel are either the products of the author's imagination or are used fictitiously.

ISBN 979-8-9873344-0-9

I dedicate this book to all of those who have suffered bullying. Stay strong, and may the ravens forever heed your call.

CONTENTS

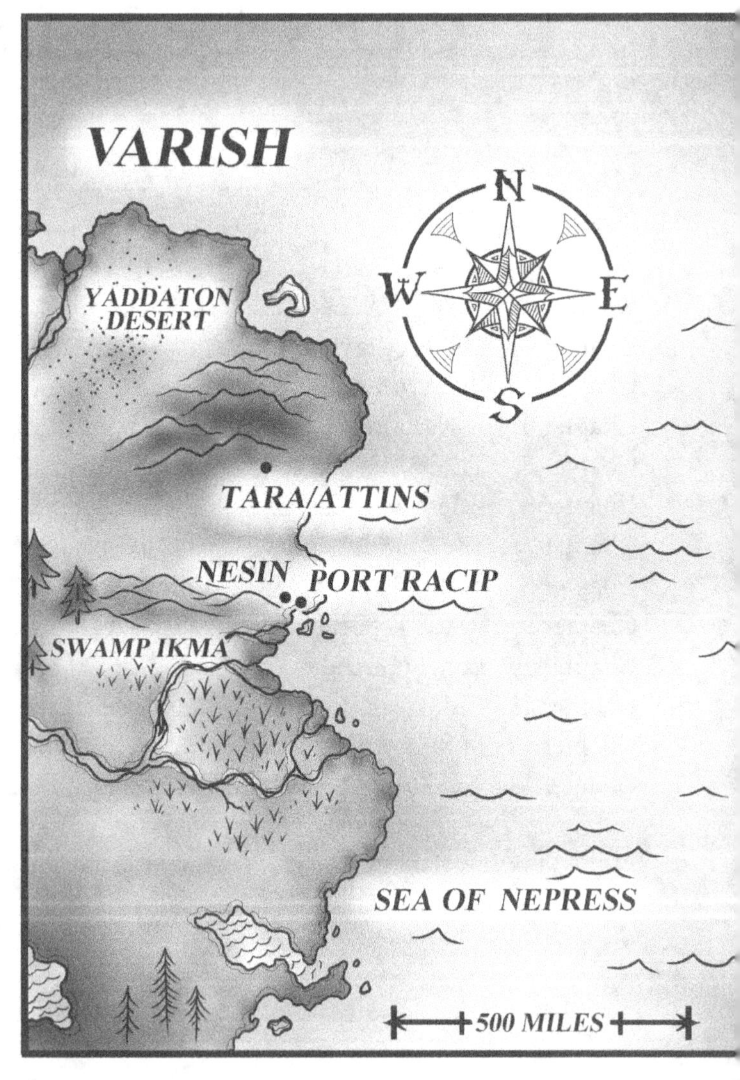

VARISH
YADDATON DESERT
TARA/ATTINS
NESIN
PORT RACIP
SWAMP IKMA
SEA OF NEPRESS
N
W
E
S
500 MILES

EA OF NEPRESS
LAKE ELFKIND
GODHOMME
PELESEA
NOVAFONTERA
DARO'S WOODS
TORLIA
OLDORBURG
FARMER'S STOP
MECCA-LORAINE

PROLOGUE

I T WAS A STORMY FALL NIGHT WHEN UNIS RHO HEARD A LOUD knock on the Oldorburg Orphanage door. She was just about to turn in, having completed her nightly chores, and was locking the front door when a sound had her nearly dropping her candleholder. It startled her so badly that she stood paralyzed for many moments, just staring at the door. It was more of a thump, as if someone had hit the door instead of knocked. She snapped out of her paralysis when she heard a baby crying right outside.

Once she summoned the courage to open the door, the wind blew in and immediately snuffed out her lone candle. It lasted but a few seconds, then relented, leaving her in the dark. She could see a large basket at the doorstep, covered with a blanket, and could hear a baby's cry within. Again, fear found a hold on her, and she stood there, gazing out into the front yard of the orphanage. It was dark and rainy, with strong gusts of wind, and only the occasional lightning strike made the yard visible for brief moments at a time. She looked around the courtyard for signs of the person who'd delivered such a precious item but found no one. Finally, however, she could *feel* something.

Something or someone was out there in the darkness, and it made the hairs on her neck stand on end. She froze there for quite a long time, not daring to pull her eyes away from the yard. The strange presence felt otherworldly and dangerous. She eventually shook the fear enough to retrieve the basket and bring it inside. Once there, she fastened the lock on the door and peered through the window to make sure one final time that no one was there.

After calming herself and relighting the candle, she unwrapped the basket to find two baby girls inside. She fell in love immediately with them, determining that they were only a few days old. They were hungry, and she quickly fed them some fresh milk to quiet them. As she rocked the newborn babies to sleep, she kept one eye on the door, waiting for another knock. It never came, and as soon as the girls were sound asleep, she quickly made her way upstairs to her quarters. She had the two babies sleep with her that night, somehow feeling safer with them beside her.

The next day, she reported the delivery to Ronnis D'Breeth, the orphanage administrator and architect. Since Unis could not prove the girls' kinship otherwise, the orphanage recorded the babies as twins. Their date of birth was estimated to be two days before their arrival. Also, since they'd come without names, Unis was allowed to name them. They took her surname of Rho, and she called them Cassandra and Kessi. She never discovered their origin and never mentioned the unusual presence she felt that night. However, because of that feeling, she knew they were somehow important and different.

She raised the girls as if they were her own, and the first five years were bliss. She taught them to read and write, and she showed them the proper etiquette for social events and how to show empathy for other living beings. The girls learned quickly, and their intelligence exceeded anything Unis had ever experienced in her years at the orphanage. Then something happened that would significantly affect them all— something that would give birth to a children's nursery rhyme called "Cassandra and the Wolves." This event devastated young Cassandra and started her down a path of mysteries and controversies that would last her lifetime. The following event is how the nursery rhyme was born.

One fateful evening, when the girls were five years old, Unis decided to take them on a small field trip to the neighboring woods just outside town. Since it was their first time out of the town limits, the girls were very excited. Unis enjoyed watching them interact with nature. They found signs of rabbits, squirrels, and deer, and the girls seemed to absorb the sights with great interest. She smiled as a proud mother might, watching the two explore the woods, eagerly finding wildlife and excitedly showing each other their various discoveries. They spent a long while in the beautiful natural theater until the light began to wane. Unis looked back toward the town as the sun set and saw that it was only a few hundred yards away. However, the town guards were lighting the lanterns on the main street, and soon it would be too dark to see in the woods.

Something about that fact did not sit well with her. She frequently dreamed of a dark man with no face who came to the orphanage, killed her, and took the girls. It was a horrible dream and one that she never relayed to anyone. After that dream, she would awaken with the same uneasiness as when she had found the girls on the doorstep. That feeling raced back to her then. She panicked just a bit, second-guessing her wisdom to take the girls out of the town limits. She silently scolded herself for losing track of time and instinctively felt the side of her boot to make sure her knife was still securely hidden there. To her relief, it was, but she still felt a sudden urgency to get the girls back to the orphanage. Something was coming; she could feel it.

"Girls, time to go back to town. It's getting dark," Unis said nervously.

Both responded with a disappointed "Aww!"

"Can we stay just a little longer?" Cassandra asked.

Before Unis could respond, the howl of a wolf that sounded entirely too close startled them. Kessi jumped and hugged her sister.

Unis's heart raced, and she turned to grab the girls' hands and head back to town. "Come along—we must be getting back."

Cassandra kept looking into the woods as Unis tried to hurry them along. "We won't make it, Mama," she said softly.

Kessi began to cry, and Cassandra's unusually calm demeanor and her own certainty of inescapable danger had Unis very upset. Another howl sounded very close, and the sound of something moving quickly through the woods had Unis turning to draw her small knife. She fumbled with it at her boot for what seemed like many moments, but she eventually retrieved it and held it with a shaking hand.

"Go ahead, girls. Hold each other's hand and run home. Send the guards out to help me when you get there."

Neither girl moved, and Kessi cried all the louder, hugging her sister and trembling with fear. To Unis's amazement, Cassandra showed no emotion and began scanning the sky instead.

Unis was getting ready to scold them for not listening, when a growl made her stop and slowly turn around to face the woods once more. She broke out in a sweat when she saw the wolf; it was much bigger than she'd anticipated, a good four feet at the shoulder. Its face was even with hers, and it was only about twenty yards away and baring its fangs. Saliva dripped from its mouth as it issued a growl and advanced slowly. Unis knew she was doomed, and her only hope was to give the girls enough time to get back to town so they could live. She tried to yell for the girls to run, but the words caught in her throat. The eyes of the beast were on her, and they showed more intelligence than that of a mere animal. Whatever it was, this creature was not just a simple wolf, and it meant to kill them—she was sure of that. She held the knife in an unsteady hand and took a step back. Kessi screamed, which Unis could only hope got the attention of the town guards.

"Begone, wolf!" came a small but stern cry from behind her, and Unis turned to see Cassandra pointing at the creature, moving in front of Kessi, who was now hiding her face in Cassandra's jacket.

Unis's eyes went wide as the creature turned its attention toward the girls, bared its teeth even more, and issued another deep growl. Unis tried to keep herself between the animal and her girls, but the creature jumped past her with blinding speed. She swung wildly with the knife, missing badly, with the momentum turning her around to face the girls once more. The wolf was heading straight for them.

"Run!" she managed to cry just before another wolf crashed into her, knocking her to the ground. The weight of the second wolf knocked the wind out of her, and its maw clamped around her throat. She managed to hold on to the knife, but the wolf pinned her arm with its massive paw. She turned her head to watch the girls. She couldn't let them die like this. A tear escaped her eye as she tried to move, tried to yell—anything to help her girls. She would die, but the wolf would let her watch her kids die first. It somehow knew that was more horrible for her than death. Somehow it knew.

The first wolf was only ten feet away from the girls, preparing to spring on them. Kessi screamed and hid her head in her sister's jacket, but Cassandra stood steadfast as a large bird flew down and struck the large wolf in the ribs. The wolf yelped in surprise and looked around for the attacker, its momentum halted. It discovered the lone raven soon enough as it circled for another attack. This time, the beast was ready and quickly caught the bird in its mouth. In one chomp, bones crushed, blood squirted from the sides of its mouth, and feathers hung from its maw. It chewed the raven, grinding its bones and crushing the life from it, just as it would do to the girls next.

"Bad wolf!" Cassandra said, shaking her tiny finger at the giant creature.

That's when it was struck again by another raven, and it yelped once more in surprise. Then another bird hit it, followed by another after that. Soon there were dozens of birds pecking and clawing at the great beast. It fought fearlessly, snipping and biting at them and killing many hateful birds, but quickly there were hundreds, and the creature was overwhelmed. Birds surrounded the girls, creating a protective wall around them. Little Kessi peeked around her sister's shoulder to witness the spectacle.

The creature howled in pain as it lost an eye to a pecking raven, and many tiny holes were bored into its fur. Cassandra just stood there watching with a frown on her face and her hands on her hips as the birds pecked it to death. Unis could not believe what she was seeing. The birds were protecting her girls. She had a glimmer of hope in her tear-filled eyes, and that was when the wolf bit down hard, crushing her windpipe. A gurgle escaped her mouth as she tasted and smelled her coppery blood. She lost all strength in her arms and released her grip on the knife. The creature dragged her away, and she was happy that the girls did not witness her death because their attention remained on the birds. Somehow, she knew the girls would live, which made her comfortable in her final moments of life.

Eventually, the birds slowed and started to disperse, leaving the fresh corpse of the wolf lying at Cassandra's feet. "Bad wolf!" she said again, still wagging her tiny finger. Then she stretched out her hand, and a raven landed on it. Kessi sniffled as the bird cocked its head back and forth, studying the girls. Cassandra said nothing but seemed to be communicating with it. The raven flew off just before the guards got there, with their torches raised and their swords drawn.

"It's fine, Mama. The bad wolf is dead," Cassandra said.

Only then did the girls realize that their mother was gone. They looked around in sudden shock, understanding that everything certainly was not fine. The guards found them shortly after, huddled together and crying beside a dead wolf that looked like it had been eaten alive, with most of its entrails strewn about the ground. They did not know what to make of the scene as they carried the scared little girls back to the orphanage.

The following day, the sheriff of Oldorburg met with the guards involved in the incident. He then questioned the girls about what had happened, but they never told him, the guards, or anyone else about the ravens. An extensive search of the area that morning found the remains of two dozen ravens near the dead wolf, as well as Unis's knife. However, they never discovered the woman's body. The sheriff deemed that it was merely an attack by wild wolves and that somehow a swarm of ravens had saved the little girls. Word of the incident spread across the region and to neighboring towns. A nursery rhyme about wolves and ravens was born from the incident, warning small children not to leave their homes at night lest they get eaten by wolves. Thus, Cassandra Rho's legend was born, and the event forever changed her life. However, no wolves, intelligent or otherwise, ever came that close to the town of Oldorburg again.

And so began the adventures of Cassandra Rho.

Nursery Rhyme:
"Cassandra and the Wolves"

Little Cassandra Rho, tromping through the forest,
Being way too loud and bringing the wolves upon us.

The wolves killed her mama without much of a fuss—
That made Cassandra mad, and she began to cuss.

The wolves circled Cassandra, ready for a kill.
They were big and mean and ready for a meal.

Before they pounced, Cassandra said one word,
And sure enough, the wolves were stopped by a single bird.

Shortly after that, many birds arrived.
They killed the wolves so Cassandra could survive.

So don't go out in the woods armed only with a stick;
It's better to take Cassandra Rho, the little raven witch.

CHAPTER 1

A WITCH IS BORN

AFTER THE DEATH OF THEIR FIRST MOTHER, UNIS, TWINS Cassandra and Kessi were assigned a new surrogate mother at the orphanage by Lord Ronnis D'Breeth. But, of course, Lord Ronnis had the final say in hiring Unis's replacement as the great facility's administrator. So it was no surprise to anyone who knew him that he hired the loveliest woman of all the applicants. Her name was Sera Jasmine, and she was much younger than Unis and far prettier.

Ronnis kept an eye on the twins and their new mother, understanding that what had happened that night in the woods was far more than some random natural event. But fortunately his fascination with Sera made him lose interest in the investigation into the events of that night, so nothing came of it. There was not much hope of finding the truth with Unis dead, anyway, especially with the girls not old enough to provide relevant information.

Cassandra did not adjust well to her new mother, having profound guilt over Unis's passing. Sera occasionally asked them about the incident, but the girls would not speak of that horrible night. So Sera let it go, hoping they would tell her in their own time. But seven years quickly passed, and nothing changed; Cassandra guarded herself against her new mother and became more introverted. Kessi, however, adjusted to life after the strange event and became a kind little girl. Lord Ronnis kept an eye on Sera from afar, making her feel very uncomfortable whenever he was around her. However, his duties kept him away from her and the girls most of the time.

Cassandra did not thrive at the orphanage as her sister did, and her time there after Unis's death was not kind to her. So it came as no surprise to her teachers when she started skipping class at twelve years of age. She was one of the brightest students at the orphanage but socially could not live up to the other children's pressures. Sera was a saint and was very patient with Cassandra's struggles. She had fallen in love with both girls rather quickly and wanted them to live happy lives. Kessi would be easy for Sera, and Cassandra would be her challenge. So when Cassandra didn't show up for her literary class for the second day in a row, Sera went to the gardens to find her, the one spot the girl felt safe and happy.

Cassandra sat in the garden, watching the birds gather for the bread crumbs she had thrown on the ground. She sat on the bench well hidden from any passersby. This part of the garden had grown full of large bushes and shrubs and offered her privacy, making her feel alone and safe. Cassandra grabbed her sketchbook and opened it to a clean page. She meant to draw a picture of the birds with the little piece of charcoal she had brought along. However, after she stared at the blank page, the symbols came into focus once more. The characters had floated around her head since her mother's death, and she knew not what they meant.

And so they swirled in her head, mainly squiggly lines and odd geometric shapes, and whenever she saw them, she always jotted them down. So she took up her charcoal and did just that. She hoped one day to discern what they were, but she kept them secret from her mother and sister for the time being. She just assumed they were part of her weirdness and people would think she was some freak—not that they didn't already think that.

She scrawled, capturing the shapes on the edge of her paper before they faded away, as they typically did. Then a rather large bird flew down and landed among the others, scaring them away. It stood just a few feet off, and she recognized it immediately as a raven. It did not peck at the bread crumbs as the others had; it just looked at her, cocking its head back and forth, almost as if it were waiting. She quickly drew it, and it stood there until she finished. Once done, she closed the charcoal inside the book and set it on the bench.

"Hello there," she said.

It just stood there looking at her, not moving other than to tilt its head back and forth. Then, finally, Cassandra summoned the nerve to hold out her hand, palm up, just like she had that day in the forest. She had felt a connection with the ravens that day, and this bird was no different. It was there for her; she just didn't know why or how. She waited for it to land on her hand, but after several moments, it took to the air as something stirred in the bushes behind her. Cassandra turned to see Sera ducking low and parting many limbs to enter the small clearing.

"Cassandra, I thought I'd find you here!" she said, trying to untangle a bit of her hair from the thorny grasp of a bush.

"Why are you here?" Cassandra asked, disappointed in the intrusion.

"Because you are skipping class, young lady," Sera said, freeing herself to take a seat beside her daughter.

"I wish you hadn't come," Cassandra said, taking her book and putting it on her lap.

She didn't look directly at Sera and instead watched her out of the corner of her eye. Her words seemed to have a profound effect on her.

Sera sighed and shook her head. "You need to be in class. I've told you many times that you may come here only with my permission and only when there is no class to attend or chores to perform."

"I hate it there!"

"But it is important for you to learn and become a model citizen," Sera explained.

"I already know more than the dolts who are teaching me," Cassandra said, then glanced at Sera briefly, realizing the unintentional insult since Sera was a teacher there.

"You are smart, Cassandra, but you must complete your education," Sera said, ignoring the insult.

"Besides, the other kids hate me."

"What? No, they don't. You need to give them a chance—"

"To do what, make fun of me? All they do is make fun and sing that stupid nursery rhyme. I want to kill them!"

"Please don't say things like that!"

Cassandra whispered something unintelligible underneath her breath and looked at Sera with a sour expression.

"What did you say?" Sera asked.

"You are not my mother," Cassandra said, this time loud enough for Sera to hear.

"Well, you are my daughter, and I love you very much. No matter how poorly you treat me, I will not stop loving you. Do you understand?"

Cassandra shrugged and focused on her book.

The two sat like that for several moments until Sera stood and offered her hand. "Come. Let me walk you to class."

"No!" Cassandra shouted, then stood and ran from the clearing, dodging the thick bushes that grabbed at her.

"Cassandra! Get back here!" Sera yelled, starting after her but becoming tangled with the grabbing limbs.

Cassandra ran full force toward the orphanage and looked behind her to ensure Sera couldn't catch her. But, unfortunately, she was so content with out-running Sera that she never noticed Lord Ronnis standing at the garden fountain.

Ronnis was on his way to a meeting with the board of owners carrying the books of affairs with him. It had been another excellent quarter financially. With the board squarely in his pocket, he effortlessly hid his bonus of one hundred gold in worker salaries. He had left Unis on the payroll and was collecting her wage. If discovered, he would easily pin the oversight on an orphanage worker. It had been seven years, so the risk of being caught now was minimal.

He ran a hand through his greasy black hair and stood at his favorite fountain in the garden. It had several cherubs pouring water back into the pool, fueled by an underground spring and strategically placed pipes. Built by the best engineers the town could offer, it was his masterpiece, having received many compliments over the years. He had commissioned the work and therefore had taken full credit for its beauty. He stopped and admired the work of art with a contented smile. The sun reflected in the pouring water, making the light dance all about. He closed his eyes and breathed in the scents of the surrounding flowers. Life was good for Lord Ronnis—very good!

He was just about to continue on his way when he heard a commotion behind him. He turned only in time to have Cassandra plow into him, knocking him down and scattering his books.

"Fool child!" He stood and gathered his books and found a sketchbook mixed among his. He held it up to the light to the open page, which depicted a raven drawing, along with some strange symbols in the corners.

"I'll take that, please," Cassandra said, now standing and holding her arm out toward the book.

"Cassandra Rho? You sure have grown," he said, looking her up and down.

He began to say something Cassandra could only assume would be a lecture about watching where she was going. However, when he saw Lady Sera approaching from behind Cassandra, picking leaves from her blond hair, the words seemed to stick in his throat. Ronnis closed Cassandra's book and tucked it under his arm with the others. He absently ran another hand through his hair and licked his lips as Sera approached.

"I'm sorry, Lord Ronnis. Are you hurt?" Sera asked.

"No, but I was about to lecture Cassandra here on the importance of manners," he said as Sera knelt and started wiping off the grass from Cassandra's dress.

Cassandra stared at him with a frown as Sera cleaned her soiled dress. He ignored her completely, his attention entirely on Sera as he took her hand and gently kissed the back of it. Ronnis then helped her to a standing position. "It has been far too long since my tired eyes looked upon you!" he said.

She feigned a smile and curtsied slightly. "Good afternoon to you as well, Lord Ronnis."

"Shouldn't all children be in class at this time of day, Miss Sera?" he said, looking sourly at Cassandra.

"Yes, of course. We were just heading to class."

"So this one is a skipper?" he said with a frown.

"Yes, no—I mean … yes, today she is a skipper," Sera said and sighed.

"That will not do. And do tell—what is this?" he said, opening Cassandra's book so Sera could see.

"It's mine!" Cassandra shouted before Sera could say anything.

Sera placed a gentle hand over Cassandra's mouth and said, "They are her drawings, sir. She means no harm. She just wanted to come to the garden and draw birds—nothing more. She is quite good."

The lord seemed unconvinced. He bent so he was eye level with Cassandra and said, "You are an unruly child, Cassandra Rho, and that simply will not do!"

Cassandra removed Sera's hand from her mouth and just stared at him, hate filling her eyes. Then she focused on her book, tucked once again under his arm. *Her book.* Cassandra knew then that he was not going to return it. The ugly man hated her, and as far as she was concerned, the feeling was mutual.

"I suggest you put on a great big smile when you are dealing with me, young lady, or I will help you learn your place," he said.

She slowly revealed a wide fake smile so that many of her teeth were showing by the effort's end. Then she whispered through those teeth, "I hate you."

She had not meant to say it so plainly, but why hide the truth if he wouldn't return her book? But the flash of anger on his face made her realize her error just before he backhanded her so hard that she fell on her rump.

"Cassandra!" Sera yelled and reached for her.

However, Cassandra regained her feet quickly, and before Sera could reach her, she said again to the awful man, "I hate you!" Then she ran off toward the orphanage.

Ronnis watched her go with a smirk on his face, shaking the sting from his hand.

"My lord, Cassandra is a good child but has had a hard time since … well, since her mother passed. But, sir, you cannot hit the children!"

"The child needs discipline, and I intend to administer it."

"But Ronnis—"

"That is Lord Ronnis to you, Sera."

"Yes, of course, my lord, but you cannot—"

"Do not presume to tell me what I can and cannot do, young lady. It is my orphanage, and that one has caused us enough trouble as it is," he said with an upraised hand, ending any debate. "I will see the both of you in my quarters this evening as the sun begins to set. Make sure you are there; your future at the orphanage depends on it. Understand?"

She began to speak again, but Ronnis waved his hand at her and shook his head, making her fall quiet and stare at her feet uncomfortably.

Her timidness brought a smile to his face. "Do you understand?" he asked calmly but firmly.

"Yes, my lord, but may I ask why? I can handle the skipping, and I shall punish her for it."

"Take a look at this scribble," he demanded, holding the book out for her to see the drawing again.

"Yes, she draws birds, my lord, as I have said."

"No, not the birds—these symbols," he said, tapping the page with his finger. Ronnis had been a well-traveled man before coming to the orphanage. He recognized the magical symbols for what they were, even if Sera did not. A collector of all things magic, he knew the symbols to be arcane. His interest in the drawings, and especially Cassandra Rho, instantly became renewed. His eyes moved from the small book to Sera, who was still looking at the symbols, not understanding their implication.

"I do not understand, my lord," she finally said in resignation.

His gaze rested on her bosom, making her uncomfortable as she drew her shirt tight around her neck. The lord bit his lip and stared lewdly at her as she fidgeted under his gaze. A long time passed before he finally asked, "Are you teaching your children about such things as wizards and sorcery?"

"I know not where she saw such symbols. We would never—"

"Enough, Sera. I will see you at sundown. Do not be late!" He turned on his heel and walked away, tucking Cassandra's book back in with his own. He walked away briskly and confidently and began to whistle as he did.

Sera hurried off to find Cassandra, happy to be away from the lord once he was out of sight. She soon rushed inside the dorms, where she found Cassandra waiting for her, arms crossed over her chest, tapping her foot.

"My book, please," Cassandra said, holding out her hand with a look of disdain on her face.

"I'm sorry, Cassandra. He kept it."

"What gives him the right to keep my things?" Cassandra asked, balling her fists at her sides and stomping her foot. Her pretty face became instantly red, boiling with anger.

Sera bent to look her in the eye. "I'm sorry, and I will try to get your drawings back, but right now, you have to listen to me." She sternly grabbed Cassandra's shoulders and made her look her in the eye. "Listen—I love you, Cassandra. Whether you like me or not, I have always loved you as my own. But now I'm telling you that you must calm yourself, or Lord Ronnis will make things very bad for you."

Cassandra studied her face, her eyes darting back and forth, looking for a sign of truth in Sera's words. Then, finally, she said, "You are not my mother." The words dripped with venom, and they seemed to stun Sera as Cassandra pulled away. Cassandra turned and stomped up the steps, but in truth, her heart ached at saying those words to Sera. She did not mean to mistreat the woman, and she refused to grow close to her only to protect herself.

"Go straight to class," Sera said.

Cassandra turned halfway up the stairs to find Sera still kneeling. Her heart went out to the woman, and she wanted nothing more than to run to her and hug her. But instead, she stubbornly kept her resolve and yelled, "No!" She then turned and continued her march up the stairs.

"Cassandra!" Sera yelled.

"No!" Cassandra said but dared not turn around this time.

By the time Cassandra reached the top of the steps, tears had streamed down her face, and she quickened her pace toward her room, not wanting Sera to see them. Once there, she slammed the door as hard as she could and fell onto her bed, finally releasing the pent-up feelings and crying hysterically. She loved Sera after all despite her actions, and her face throbbed where Ronnis had struck her. She needed a mother at that point and hoped Sera would come in and catch her crying. She hoped she would rush to her and make her feel better. She cried for a long time, but the door never opened.

~

Later that evening, Kessi brushed Cassandra's hair as they sat at the tiny vanity they shared in their room. Spying the frown on her sister's face through the mirror, Kessi tried to ease the tension. "You know, you should be nice to Lord Ronnis. He is our protector and provider."

The words only made Cassandra's mood worse. "I hate him. He is evil, and he took my book!"

"He will give it back, I'm sure," Kessi said and smiled.

"No, he won't," Cassandra insisted, shaking her head. "I remember him, don't you? He asked us lots of questions after Mother died."

Kessi shook her head. "No, I don't remember him. I think he spent more time asking you questions than he did me."

"Do you think he knows about the ravens?"

Kessi stopped brushing and stared at her sister for a long while before finding her voice. "No, of course not. How could he?"

"I don't know. It just seems that in the past, he was suspicious of us, and now he's back, asking more questions. I hate him."

Kessi let out a long, exasperated sigh. "You know you shouldn't hate, right? I like everyone!"

Cassandra had no response and would have probably punched Kessi in the mouth for saying something so ignorant if she weren't her sister. However, Cassandra loved her very much, and Kessi was the only family she had. Watching her lovingly brush her hair made a tear form in her eye. She wished she could feel happiness the way Kessi did. But the fact was she could not; they were two different people. Cassandra saw great things in her sister's future but was not so sure of her own. A knock on the door interrupted her thoughts and made her jump. Kessi placed the brush on the vanity and skipped to the door, happy as a lark. "Who is it?" she asked.

"It's me, Kessi," Sera said.

Kessi opened the door excitedly and nearly knocked Sera down with a big hug. Cassandra sighed and instinctively picked up her brush and started running it through her hair. She watched Sera through the mirror, though, judging her movements, observing how she interacted with her sister. Cassandra liked Sera more than she let on, that was true, but she would never consider the kind woman her mother. Cassandra kept her distance because she would not suffer losing another mother.

"Are you ready, Cassandra?" Sera asked, approaching her from behind and kissing the top of her head.

Cassandra wanted to cry, wanted to scream out that Sera was not her mom. But at the same time, she longed to wrap the woman in a big hug and never let her go. So she did the only thing that came naturally and responded with an unenthusiastic "I suppose."

Sera took her brush and worked out a few kinks, all the while staring at Cassandra through the mirror. "I want you to be on your best behavior tonight. Do you understand?"

"Of course I understand your words—I'm not an idiot!"

"That's not what I meant, and you know it."

"I hate him."

"You must not say that! He simply wants to find out about your drawings. Just answer him honestly, and I'm sure we'll be home before nightfall."

"You're wearing makeup … and perfume."

Sera blushed slightly and nodded. "I am, but only because it may help our cause."

"Are you a streetwalker?"

"Cassandra Rho! How dare you say such a thing! That is enough!" Sera yelled, slamming the brush down hard on the vanity.

The sound startled both girls, which made Sera's anger quickly dissipate. Her face was flush from anger and embarrassment as she made eye contact with both girls. Cassandra had a smirk on her face, while Kessi looked as if she would cry.

"I'm sorry for that, girls. I have made myself up, to answer your question, Cassandra, hoping that Ronnis will notice me and go easy on you. Unfortunately he fancies me, so I will try to distract his attention from you in the hopes that this nonsense concerning your drawings will die down after tonight."

Kessi stood a few feet behind Sera and looked at her feet uncomfortably.

Sera saw this in the mirror and turned to the child. "What's wrong, Kessi?" she asked and knelt beside her.

"Nothing. I just want to know what a streetwalker is," she said with a sniff, trying to stifle her tears.

"It's nothing for you to be concerned with, my dear," Sera replied, hugging Kessi.

Kessi hugged her back and made eye contact with Cassandra through the mirror. Then she mouthed the words *be nice* to her.

Cassandra rolled her eyes and made her way for the door. "Can we please get this over with?"

"Yes, let us be done with this nonsense," Sera said, ending the hug and standing up. She looked at Kessi with a smile as Cassandra opened the door and left the room without looking back.

"I will be back soon, and perhaps you can tell me a little more about theology before bed," Sera said with a smile. Kessi's eyes went wide, and a smile spread across her tiny face. Sera wiped the girl's tears away and kissed her on the forehead. "I'll see you soon."

Sera made her way to the door and was about to walk into the hall when Kessi said, "She loves you, you know."

Sera stopped and looked back at the always surprising little girl.

"Cassandra, I mean," Kessi said.

"Yes, I'm sure she does in her way. And you know that I love you and your sister very much, don't you?"

Kessi smiled and nodded, and Sera left the room, closing the door gently.

Cassandra was already downstairs and near the front door when Sera caught up with her. As expected, Sera had a few ground rules for her as they made their way to Ronnis's office. Cassandra tried to listen but simply wasn't interested. She just wanted the meeting over with and for Ronnis to creep back into his hole and leave her be.

~

Ronnis pored over his notes from all those years ago: Unis had disappeared, her body never found; the girls saw a wolf but did not see how it died; and the dead ravens found at the scene suggested that the birds had attacked the wolf. Ronnis had determined that there was more than one wolf and that the ravens had protected the girls. He had known at the time that it was impossible without the help of some kind of powerful magic, so he had thoroughly interrogated the young girls over the next six months. Neither seemed to remember anything, and in the end, the sheriff of Oldorburg had ruled it a wild animal attack and a miracle the girls weren't hurt. Ronnis knew better but had not been able to prove it.

He had collected many things in his travels, including a particular spell book that he had taken from the corpse of a young wizard many years ago. He had never fully learned how to read the symbols found inside the book, but he recognized Cassandra's drawings as some of the ones he had seen there. Sure enough, comparing the spell book to Cassandra's book of drawings confirmed that the symbols matched. He had counted nineteen matches but had no idea what they meant, as he had no official training in the arcane arts. However, with the girl now being twelve years old and with this discovery, he could probably convince the good sheriff to reopen the case.

A knock on the door had him piling the various books and scrolls on his desk neatly on one side. He ran his hand through his greasy hair and took a sip of his favorite drink—honey brandy. Then he straightened his shirt, tucked it in, and opened the door with a large fake smile and a gleam in his eye.

Cassandra noticed the stupid look immediately and rolled her eyes. Ronnis didn't seem to notice the eye roll or even Cassandra in general; his gaze stuck on Sera, who wore her hair in a ponytail tied with a blue ribbon, which matched her modest dress. She wore makeup—not too much, but enough to make the lord notice her. Her perfume wasn't too strong, but Cassandra was sure he caught the scent. The pretty package that was Sera seemed to garner the lord's attention, and Cassandra was grateful for that. However, it made her a little nervous about the way he looked at her mother.

"Good evening, my lord," Sera said with a slight curtsy.

Ronnis took her hand and kissed it and ushered her into the room. "It is lovely to see you, Sera. You look as beautiful as ever."

Although Cassandra appreciated Sera's efforts to draw the lord's attention from her, she didn't like how he was acting, so she decided to take the attention away from her mother just a bit. "It stinks in here," she said calmly, looking around at the stuffy room.

Ronnis gave her a sour look, and she smiled on the inside but did not dare to change her expression as she curled up her nose and sniffed the room. Then, ignoring Cassandra, Ronnis led Sera to a chair at his large desk and pulled it out for her. She sat gracefully, and he took in a long draw of her perfume before moving to take his place behind the desk.

"You need a bath," Cassandra said flatly, taking a seat in the chair next to Sera again, trying to keep the dull man away from her mother.

"Cassandra, please watch your manners!" Sera said.

In response, Cassandra just carried an air of boredom and disgust.

"I will have the truth from you this evening, child, or you will face the consequences of being rude to me. Do I make myself clear, Cassandra Rho?" Ronnis said through gritted teeth.

Sera tried to diffuse the situation by placing a hand on Ronnis's arm as he gripped the edge of the desk with white knuckles. Her touch calmed him immediately, and when he looked at her, he seemed to relax. However, the two stared into each other's eyes, and Cassandra noticed Sera smile and then wilt under his gaze. It dawned on her then what Sera might be doing. Her words at the room before they left had indicated that Sera would try to draw the lord's attention from her. Did she mean sexually? Cassandra didn't fully understand sex, but she understood the gist of it. She could not let that happen to Sera.

"Can I have my book back?"

Ronnis glanced angrily at her then, and Cassandra felt as if she had pressed too hard. She didn't care, though; she could not allow Sera to make this sacrifice for her. Then Cassandra noticed her book lying atop a stack of papers on the desk, and she summoned the courage to reach for it. As she did, Ronnis smacked her hand away. It was a powerful hit, and it stung her hand, making her jerk it back with a yelp. Tears formed in her eyes, but she stubbornly held them, not wanting to give the awful man the satisfaction of seeing her cry.

"Please, my lord—she is just a child and doesn't understand what she may have done. She just wants her book back," Sera said.

"No, Sera, that book is now evidence in my investigation, and the child is making things much worse for herself."

Cassandra crossed her arms over her chest and looked away, still fighting back the tears of pain and anger. The smack had hurt her, but she didn't want him to know that. More important, the lord had just mentioned something about an investigation, and that tugged at her memories of long ago when he had investigated the death of Unis. Would he reopen that tragedy once again just because of a few symbols she had drawn? Finally a tear rolled silently down her cheek, and she quickly wiped it away.

"Lord Ronnis, what investigation are you referring to?" Sera asked.

"Witchcraft, my dear lady," he answered with an evil smile.

"Witchcraft?" Sera shook her head, confused.

He grabbed up Cassandra's book and opened it, shoving the open pages toward the girl. "I want to know where you learned how to draw these symbols, young lady. Unfortunately my orphanage tolerates no magic, and I will not have a smart-mouth brat such as yourself defiling the other children with it!"

Those comments sparked a wave of emotions from Cassandra, and she turned hatefully toward the lord. She could feel her cheeks redden with anger as he looked on with disgust, trying to intimidate her. But that was when she saw the symbols floating in the air, dancing all around the man. They almost seemed to call to her to offer assistance if needed. But as she watched them bounce around, trying to figure out whether they were truly there, the lord snapped.

"Don't look at me that way, Cassandra, or I will tan your hide!" he yelled, suddenly standing and lunging to smack at her from across the desk. But Cassandra was just quick enough to fall back in her chair, and the wild swing missed her and instead knocked over the books and scrolls stacked on the desk. Then Ronnis unfastened his belt, removing it with one swift motion and folding it in half, making it a weapon of control. "Pick all of those items up right now, Cassandra, and place them on the desk, or so help me, you'll get a tanning you'll never forget!"

His face was red with anger, and it truly scared Cassandra. Had she done something to provoke this level of wrath? Yes, she had insulted him and his smelly room, but they both stunk, so why be mad about that? She was frozen to her chair, not knowing what to do. Sera said something to her, but she did not hear it, so consumed was she with the lord. Then she took note of his belt and somehow found the courage to fall from the chair and start picking up the items as ordered.

Ronnis took a step toward the pile of books, which made Cassandra work faster and finally begin to cry. She was genuinely panicked, and fear washed over her—not only at the possibility of being whipped with the belt but also for Sera's safety. She understood then that they were in grave danger. As Cassandra's young mind tried to register those thoughts, Sera was suddenly there with her and hugged her tight. It was the moment that Cassandra had hoped for earlier that day; Sera was there to rescue her and comfort her. The emotions overwhelmed her then, and she hugged Sera back and buried her face in her mother's shoulder. Cassandra bawled for a very long time, sobbing uncontrollably, letting out years of fear and frustration. But more important, she was finally letting her guard down and accepting Sera as her mother.

Ronnis calmly put his belt back on, then picked up the rest of the books and scrolls and stacked them neatly back on the desk as Sera kept one eye on him. Cassandra was still crying when he finished, and he plopped back down in his chair. He sighed and reached into a drawer, finding his bottle of brandy and an unclean glass. Ronnis filled the glass and took a long sip. Then, without any emotion, he finally said, "Enough of this," waving a hand at Cassandra.

"You struck her once in the garden already today, my lord, and now you try it again. Striking her is no way to punish her and certainly no way to treat a child who has done nothing wrong!"

Cassandra looked up from Sera's shoulder and could tell the comment did not sit well with the lord. Ronnis sat there eyeing Sera as he downed the remainder of his drink in one large gulp and then poured himself another one. Cassandra tried to gather herself, to stop the childish crying, for the more she did it, the worse the lord's mood seemed to get. She had to pull herself together not just for her own sake but for Sera's. Cassandra noticed the way he looked at Sera, and it made her afraid. As the seconds ticked by, the tension grew. Finally, just as Cassandra was gathering the nerve to apologize, Sera said, "Why don't we discuss this in your private chambers, my lord? I'm sure we can find a resolution."

Cassandra noticed the sick look that spread across Sera's face immediately and saw Ronnis smile.

"No," Cassandra whispered in her mother's ear.

Sera smiled and hugged her tight, whispering, "It will be all right. Do not fret." She pulled Cassandra back to arm's length. "Take a deep breath. Everything will be fine."

Cassandra did just that, and as she looked into Sera's face, she felt safe and happy; she felt as if things really would be fine. They hugged once more, and there was not a better feeling Cassandra had ever known.

She could have maintained that hug forever, but unfortunately they were in the lair of Lord Ronnis.

He cleared his throat. "Uh … yes … that would be a splendid idea, Sera."

Sera knelt by Cassandra with a sick look on her face. She did not rise, and Cassandra watched as Ronnis fished around his pocket and produced a key. He then stood and locked the door to the room. As he did, Cassandra whispered to Sera, "Let's go home."

Sera stroked Cassandra's hair and wiped the tears from her cheeks. Then she whispered, "Be strong, and know that I will be safe."

"Shall we begin our negotiations?" Ronnis said, holding an arm toward the door to his chambers at the back of the room. He downed the rest of his brandy and held his other arm out to Sera to assist her up.

"No," Sera replied, ignoring his gesture and standing on her own. "Cassandra must be sent back to her room first."

"I'm sorry, Sera. She must stay. Of course, I will forgive her for her actions, but only if our so-called negotiations work out for the best. And I have a feeling they will work out quite splendidly," he said and stroked her face.

Sera recoiled from his touch. "You can't be serious! She is a child. Let her go. You've scared her enough, and I'm sure she has learned—"

"Silence!" Ronnis said. "She has practiced the dark art of witchcraft—that is abundantly clear—and knows information concerning the disappearance of Unis Rho. Therefore I am heavily suspicious of this girl, and she stays until I say otherwise."

Cassandra looked on as her mother tried to stand up to the evil man. In the end, she seemed to wilt under his gaze, defeated. She glanced at Cassandra briefly and said, "You sit here while I talk to the lord in private. We will not be very long, and we will leave after our talk—understand?" Cassandra nodded, so Sera walked toward the door at the back of the room.

Ronnis followed and gave Cassandra a stern look as he did. Cassandra tried to remain strong and stared back. She had to be the strong one; she could not let him intimidate both of them. They held their silent gaze as Ronnis led Sera into his room, followed, and slowly shut the door, allowing Cassandra to see his face for as long as possible. Cassandra balled her fists at her sides, wanting so badly to do something. She knew that whatever was going to happen behind that closed door, it would not be a good thing for Sera. In the end, all she could do was take a seat and cross her arms over her chest.

Cassandra could hear the door lock from within, and she heard muffled voices as they began their talk. Soon it was quiet—eerily so. She nestled back in her chair and looked around the room. She hated being there and wanted to take her book and go home. She spotted her book on the desk just then and stared at it. Everything about this situation was wrong. Why was she being singled out? Kessi had never gotten in trouble for the wolf incident. She'd been there too, but somehow everyone knew that Kessi had nothing to do with the ravens. Somehow everyone knew! Cassandra herself knew that Kessi had nothing to do with it—it had been so long ago now that she wasn't sure even she had had anything to do with it. She vaguely remembered sharing a connection with those strange birds, and that was it. It never happened again, so she was beginning to believe she was innocent of any involvement as well.

A moan from the back room had her sitting up in her chair. "Sera?" she whispered. No response came, so she listened more intently. Then, finally, the moan came again—this one a little louder. To her delight, it wasn't Sera but Ronnis. She smiled, thinking that perhaps Sera had finally backhanded the man a couple of good times, but she had a feeling it was nothing of the sort. She slumped back in her chair and covered her ears with her hands. She just wanted to go home.

That's when she first noticed the book—a magical book. It lay on the floor just under the desk. It must have been among those that had fallen when Ronnis tried to strike her. She sat up, and her mouth dropped open. She could see only part of the cover, but there were two symbols on it she recognized immediately—magical characters, to be more exact, similar to those she had drawn in her book. The images in her head were on that book!

She tuned out the moans from the back room that were now constant, and she didn't hear the lewd noises accompanying them. She was mesmerized by the book now, and it seemed to call to her. She slid off the chair and reached for it tentatively, afraid somehow that it might hurt her if she touched it. When she finally found the courage to pick it up, it felt warm, and she could almost feel the energy flow up her arm. It didn't hurt her but instead seemed to make her a little stronger. The truth was, it felt good!

It was the most magnificent book she had ever seen. The cover seemed simple enough, made of plain leather, but it felt otherworldly, and she could feel the power pulse within it. She traced her finger over the symbols on the cover. Some she recognized, others she did not. As she opened the book, her young mind did not understand that those symbols created a glyph of protection that would have killed her. However, Ronnis had already had it dispelled so he could browse through the pages. He had paid a fair amount of gold for a wizard from the north to remove the protection, but the old, now harmless symbols remained, and she saw them.

Her eyes went wide at the sight of the pages. Symbols seemed to move and create a structure that she understood, instructing her on certain hand gestures, and required components to create magical effects. Some of them even led her to say a particular phrase or speak the names of the symbols themselves. It was incredible, and she understood every bit of that first page immediately.

She hungrily read through the pages, knowing her time to be limited. She had no problem reading the first several pages, which seemed to describe various spell effects. Next, she read and reread the pages related to the first two spells, trying to memorize what she saw. Once satisfied with that, she moved to a third, more aggressive spell. This one was harder and gave her some trouble, but she eventually figured out the intricate hand gestures required to cast it, and she practiced them as her mind absorbed the information.

She studied the book for almost an hour, although it felt like just a few minutes to her. Lost in the spell book, she absorbed the information, and she never heard the door in the back of the room open. Only when she heard Ronnis laughing did she realize she was no longer alone. She quickly shut the book and tossed it back on the floor, trying to make as much of it as possible slide about under the desk.

When Sera approached her and put a hand on her shoulder, Cassandra jumped. "It's fine, Cassandra. We may go now," Sera said and smiled.

Cassandra looked up at her and noticed several unusual things right away. Sera's hair was a mess, and her clothes were wrinkled, her dress even torn in one place. Her face was flush, and her neck had what appeared to be red splotches. Ronnis plopped back down in his chair and poured a new glass of brandy. His face was red too, and he was sweating even more than usual. Cassandra had a good idea of what had transpired in that room. So she stood up and moved to Sera's side, ready to leave the vile place.

Sera looked at Ronnis. "We are done with this silly business, and you will leave Cassandra alone, correct, my lord?"

He smiled and leaned back in his chair. Cassandra took a step behind Sera, not knowing what would happen next. But then she felt her eyes drawn toward the book of spells that still jutted out from under the desk. Cassandra became mesmerized by it, seeing the symbols form around it once more, sensing its magic. She barely heard Ronnis when he finally spoke.

"Yes, of course," he said, sitting up in his chair. Then he looked at Cassandra and said, "You be sure not to draw symbols such as the ones in your book again, you hear? They are dangerous and very much against the law. Sera here has convinced me, temporarily, that I can trust you not to do this. Do you understand?"

Cassandra looked at the book and nodded, unable to make eye contact with the evil man.

"Very well. You may leave now, but understand I do not take witchcraft lightly, Miss Rho. I will have my eye on you, and one false move will lead you right back here to my office. I won't be so forgiving next time—I promise."

Cassandra continued to avoid eye contact, gazing instead at the spell book, wanting desperately to grab it and run. She nodded her agreement, but really, she had no idea what the lord had just said and couldn't have cared less. Ronnis moved toward the door and unlocked it with a smile. Cassandra never looked at him as she and her mother left the dreadful room, finally making their way home.

They did not speak as they walked across the courtyard and back toward the dorms of the orphanage. The evening had been a plethora of emotions for both of them, but most important, they had shared that hug. Cassandra took Sera's hand as they walked, and they smiled at each other, no words necessary. It was the best walk Cassandra had ever taken.

Once at her room, Cassandra immediately grabbed her quill and ink and a small book similar to the one Ronnis had confiscated. She sat at her desk and began writing in it. Sera spoke with Kessi as Cassandra worked hard to jot down the spells she had read at the lord's office. Kessi was dramatic as usual with her discussion of her god, but Cassandra welcomed it this night; she had to write down these spells before she forgot them.

"Listen, Kessi," Sera said after many moments of listening. "I am not feeling well. I must be going to my room to clean up and go to bed. I wish I could listen some more, but we will continue this conversation tomorrow. I promise."

Kessi smiled and hugged her. "I love you, Miss Sera. May Adlesk heal you of all your pains."

Sera smiled and kissed Kessi's forehead. "Good night, Cassandra!" she called out.

Cassandra turned and smiled, a genuine smile at that. Then Cassandra closed the book and ran over to Sera, giving her another big hug.

Sera hugged her back and then bent to eye level once the embrace had ended. "You know, I could get used to all these hugs."

Cassandra smiled. "Me too." Then she hesitated and fidgeted with her hair, wanting to know more about what had transpired in that stinky office.

Sera waited for her to speak what was on her mind, and when Cassandra could not find her nerve, Sera coaxed it out of her. "Is there something on your mind?"

"Yes. Did Ronnis hurt you?" Cassandra finally asked, looking at Sera's neck, which displayed several red marks and maybe a bruise or two.

"No, he did not," Sera said and smiled, but Cassandra had a feeling she was lying.

"Well, thank you for helping me," was all Cassandra could think to say.

"Of course. I will always be there to protect you and your sister. Do you understand that?"

"I do now," she said with tears in her eyes. She gave Sera another hug and then went back to her desk.

From the corner of her eye, she could see Kessi watching her with a shocked look on her face. Sera and Kessi spoke for a few moments, and Cassandra could not make out everything they said, but she did hear Sera whisper, "I'll tell you later."

"All right, girls, I want you both in bed by the time that candle burns another inch."

The girls moaned and complained but agreed to Sera's wish. Sera opened the door and was ready to step out into the hall when Cassandra found the strength to say, "I'm here to protect you as well, Sera. So don't worry; I won't let him hurt you either."

With a shocked look on her face, Sera nodded and smiled once more. She left the room in the hopes of taking a bath and washing the filth that was Ronnis D'Breeth off her.

After Sera had left, Kessi ran to her sister excitedly. "What happened at Lord Ronnis's house?"

"Something amazing!" Cassandra said but never stopped her work with the pen and ink.

"What are you doing?"

"Scribing magic spells."

Kessi laughed, perhaps thinking Cassandra was joking, but Cassandra did not return the laugh and continued her work. Her tongue stuck out slightly from her lips, which she tended to do when concentrating on a particular task.

"Tell me more! What about you and Sera? You've grown close?" Kessi asked, coming over to stand at the desk and observe Cassandra's work.

"Yes, yes, I will tell you, but not now. I have to write down these spells before I forget them."

"I don't understand—you're writing spells? I thought Ronnis forbade it! I'm confused."

Cassandra sighed and dropped her pen into the inkwell. "Confused you must stay until tomorrow, dear sister. I have to do this, or I will forget. Now please go to bed. I'll do the same soon."

"Sera said in one inch of the candle melting. That won't be much longer."

"I know, and you're making this more difficult! Now good night, Kessi."

Cassandra grabbed her pen and began the work again. She noticed Kessi watched for a bit but seemed to lose interest and tucked herself in. She vaguely heard Kessi say her nightly prayers, then quickly doze off.

Cassandra worked through the night, penning the three spells in her tiny book. She stayed awake until the first light of day began to crest the eastern horizon. Then, exhausted but satisfied, she smiled and hid her book in a secret compartment in the wall. For the first time since her mom's death, she felt happy and complete.

CHAPTER 2
THE PRODIGY

As Cassandra was discovering the delights of arcane magic, in another part of the world, a young boy her age was gaining a reputation as a child prodigy. His name was Greyson Kavince, and similar to Cassandra, he was orphaned when he was born. But unlike her, he'd been left at the doorstep of a temple, not an orphanage. The priests of that temple, located in the small village of Tara, took him in and raised him under the god Plath's tenets. Plath provided the priests with defensive magic and healing, as opposed to some gods' more aggressive powers. The priests referred to him as the god of art and light.

Tara, home to approximately five hundred priests of Plath and their families, was a simple community. The inhabitants were self-sufficient, growing their crops and livestock and living peacefully in celebration of their god. The temple, designed with many windows so the sun could illuminate its rooms, was the heart of the village and the only structure with multiple levels. It was the oldest building, as well as the most decorative, as the priests' artistic abilities shone through its fantastic design.

Tara's visitors were rare indeed, but the priests refused no one's entry into the village, as they believed their god favored travelers. The closest town, Attins, was located only a mile southwest of their home, but no roads led to Tara. That was primarily due to the lack of trade between the two locales. Tara was self-sustaining, with rich soil for crops and plenty of livestock. However, the rougher terrain made travel to and from the village very difficult by horse. Thus, the priests maintained a solitary existence.

Tara's priests believed Plath blessed Greyson upon his birth, and as he approached his thirteenth birthday, they held a special meeting to discuss his future. Those in attendance included Berro, the giver of light; Sebe, the mother of travels; Jak, the creator of art; Talis, the giver of hope; and a fifth priest, who was much younger than the other four, by the name of Darian Dulin. Unlike the others, Darian was not a high priest, and at only twenty years old, he was the youngest member of the village ever to be dubbed a priest.

So, as the sun flooded the temple room and the priests completed their prayers, their business began. "Brothers and sister of Plath, we have gathered here on this glorious morning to discuss the fate of young Greyson Kavince," Berro said.

"And a glorious morning it is, Brother Berro," Sebe replied, followed by mumbled agreements from the others, as the sun bathed the room and the spirit of Plath filled each of them.

"So we must handle the prodigy the way Plath sees fit," Berro said. "We have all had the vision, excluding young Darian, of the future of this child. We know what is to come and how much glory he will bring Plath!"

His words were followed by calls of "Praise Plath" and "Amen" from among the gathered priests, with Jak kissing his holy symbol in response. Each of the five wore a similar medallion, depicting an eight-pointed star. The higher the priest's rank within the sect, the rarer the metal used to craft the holy symbol. Berro, the highest ranking, wore a star made of pure gold; Sebe, Jak, and Talis wore stars made from silver; and Darian wore one made of copper.

The priests had summoned Darian to that meeting to discuss the critical need for him to take Greyson under his wing as a mentor. He did not know that yet, so he attended the event without knowing why he was there. As the powerful disciples of Plath celebrated their holy gathering, Darian kissed his sacred symbol, then closed his eyes and said a small prayer of thanks. When he opened them, the others were all looking at him. The moment of truth was upon him.

"Brother Darian," Berro said, "we have asked you here this glorious morning to witness the will of this council and to take young Greyson under your wing."

"We know how close the two of you are," Sebe added.

"Yes, of course, he is like a brother to me," Darian said. "I will show him the proper behaviors and rituals of a priest of Plath, and when he reaches the age of his trial, I promise to have him ready."

"Good. We were hoping you would say that, young Darian, because that day has come," Jak said.

"Wait, you mean today?" Darian asked.

"In three suns' time," Berro said.

"Forgive my ignorance, but I do not understand. I thought the trial was given to our upcoming priests when they turned eighteen. Unfortunately Greyson is only twelve."

"We are well aware of our customs, dear boy," Berro said and smiled.

"Of course, and I do not mean to offend any of you. Please forgive me," Darian said, his face flush with embarrassment.

"There is nothing to forgive. You have accepted our offer to be Greyson's mentor, and so you have pleased Plath this very day," Sebe said.

"We have all shared a premonition about Greyson from the day he first came to us. We have seen a glimpse into his future, and he will be a powerful force soon. We have seen this and believe there can be no more delay," Talis said.

"Why now?"

"He will be old enough to procreate soon. He must have the early years of training under his belt when he reaches eighteen. At that time, you will take him on his lifelong journey to sample the world," Berro replied.

"But isn't it custom for the disciples of Plath to travel alone?"

"Not Greyson. You will be the insurance that he not only survives but thrives as a priest. We have chosen you to walk beside him. You will have the greatest opportunity to experience the miracles he will perform in the name of Plath!" Berro replied, and the other high priests nodded. "Go with young Kavince and document his miracles so that others may learn of his greatness!"

"Very well. I will do as you ask, and I feel honored to be chosen for this most important of tasks," Darian said.

"Go and speak with him now. Tell Greyson that he must prepare his mind, body, and soul for his trials," Sebe said.

Darian stood and bowed, then kissed each aged hand. Once he was gone from the temple room, the high priests of Plath began to undress. The burdens placed on the god's followers included being skilled in the arts and well traveled. He demanded each be a beacon of knowledge and wisdom. The small village of Tara had taken that oath one step further and had decreed sex to be one of the best ways to please their god. With Darian gone, the four used the temple to expand their knowledge and satisfy their god, as they had many times before.

~

A few days after that meeting, on the night before his trials, Greyson slept very peacefully. He dreamed of Plath and never felt closer to his god than that night. He was not worried about the coming tests and knew there was no way he would fail. He awoke to Darian gently shaking him, and he quickly rose, excited that the day was upon him. Darian had been like a brother to him since he was very young, and he looked up to him as a friend and mentor. So he greeted the new day with a smile at the sight of his dearest friend. Darian, however, looked very concerned.

Greyson sat up in his bed. "What's wrong, Darian?"

"Nothing—it's a most glorious day!" Darian exclaimed, unsuccessfully trying to change his expression from worry to joy.

Greyson sat unconvinced. "What are you not telling me?"

Darian sat down on the edge of the bed. "I'm worried, Greyson—worried for your safety today."

Greyson smiled, stretched, and yawned as if nothing in the world bothered him. "Is that why you come to me on my day of trials with a long face? Don't worry, Darian. I'll be fine."

Greyson got out of bed, totally nude, and noticed Darian shake his head with a smile as he dressed. The upcoming trials did not faze him, but at just twelve years of age, Greyson would be the youngest person to take the tests into the priesthood. However, he did not feel young, and truth be told, his physique was closer to that of a man's, even at his young age. That blessing from Plath was just the beginning of why the village hailed him as a prodigy. He would do well with the ladies once he set off to explore the world; he was confident of that.

"It's dangerous, you know," Darian finally said, breaking Greyson's thoughts.

"Yes, you told me it would be."

"Many people have died taking the trials. Those who failed are still there in the holy cave."

"Yes, yes, I am aware, Darian," Greyson said with a wave of his hand and another yawn.

"Berro and the others will be here in moments. I want to say a prayer for you before they come, not only as a priest but also as your brother."

Greyson smiled with a nod and knelt at his bedside. Darian came over, knelt beside him, and draped an arm around him. "Dear Lord, please bless Greyson today as he takes his trials. We both know that he will pass because you will see him through, but I pray for his safety in this most dangerous of tests."

When finished, he kissed his holy symbol, signifying his dedication to Plath. Greyson then looked him in the eye and said, "Thank you, Brother. But fear not, for I will be safe today. Plath told me so himself."

Greyson knew that Darian did not know how to react to that. None of the higher priests had ever hinted that Plath had spoken with them, and perhaps he had not. However, Greyson had frequent vivid dreams in which his god talked to him. They made eye contact, Darian trying to read his face. The look in Darian's eyes told Greyson that his friend believed him. That meant more to Greyson than his friend could know.

A tear came to Darian's eye, and he whispered, "You are a prodigy, aren't you?"

"That's what they tell me."

After a brief moment of silence, they both shared a good laugh, and by the time the high priests entered the room a few minutes later, Greyson and Darian were both relaxed. Greyson knew then that everything would turn out fine. It had to; he was the prodigy of Plath.

Berro, Sebe, Jak, and Talis were all dressed in their ceremonial robes, which consisted of many bright colors and depictions of the eight-pointed star. But unfortunately, Berro did not share the joy that Greyson and Darian were experiencing before he entered. Soon his stern mood rubbed off on all, and things became serious for Greyson.

"It is time, my young disciple. Are you ready?" Berro asked him.

"Of course, Brother Berro. I have never been readier."

Darian then assisted with preparing Greyson for the task, which included many prayers. As the priests looked on, Darian also informed Greyson that the high priests were the only ones allowed to know the actual location of the holy cave. "Do you understand, young prodigy?" Darian asked once he completed the instructions.

Greyson nodded with a smile.

"Berro will now blind you," Darian continued, "using the power offered him by Plath. But of course, the effect will be temporary and undone once we reach the cave entrance. After you, I, too, will be so blinded to maintain the secrecy of the cave location. Do you understand?"

"Of course, and I accept the blindness as a humble beginning to this magnificent day."

Darian patted him on the shoulder. "Then let us begin." He then stepped away and nodded to Berro.

Berro approached Greyson and said, "I am the giver of light, and as such, I take your sight with the holy light of Plath." Then the high priest waved his hand in front of Greyson, and suddenly his vision became filled with a bright light, and he could see nothing but white. It was magnificent, and Greyson felt so blessed by the action. Satisfied that the blindness had appropriately taken Greyson's sight, Berro instructed Sebe to do the same to Darian, which she did. Soon both were unable to see and were escorted gently outside to begin the trek up the mountainside to the secret holy caves.

Tara was a small community carved out of the side of a mountain, hard to reach by foot and impossible to get to by horseback. The trip to the caves was even more treacherous, and so the going was slow as the high priests took their time escorting their blinded friends higher up the side of the mountain. But by midday, they reached their destination.

Once there, Berro and Sebe restored vision to the two friends, and they found themselves in a heavily wooded but flat area on the mountainside. A hole in the ground, about fifteen feet in diameter, was near them. A bracket spanned the entrance with a pulley system installed with a seat large enough to lower one person at a time into the pit. Greyson soon realized that this was the entrance to the holy cave.

He dropped to his knees, overcome with emotion, and kissed the most hallowed ground. Then, after a brief prayer, he stood once more.

Berro came over to him and smiled, placing his hands on his shoulders. "Dear boy, each experience in the caves is unique. I cannot tell you what you will find within. All I can say is that if Plath is with you, you will survive. If he blesses you, he will offer treasures beyond your dreams."

He fished something small out of his vestments and produced it for Greyson to see. "This was my reward all those years ago." In his hand was a small chest made of some sort of rare metal. It reflected the light of the midday sun as a diamond might, and it looked to be as durable as steel. Berro placed it on the ground and whispered a magical command. The chest immediately began to grow, and Greyson had to step back as it grew to full size. During the transformation, the chest's material changed, with metal giving way to simple unadorned wood.

Berro smiled and produced a key to unlock the magnificent chest. Inside he showed Greyson that there was a suit of chain mail, a large shield colored a bright gold with an eight-pointed star etched onto it, and a beautifully constructed mace.

"These are my gifts to you for today's test. You cannot take magical items with you into the cave, so these have no unique properties. However, they are made from the finest materials in the land and constructed by the best smithies Attins offers.

"Darian, help Greyson don this most wonderful suit of chain mail while the other high priests and I say one last prayer for the boy."

Darian bowed and went to the chest. Before he reached it, Greyson already had the mace out, holding it before him. It was incredibly light but made from a rare metal that gave it tremendous strength, and the head was cut into an elegant eight-pointed star.

"Do you remember how to use one of these?" Darian asked as he reached into the chest to produce the shield and armor.

"Yes, vaguely, but only from the few times you have instructed me. This one is different; it is much lighter than the practice maces I have used."

"That means it is of much higher grade and will therefore be a better weapon for you. Hopefully you will not have to use it."

"Hopefully," Greyson said, but with not much conviction. He knew the trials would be difficult, and Berro offering a weapon and armor meant he would need them. It was at that point that he began to realize the dangers of the ritual he was undertaking.

Darian noticed his concerned look and grabbed him by the shoulders. He looked into Greyson's eyes. "Do not worry. I'm sure Plath is with you, and you will defeat any obstacles that stand in your way."

Greyson forced a smile and nodded. In truth, he still felt confident, but the reality of the dangerous test was now upon him. No one said a word as Darian helped Greyson dress into the fine chain mail. It was a little large for him, but for the most part, it fit comfortably, and Darian helped to make him as flexible as possible in the ill-fitting armor. Once Greyson was fully donned, Darian showed him how to hold the holy shield securely and attach the mace to a belt loop for easy access. Darian then clasped the young boy on the shoulders, looked him in the eyes, and smiled. He did not speak but nodded to let Greyson know it was time. Greyson smiled and nodded in return.

Berro then instructed Darian to move a nearby plank across the pit so that Greyson could use it to access the seat. Greyson took his time to thank each of them, lastly Darian, before he moved to the edge of the pit. He looked up to the heavens, closed his eyes, and said a silent prayer. Once he felt he was ready, he nodded to Berro.

Berro approached the edge of the pit and stood beside him, looking into the darkness below, and then said softly so that only Greyson could hear, "It is time, my son. Are you ready?"

"I am ready, my brother."

"What you find beneath is for your eyes only. Plath will decide if you survive, and if you do, he will enlighten you on many things. But, my boy, this is a test of faith, which means this could be the last time we see each other. I have lowered many potential priests to their deaths in that seat, but I believe you will be fine and we will be celebrating your victory very soon. Do you have any questions before we begin?"

"Yes. How will I know when the trial is over?"

"There is only one way out of the caves, and Plath will show it to you if it is his desire. If you do not find the exit, it will mean certain death. Otherwise, we will see you once you complete your trials."

Greyson nodded grimly. "I am ready."

"Good. Your first test is to walk this plank and find your seat that will take you below. If you lose your balance, then you will fall to your death. If you find the seat, we will lower you into the most magnificent cave. You may begin when ready."

Then Berro stepped back to join the others and watched as Greyson took his first steps onto the plank. His moves were nervous and shaky at first, and the chain mail made him unbalanced on the plank. It bowed under the armor's weight, and the plank shook more and more with each step. He stopped after a few steps and found his balance as the shaking slowly subsided. He closed his eyes, refusing to look down into the darkness, and instead focused on taking easy steps and not rushing the short but dangerous trek. He opened his eyes and focused on the chair connected to the pulley system ahead of him. He began to walk deliberately and covered the remaining distance in five steps, but it felt like an eternity. Finally, he grabbed the chair and tentatively took a seat.

He now found himself facing his friends. He did not show any emotion but felt very relieved to have made the seat. He sat calmly, still refusing to look down, as Berro and Darian made their way to either side of the pit to where the cranks would lower him. After a few moments of releasing the brakes, the cranks creaked into action, and the chair lurched slightly forward, making Greyson tighten his grip on it. A moment later, he was moving slowly down.

The darkness enveloped him, and panic took him briefly. The cool air encased him, and his vision began to fail as the daylight lost its battle against the darkness of the cave. He glanced up and focused on the bracket and chain attached to his chair. He realized he was too afraid to look down and instead continued to focus on the ever-shrinking hole above him. The descent seemed to go on for an eternity, but eventually, his feet touched something substantial, and shortly after that, his chair stopped moving. The chain had reached its length, and it would take him no farther. He looked up at the hole and saw Darian, and it was evident by how his friend squinted into the cave that he could not see Greyson in the darkness below.

"The chain is at its end; you should be able to reach the cave floor now," Darian called to him.

Greyson had instinctively lifted his feet straight out in front of him when they first touched the bottom of the pit and slowly relaxed them feeling the ground beneath his feet. He moved them around to make sure there was a floor beneath him. He dared not call out to Darian but gingerly moved off the chair. He did not let it go until he was sure he was on solid ground. He still could not see anything around him and had to summon the courage to yell back at the hole, shakily, "I am here!"

Darian, who appeared tiny and many miles away, waved and disappeared. Then the chair began to move up toward the hole as the crank started to rewind the chain. He watched until it was back to the starting point. Then, although he did not see anyone, he saw the plank that spanned the hole move away. Once it was gone, he knew he was truly alone.

"Hello?" he whispered to the opening that seemed so far away now. There was no answer—not that anyone could have heard his soft call, anyway. He waited and hoped to see Darian one last time; he needed to look on his friend once more before starting this test. He suddenly second-guessed his decision to do this. Was he ready to fight for his life? He waited many moments, staring at the tiny hole in the ceiling, but Darian never came back, and fear began to creep inside him. He felt small, alone, and terrified, whereas this very morning he had felt like a seasoned priest of Plath who could face anything. Greyson closed his eyes and focused, trying to find that feeling once more. The peace of Plath washed over him, erasing his doubts, and he could feel the warmth spread through him as his confidence returned. He would have to focus and have faith. He let out a small chuckle and shook his head. How could he doubt the powers of his amazing god? Finally, he found the courage to begin the test.

But where should he start? He could not see, and the traces of light from the small hole in the roof grew dim because of the sun setting in the western sky. He would need to find a source of light before nightfall. He took out the mace and, for a moment, marveled at its lightness. Then he used it to reach out in front of him into the dark, treating it as an extension of his arm. He swept it back and forth in an arc in front of him and proceeded to walk. After about fifty paces, it struck the cave wall. Then, using the hole in the ceiling as a guide, he started the same process but walked in a different direction.

After Greyson hit the wall several more times and started on his fourth line of movement, the mace struck something metal. The object gave way and moved with the sweep of the mace. He stopped and held his mace in front of him, defensively, and prepared for some attack. There was only silence. After what seemed like an eternity, he found the courage to reach out in front of him to find out precisely what he had discovered.

To his relief, he found a wooden table with a small rope and metal lantern on top of it, which he determined must have been the object he had struck with the mace. He attached the mace to his belt and quickly felt around the table. He found some oil for the lantern, as well as some torches and some flint and steel. He would have light! He used the flint and steel to light a torch first. As it flickered to life, it took several moments for Greyson's eyes to adjust. Once they did and he could see his surroundings, he realized he was in a vast room, clear of any obstructions other than the table. Three passageways were to his left. Other than that, it was empty.

He realized then that he was a beacon in the dark, alerting anyone and anything to his presence. He did not care; he could not stand being blind any longer. Besides, Plath was with him—he could feel it, his confidence fully intact once more. Now he needed only to decide which passageway to take.

~

Darian and the others traveled to another smaller opening into the caves. This one had no bracket or chair but instead had ladder rungs nailed into the cave wall to allow Greyson to climb out of the caves if he made it this far. There was a steel grate over the top, and Berro knelt and unlocked it. Then he and Darian moved the heavy grate to the side of the hole, offering an escape route to their young prodigy.

The place offered profound memories for all of them as they silently recalled their trials within those caves. Then, as they set camp, Darian looked to the sun, slowly setting in the western sky, and asked, "What is the longest anyone has stayed in the caves … and survived?"

"I was in there for four days," Berro said. "It is the longest stint on record and a tremendous blessing for me."

Darian nodded his understanding but said, "He is only twelve. Can he survive the ordeals found within?"

"That is for Plath to decide, young priest. Besides, if Greyson is truly a prodigy of Plath, he will have no trouble making it out alive. So have faith, Darian."

The young priest put on the best smile he could muster and nodded. None of them said it, but all the high priests shared some of Darian's doubts. They all loved Greyson but agreed that twelve was far too young for him to enter the caves. Plath had communed with them to do just that, so they had. But had they delivered the boy to his death?

"Well, we should finish making camp," Talis said after many long and silent moments. "It is going to be a long night not only for Greyson but for us as well."

The others agreed, so they built a fire and set their camp around the cave exit. They took turns watching over the pit and put several mystical guards around the base to alert them to intruders using their powers from Plath. Darian took the first watch and nervously awaited Greyson's appearance. Unfortunately it did not come that night.

~

After studying the three passages, Greyson decided that the left represented the setting sun because of its placement. Likewise, he felt the one on the right represented the rising sun since it was on the cave's east side. Following that rationale, he felt it only made sense that the middle one represented the sun at midday. He was confident in his deduction and took the lit torch in his shield hand and his mace in his right hand and approached the passage in the center. Plath would prefer the sun at its peak, and therefore the center passage was the correct choice, he reasoned.

He had tucked the lantern oil in his belt pouch and had an extra torch looped in his belt as well. He also pocketed the flint and steel, knowing good and well how valuable it would be down there. He left the lantern and turned to look at it one last time before exiting the room. It called to him as if beckoning him to take it, and he had a feeling that he was failing part of the test by not doing so. He shrugged it off and turned back toward the passage, convinced his mind was playing tricks on him. It was time to leave this entry room and explore the depths of the cave.

He walked slowly and quietly down the passageway. There was a slight curve to it, and he fully expected to see some sort of monster around every corner. The shadows from the torch danced on the stone walls, fueling his imagination. The passageway made several turns before it finally branched into a four-way intersection. The left and right passages seemed to go on forever, being swallowed up by the dark. He stopped there to listen but could hear only the beating of his own heart. There were no clues as to which way to go, and the silence was deafening. After some contemplation, he decided to continue straight ahead.

Once he cleared the intersection and had taken about twenty steps down the passageway, a section of the floor sunk about two inches as he stepped on it. He realized it was a pressure plate and he had triggered something—and probably something terrible. He readied his mace for action and fully expected some creature to come rushing out at him from the dark.

He listened intently, knowing that he had set something in motion, and he finally heard what sounded like cogs grinding together and the sound of heavy chains moving metal. Then, after what seemed like forever, it stopped with a crash of metal against metal. He imagined that a portcullis had been lifted somewhere up ahead in the infernal darkness, releasing a terrible monster on him. Suddenly he felt that this was not the correct passageway at all. The image of the lantern called to his subconscious, and he felt the urge to run back to it.

He tightened his grip on the mace and realized it was a sweaty grip, his fear getting the best of him. He took a deep breath to steady his nerves, but that uneasy feeling that this was the wrong way grew with each subsequent step. He cursed his poor choice and understood he would now have to deal with the consequences, whatever they might be. He thought of the lantern once again, and suddenly he knew what he had to do—he knew precisely why the lantern was meaningful. He turned and ran as fast as he could back to the entry room. He sensed something coming slowly from behind. He would have time, though, he hoped.

Once more, when he reached the entry room, he hastily laid the shield and torch on the table and went to work. He made sure he was facing the passages, waiting for the unknown horror to appear. He quickly worked to take the top off the lantern and then removed the glass windows and glass oil chamber from it. He discarded them quickly, leaving just the metal frame and bottom of the lantern. He had some training in the art of metal crafting, and using that knowledge and his mace, he began to hit the lantern frame, bending it to his will.

Soon he had the bottom removed completely, and he worked feverously to shape the frame. His hammering echoed down the passageways, summoning the evil that lurked there. He worked so long with the lantern that he didn't realize his torch was burning low. How long had he been at work? He did not know and dared not stop, knowing that the lantern was the answer to his success. It was more important even than the torch, which barely produced light now. Sweat dripped from his brow, and he hurriedly continued his work, not slowing even when he sensed the evil coming down the passage. He dared not look up, for any delay might cost him his life.

Hit after hit rang out, and as his project came together, the evil made its appearance. Greyson could see an outline in the passageway, a human figure that moved slowly and methodically. It limped, and he could hear the thud of its uneven gait as it landed hard on its left foot each time it stepped. He used his peripheral vision as much as he could to trace the creature's path but focused on the lantern, hitting it hard over and over and bending the metal to specific angles. The torch puffed out. Total darkness filled the room, and then the smell overcame him. Not the scent of the extinguished torch but the smell of rot and decaying flesh. It was the smell of evil coming for him—a creature of the undead.

He removed the small rope from his belt and took the newly shaped lantern into his hands. He felt its eight uneven points in the dark, and although not nearly perfect, it would have to do because he was out of time. He quickly ran the rope through the lantern and then tied it, formulating a primitive holy symbol, the eight-pointed star of Plath. He put it around his neck and picked up his shield and mace. He heard the creature grunt as it hit the table and felt a breeze above his head as the creature swung at him. He could not see it, but he could hear it move now and could smell it.

He held the symbol with his shield hand and started a prayer to Plath. He spoke softly at first, backpedaling to the far reaches of the room. His prayer got louder and louder as panic found its icy grip on him. Then, sensing the creature was close and using the moonlight from the ceiling's entrance hole, he vaguely made out a swing from the beast. He ducked, and something metal scraped the wall above his head. It had a weapon.

As it prepared to swing again, Greyson yelled as loud as he could, "Let there be light! By the grace of your will, Plath, give me sight against this beast!"

Energy washed over his body, and immediately the room flooded with light equal to that of several torches—and not a moment too soon, as the creature became visible, and Greyson let out a yelp of terror. It was human, or at least used to be, female and young, but now it was misshapen and rotting, with half her face peeled off, revealing bone underneath. Her left eye hung uselessly from its socket, her hair caked with dried blood. In the creature's right hand was an axe, already swinging as the room lit. He had just enough time to raise his shield to deflect the blow, but the force of the hit knocked him onto his backside and, worse, tore the holy symbol from his grasp as it came free of his rope necklace.

He could see out of the corner of his eye the hunk of metal that was once a lantern frame sitting just a few feet away. It looked nothing like an eight-pointed star. It merely appeared to be a hunk of metal now, beaten and distorted. However, it was the light source as it glowed as powerful as any lantern he had ever seen. Plath was with him. He had granted him this power of light.

The creature struck again, and this time the shield absorbed the blow, but it racked his left arm with a wave of pain. The beast was powerful, but the sight of the glowing holy symbol motivated him and lifted his morale. He swung at the creature's knees, striking it hard with his mace, tearing flesh and a bit of bone from the undead thing. Although gore now clung to his mace, the hit seemed not to have affected the zombie at all. It neither acknowledged the impact nor slowed its attack.

It reached down and pulled the shield away while preparing another strike with the axe. Greyson was trapped, and he could not remove his left hand from the shield at the current angle. Then he noticed an overhead chop from the axe aimed for his skull. He swung the mace with all his might, batting aside the swinging axe enough so that it sliced the stone beside his head, then hit his left shoulder. The spray of pebbles from the near miss cut his face, and the axe hit him hard, not penetrating the chain mail armor but nearly dislocating his shoulder. The parry had saved his life, but the impact had taken the mace from his grip and knocked it several feet away.

He screamed in agony, and he almost blacked out from the pain in his wounded shoulder. The zombie sensed his distress and leaned down to look him in the face. It showed no emotion, but the smell was worse than anything he could have imagined. It pulled the shield even farther away, manipulating his injured shoulder, which made him scream out again. The creature dropped the axe and grabbed him roughly by the hair, clawing his scalp and drawing more blood. It then forced Greyson's head back and opened its mouth. It was going to bite his face, and he could not stop it.

He thought the end was near and closed his eyes. He knew Plath was with him, but he simply was not strong enough to defeat even one zombie. He had failed. As quickly as the test had begun, so it would end. He would not see Darian or the other priests again—never see the light of day, never become a Plath priest. As he felt the creature close, he remembered the gait. The filth had a bad leg, and he had just hit it with the mace. Seeing only one way to survive this encounter, Greyson kicked with his right leg at the thing's wounded knee. He couldn't see the target clearly with his head pulled back, but his aim was perfect. He heard the bone snap, and the creature wobbled, falling headfirst into the stone wall. That impact did little to hurt it, but the fall made it release his hair. Greyson moved frantically to remove his wounded arm from the shield as the creature fell on its face, its left leg sticking out unnaturally to the side.

He fought through the pain, screaming several more times in his haste, and managed to free himself from the shield eventually. He backed away to look at the creature, which was now trying to stand again. It did not feel the pain, and it did not understand the damage to its leg as it toppled over immediately. Greyson backed away from it, and then a calm feeling came over him. He had almost died. He had nearly failed, and yet, as he watched the thing struggle, his emotions changed from fear and anger to pity. He felt sorry for the creature even though it had nearly killed him. Greyson watched it struggle to regain its footing and looked over to the axe, which he could easily use to hack it to pieces now. But instead, he had a better idea. Plath was with him, and now he would harness that power.

Instead of the axe, he picked up the holy symbol he had created. He held it tight and whispered a prayer to Plath, and then he kissed it and presented it before him. "By the power of Plath, I rebuke you!"

The creature stopped struggling and looked his way. It showed no emotion on its rotting face, but he could sense that it understood his words. After a few moments, it began its struggle anew, this time crawling toward the axe. Greyson calmly walked over to the weapon and picked it up before placing it on the table, out of the zombie's reach. The creature continued to crawl, this time toward him.

He reached deep within himself to harness Plath's strength and presented the symbol once again. With more conviction this time, and all his faith in his god, he yelled out, "Begone from this world, you creature of undeath! I rebuke your existence!"

The zombie stopped immediately and managed to look at the holy symbol, and he thought he saw a hint of peace there. Unfortunately the expression didn't last long, as the creature quickly began to disintegrate. It kept its one functioning eye on the holy symbol as if in a trance, and within seconds, the zombie was gone, and there remained only a pile of ash. He kissed the sacred symbol again and replaced it around his neck. It was then that he understood he was indeed a priest of Plath, gaining an extraordinary amount of power in the short time he had been in the cave. He stared proudly at the pile of dust for a few moments, letting the turn of events sink in.

His shield arm was useless, so he decided to leave the shield. He used it as a marker for the zombie's grave and said a quick prayer for the creature just in case it was a poor soul trying to make its way into the afterlife. He couldn't forget the look on its face just before he had destroyed it. After the brief ceremony, he prepared himself for the next test. Knowing that the middle passage was terrible luck for him, he took the one to the right, which, he reasoned, represented the sunrise. Tara's high priests would have chosen that one, he did not doubt, so that was the path he took, his hope renewed.

He tucked his left arm against his chest, with any movement of that arm causing excruciating pain. His right arm held a tight grip on the magnificent mace, and the poorly made holy symbol that he wore around his neck still shone brightly. He made his way down the dark passage, his star symbol casting enough light for him to see the twists and turns. After he had gone about one hundred yards, he heard the familiar sound of a portcullis being raised or lowered, this time from behind him. Thinking that was curious since he had not seen any on his short trek down the corridor, he turned and went back once more to the entry room.

He was confident enough not to be afraid of any zombies now, but what he finally saw sank his heart a little. A portcullis had dropped at the beginning of the passage, cutting him off from the entry room. He walked up to it and laid his forehead against the cool metal. It was then that he realized he was sweating profusely. Whether it was from pain or fear, he did not know. All he knew was that the metal felt good on his forehead.

He peered into the room where he had twice left and twice returned, seeing the table, his shield at the pile of zombie ash, and, in the distance, the hole in the ceiling. In a short amount of time, that simple room had become his home away from home. It was the one place in the caves where he felt a little safe. Perhaps because that was the place where he had last seen his friend Darian and the place where Plath had given him the power to create light and had defeated evil in the face of death. He sighed, understanding that this part of the test was now over. He would have to continue into the unknown passage behind him. Greyson could see the night sky through the small hole, and the stars twinkled at him, reminding him of the power of Plath that he was learning to wield. After looking around the wall and not finding a mechanism to open the heavy gate, he said his final goodbye to the room, the zombie, and Darian, whom he assumed was still near the hole. Either way, he was now on his own. He turned and proceeded with his test, taking confident steps down the dark passage.

Unlike the other one, this passage had many branches to it, and one did not seem more correct than the other, so Greyson wandered through the maze of passageways. He did not encounter anything but could occasionally hear another portcullis open or close in the distance, somewhere deep within the cave, or sometimes behind him as he would trigger another pressure plate in the floor. He lost count of how many he heard and soon lost his way, not remembering which turns he had taken. He panicked as minutes turned to hours, and he cursed himself for not trying to mark the walls with his mace, to leave some kind of trail. Sometimes he would come to a fork in the passage that looked familiar, as if he had been there before, but he simply couldn't tell for sure.

With his shoulder throbbing and his hope diminishing, he finally found himself at a four-way intersection. Knowing that he had not encountered this particular section of the cave yet, he felt a bit of hope. He kissed the still-shining makeshift holy symbol and blessed Plath once more. "I am sorry I doubted you, my most wonderful god! Now please give me the wisdom to make the correct decision. Please show me the way out of the cave. Give me some sort of sign!"

He listened intently for a few moments, his heart pounding as he felt each beat in his wounded arm. Then he heard it—another portcullis to his right opened or shut. "Thank you, my lord," he whispered. Then he kissed the symbol once again and let it hang from his neck, still a shining beacon in the dark.

He moved into the passage on his right, knowing without a doubt that the sound was a sure sign from Plath himself. He had taken only a few steps down this passage when he sensed something was in front of him. He stopped, swallowed, and composed himself. He could handle a zombie—Plath would not let such a foul creature kill him—that he knew now. Perhaps the presence in front of him was another undead creature. Maybe not. Although he could not see anything beyond the light of his holy symbol, he knew something evil lurked in the shadows just a few feet away. He propped the mace against the wall next to him, leaving it within easy reach, and then held out his symbol in front of him, drawing on the power of his god, hoping it would have the same effect on this new adversary as it did on the zombie. Finally, he said sternly into the darkness, "In the name of Plath, I rebuke you, creature!"

Nothing happened. He could not hear any sound from the pitch black, but his uneasiness grew as something unseen in the dark drew nearer. "Show yourself, you creature of the dark! I renounce your existence, foul beast!"

His voice was loud and echoed down the passage before him. Then he heard something bellow from within the dark that sounded like a beast, possibly enraged by his words. He knew then that what he faced in the darkness was no simple zombie as before. He swallowed hard and then reached for his mace. But before he could grasp it, he heard the sound of heavy footsteps running toward him from the darkness.

His eyes went wide as he finally saw the great beast emerge from the shadows. It was not a simple zombie as before—that much was sure. It had the head of a great bull, the horns curving out from its forehead, and the body of a muscular man. It wore no shirt, donning only a tattered pair of old pants. It was shoeless as its hooved feet poked through the ends of the pants. It also had a large axe hanging on its belt, but this one was much larger than what the zombie had carried and was double sided. Muscles bulged from its arms, chest, and abdomen. It was a perfect killing machine, and it looked enraged. "Minotaur," was all Greyson could whisper before the creature was on him.

Instead of grabbing the mace, he backed away on instinct as the creature was in a full charge, head lowered, and horns aimed straight for him. Unlike the zombie, this creature was swift, and Greyson had just enough time to maneuver himself so that the horns would not impale him. Unfortunately, that did little to avoid the full brunt of the attack as the minotaur's forehead struck him on his wounded left shoulder.

Pain shot through Greyson's whole body as he was thrown back into the four-way intersection with the tremendous hit. His collarbone snapped, and his wounded left arm hung uselessly, any movement causing him insufferable pain. He had hit his head hard on the rock floor, and he nearly lost consciousness. He lay on his back in the middle of the intersection, fighting the pain, his screams of agony echoing through the cave. Finally, the minotaur let out another beastly roar, and that snapped him out of his stupor.

He managed to gain a sitting position somehow, his wounded arm screaming at him. He heard the creature begin another charge, and there was nowhere to run. He tucked his arm and crawled toward the passage opposite the one with the minotaur. He managed to gain his footing for a short while, but the dizziness from the hit had him falling before he realized it. He fell just inside the passageway, triggering another portcullis to crash down behind him and seal off the intersection. However, the creature knelt and reached for his foot as the steel portcullis continued its fast descent.

Greyson tried to back away, but he could not do it fast enough with his wounded arm. The creature grabbed him by the foot, and its strength was beyond anything he could have imagined. With one swift tug, it had him moving toward the intersection and the falling portcullis. Greyson clawed with his right hand at the stone floor, trying to find a grip to slow things down. He kicked at the creature's hand with his other foot. The portcullis was almost closed, the animal now on its stomach as it pulled him closer.

The portcullis slammed shut, and Greyson closed his eyes, waiting for the pain to hit. He just knew the heavy iron gate had crushed his legs and the pain was about to overtake him. But instead, the minotaur let out a terrible roar. The creature had not been quite fast enough, and the portcullis had slammed right down on its wrist. Greyson's foot was just a few inches from the closed portcullis, and he knew he had narrowly avoided a terrible injury. The minotaur's hand still held him tight, and it let out another frustrated roar. It could not move its broken arm, but it still held on to him with incredible strength. Greyson managed to sit up again and found himself just a few inches away from the beast. The portcullis kept the creature from tearing him apart, but it could not protect him from the fear he felt welling inside him. Greyson could now see the hate in its eyes. It hated him and wanted nothing more than to kill him.

Once he gained enough courage, he tried to pry the great beast's fingers open with his right hand. The grip was as firm as the iron portal, and he had no hope of breaking it with only one hand. There was no use; he could not free himself from the creature's grip. He looked desperately around for a tool he could use, having now lost his mace, just like the shield. His left arm still hung limply beside him, and if anything came down the passage behind him, there was no way he could defend himself. The only hope he held on to was that the star around his neck still shone brightly.

He gave up his struggling and sat there, looking the minotaur in the face. He was battered and bruised and knew that if the portcullis weren't in place, this creature would have already killed him. He thanked Plath for the narrow escape and asked again for wisdom to escape his current predicament. The answer came from the minotaur itself as it smashed its head against the metal portcullis. It did minor damage to the structure, but one horn stabbed through one of the four-inch square openings. The horn nearly hit Greyson's face, and he dropped to his back and lay as flat as possible. The creature hit the portcullis several more times, trying to get its horn to gore him. Finally, it stopped and let out another roar that echoed many times down the corridor behind him.

Greyson assumed the constant noise from the angry creature would summon a predator that would rip him to shreds as he lay there on his back. But instead, the animal changed its tactics. Determined to kill its prey and furious to be so close without accomplishing its objective, it moved to a kneeling position and withdrew the large axe from its belt. Greyson watched in wonder, thinking that it might try to cut through the solid steel portcullis. But it chopped at its trapped arm, cutting it cleanly at the elbow. Blood sprayed everywhere, and the grip on his foot immediately loosened. He kicked his foot free of the severed arm and moved back from the gate.

The minotaur stood and roared again, looked at him for a moment, then snorted. Blood poured from its wound and splashed onto the rocky ground. Greyson looked on, dumbfounded, waiting for the creature's next move. He didn't have to wait long. It suddenly moved to the passage at its right, sprinting into the darkness. Greyson stood slowly and made his way to the portcullis. What had scared it off? At first he thought maybe another creature, even fiercer than the minotaur, had moved up behind him. Slowly he turned his head so he could view what terribleness awaited him there. To his relief, there was nothing but darkness.

"Why did you run, minotaur? What spooked you?" he asked the darkness of the corridor.

He turned and laid his head again on the cool iron of the portcullis and sat for a moment to catch his breath and straighten out his thoughts. He could barely see the outline of his mace, still propped against the far corridor. To his right, how he had come, nothing stirred. To his left, a similarly empty hall in which the enraged minotaur had run was utterly silent. There was simply nothing that had spooked the creature, if scaring it was even possible.

That last thought made his heart skip a beat: the creature wasn't spooked but was hunting. It knew the riddle of the caves and was circling to come in from behind him. He turned, and as quickly as his legs would take him, he ran down the corridor, not knowing what he might find or what portcullis might be triggered. His arm and collarbone throbbed with each step, and his legs tired quickly from the cumbersome chain mail. A growing fear of the creature appearing suddenly ahead of him had him running faster than he thought possible in the heavy armor.

He passed several more four-way intersections but did not pause to consider his path. He could hear the cranking of triggered pulley systems as an unseen portcullis was lowered or raised from the various hidden pressure plates he was activating. After what seemed like an eternity, and after Greyson passed several more intersections, his fear finally came true; the roar of the beast was behind him again—and very close.

He dared not turn around and instead focused on moving forward. That was his only hope, to keep moving. He could hear the creature gaining on him and could picture the thing readying its axe for a swing that would split his head. That thought would have been frightening enough for a seasoned warrior, but to a twelve-year-old kid, who knew little of melee combat and fighting to the death, the image more than scared him. The fear finally gripped his heart, and he lost all confidence and all hope as he began to cry uncontrollably.

The roar came again, and this time it was very close. Greyson estimated the great beast was within ten feet of him. Then he entered an entirely different place as the rock passageway emptied into a vast cavern. The ceiling was so high the light of his holy symbol could not detect it, and there was a polished stone floor that stretched out in all directions and seemed to go on forever. A final portcullis clanged shut as he entered the gigantic cavern. Still running, he looked behind him to see that the minotaur had indeed made it through the entryway before the path was sealed and was right behind him. It had its axe at the ready, and Greyson's life was at its end. There was nowhere to hide.

Greyson screamed in fear and frustration, not understanding how his god could have put him up against such a great foe—unless, of course, he was incredibly disappointing Plath and falling well short of the god's expectations. All he could think of was to continue running as fast as possible. As he turned back around, he found that the floor was at its end and there was a drop-off into darkness. He was at the precipice of a cliff, and there was no way to stop his momentum. He felt the swing of the axe just inches from the back of his head, then the scratching sound of the creature's hooved feet sliding on the polished rock floor. It knew to stop and would not topple to its death. Greyson gained some satisfaction knowing that he had escaped the creature and would not die at its hands.

Then he spotted a rope bridge about five feet to his right as he neared the drop-off. Unfortunately, he could not see the end of the bridge because of its length and the limited visibility of his star-shaped holy symbol. Nevertheless, it was his only hope, and as he found himself at the last step, he lunged for the bridge with what little strength he had left. The rickety thing was made of wooden planks and supported by rope, which held the planks together, and smaller cords created handrails on each side. He managed to grab the left-hand rail with his right hand, making the bridge swing wildly.

In the process, Greyson lost his holy symbol as the rope necklace came undone once again, then plummeted down into the darkness. It did not fall as far as he expected—only about fifty feet before crashing to the stone floor. He hung from the bridge with his one good arm and looked below to see where his precious symbol had finally come to rest, and what he saw made his heart ache. Many stalagmites lined the floor, which appeared very sharp and deadly in appearance. His holy symbol produced light even still, and though it barely benefited him at all that far away, he could see the floor of the great pit. There lay many skeletons, all armored with similar chain mail as he now wore. They were the remains of hopeful priests before him who had failed their quests in the cave. He was mesmerized by the tragic view and could only stare at the awfulness as he swung from the bridge, understanding he had almost become the latest addition to the collection.

The minotaur roared right behind him, and he realized he was still very close to the edge of the cliff. He could vaguely see the beast's outline in the dark and was almost in striking range of that vicious axe. It was standing at the edge of the bridge but would not walk on it. Greyson considered that a terrible sign indeed. He found the strength to pull himself up, grasp the bridge's wooden floor, kick a leg up over the side, and hook it onto the rope railing. The swinging increased with the movements, and he struggled to hold on. He smacked his wounded arm on the bridge several times as he hoisted himself up, a scream escaping his parched lips with each hit. As he made his way to his knees, he realized he was only about ten feet from the creature, and it was furious. The stump where its arm had been still gushed blood, and he could hear it splatter on the smooth floor. He was hopeful that the wound was mortal; however, he could sense that the creature was far from dead. He decided that it would be best to move along as quickly as possible. He wanted to leave the minotaur behind him, regardless of what might await him on the other side. As he turned and walked away, the creature let out a huge roar that echoed for many moments through the vast cavern. That only made Greyson walk a little faster on the still-swinging bridge.

He had taken no more than a few steps when something huge swung at him from his left. He could not see very far into the dark without his holy symbol, so the gigantic missile was on him before he knew it. He saw it just before it struck the bridge not six inches in front of him. He barely had time to register that it was a giant version of the minotaur's axe. It sliced through both handrails and scraped the wooden plank in front of him. Another few inches, and he would have lost his toes.

As the giant axe flew past him, Greyson estimated it was at least six feet long and shaped like a battle-axe, with the sharpened part of the blade formed in a semicircle. He was also just able to realize it was attached to the ceiling somewhere above in the darkness and was razor sharp, as it had severed both handrails with such proficiency that it hardly moved the bridge at all. However, without the assistance of the handrails, which now hung limply off the sides, he lost his balance.

He fell backward and luckily landed on the wooden planks that formed the bridge. He quickly turned onto his stomach to hug the bridge with his right arm. That's when things became worse, as the axe came back from the other direction, nearly hitting the bridge again and coming very close to his toes. To his horror, he realized the axe was part of a pendulum system, and it was swinging back and forth with tremendous speed, daring him to advance across. What was worse was that he could hear more of them ahead in the darkness, and all seemed to pass by the bridge within seconds of one another. Now he knew why the minotaur had refused to advance onto it.

The first pendulum swung by again and was not slowing down at all. The blades made the bridge swing slightly with each pass, enough to keep the young priest facedown and hugging the bridge. That's when he heard the chopping of the other axe—the minotaur's axe. Greyson looked up and could barely make out the shape of the creature chopping at the ropes that secured the bridge to the cliff edge. He was chopping the bridge down! Greyson knew that if that happened, he would join the others at the bottom of the gorge. He felt anger flood over him at the thought of the stupid beast ending his life. He had been afraid this whole time of the crazed monster, but suddenly he had had enough.

"Stop!" he yelled from his hugging position. The creature snorted back at him and kept at his work, which only made Greyson angrier. Then he thought of the trip to the caves and how he and Darian had been temporarily blinded. But of course—Plath was the god of light and hope, so indeed, he would grant his prodigy the power of light.

"Nice trick," he whispered to himself with a smile. He struggled to kneel on the bridge, which was very difficult to maintain with the pendulums swinging fiercely behind him. The direct strikes from the minotaur's axe made the bridge very unstable as well. Greyson was determined to concentrate, though, and so went into a trance, holding on to the bridge the best he could with his knees. He could hear the furious swipes of the minotaur's blade, and it only made him more determined to pull off this trick. "Let there be light and you have no sight!" he screamed, holding an outstretched hand at the beast.

He could see only the outline of it in the dark, but he knew the potent trick had worked, as the creature immediately lost the grip on its axe, which clanged against the stone, then bounced over the edge, plummeting to the bottom of the gorge, right next to Greyson's holy symbol. He could hear the creature grunt in surprise. Then it started swatting at the empty air with its uninjured arm. It was the one that was afraid now; the dumb beast didn't understand that he was up against a prodigy!

"I made you take your arm, and now I take your sight. You are weak and pathetic!" Greyson yelled over the wind of the swinging pendulums and slowly stood once more.

The minotaur roared and turned toward him. Even though Greyson was well out of reach, it swung its massive arm out in his direction, then the bleeding stump, trying desperately to hit him and end the taunting. It took a step toward the bridge, all the while swinging wildly at him. It took another step and lost its footing, slipping off the edge. Greyson watched with great satisfaction as the creature let out a surprised bellow and then reached for the bridge as it fell. If it had used its functioning arm, it would have caught hold, but the thing was blind and desperate enough to try to grab it with its wounded arm. It roared in anger as it fell fifty feet and landed onto two sharp stalagmites, one puncturing its abdomen, the other impaling its throat. It struggled for a few moments before finally becoming perfectly still. The holy symbol shone brightly on the tragic scene, and Greyson almost felt bad for it. Almost.

With a sigh of relief, he collected himself and gingerly turned back toward the ledge where the dead creature had stood just moments before. It took a long while, but he eventually found himself on the polished floor of the rock cliff. It felt good to be off the unstable bridge and back on solid ground. He lay down, staring at the unseen ceiling somewhere above him. He could still feel the breeze and hear the giant pendulums' whooshing sounds. He closed his eyes for a moment and realized then how exhausted he was. How long had it been since he had first entered the caves? How long had it been since he had eaten or taken a drink? He wanted at that moment to be back in Tara, sharing breakfast with Darian. He couldn't wait to tell him about the minotaur and the zombie and the rope bridge. But first, he had to complete the test and get out of the caves.

He sat up, crying out in pain, his shoulder throbbing even worse than before. He gazed into the darkness and was glad for the little bit of light his holy symbol continued to give him from below. But he just couldn't see much past the first pendulum. By the sound and the shadows, he could tell that there were at least two more, maybe three. He watched the dim outline of the one closest to him and saw it climb to the left out of sight for just a few moments before swinging back down, out of the darkness, with tremendous speed. Then he watched it do the same thing to the right. He tried to measure the timing of the obstacle and soon fell into its rhythmic pattern. He closed his eyes and listened for a while. He would get one chance to cross, and he could make no mistakes. He needed light!

He stood and summoned the power of the light again, this time focusing his effort on the first pendulum. Nothing happened. He closed his eyes and concentrated, calling forth the power to produce light as he had twice before, but still nothing happened. With a sigh, he came to terms with the fact that he would have to make the venture without seeing well. He understood that limitation because even the high priests could not call forth light more than a few times a day. He was satisfied with Plath's help and understood he would have to continue alone.

The first step was to remove the chain mail armor somehow; there was simply no way to keep his balance with it on. He knew it would be challenging to remove it with two hands but nearly impossible with only one. So he began the tedious and painful task. It took him almost two hours to get it loose enough to slide out of, and by then, he was sweating profusely from the pain. He still had a small flask of oil and some flint and steel in a small belt pouch but had no torches or lantern. He decided to keep the items anyway and secured the small bag to his belt. He now wore only breeches and a heavy white shirt. He felt like he had lost a good twenty pounds by removing the armor, and with hope renewed once more, he started across the bridge.

His first thought was to use the hanging rope handles as tightropes as he clung to the side of the bridge. That way, he could bypass the pendulums altogether, but in the end, he was just too afraid to try it, knowing that he wouldn't have much of a grip and that the damaged handrails provided no help. His only hope was to walk the bridge and try to dodge the massive blades.

He took his time and walked to the first pendulum. The bridge swayed gently as the blade passed it, but he grew accustomed to the slight movement, and he made his way to the giant axe quickly. He looked straight ahead and used his peripheral vision to watch for its return each time it passed him. Without a handrail or anything to hold on to, he could not look from side to side, especially with his left arm tucked in tight to his chest. The blade passed, and he counted; it passed again, and he counted the seconds of each pass. Each time it crossed the bridge, it took ten seconds to come back and swing in the other direction.

It was not speeding up or slowing down; it kept the same time. As the pendulum swung past, Greyson took two quick steps, leaving it behind him. He breathed a sigh of relief but kept his concentration on the next one. He walked up to within a few inches of its path and did the same thing as he had done with the first one, counting the time of the swing. Satisfied that it was not changing speed, he took two steps and was past that one. He peered into the darkness, and it looked like he had three more to go through. He was happy with himself until he realized that, just as it had back in the cave passages, his progress had triggered something. He heard the grinding of metal sprockets above him and, to his horror, realized the blades were moving lower!

The one in front of him skipped off a plank, slicing it in half in the process and hitting the bridge hard. He fell to a sitting position just before the pendulum behind him hit the bridge as well. The bridge swung wildly, tossing him over the side. He managed to hold on to a plank with his right hand, but the bridge moved now as each blade took turns slicing it. It was chaos, and Greyson felt like he was in the middle of a great storm, tossing around like a leaf. He tried to keep his bearings, but he was out of ideas and knew that he could not turn back or make it across before the bridge fell in half.

He held on for dear life and tried to think of what Berro had taught him. The high priest had shared an old tale with him about how a priest of Plath never travels the straight line and always takes a long way around. There was more one could experience and learn about life by taking a long way.

"That's it!" he cried out to the darkness, which seemed to be his only companion in this cavern.

He knew he had precious little time to do this, so he scrambled up to the bridge, still lying flat and tucking his legs under him, so the blade behind him would not cut them off. The one in front of him skipped off the bridge violently, and he could feel the integrity of the thing give way beneath his feet. Then, just as the bridge collapsed, the pendulum came back into view. He jumped with all his might and hit the blade hard in midair. It knocked the wind out of him, and his face cracked the side of the bar that held it in place. He draped over the pendulum as a rag doll might, and he held on to the holding bar for dear life. The blade flew up into the darkness and slowed quickly, coming to a stop almost parallel to the floor, and then it swung back the other way.

He held on as best he could as blood gushed from his now broken nose, filled his mouth, and covered his chin. He caught his breath and tried to think of what to do next. Then he looked down and could see his lantern, which looked very far away, and he could tell the bridge was no more. Instead, he could see a tunnel full of light somewhere up ahead, past the pendulums, precisely where he imagined the bridge would have taken him. His heart pounded in his chest. Was that the way out? Was he this close to finishing the trial?

He tried to climb atop the blade to gain a better view of the magnificent tunnel. He struggled a great while but finally made it to the top of the pendulum and stood there, hugging the bar with his one functioning arm. That's when he found the lone rung on the bar. It made it easy for him to stand and hold on to the swinging pendulum. It was as if Plath intended for him to ride the giant blade, and he knew that he had made the right decision to jump onto it. However, it took him several minutes to orient himself to its movements as it paused briefly with each swing, horizontal to the cavern floor, before moving back the other way.

He eventually mastered it and then tried to determine what his following action should be. Each time the pendulum stopped for just a second, Greyson tried to look below to see whether there was some kind of ledge or something he could stand on. It was simply too dark to see with his holy symbol so far away now. Then, after many swings, he had an idea. He rummaged around for the flask of oil. He had to use his bad hand, but he eventually retrieved it from his belt pouch. Now he had to decide where to drop it. After thinking for a while, he went with the cavern's right side since that had been the better choice of passageways back at the beginning of this ordeal. It also correlated with an easterly direction, where the sun rises, and he felt that to be the correct choice.

The next time the pendulum stopped on the right side of the cavern, he dropped the flask. He made the count to three before it smashed on something just beneath him. He had to believe it was a ledge and decided he would jump off when the blade stopped on the next swing. He said a small prayer to Plath and did just that. He fell for just a moment before landing on a stony ledge. The glass from the flask cut him in several places on his hands and knees, and the impact made him nearly lose consciousness as his bad arm took another hit, but he did not care, as he was finally off the swinging pendulum.

After catching his bearings, Greyson sat down and retrieved the flint and steel. It was awkward trying to generate a spark with only one hand, but luckily, enough oil had saturated the ledge, and he was able to ignite it with just a tiny spark. The oil lit, nearly engulfing him, and he had to move quickly to get out of the way. But he could now see! As the oil burned on the stone ledge, he could see that it paralleled the path that the bridge had taken and continued far into the darkness. He decided to crawl since the ridge was narrow and it was a long way to fall. As he passed the swinging pendulums and the fire got farther behind him, the tunnel of golden light got closer. He took his time and tried to pace himself, always reaching before him to ensure the ledge did not stop. When he finally made it by the last pendulum, he found that the ridge stopped and a set of stone stairs led down toward another polished floor. The tunnel of concentrated light was on the far side of that polished floor.

He followed the stairs, and as soon as he left the steps, the pendulums stopped their swinging. He collapsed on the polished stone floor at the edge of the cliff and cried in relief and joy. He said a prayer to Plath and then stood on shaking legs. His shirt, now covered in blood from his broken nose and his arm, bruised and swollen, made him appear quite pathetic, but he was alive. He made his way to the tunnel, weak from exhaustion and hunger, the golden light bathing him as he got closer. A terrible thought briefly filled his head: What if this wasn't the end? He stopped and frowned at the possibility. Then he decided that his test was complete regardless of what happened next, so he walked into the tunnel. He may find an exit or perhaps death—it didn't matter to him which one it was at this point. As far as he was concerned, the trial was over.

~

It had been three days with no sign of Greyson, and the priests were worried. On the day his trial began, Greyson's confidence had been contagious, but now, none were sure that was well placed. Darian sat just a few feet away from the cave exit, a solemn expression on his face. Even the high priests had grown concerned at the idea of their prodigy not making it out alive. None of them had considered that to be a possibility, so the trial taking this long was unexpected. Sebe approached Darian and took a seat next to him on the grass.

"He's not dead, you know," she said.

"How do you know?" Darian asked, never taking his gaze from the hole in the ground.

"Plath would have given us a sign. But fortunately, none of us have received such a sign. Remember—he is the chosen prodigy, and we are all confident he will pass his trials." She put her arm around the much younger man, and they shared a bonding of sorts, and neither said a word for the next several hours. However, both had plenty of doubts.

~

As soon as Greyson entered the bright tunnel, his mood changed for the better. The smell of a fantastic stew invaded his blood-caked nostrils, and his stomach growled to remind him he had not eaten for a very long time. A sweet burning log created a magnificent scent but one he could not place. The temperature in the tunnel also changed, as it became warm and comfortable. He felt very relaxed and wanted nothing more than to lie down and sleep, but the smell of food kept him moving on tired legs.

Eventually, the tunnel spilled out into a quaint room complete with a fireplace and a burning fire to his right, a warm fluffy chair to his left, and a wooden door on the far side of the room. Most important, a table sat straight ahead and had a large pot of stew, a loaf of bread, and a pitcher of water adorning it. He moved quickly to the water and did not bother pouring it into the goblet next to it but instead brought it up to cracked lips and drank. He gulped it down fast—too fast—and threw it back up all over the lovely floor, which he realized now contained a goatskin rug.

His eyes went wide at the sight of it, and he dropped the pitcher, spilling the rest of the water all over the rug and floor. He hardly noticed his actions as he stared at the beautiful goatskin. He'd been taught at an early age that a goat sighting was the surest way to know that Plath truly blessed you. He felt so blessed at that moment, and tears filled his eyes. He took the rug into his hands and tried to wipe the water away, only to find it dry, as well as the floor around him.

"Come, child—rest on the comfortable chair," a calming female voice whispered to him, and a woman's hand gently took his. He looked up to see a woman standing above him, but she seemed out of focus. He rubbed his eyes and tried to shake away the blurriness with no success. He felt as if he were dreaming as if she were just a hallucination. He could tell she was smiling, but her face was a blur. She had dark hair and wore a red dress, but he could not make out her features. All he knew for sure was that she was beautiful and kind. He let her guide him to the chair, and he sat, nearly dozing off right away. He watched the blurred woman pour him some water from the full-again pitcher and bring the goblet to him.

"Mom?" was all he could think to say as he looked up at her with tears streaking his cheeks.

"No, but I am a friend. Just sip it this time, young one," she said.

He nodded and sipped the refreshing liquid. The woman followed with a bowl of stew, taking his goblet so that he could eat. And he did. She had to remind him not to eat too quickly or risk being sick again. He tried to oblige, but the stew was so delicious, and he was so hungry. After his meal and another sip of water, he lay back in the chair and closed his weary eyes.

"Are you an angel?" was all he could think to say, although he did not use his voice since he was now viewing things through closed eyes.

So instead, he just thought of the words, and they were there in his mind and hers.

With his eyes closed, Greyson could view the room in focus in his mind. He could see the beautiful woman, and she was far prettier than he'd imagined she might be. She wore a bright smile on her face and looked at him lovingly. "That is as close to the truth as anything else you could have called me, Greyson. The truth is, I am the keeper of the caves, and I have to say you made a glorious mess for me to clean up."

"You're welcome."

She laughed at that, and it sounded magical to him. He smiled and tried to get up to get a closer look at her. He wanted to hug her and thank her for the food. He felt so close to Plath, and this woman had to be some kind of disciple. He felt love for her on many levels, and he wanted to express it with a hug. However, he found that he could not move; he was too relaxed.

"Greyson, do not try to move. Your body is preparing to receive a vision from Plath himself."

"A vision?" he heard himself ask, but with little excitement in his voice. He was dizzy, and the feeling was all too surreal, almost as if he were dreaming but awake at the same time.

"Yes, the food, water, and smoke all serve as inhibitors for you to open your mind and receive his message. The only question remaining is, what do you wish to learn? You have three choices: the past, the present, or the future.

"To learn who you are, where you come from, and even who your parents are, choose the past. To discover a safe path and be reunited with your friends, choose the present. Furthermore, if you wish to learn about what will happen to you during your lifetime, choose the future."

He could not react and had not the energy to answer her. She repeated the question and shook him slightly. He opened his eyes briefly. He wasn't sure if he opened them in the vision or opened them for real. "Future," he finally managed to whisper.

The vision then flooded his mind. He saw lots of images after that, things that he was sure were real but felt like a dream. It started with the faces of many beautiful women. He somehow knew that some would be his lovers, some would be his enemies, and others would be companions.

They were gorgeous, and that made him happy. Then the visions became strange yet fantastic at times—but very strange indeed. He saw a raven, beautiful and powerful, soaring in an open sky over a beach. On the beach was a king—or what appeared to be a king; it was a man wearing a crown. Then he envisioned a dark evil that stole all his hope; it was faceless but genuine. Finally, in the mass of darkness, he saw a lone flower of white blossom in the middle of all the despair. He heard cries of pain and anguish give way to cheers of joy and laughter. The last thing he saw was a reflection of himself in the mirror. He was older, maybe in his thirties, with a chiseled chin and flowing blond hair. He was quite a good-looking man, and this made him proud. Then his appearance changed: his eyes grew black, he sprouted horns from his forehead, and bat-like wings stretched out from his back.

That's when he woke up, covered in sweat and panting heavily. He looked around the room, and the fire was now just hot embers, and the food and water were all gone. Had he eaten it all? He did not remember. The beautiful woman was gone, and the wooden door was open, revealing more caves. The tunnel he'd entered the room from was dark and uninviting. There was only one way out, and that was through the wooden door. Worst of all, his pain was back, as his shoulder throbbed and his nose was very sore. His only light source came from the fireplace's low-burning embers, which barely lit the room. The caves outside the door seemed very dark indeed. He desperately tried to go back to sleep, to catch a glimpse of the angel, but he could not. It was time to move on.

He stood and felt very stiff, as if he had sat on the chair for a long time. How long had he been there? The vision had seemed to take only a few minutes, but Greyson figured he must have been asleep for a while. He went to the door and stood, peering into the gloom of the dark cave. So his trial wasn't over? He thought about staying in the room and just giving up. He could not take much more of this, but then again, he knew that Plath would not give him more than he could handle.

He thought of the vision and how blessed he was to have had a glimpse into his future. The most significant parts to him seemed to be the images of the raven, the king, and the white flower. But he didn't understand them, and he certainly didn't understand his vision with horns and bat wings. He wished he had asked to see the present, which included the way out, but that didn't matter now. He would have to find that himself.

"Well, if any of the visions are going to happen, I have to get out of here," he whispered to himself.

"You chose the future, young Greyson, and so the way out is not revealed to you. The only way those things you saw will happen is if you survive the trial," came the woman's voice in his head. He looked around, and she was not in the room, at least not that he could see. He could feel her presence, though, and it made him happy.

"I have no weapons, no armor, no holy symbol, and no light. Am I to venture forth to face the next monster with no hope of survival?"

"None of those things matter now, young Greyson. You have lost all of your material possessions, but have you lost your faith? That is the bigger, most important question."

He let those words sink in for a moment, and before he could respond, an unburned stick in the fireplace ignited on one end. He knew it to be a gift from the angel. She had just offered him a torch, so he fetched it out of the fireplace and smiled. "Thank you, beautiful lady. I hope we get to meet again someday. And no, I have not lost my faith!"

"Good luck, Greyson Kavince."

Then she was gone, and he could feel her presence no more. He was alone once again and would now venture out into the unknown, hoping that this ordeal was almost over. The cave opened into many options all at once. He chose randomly, as one passage seemed just as good as the next. Many intersections led to many more hubs. There were too many options, and he quickly lost his way. He decided to press on in one direction the best he could, and lots of times, that led him to a dead end, where he would have to go back and start again. After a while, the passages began to look the same, and he felt like he was going in circles.

After what seemed like hours, Greyson took a seat. His torch was burning low, reminding him he would soon be alone in the dark once more. He was thankful that he had encountered no creatures since leaving the comfortable room. It was also nice not to hear the rise or fall of a distant portcullis with each step he took. But he was lost nonetheless, and he would need help finding his way out. He cursed himself, not for the first time, for not asking for a vision concerning the present. He would have been out by now if he had. And what was the point of the images shown in his dream? He did not understand any of them, and some of them frightened him.

He waited while the torch slowly burned down to nothing. Soon it was just a stick with a red ember on one end. He watched it as it smoked, feeling the darkness surround him. "Why, my god, why?" he asked the dark. "I passed all the trials, and I have seen what you have planned for me. Why, then, would you let me die in here alone? Have I not done everything the right way? Have I failed you? I am still faithfully your servant, but I do not understand what I am to do now. Please show me a sign so that I might do your work in the world."

The torch then burned out, and it was pitch black. The young priest let out a sigh and put his head on his knees and waited for some sign from Plath. As he sat there, he began to feel cold and had the feeling something was watching him. He was afraid to lift his head, and it took a good while for him to actually do it. He began to chill and even shake as the temperature continued to drop. Finally, he lifted his head.

Before him, in the passageway, was a ghostly figure. Again it was the zombie he had turned to dust. But this time, the girl did not smell bad, have rotting flesh, or intend to kill him. This time, she looked more like a girl, someone about his age, and she wore a smile on her face. She seemed almost translucent, and he guessed it was the spirit of the zombie making its way to the afterlife finally. But she wasn't going to the afterlife; she was standing there, looking at him.

He stood, and she turned around and floated down the passage. He stood there, watching her go, but she did not go far. Then, finally, she stopped and turned toward him again and offered another smile. He slowly realized she was guiding him. He followed her, mesmerized by her changed demeanor. She had nearly killed him earlier, and now she seemed as sweet and innocent as a child. He followed her for many hours through the winding paths, and all he could think of was that she was returning the favor for him freeing her. Was it because he'd prayed for her after he'd destroyed her? He believed that was the reason, and that made him proud. If that was the case, then she was indeed a gift from Plath.

Eventually, she led him to ladder rungs nailed to the wall that went straight up to a hole in the ceiling, which let in one giant ray of sunlight. It was the first time he had seen daylight in many hours, perhaps days. He squinted against the brightness, and it was the most beautiful thing he had ever seen. He turned to thank her, but her form was dissipating, turning into nothingness. Then, before she disappeared entirely, she smiled again and waved, and he knew her soul was whole, finally finding peace in death. That made him smile, and he began to climb the long ladder that would lead him out of the caves once and for all.

~

After six days, the high priests decided that it was time to leave the cave exit. Collectively, their morale was down, especially for Berro, who had known without a doubt the prodigy would exit the caves well before then. They had not received a sign from Plath that Greyson was dead, but they held little hope that he still drew breath. They were now out of rations, and the high priests made the difficult decision to leave. However, they kept the locking grate off the exit just in case their prodigy showed up.

"Come, Darian. We will leave the grate off so that young Greyson can come out when he finally finishes his trial," Berro said.

"No, my place is here. He is like a little brother to me. He deserves someone to be here when he exits, and so I shall be. I owe him that much."

Berro nodded appreciatively at his faith. "Very well. We will send food and supplies to you once we get back home. We look forward to seeing you and Greyson very soon."

Berro's tone wasn't exactly uplifting and cheerful, and all knew that hope was fading. So just like that, they packed their things, preparing to leave Darian alone with his thoughts and his guilt. Even though none had said it, the general attitude was one of defeat. They had all given up. Six days was just too long. So as the priests packed their things, Darian sat by the exit, his head on his knees, silently praying to Plath to return his friend to him.

Then he heard a noise come from the cave. He snapped out of his trance and craned his neck to look at the exit. He saw nothing, but he knew he had heard something come from the hole.

"Wait!" he exclaimed with excitement, gaining the attention of the departing priests, who all turned to regard him.

He stood and made his way to the hole, hoping beyond hope that he would find Greyson there. He stopped suddenly, his eyes going wide as one hand reached out of it and grabbed a handful of grass. Soon after, Greyson's face appeared, grime and blood covering him. Darian ran over and helped pull him up. Once the boy was standing, Darian realized how serious Greyson's wounds were, as blood covered his shirt and he seemed to favor his left arm.

"You look terrible," Darian whispered.

"It's good to see you too, my brother," Greyson said.

They both shared a good laugh, which eventually led to tears of happiness. They embraced and then said a prayer of thanks to Plath, the high priests returning to join in their celebration. Finally, Berro hugged Greyson and exclaimed, "My prodigy has returned!" The other priests followed suit, all excited to have him back.

After enduring many hugs and handshakes, Greyson eased himself to the ground and rested on his back. Darian joined him as the priests continued to yell praises of thanks to Plath and share what appeared to be an endless amount of hugs. Greyson and Darian could only laugh at the spectacle; it was indeed the most fantastic day of their lives.

After what seemed a very long time, the priests realized Greyson needed healing and attended to his wounds. Afterward, Darian put the grate back in place, and Berro locked it. Then the tiny contingent of priests traveled home, all singing loudly to their god.

CHAPTER 3

BAD WOLF!

NEARLY SEVEN YEARS PASSED, AND SERA'S LIFE BECAME A routine of misery and suffering, as she spent more and more of her free time with Ronnis, which meant less time was available to spend with her girls. Not just Cassandra and Kessi but all the orphans under her charge suffered from her absence. Nevertheless, she kept up the routine and obeyed Ronnis's demands for Cassandra's sake. Cassandra knew all too well what her life would be like if Sera did not. She and Cassandra had grown close since that night at Ronnis's quarters. That hug had started a flood of Cassandra's emotions, and now they were very close because of it. So Sera lived that life of suffering so that Cassandra could live hers to the fullest.

The girls meanwhile remained close even in Sera's absence. Cassandra dived deeper into the art of magic, learning everything she could about the craft while keeping that and her spell book a secret from everyone except her sister. Kessi quickly became overly devoted to the god Adlesk, and although there were no temples in the small town dedicated to him, she became a self-proclaimed worshipper of the god. Cassandra witnessed that devotion on nights when Sera came home late with bruises on her arms or neck.

After Sera was sound asleep, the girls would sneak into her room so Kessi could practice her holy rituals of healing. The young girl would heal her mother's wounds while she slept, and the bruises would be very faint by morning. Even though they never asked her about the marks, the girls could only imagine what Ronnis did to her behind closed doors.

Cassandra knew that Sera did this to protect her, which made her love for the woman grow more and more each day—and her hate for Ronnis grow just as fast.

During that time, Cassandra finally outgrew the traumatic event that had taken Unis from her. But her life was far from easy, as she endured teasing from the older orphans. So she kept to herself and secretly studied her magic. The girls were two of the brightest students at the orphanage and gained plenty of attention from the teachers. For Kessi, that attention spilled over to the students as well, many of them of the male persuasion. But she did not partake in those temptations and always remained by her sister's side. The two were inseparable.

One evening, with their nineteenth birthday just a few weeks away, the girls found themselves in a small tavern in the town, mixing with the townsfolk. The Happy Harpy pub had quickly become one of their favorites since they turned eighteen. The orphanage rules were strict and very clear: any orphan who reached the age of eighteen could venture into town as long as the sun was still in the sky. Leaving the orphanage's property without supervision was a privilege they took full advantage of, as they had spent almost every evening at the Happy Harpy over the last few weeks. They made a point to head straight into town after their classes ended each day. They enjoyed the freedom, but more important, Cassandra was able to get away from the prying eyes of Lord Ronnis, who always seemed to be around, watching her suspiciously.

They sat near a window on this particular evening, looking out at the marketplace that lined the town's main street. There a person could find various goods, ranging from fine cloth to dried meats and spices. Unfortunately, neither of them had any coins, so sitting at their favorite table and drinking nothing more than water, Cassandra and Kessi could only watch the traders. The barkeep had watched the two come in almost every day and noticed them right away because they stood out from his usual patrons. Their faces were fresh and very attractive, and the two were much younger than most people who frequented his establishment. At first he found it charming that two orphaned sisters would choose his tavern to spend their time, but after two weeks of their ordering nothing but water, he decided their charm had worn off.

Barkeep and owner of the Happy Harpy, Brutus was a patient and fair man but did not seem pleased this evening as he draped his hand towel over his shoulder and made his way to the table. Cassandra and Kessi had been whispering, leaning into the table to keep their conversation private, when Kessi noticed his approach. They both sat back and stared out the window as if he weren't there. Then, finally, Brutus walked up to the table and stood there, arms crossed over his massive chest. Both young women could see his reflection in the window but pretended not to see him.

He cleared his throat loudly to end the facade.

Both slowly turned to look at him nervously. Finally, his grumpy exterior faded, and he let out a sigh. He uncrossed his arms and shook his head. "Listen, girls. I love having you as patrons, but I need you to order something other than water. If you are going to be here every day, I need you to order something. Understand?"

"We will be upstanding citizens one day and are trying to find places we enjoy visiting where we can spend our coin. But as of yet, we are undecided on this establishment," Cassandra said with a little more attitude than she'd intended.

"Cassandra!" Kessi whispered and put her hand over her eyes while tilting her head toward the table in embarrassment. Cassandra stared defiantly at him.

"You may stay today, but you are no longer welcome here if you do not order. Bring some coin tomorrow," Brutus said, then took his towel from his shoulder and wiped his hands. He kept his stare on the girls a little longer and then walked back to the bar.

Once he was gone, Kessi said, "Why must you always do that?"

"Do what—take up for myself?"

"No, be rude to people. He has a point, you know."

Cassandra let out a sigh, and her shoulders slumped a little. "I know. I'm just sick of always being the little orphan that everyone walks on."

"What do you mean?"

"Well, for one, our parents abandoned us."

"We are probably not even related, and you know that."

"So my point is made twofold. Our parents abandoned us. The incident with the wolf killing our mother, Ronnis always watching me, and Sera a prisoner to that monster."

"Sera does that for you!"

"I know that! Do you think I'm stupid?"

The girls had let their voices rise and now realized that some tavern patrons were staring at them. They both slumped in their seats, and Kessi noticed Brutus staring at them with a scowl.

"Listen—all I'm saying is that we are always the oppressed ones," Cassandra whispered. "You told me that your god defends oppressed people, so why don't you see it?"

"I do see it, and I agree with you for the most part, but I also have compassion for people. After all, we are taking up his space and not spending any money, so why shouldn't the barkeep be mad?"

"Well, I make you a promise, dear sister, that one day I will be powerful enough to protect both of us. No one will walk on us again when I am a grand wizard, and our purses will overflow with coin!"

Kessi sighed and returned her stare out the window. Cassandra meant every word of what she told her sister. For far too long had they endured mistreatment. However, Cassandra had been the brunt of that. She was happy her sister did not have to take the bullying tactics of the older orphans or the monster Ronnis D'Breeth. But Cassandra refused to live her life like this. She would someday become a powerful wizard, and woe to anyone who defied her then! And she would take care of Kessi if need be, but something profound inside her knew that Kessi would be just fine.

"I want to leave this town," Cassandra said after a long pause.

"When?" Kessi asked, her eyes wide with shock.

"As soon as possible."

"But what of your schooling? What of Sera, and what of me?"

Cassandra smiled and took Kessi's hand. "Dear sister, I would not leave without you!"

Kessi smiled and squeezed her sister's hand. It seemed to Cassandra that relief washed over her sister at hearing those words. The truth was that Cassandra could not imagine life without her sister beside her and would never leave her.

"Besides," Cassandra said, "Sera will be better off without having to protect me from Ronnis. Also, the schoolmasters at the orphanage have nothing else to teach us. They say we have a few more years of education to obtain, but I say they are boring and their teachings are elementary."

Kessi had no response to that and turned her gaze out the window as the trade vendors began to pack their things. The sun would be down soon, and they would have to go back to the orphanage before it fully set. Cassandra knew that Kessi liked this little taste of freedom, venturing from the orphanage grounds. Also, her god required her to travel to various places in the world to help those in need. She knew her sister would leave this town, given the opportunity. Cassandra joined Kessi then in watching the vendors and envied them because they had plenty of coins to go where they wanted, and some did just that, moving from town to town to sell their goods.

"We have no money," Kessi said. "There is no way for us to travel right now. How far could we make it without food, water, or money?"

Cassandra didn't answer at first, and she became lost in thought, mesmerized by the trader activity outside the window. She struggled to find a good answer. She needed her sister to side with her on this decision. A solution did come to her then, and she blurted out, "We'll take her with us!"

"Shhhh! Who? What are you talking about?" Kessi asked, looking around to ensure no one was watching them again.

"Sera!" Cassandra whispered once more. "She'll have money, and she'll come with us! She hates it here now because of that monster. We can move and start our family anew."

Kessi's smile widened, and she grabbed her sister's hands again, squeezing them tight. "Sister, you are a genius!"

Cassandra agreed, and the two hugged each other over the table, excited about the possibility of leaving Oldorburg and getting a fresh start somewhere else. They were ready, and the time seemed right.

~

Baxter Von Glord sat on the other side of the small tavern and chewed on the succulent duck, closing his eyes and savoring the flavor. The Happy Harpy offered quite excellent food for a small town like Oldorburg, and he was impressed. He made a vow to himself then to revisit the establishment if he ever came back. He listened intently to the conversation the two young girls were having. Although he was not within earshot of them, he had secretly cast a spell that allowed him to hear every word for the last few minutes, as if he had been sitting at their table. As the magic faded, he knew it was time to move. He frowned at the thought of leaving his dinner unfinished but took a sip of wine to wash his palate and stood. He left a silver piece on the table as a tip, straightened his vest, and brushed off a few crumbs from his pants.

Usually an experienced wizard such as Baxter would sport his wonderful wizard's robes, complete with mystical symbols and wards of protection. Not here, though—not in Oldorburg, where magic was taboo. He tried to keep a low profile, so his travel attire seemed quite average to the untrained eye. His neatly trimmed goatee showed the slightest hints of gray, and his well-styled short hair gave him the appearance of a wealthy traveler. He walked toward the two girls, who looked like they were preparing to leave. As he approached, he couldn't help but notice how attractive they both were, especially the one called Cassandra. She was the target of his travels, and he was thrilled that he would get to interact with her, even though she was twenty years his junior.

Just as they were getting ready to rise, he said, "Dear ladies of Oldorburg, I have something to show you before you leave."

"We don't have time, grandpa," Cassandra said. "We have a curfew."

"Grandpa? Why, I am only in my fourth decade, dear lass. Why would you call me that?"

"She is sorry, dear sir," Kessi said. "She is correct, though; we have a curfew and must leave."

"Yes, of course. Don't let me stand in your way," Baxter said with a bow.

When they stood, he stepped in front of Cassandra and cast a simple cantrip, which he knew would impress the fledgling wizard. He held out his palm and blew on it. A small flame soon followed, dancing on his upraised hand yet not burning him.

Kessi gasped and whispered, "That is illegal!"

Cassandra seemed unimpressed, looking Baxter in the face and not at the flame at all, as if she had seen the trick a million times. Baxter relaxed his dramatic stance, puzzled at her lack of enthusiasm. "Do you not want to know how I did this? Do you not want to learn to do it yourself?" he asked.

"Hmm, let me see. How did you do that?" she asked, feigning intrigue. "Maybe like this?" she said with a wave of her hand.

She ended the wave with her hand just beside Baxter's, and the flame jumped from his hand to hers. He had never in his life witnessed something like that. Never had someone stolen another wizard's trick. That was simply impossible! When two town guards entered the tavern, Cassandra quickly waved her hand, and the flame disappeared. Then she looked him in the eye, smiled, took Kessi by the hand, and strolled out the door. Kessi gave him a small curtsy and a kind smile before being tugged away. Baxter stood there in the middle of the tavern with his empty hand before him as a few nearby patrons whispered and giggled at the spectacle. Then he snapped out of his trance and ran outside.

"Cassandra Rho!" he called to the girls, who were now walking swiftly down the town's main road. They both stopped and turned, wearing equally puzzled looks. The wizard tossed Cassandra a small bag of coins, which she caught. He then approached them once more and bowed. "I am a messenger."

"I'm listening," Cassandra said. "How do you know my name?"

"I know a lot about you. After all, you are the one the nursery rhyme is about, is it not?"

Cassandra didn't answer, and Kessi let out a gasp.

"My name is Baxter Von Glord, and I serve Lady Victoria of Pelesea."

"I have never heard of you, her, or Pelesea."

"You will want to. I mean, you will want to know Lady Victoria, that is," Baxter said as his face reddened. Although he was much older than Cassandra, he felt physically attracted to her, making him feel like a bumbling teenager.

"Why?" Cassandra asked.

"Because she is the most powerful wizard in all the land, and she wants you to come to Pelesea. That is a gift from her to you," he said and pointed to the sack of coins.

For the first time, Cassandra seemed interested in what he was saying, and she took a step toward him with her eyes wide. "You say she's a wizard—a powerful wizard? She knows of me?"

"She only knows of the tale of the wolf and the ravens. You see, each year, she invites five lucky individuals who are blessed with arcane abilities to join the school tuition-free. She has known of you since you were five and has waited to make contact until you were old enough to join the school."

"She wants me?"

"She knows of the unusual circumstances with the wolf, and from what I saw you do with the spell in the tavern, I agree that there is something extraordinary about you, young lady."

"But that was nothing, and I don't know how the ravens play a part in this. I cannot summon them or control them. The tale is tall, I am afraid, and that was a very long time ago."

"Do not underestimate your worth, Cassandra; you have a gift."

The two stood there staring at each other for many moments. Cassandra was speechless and had a quizzical look on her face, as if she was contemplating his words.

"Hello, you two!" Kessi said. "The sun is setting, and we are past curfew. So we should go, Cassandra."

"And you, Kessi Rho—you are welcome as well," Baxter said, snapping out of his trance with Cassandra. "There is a temple there dedicated to Adlesk, and you are most welcome to join your sister in our grand city."

"A temple to Adlesk?" Kessi asked excitedly, now the one with the stupid look on her face.

"Yes, and you would love it there!"

Neither girl responded for quite some time, and Baxter, having deemed his message delivered, said, "I bid the two of you farewell and hope to see you both in Pelesea one day. It is about eight hundred miles northwest of here. Just follow the main road to the sea, and there you will find our grand city." Then, with another bow, he turned and walked away, disappearing into the night.

The girls watched him leave and then looked at each other wide eyed.

"This cannot be a coincidence, Kessi!" Cassandra said, hardly able to control her excitement. "Just think—the very moment we decided to leave the town, this strange man approached us with a most desirable destination for us!"

"Yes, it sounds too good to be true. Do you think the wizard is trustworthy?"

Cassandra pondered that for a moment and then looked at the bag of coins in her hand. "Well, he did give us money, unconditionally. Let's ask Sera tonight if she knows anything about Pelesea and perhaps this Lady Victoria."

The girls turned and ran toward the orphanage, their minds already made up on what they should do. They could hardly wait to tell Sera; they just hoped she wouldn't say no to such a radical idea.

~

Late that night, when all the other orphans were asleep and only a few staff remained awake, the girls made their way to Sera's room. She was fast asleep, and as was the routine, Kessi performed a healing spell on her bruised arms. Both girls noticed they were terrible this particular night, and they shared a concerned look. Then Kessi gently shook Sera, and she jumped, eyes wide, and pushed Kessi away. It took her a moment to orient herself and realize what was happening.

"It's just us, Kessi and Cassandra," Kessi whispered.

"Oh, Kessi, I'm sorry. Did I hurt you?"

"No, you must have been having a nightmare," Kessi said and smiled.

"Or maybe you thought it was a bad person who might hurt you and leave bruises," Cassandra added with a frown.

"Cassandra, I'm fine. See?" Sera said, holding her forearms out for the girls to see. "My arms don't even hurt, so it looks worse than it is." The girls shared a knowing look but said nothing about the healing.

"We need to talk to you," Cassandra said.

"At this late hour, whatever for?"

"We have decided to leave," Cassandra said.

"But not without you!" Kessi said.

"Wait for just a second! Where is this nonsense coming from?" Sera said, sitting up and putting on the shawl she kept by her bed. Cassandra opened the hooded lantern a little more to give them extra light in the room. The girls used the lantern each night because it gave them enough light without waking Sera, but now, both girls noticed the severe expression on Sera's face with the brighter light.

"It's not nonsense, Mother," Kessi said. "We decided just this evening, and it will be a solution to our problems here and at the same time will provide a great opportunity for us."

"Solution to what problems?" Sera asked, seeming to struggle to register the information.

"To this!" Cassandra said, gently taking Sera's arm and turning it to reveal faded bruises.

Sera smiled and kissed Cassandra on the head. "You know, sometimes I forget how smart and how amazing you girls are for your age. But I cannot condone either of you leaving the orphanage before you turn twenty. The world is simply not safe for two young girls with no experience and no money."

"Of course not. That's why we want you to come with us!" Kessi said.

Cassandra nodded. "We need you, Mother."

"We won't leave without you, and we won't take no for an answer," Kessi added.

Sera looked into both girls' eyes, seeing the excitement mount in each. Then, finally, she sighed and said, "You girls have put a lot of thought into this but in too little a time frame. I don't think we should rush into a decision like this without really considering all the circumstances."

"We need no further schooling. We're smarter than most of the instructors at the orphanage, anyway," Cassandra said.

"Yes, I suppose you are," Sera said and smiled.

"More importantly, we are family, and we will all be happy together somewhere else. But we must stay together," Kessi said.

"Where are you girls thinking of going, and how will you get there?"

"Pelesea!" they said in unison.

"We can pay for a ride from one of the merchants," Cassandra added.

Sera looked very confused. "Pelesea? I've never heard of it, and I know you girls don't have enough money to pay for a ride anywhere. So I think you have some explaining to do."

"There was a man—" Kessi began before Cassandra elbowed her in the ribs. "Ouch!" she said, grabbing her side and staring hard at Cassandra.

"What man? Cassandra, who is your sister referring to?" Sera asked.

Cassandra gave her sister a nasty look and said, "His name is Baxter, and he claims to be a wizard from Pelesea."

"A wizard? If Ronnis or Sheriff Quinn finds out you are dealing with a wizard, you will be in huge trouble!"

"Don't worry. He didn't look like a wizard. Besides, I think he's leaving town soon. He said the head of the wizard school there wants to meet me for possible enrollment!"

Sera studied Cassandra's face, looking for hints of a lie or omitted facts. She was hiding something, but before she could ask her, Kessi exclaimed, "He knew of the tale of the wolf and the ravens!"

"Kessi!" Cassandra moaned.

"She needs to know, sister."

"Yes, I do, and I'm glad you told me, Kessi. However, we must consider this man dangerous until we find out more about who he is. Until I discover the truth of this man, you are both grounded from leaving the orphanage."

Bickering ensued as the girls tried desperately to convince Sera to leave Oldorburg, but she would hear nothing of it. The conversation continued for quite some time, and it quickly became heated. In the end, Sera remained firm; she would not allow them to leave until she learned more about Baxter and Pelesea.

Prudence Palence was one of Sera's coworkers at the orphanage. She had been there only a short time—nearly five years—and had made few friends. She was a loner and cared little for her coworkers, especially Sera, whom she considered a simple tramp. However, she knew of her relationship with Lord Ronnis because Prudence was very close to the man. Not in a sexual sense as Sera, but in the sense that she was one of his most resourceful spies. Prudence informed him of all the goings-on in the orphanage, from children misbehaving to other workers' failures, but mostly what Sera and the Rho girls were doing. Yes, she had grown close to the lord over the last few years, and he trusted her word.

Cassandra had left the door to the room ajar. It was only a crack, but it was enough for Prudence to steal a peek. She had been shadowing Cassandra for the last few years, per Ronnis's orders. So when the sneaky woman saw the girls leave their room so late at night, Prudence eagerly followed them, always staying in the shadows and being extra quiet. From her location, she picked up the entire conversation, from discussions of Pelesea to the gold given to the girls and even the name Baxter. Then, as the conversation started to wind down and the girls were being herded back to their room by Sera, she quickly made her way down the hall and out of sight.

~

The following day, Prudence found herself in Ronnis's office as the sun crested the horizon. She ran down her usual morning report as Ronnis tried to wake himself by pouring a little brandy into his morning tea. He seemed not to be listening much as his chief spy told him about Lady Mileah stealing linens from the orphanage stores and about how one of the orphans, little Thomas McLilly, was still wetting the bed at eight years old. He seemed not to care about anything she was saying until she got to the news of Lady Sera and the girls.

"Your plaything and the Rho girls are planning on leaving Oldorburg," Prudence said with a grin.

He sat up in his chair and leaned toward her. "What did you say?"

"It's true. I heard it with my own ears, my lord. They plan on leaving soon to a place called Pelesea."

"Why did you not tell me this to start with?"

"I thought you would like to save the best part for last, my lord."

"I'm not paying you to think, so don't do it again, understand?"

"Yes, my lord," Prudence said, becoming flush with embarrassment.

"Tell me all you heard about this, and do not leave out any details."

Ronnis listened for the next thirty minutes as she told him about the conversation she had overheard. She told him of the strange man named Baxter, of the promise of a place for Cassandra at the school of magic in Pelesea. She did not mention how resistant Sera was to the idea. There seemed to be no need to disclose that piece of information. The ensuing friction between those two would only strengthen Prudence's relationship with the lord. It was common knowledge that Prudence did not care much for Sera. His wrath would be swift and harsh with her, and a few bruises on her pretty face were sure to follow.

Once she had told him Sera's secret, and his mood had turned foul, he paid her five gold pieces and hurried her out of his office. As she left his private quarters, she stuffed the gold in her pocket and walked with a bit of extra kick in her step.

~

A few hours later, Ronnis found himself at the sheriff's office. Oldorburg was a strict town, and the one man who would uphold and maintain the town's laws was Sheriff Quinn. He was a just and fair man but would punish anyone he caught using magic. The board at the orphanage had many influential, wealthy citizens, and Ronnis had all of them in his back pocket. Ronnis's threat of the sheriff not being elected to office in the next term would suffice for what the lord had in mind. If the sheriff required reminding of this and who was really in charge of the town, Ronnis would be glad to oblige.

This particular morning, Quinn and Magistrate Sams, a little wormy fellow Ronnis did not care for, dealt with some emergency concerning a territory dispute on the main street between two vendors. Ronnis had very little patience for such nonsense, especially with such an urgent matter at hand, so one of the town clerks had hurried him right back to the sheriff's office. However, instead of seeing the sheriff right away, he sat on a hard bench near the open door and listened to the heated discussion. He watched through the cracked door as Sams described facts about the dispute at hand as they both pored over a map of Main Street.

After a few minutes of this, Ronnis got up and knocked loudly on the door, clearing his throat. "Uh-hum, excuse me, Sheriff, but I have an urgent matter to discuss with you!"

Magistrate Sams looked up from the map, his beady little eyes peering above his round glasses. As soon as he saw who it was, he nodded to Ronnis and gathered his things.

Sheriff Quinn said, "Split the lease lines in a way that both vendors will be happy. Then offer them both a discount for this quarter's lease as a sign of good faith."

Sams nodded and collected his maps before quickly walking toward the door. He paused just long enough to ask Ronnis, "So how is that sweet little lady of yours doing?"

Ronnis knew that Sams was sweet on Sera, and most days, this kind of question would only stroke his ego. However, today was not a good day for such banter, and he quickly dismissed it. "She is well, very well indeed!"

Sams licked his lips as if lost in thought, then looked up to meet Ronnis's stern gaze, and that broke his train of thought. "Uh, yes, well, good!" he said and scurried off.

"Worm," Ronnis muttered when the magistrate had gone. He then entered the room and shut the door behind him. "Good morning, Sheriff," he said and gave his best fake smile.

"Good morning, Lord Ronnis. How may I be of service?"

"I have an important matter to discuss with you—one that is of higher importance than a simple vendor's squabble."

"Well, it seems that everyone has a problem that is more important than anyone else's," Quinn said with more than a bit of aggravation in his tone.

"If I am obtrusive, then perhaps I should take this business through the proper channels and visit your little friend Sams. You know, get an official document so things are legal. However, that will take too long, so I sit before you, asking that you hear me for the sake of saving time!" Ronnis said, his voice rising as he spoke.

"Calm down. I'm listening," Quinn said, patting his hands in the air to quench the lord's anger. "Please sit down and tell me what is on your mind." He walked around his desk to sit on the corner of it near Ronnis's chair.

Ronnis did not like the way Quinn carried himself. From his shiny scabbard, polished boots, silk shirt, and waxed mustache, it was evident the man had too much time invested in his appearance. He snorted when Quinn moved up to sit on the desk, catching a whiff of cheap cologne as he passed.

"The first order of business is to send a messenger to the gates and stop Sera or the Rho girls from leaving the city," Ronnis said.

"On what grounds are they to be detained?" Quinn asked, now seeming interested.

"How about suspicion of witchcraft, dear sheriff?"

"I hardly think that Lady Sera is a witch."

"You don't get paid to think, Sheriff!" Ronnis said.

Quinn stood immediately, a flash of anger on his face. "I get paid to uphold the law, and you get paid to sit in your cushy office at the orphanage."

Ronnis stood now, and the men eyed each other, neither giving ground until Ronnis finally said, "Do you want to bite the hand that feeds you, Quinn?"

Sheriff Quinn squirmed a bit after that comment. Ronnis knew that the sheriff would bend to his will, having served as the lord's puppet for the last dozen years. Of course he carried the title of the sheriff, but both of them knew who held the real power in their relationship. "Very well. I will hear you out. Now sit back down and let me get you a brandy," he replied with a smile and a friendly slap on the shoulder.

"Now we are getting somewhere," Ronnis said, retaking his seat.

Quinn moved for the door and summoned the clerk. "Send word to both gates to be on the lookout for a group of female travelers looking to leave the city. This group will consist of one woman and two teenage girls, and the guards should deny their exit. Have the guards report to me immediately if they discover someone of this description. Have them be vigilant until I send word otherwise."

"Yes, sir!" the clerk responded and then hurried off, shutting the door behind him.

Quinn produced a bottle of liquor and poured Ronnis a glass.

"Are you not drinking?" Ronnis asked.

"No, not on the job. Now let's discuss this claim of witchcraft you seem all riled up about."

"Riled up? Do you not take my accusations seriously, good sheriff?

"Of course I do, but witchcraft is such an outdated law, not to mention completely unfair. Unfortunately most of our neighboring cities and towns support the art of magic."

"Let me stop you right there, Sheriff. Is witchcraft illegal in Oldorburg?"

"Yes, of course."

"And are you required to uphold the laws of Oldorburg?"

"Yes, but—"

"Then you will listen to my reasons with great care and concern for the well-being of the citizens of our great town, correct?"

Quinn nodded and sighed. "Yes, why don't you just tell me why you think Sera and the two orphans are witches."

"Let me make it very clear, Quinn, that no harm should come to Sera. I do not believe she is practicing witchcraft, and I feel she is being dragged into this situation by that little witch, Cassandra!"

"So you feel Cassandra Rho is the witch?"

"Of course she is! You remember the day of Unis Rho's death. You let that event die, declaring that it was an act of nature that saved the girls that day. But you and I know that you did it because you couldn't face the fact that a little girl could be a witch, now, could you?"

"First of all, Ronnis, do not question my judgment as sheriff. What happened in those woods nearly fourteen years ago still haunts many townsfolk, including myself."

Ronnis watched as Quinn sat back in his chair and reflected on that strange night. There had been something supernatural at work then, but the sheriff could never trace anything back to either of the girls. Ronnis had a personal vendetta against Cassandra from that day forward, but Quinn did not seem to understand the severity of that obsession until this very moment.

Ronnis leaned forward and downed his glass. "You are going to have to make some tough decisions soon, Sheriff. Cassandra is becoming powerful, and I have reason to believe she is practicing magic under your nose. You know the penalty for practicing witchcraft, don't you?"

"I am the sheriff; I know the law."

The two men sat there a moment, studying each other, feeling each other out. Neither thought much of the other, and the conversation had become a little heated as it progressed. Ronnis knew that the sheriff had to take his claims seriously and, in doing so, would have to make some decisions that would affect the lives of two young girls. Ronnis smiled on the inside at the prospect.

"So what is the penalty, then?" Ronnis asked.

"Death," Quinn whispered after another long, uncomfortable moment.

"That's right," Ronnis said and smiled as he sat back in the chair.

"You want me to kill a young girl over some harmless magic? Is this what you're getting at?"

"Of course not!" Ronnis replied angrily. "What I am getting at is that Cassandra Rho is practicing magic, which is highly illegal, and she, her sister, and Sera are planning on leaving the city in secret to go to a place called Pelesea. Furthermore, dear sheriff, there is a wizard on the loose in your town by the name of Baxter. He is the one who has come to take them to Pelesea. He promises Cassandra great power if she leaves with him, and I believe he is trying to convince Sera and Kessi to come as well."

Ronnis didn't mind stretching the truth a little. The mention of a wizard in the town was enough to grab Quinn's attention, but adding that he was recruiting townsfolk was finally enough to make him take the matter seriously.

Quinn stood again and went to the window, rolling the end of his mustache, deep in thought. Then, after some time, he asked, "What evidence do you have of any of this?" and turned around to face Ronnis.

"I have plenty against the troublesome Cassandra, and I feel that Sera and Kessi are, as of now, innocent. However, I feel that their segregation from Cassandra is of utmost importance. Therefore, arrest that little witch, and the rest will take care of itself."

"You feel, then, that the whole issue is with Cassandra Rho?"

"Of course it is. I would not be seeing Lady Sera if I thought she was a witch. She is a good woman whom I plan to marry," Ronnis said, getting up and helping himself to another glass. "Furthermore, we will probably adopt the other Rho child. She seems sweet and has never caused me issues at the orphanage."

"I find it interesting that you have such a profound hatred for Cassandra and yet are perfectly at ease with her sister," Quinn said, making his way to stand in front of Ronnis once again, still rolling the end of his mustache.

"Well, the evidence suggests that Cassandra is the witch. Little Kessi Rho is an acolyte of some insignificant god. Since our town's laws suggest that healing is not witchcraft, she is innocent of any crimes—in my opinion, of course."

"Of course," Quinn said as he walked around his desk to once again take his seat, all the while playing with his facial hair and giving the matter serious thought. "You know, Ronnis, it was never proven what happened out in the woods that night. If witchcraft was involved, we do not know which child is guilty of the crime. I dismissed it as an accident and nothing more. If this is the evidence you have against Cassandra Rho, then I'm afraid I cannot allow it."

"Remember—I helped you with that investigation, including spending time with the Rho girls. It did not take me long to determine Cassandra was the source of the mystery. I have been watching her intently while you have attended to your affairs as sheriff.

"That night, all those years ago, was only the beginning, Sheriff. I have more evidence that I have documented over the years that incriminate her as a witch. I have it in my study and can show you all you need to see. However, the most damning piece of evidence will rest with your search of her room. Every witch has a spell book, and I know she has one in her room somewhere."

Quinn let out a long sigh and then sat up in his chair. "Enough of this talk, Ronnis. I need proof."

"I can take you now, if you're ready, good sheriff."

"Let me grab some men, and we'll go," Quinn said and opened the door to address the clerk once again. "I need four men—send word that there is a potential wizard in the town. I want all guards on the lookout, but no one is to engage without my permission. I'll be at the orphanage for a bit."

The clerk nodded and quickly sent a page with the message. Ronnis smiled at what was to come. His relationship with Sera had been one he had controlled over the last few years. He was able to exert that control because of her love for Cassandra. He had taken full advantage of that, and Sera had been very submissive up to this point. However, she had become more confrontational about some of the things he demanded of her as of late. She was rediscovering a sense of independence and needed reminding of why she was with him in the first place. Cassandra would be that reason, of course. Once they jailed the brat, his hold over Sera would only strengthen.

Now, as Ronnis sat in the sheriff's office, sipping brandy and poisoning the lawman's mind against Cassandra, Prudence was busy planting spell components in Cassandra's room. Ronnis had a few pieces in his possession that he had "liberated" from a wizard years ago. He knew not whether they were fundamental components, but the fact that they had that mysterious, wizardly appearance would suffice. With Cassandra locked up, Ronnis would enjoy a whole new hold over Sera. As he sat back in Quinn's office with a smile, the sheriff prepared his posse.

Ronnis and Quinn headed for the orphanage a few minutes later, escorted by four city guards dressed in chain mail and brandishing longswords on their hips. Ronnis smiled as they made their way, thinking how he had outsmarted them so quickly. How surprised would Sera be when she discovered he had learned of her vile plans so quickly? What a glorious day this would be, for Cassandra Rho would finally get the punishment she deserved. Yes, it was a fine morning for Lord Ronnis as he basked in the warm sun and strolled toward the orphanage. Little did he know what dangers were in store for him there.

~

As Ronnis and Quinn made their way toward the orphanage, Sera was busy teaching a class of kids she had watched grow up over the last thirteen years, Cassandra and Kessi among them. Cassandra knew that her mother truly loved all of them, and the thoughts of leaving them troubled her. However, Cassandra knew it would be best for Sera to break free of Ronnis's grasp and leave the town. They had continued their discussion of Pelesea that morning after Sera had had a chance to sleep on the issue, and she seemed more willing to listen to their plan. The more they discussed it, the more their mother seemed to approve of the idea. She had insisted on the three of them going to the library to research Pelesea before classes began. All were delighted to discover that Pelesea was real and ruled by just people.

Furthermore, they discovered that Pelesea did have a school of magic—one of the best and most reputable in all the lands. Afterward, Sera did not come out and say it, but the girls had a good idea she would go along with their plan. Cassandra looked forward to continuing their discussion after classes were over.

For now, they were writing essays, and the students had their heads down as Sera walked lightly around the room. Cassandra watched her stop at the large windows with sunlight bathing that part of the room. Her mother seemed content, more so than Cassandra could ever remember. She also looked like an angel as the sun bathed her with its golden rays. Sera finally noticed her and smiled. They locked eyes for a few moments, and Sera's smile widened, a perfect clue as to what her decision was. Cassandra beamed, her heart raced, and she wanted to run up and hug her right then. However, Sera pointed to the book on her desk, and Cassandra nodded and went back to her work, but now with renewed vigor. Then suddenly the door burst open, interrupting the class.

~

As they entered the orphanage, the troupe of soldiers, led by Ronnis and Sheriff Quinn, were met by a surprised Prudence Palence. She looked and acted astonished, by all accounts. However, Ronnis had told her what he had planned and had instructed her to maintain proximity to the door. So when they entered, she was busy sweeping the floor and feigned surprise at the intrusion.

"Miss Palence, come with us. I have a task for you," Ronnis said, never breaking stride.

"Yes, my lord," she said with a curtsy and quickly handed the mop to Ruthie Parks, another orphanage employee, who now stood with a broom in her hand, gawking at the strange sight.

Other workers of the orphanage began to follow and whisper among themselves. It was not every day that they saw a contingent of soldiers enter the building. Rumors began quickly spreading among the employees. Ruthie passed the broom to Anka May and whispered, "Someone's in trouble, and I'm gonna see who it might be."

Anka never even reached for the broom as it slowly fell with a loud smack to the floor. None of the women noticed it, as cleaners, cooks, and other workers began to follow the parade of soldiers, all the while whispering about what this could concern. The troupe made their way to the classrooms as a dozen employees followed to witness the spectacle. Ronnis smiled, liking the attention they were gaining, knowing that the dramatics would play in his favor.

"All right, good sheriff, this is the room. I will enter and replace Sera with Miss Palence here," he said, waving a hand at his secret spy. "After Sera is safely out here with me, you may apprehend that nasty witch, Cassandra Rho."

Quinn nodded and turned to his soldiers, who were now brandishing small crossbows. "Remember, soldiers, these are children. You are not to raise these crossbows at any time unless I am attacked or give you the go-ahead. We do not want any violence, and neither of the girls has broken any laws unless we find evidence otherwise."

The guards nodded and lowered their weapons. However, Ronnis did notice that the crossbows were loaded and ready in case their use was required. He looked at Prudence, who gave him a reassuring nod, confirming that she had planted the spell components among Cassandra's possessions. Then he opened the door to the classroom, rushing in with Quinn and Prudence close behind.

Sera was standing at the window, lost in thought. Ronnis barely registered the sight as he quickly surveyed the room, looking for Cassandra and Kessi. They sat next to each other, which he found convenient. Unfortunately, the sudden entrance startled all the children, especially after seeing that the new arrivals included the sheriff. Ronnis crossed the room to Sera, who now looked surprised and wore a worried expression on her face. As he walked, he made an announcement. "Students, Lady Sera is leaving school early today. Miss Palence will finish your instructions."

Sera met him halfway across the room. "What is the meaning of this, Ronnis?" she whispered.

He smiled and took her by the arm with a steel grip.

"Sheriff, there are the girls," he said, pointing to the Rho sisters, who were now looking very surprised, trying to register the events, just like all the other students. Ronnis then escorted Sera toward the door, forcefully pulling her along. He never noticed the look on Cassandra's face, but if he had, it would have made him think twice about the events he had set into motion.

As Ronnis forced Sera out into the hall, the sheriff approached the front of the room where Cassandra and Kessi were seated and said, "I'll ask that the two of you come with me." Behind him, four men armed with crossbows who the children could only assume were part of the town guard flanked the sheriff. Their weapons pointed to the floor, but Cassandra knew that if they were out at all, this had to be serious. Kessi obediently stood to go with the sheriff, but Cassandra did not.

"Why should we go with you?" Cassandra asked. "We have done nothing wrong."

Kessi's eyes widened, and she whispered, "Cassandra, please get up! This issue has to be important. As you said, we have done nothing wrong, but resisting the sheriff will get you in trouble!"

The sheriff smiled. "You would be wise to listen to your sister, for I will not repeat myself."

Cassandra stubbornly held her seat a bit longer, trading stares with the sheriff. She had never met the man but immediately did not like how he looked or handled himself. He returned her stern look, and it made her feel uneasy. She squirmed in her seat for a bit, then finally slammed her book shut and shouted, "Fine!" and stood.

Sheriff Quinn stepped back and, with one arm extended toward the door, motioned the girls to exit the room. Kessi led the way, but Cassandra didn't move immediately. She could see that the four men behind the sheriff looked a little nervous, and she wondered what this could concern. Perhaps it had something to do with the wizard from last evening? It had to be! Somehow that idiot Ronnis had seen them talking to a wizard and had turned them in.

"Any day now, Miss Rho," Quinn said.

She rolled her eyes at him and said, "Fine, but your mustache is stupid looking!"

It was all she could think to say, but as she stomped past him and toward the door, she could tell that the comment bothered him. Once outside, she overheard Ronnis saying something to Sera about trying to go behind his back. That's when Cassandra knew her guess was correct; he had learned of their plan to leave the town. She looked to Kessi, who shrugged to indicate she was just as puzzled as Cassandra was.

The sheriff and the guards came out of the classroom, and as the last guard was shutting the door, Cassandra could hear Prudence begin her teachings. "Now, orphans, let me have your attention." The door closed before Cassandra could listen to anything else, but she wondered just exactly what the woman would tell her classmates. She sighed and dropped the thought; the only people who mattered to her were Sera and her sister. She couldn't care less what the other students thought of her.

"Girls, walk to your room, and please don't make any sudden moves or stupid comments," the sheriff said, looking only at Cassandra, as if to make the point he was talking just to her.

Being singled out infuriated Cassandra even more. Why was she being addressed? They both had spoken to the wizard, Baxter, the previous night. Why was Kessi not being treated with the same disdain? In the end, she was glad they didn't treat Kessi that way, but it still made her mad at how unequal it felt.

She did manage to bite her tongue this time, but it was because she caught a glimpse of Sera over the sheriff's shoulder, a solemn expression on her face. Cassandra knew that her actions might affect Sera negatively, so she tried to do as instructed. She rolled her eyes again and turned to walk down the hall with her sister. Quinn had the girls walk in front of them, and Ronnis walked beside the sheriff, still roughly dragging Sera with him. The guards followed behind, weapons lowered.

Now packed with teachers, orphanage workers, and even some orphans, the hall was challenging to traverse. They all looked on in amazement, for nothing like this spectacle had ever occurred in those halls. Like fish swimming away from a predator, the onlookers parted as the girls made their way toward their rooms, which only fueled Cassandra's anger. But she bit her tongue once more, and they finally made it to their room.

Ronnis barged past the girls, who had stopped at the entrance. He roughly dragged Sera in with him. "Sheriff Quinn, please search the room. Now we'll see what proof we have of this one breaking our laws!" he said, pointing toward Cassandra, whose temper only simmered even more at the stupid comment. Given the opportunity, she would have killed him then and there, eliminating the source of all their troubles.

She saw the look on Sera's face, and she could take no more. "Release my mother! If this is all about me, then release her and my sister!" she said, entering the room and pointing toward Ronnis with a shaking finger.

Sera jerked her arm out of his grasp, seeming to find her strength then, while giving him a hateful expression. "What is this about? These girls have done nothing," she said, but Cassandra noticed her tone was meek, as if she was scared.

Cassandra noticed Sera rub her arm after prying it loose but said nothing more, Ronnis's intimidating glare silencing her. However, he did not try to grab her arm again. If he did, Cassandra was ready to unleash her rage on him.

"Easy, now!" Quinn said, entering the room behind Cassandra and gently lowering her hand back down to her side. "I said no sudden moves—remember?"

The sheriff then escorted the girls near the center of the room, which was small and unadorned. It contained Cassandra's bed on the west wall and Kessi's on the east. Each had a chest of drawers next to her bed, and there was one table near the lone window in the room where the girls performed their studies and where Cassandra had penned her spell book nearly seven years ago. Kessi also had a small chest at the end of her bed. Cassandra had let Kessi have the one chest since she had the secret compartment behind her headboard to hide her most precious items.

"For now, both of you girls are under suspicion of witchcraft," the sheriff said.

"That is ridiculous!" Sera said, unable to control her tongue. "These girls have done nothing! You have no proof of them being witches." She glared at Ronnis as she spoke, but he just stood there confidently with a sly grin.

Cassandra had never seen her mother that mad before, and it made her feel good to know that she was protecting them. She looked at Kessi, who seemed very nervous. Cassandra understood what could happen over the next few moments—as did her sister. Their plans of leaving the town and starting a new life all hinged on what happened next.

Ronnis looked too confident and too smug, Cassandra realized. They would find nothing to condemn her unless he somehow knew about her secret compartment in the wall. It was almost as if Ronnis knew about that as well. How did he know all of this? Her heart raced at the sad realization that he may have outsmarted her. She had been so careful to keep her spell book a secret, but now she wasn't so sure she had been thorough enough.

"We are going to search your room, and if we find anything that looks like evidence of witchcraft, I will arrest you," Quinn said calmly. "Lady Sera, if you interfere, I'll have to arrest you as well. So please stand back with Ronnis"—he motioned for her to return to his side—"as we perform our investigation."

It looked like she wanted to say something then, maybe to argue the decision to search the room, but in the end, Sera just folded her arms in front of her chest and walked back to Ronnis's side. She stood nervously, watching as her two girls stood on either side of the sheriff. Cassandra glanced back with a worried look and made eye contact with Sera just briefly. She knew this would end badly as well; Cassandra could read it on her face.

Quinn motioned for the four guards to begin the search. He split them up so that two searched Cassandra's area while the other two searched Kessi's things. On her chest of drawers, Kessi had a vase that depicted her god, Adlesk, breaking free of a torture device. She had made it herself, and it carried a lot of sentimental value to her. One guard grabbed it and looked inside, even turning it over to pour out its contents. Nothing came out, so he began to shake it.

"Please be careful—that's breakable!" Kessi said.

The guard looked up and nodded, gently placing the two-handled vase back in its place. The other guard was busy going through her drawers, revealing undergarments and other clothing, making her blush. Nevertheless, she somehow managed to keep silent as the intrusion continued. She did not want to make anything worse for her sister, who was almost certain to say something upsetting.

"I found this, Sheriff," one of the men said, holding up several vials of clear liquid he had taken from Kessi's top drawer.

The sheriff made his way over to Kessi's chest of drawers and took one of the vials. He opened the top and smelled the contents. "Odorless."

"It's holy water, Sheriff," Kessi said. "I am an acolyte, and I need it to heal and protect others."

The sheriff smiled at her and nodded. Cassandra noticed the way he looked at her sister. She had witnessed that look her whole life—the one that indicated Kessi was the more likable between the two of them. Cassandra agreed with that; she just hated having to endure that treatment all the time. Cassandra crossed her arms over her chest and sighed in frustration.

"Is that illegal?" Sera asked before Quinn could respond.

"No, quite the contrary, Lady Sera," Quinn said with a smile. "The founding fathers of this town believed healing to be a necessity, so priestly magic is not forbidden."

He looked in the top drawer then, where a small metal mirror and a hairbrush lay among Kessi's clothing. The other guard found a blanket and more clothing in her chest. "I believe this one is innocent," the sheriff said. "Put her things back nicely, exactly as she had them."

The two guards followed the directions, and Sera breathed a sigh of relief. She was worried that Kessi, a fledgling priest, ran the most risk of being found a witch. She looked at Ronnis with a smirk. "Well, I don't guess your evil plan worked out too well, my lord."

Ronnis wasn't looking at her. Instead, he focused on the search through Cassandra's personal effects. "I wasn't trying to catch her; Cassandra is the one I'm concerned with."

"Why don't you leave her alone? She has done nothing to—" Sera began, but that was when one of the guards produced from Cassandra's bottom drawer a small sack hidden beneath some clothing. He proceeded to pour the contents onto her bed while Quinn watched. Pouches of various sands, animal parts, dried insects, and such now littered it.

Quinn shook his head. "Inspect her bedding. Look under the chest of drawers as well. We are looking for a spell book," he said while picking up a pouch and pouring some of the contents into his hand. It was reddish-colored sand and felt sticky to the touch.

Cassandra was there in a flash, her face beet red. "These are not mine! I don't know what these things are!"

Quinn turned to her and said, a hint of anger in his tone, "Please step back, Miss Rho, and do not interfere with the search. You will have your say in our court, if it comes to that."

Cassandra backed away slowly as now all four guards were tearing up her bed and moving the chest of drawers. They were rough with her things—much harsher than they were with Kessi's, she noticed. They threw her bedding and clothing on the floor with little to no care. She could feel anger welling up inside her.

Behind her, she heard Sera say, "Cassandra, what is that stuff?"

Before she could answer, even before she could turn to her mother, Ronnis said, "Can't you see, my dear? She is a witch, just as I said all along."

"You did this, didn't you?" Cassandra whispered to herself as she slowly turned to regard him. She directed the question to Ronnis, but she barely spoke at all. No one heard her, but Cassandra already knew the answer. Everything became a blur at that moment. Sera and Ronnis were in a heated discussion, but she couldn't make out the words. The men had found her secret compartment and were now moving the bed to access it. The sheriff was standing there with his hands on his hips, surveying the progress. Kessi stood nearby, near to tears, watching the spectacle. She realized there were people at the door, orphanage workers peeking in, orphans too. She registered all of that, but she felt far removed from the situation. Her entire focus was on Ronnis at that moment. He, and only he, mattered then.

"Bad wolf," she whispered.

Kessi was the only one who heard her, and her expression turned from one of confusion to one of fright. Kessi seemed five years old again, in those horrible woods on the night Unis died, watching her sister stand up bravely to the evil creature that threatened them. Cassandra knew that scene unfolded in Kessi's mind again, but she could not focus on that. Instead, she had to defend herself once again.

She now faced Ronnis and Sera, who were only about ten feet away from her. He had Sera by the arm, gritting his teeth and saying something under his breath to her. Sera was trying to pull free, and the grimace on her face reflected the pain he was causing her. That was enough for Cassandra. She decided she would put an end to it once and for all.

"Bad wolf!" she yelled, and this time everyone heard. Everyone stopped what they were doing and looked at her, mouths agape and eyes wide.

Ronnis noticed her then and let go of Sera's arm. Cassandra vaguely saw Sera's face and the concerned visage that it took. "Bad wolf?" Ronnis said. "I think you are the bad wolf, young lady, and now you will—"

Cassandra raised her right hand, pointing a finger toward him, and yelled even louder, "Bad wolf!" She felt the energy in the room, and everything seemed to slow down. The magical symbols danced in her head, and her arm tingled as the energy built in her small frame. Ronnis took a step toward her, that smug smile still on his face. Time seemed to stop for her then as she called forth all the energy she could muster, quickly remembering the spell she had taken from Ronnis's book those years ago. A small green ball of energy formed at the end of her finger.

"Bad wolf," she whispered once more as the bolt of energy flew from her finger and hit Ronnis square in the chest so hard that he flew back into the wall and dropped to his knees. A hole in his shirt showed burned skin and splotches of blood. Smoke wafted up from the hole in his chest, and his expression was one of shock and pain. Cassandra barely heard her sister screaming at her to stop, and she saw Sera yelp and jump back from the sudden attack. Several people in the hall yelled out in surprise, and the mob became like ants scattering from danger. Pure chaos had erupted around her, but Cassandra saw and heard none of it. Instead, all she saw was Ronnis, the source of all her problems. She advanced on the nasty man as he looked up at her, the smug expression on his face now gone. At that moment, she truly hated him.

"Bad wolf!" she said with finality as another missile flew from her tiny finger, this one slamming the right side of his face, knocking him hard against the wall again, and then he fell facedown, blood pooling around his head.

Sera screamed, "Cassandra, stop!" as two of his teeth bounced around her feet.

She was summoning another magical ball of energy when she felt a shock of pain and heard the crack of her skull as something slammed into the back of her head. She felt herself falling to the floor, but only for a moment, as her world became black before she ever reached it.

Kessi went to Ronnis quickly and began to cast her healing magic. Sera made her way to Cassandra's crumpled form and held her. At that point, she was no longer able to hold back her tears. She sat on the floor at the sheriff's feet, rocking Cassandra's unconscious form, sobbing uncontrollably. Quinn, who had just struck Cassandra unconscious with the pommel of his sword, slowly sheathed it.

Kessi's hands gently took Ronnis's head, and as healing energy flowed through her, she heard him groan. He was alive! She cast again, her healing energy washing over him a second time, perhaps in time to even save him.

"Bind her!" the sheriff said, pointing at Cassandra. "Be sure to bind her hands and gag her so that she may not spit out another deadly spell!" He yelled through the chaos to a nearby teacher, "Go fetch the priests, woman, and hurry!"

The young woman darted off to find the help that would possibly save her lord's life.

Quinn pulled Sera away from Cassandra as the guards bound her limp form. Sera screamed and fought to stay with her daughter, but the sheriff, having seen enough, forcefully pulled her to a standing position and said, "I'm sorry, dear lady, but I'm going to have to take my prisoner now."

CHAPTER 4

NOVAFONTERA

OVAFONTERA WAS A LARGE CITY LOCATED ABOUT SIX hundred miles northwest of Oldorburg and about two hundred miles south of the grand city of Pelesea. It had once been home to thousands of goodly races, humans, elves, and dwarves included. The vast city was also one of the major capitals in the civilized world, ruled by a fair and just half-elven king named Spring Goodwright. He was not only the king of the magnificent city, but he also led a righteous group of warriors, priests, and wizards against the demon lord Marnelphion when the demon had invaded the world centuries ago. This brave group called themselves the New Order and protected the world from that awful demonic invasion. With the help of thousands of brave warriors, the New Order had led a charge straight to hell to stop the attack, but it had cost all of them their lives.

That was long ago, and the great city was now just a pockmark on the landscape. When Marnelphion was defeated and sent back to hell, he'd cursed the city in his final moments, making it uninhabitable by any living creature. Now a fog of poisonous gas blanketed the entirety of the kingdom, with no wind strong enough to blow it out and no magic powerful enough to dispel it. The only known way to break the curse was for a direct descendant of Spring's to set foot in the city. Unfortunately, after the great battle, Marnelphion had made sure that all of Spring's relatives were hunted down and killed, so there was no way to break the curse afflicting the once-grand city of Novafontera.

And so it sat dormant for hundreds of years, the beautiful architecture now crumbling and the city uninhabitable by any living creature. The king of Pelesea kept a watchful eye on the place but was helpless to remove the curse, so he accepted that the dead city was his closest neighbor to the south. The roads leading to and from Novafontera had long since been overgrown with vegetation. Travelers refused to venture anywhere near the place. New roads developed long ago and took a much wider route around the cursed site.

Located along the coast, like Pelesea, the harbor had also become a wasteland, with giant galleys half-submerged near the rotting docks. It was an actual ghost city in every sense of the word. Marnelphion's curse had endured. But now a human stood at its threshold for the first time in nearly seven hundred years.

Matilda, a small but powerful priestess of Marnelphion, waited anxiously at Novafontera's docks as her spell to neutralize the city's poison slowly affected her body. It was not nearly powerful enough to protect her, but she hoped it would slow the toxins long enough for her to reach the pit.

"This is crazy, you know," Cerus said, standing between her and the small rowboat that had delivered them to the rotting docks.

The two oarsmen in the boat looked around nervously at the ghostly waters, anxious to leave. Instead, they waited dutifully for their general, Cerus the Gray, a magnificent specimen of a man. He had chiseled good looks and the strength of a bull. Cerus knew no fear and led Matilda's army.

Matilda and Cerus stood facing each other, poisonous gas lapping at the woman's heels. She smiled and said, "I *am* crazy—remember?"

Cerus looked into her big brown eyes and did not flinch. He showed no emotion, but she knew he was generally concerned for her. She turned and put her face in the gas, breathing in deeply. The gas ate at her lungs, and she coughed it out. Unfortunately, her spell offered little protection, just as she'd expected. She turned back to Cerus, who was frowning. It took her several minutes to control her coughing fit.

"This is ignorant. If the gas doesn't kill you, the vampire lord who resides within the foul city will. Is the legend of the vampire lord real? Does Heinsvick the warlock truly live in this toxic gas, or did he perish all those years ago alongside your god?"

Matilda just smiled at him and began casting again. He was ever the pessimist when it concerned her god, and she'd learned to ignore his snide remarks. She would prove to him what a valuable and essential trip this was to their cause. But first, she would have to reach the pit of Marnelphion, near the center of the city, where her demon-god banishing had taken place nearly seven hundred years ago.

"The legends are true," she said. "And my god is far from dead."

"The vampire will kill you, then, assuming this gas doesn't," Cerus said.

"Don't fret so much over me, Cerus. I will return before nightfall. He'll never know I've been here."

Matilda's spell took effect after a few moments, and her insides began bubbling and churning, the magic having her change shape. She cringed, expecting the excruciating pain that always accompanied this particular spell, and suddenly she doubled over, screaming in agony and falling to her knees. The pain subsided for a moment, and she lay there panting, knowing it would return soon. She squinted her eyes and willed away the awful pain as two more arms tore from her sides and planted their palms facedown on the ground. These new limbs were muscular and much darker than her naturally fair complexion. Only the high priests of Marnelphion gained the power to cast such magic.

Moreover, the appendages allowed for swift movement and short bursts of strength. The magnificent blessing was called demon crawl. The grotesque arms were entirely disproportionate to Matilda's petite frame, and once the pain had subsided, she tested them. She rose quickly and remained in a horizontal position that was more animal-like than human. She turned to Cerus with a crazed look in her eye, and he just stared at her, seemingly repulsed by the spell's effects.

"I will go now, to the spot of banishing, completing my unholy journey—something that no other human has ever done or even attempted!"

"That's because it's crazy," Cerus said.

Matilda had completed all prerequisites to become a high priest, and visiting the pit of Marnelphion was the final feat before she could call herself such. All she had to do now was see the bubbling pit that gave off the toxic gas, the essence of Marnelphion himself. If she could reach it without the gas eating her alive, she would gain his blessing. If he did not bless her—well, the gas would then make short work of her. She was ready for the test, the risk perfectly acceptable to her.

Cerus nodded. "You are a fanatic, and you will get yourself killed one day, Matilda. I will wait until the sun reaches the afternoon sky in two days' time before we set sail back home. Good luck."

"Always the optimist," she said with a smile. She then took a deep breath, turned, and rushed into the gas, her grotesque demon arms carrying her faster than any horse could hope to run. Once the gas closed in behind her, obscuring Cerus's view, he turned and headed to the small rowboat. Once he was aboard, the two oarsmen quickly paddled back out to sea to the giant ship anchored safely away from the haunted waters. Cerus stood and watched the gas as they rowed. She had not returned to the docks, so she would either make it or die. There was no turning back now.

Inside the poisonous gas, Matilda made her way hastily toward the pit. She had memorized the old city map, and the site was deep within the city. She couldn't hope to hold her breath long enough to reach it. She hoped only that her demon arms could get her there before she perished. The muscular arms bounded a half dozen feet with each stride, and they worked in perfect harmony. She jumped quickly over the various piles of debris that lined the streets, and it barely registered in her mind that these piles of stone were the remnants of the wrath of Marnelphion all those years ago. She wished she had time to savor the sights, but already she was losing her battle to hold her breath. Although she was making incredible time with her magical appendages, she was still far from her destination. Again, she could not hold her breath that long.

~

Heinsvick sat on his throne in Novafontera's majestic castle, located in the city's northern reaches. He had ruled ever since the demon lord Marnelphion's banishment all those centuries ago. What a remarkable rule it had been! All of the castle's treasures were his, as was evidenced by the multiple rings he wore on his long pale fingers. His harem totaled sixteen beautiful women, forever young by his bite. He had been selective over the years in his choice of brides, taking only the most attractive to share his bed and the afterlife with him. He'd possessed a unique set of skills in his former life that allowed him to cast spells without the need for clunky components or spell books. He had been a warlock—and a mighty one, at that. That uncanny ability had stayed with him in the afterlife, making him the most dangerous vampire ever to exist.

He sat back in his throne, the old throne of Spring Goodwright, as his brides lay around the room, adorned in the most delicate garments of the ex-queen. They grew restless, having not eaten in several days. He made them wait as long as possible so that they would be worked up into a frenzy, ready to tear their prey to pieces. They patiently awaited his command to feed, but he knew they were pretty ravenous at that point. They were all agitated, some even becoming brave enough to venture near the heavily draped windows.

His favorite and most recent bride, a young elf maiden named Emiline, approached him. She fell at his feet, dropping her head and looking only at his polished shoes, for she had been trained like all the others to respect their master. She whispered something soft and delicate, typical of her race, but too weak for him to hear. He leaned forward and stroked her hair. "Look at me, my love," he said.

She slowly lifted her head, and he looked into her large blue eyes, which he found more beautiful every time he did so. Her slightly parted red lips revealed the tips of her tiny fangs. She was not a savage killer like the rest of his brides could be, but she was his best lover by far. She would kill to feed only as necessary, whereas the others would have so much bloodlust on those nights out of the city that they would ravage everything in sight. Not this one, though—her gentle nature had carried over to the afterlife, and he loved her for that.

"What did you ask me, my love?" he asked, cupping her chin.

"I … we are hungry, my lord."

Heinsvick smiled at her innocence. "I know this already. Do you think I am treating my brides poorly?"

"No, my lord. I only ask because …" She lowered her face again.

He gently lifted her pretty face, those blue eyes burning holes into him. He loved this one—the others were special to him, but he loved this one. "Finish your question, my dear Emiline. Do not be afraid."

"I … we … are just so … hungry, my lord. May we hunt?"

"Yes, my love! This very night, you shall feed!"

Her face brightened, and she became excited like a child. "We may drink this night?"

Heinsvick smiled and leaned back on his throne. His other brides now closed in on him, growing very excited and hopeful that they would be allowed to feed soon. He watched them gather at his feet, lowering their gazes to the floor and gently stroking his legs and feet. He marveled at how innocent they all seemed, how needy they were of him, and yet how very dangerous they were. Each of his brides could quickly kill a mortal human with her bare hands, and he had witnessed that on more than one occasion. Finally, he stood, and they all grew silent.

"Listen to me, my lovely brides. You will feast well tonight!"

There were several squeals of joy at the proclamation. He motioned for them to calm down, gently patting his hands in the air. They obediently sat at his feet, their beautiful faces looking up at him hopefully. When he had their full attention once more, he continued. "Tonight, ladies, we feed, we hunt, as a family. This very night, you shall taste blood!"

That started a near riot as the lesser vampires fell over themselves, shrieking as they did, and came close enough to touch him, to thank him. He sat back down and let them rub him. He closed his eyes and enjoyed the caresses as they purred and squealed with delight. Then, after a few moments, he calmed them. "Now go and rest. To your coffins, my lovely brides. Become rejuvenated. You will need your strength tonight."

They all eagerly rushed from the room, happy to follow the commands of their master. However, he grabbed Emiline before she could turn and go. He pulled her gently to him and looked into her beautiful eyes again. "Not you, my dear. You will stay and share my coffin this day." The confused and innocent look on her face told him that she didn't understand what he meant, but she complied, always happy to please him.

~

Unable to hold her breath any longer, Matilda sucked in a massive amount of the poisonous gas and felt it immediately eating her throat and lungs, and her protection spell offered little help. She inhaled deeply again, trying not to cough out the little bit of oxygen she took in with that deadly breath. The fanatical priestess was close to her destination, but the pain was significant, and her breath couldn't hold. She could see the castle to her left, standing proudly in the poisonous gas and rising high into the veil of fog. That meant she was close, and that spurred her on even faster. Soon after, she saw it—the pit of Marnelphion.

It was only a few hundred yards away, a simmering tar pit spewing the deadly gas into the air with each bursting bubble. It roiled with the demon god's remnants from centuries before, still functioning powerfully and effectively. To reach it would please her god.

The sight inspired her to quicken her pace, pushing herself faster than she could imagine. She coughed out the last little bit of oxygen in her lungs, and blood came with it, running down her chin. The poison was eating her up from the inside out. She believed that Marnelphion would bless her with more power than she could imagine and save her from the gas if she reached the pit. If this was false hope, then she was already dead. Her only chance now was to get to the hole before the gas killed her. She had precious little time.

One arm buckled as she swooned from the toxic fumes. She nearly fell but somehow managed to keep crawling. She knew that if she stopped, she was as good as dead. When Matilda was fifty yards away from her destination, the poison became more concentrated. Her skin began to smoke and even blister in some parts. Then, at only forty yards out, her vision failed, the gas blinding her. She ran into something tangible, perhaps a building or maybe just a street post. Either way, it knocked her off-balance, and she fell to the cobblestone street. She felt the pain in her sides as the arms withdrew, her spell ending abruptly. She crawled as best she could, now in earshot of the bubbling. She followed the sound, desperately needing oxygen.

She tumbled over broken ground, stubbing a finger in her crawl. She remembered learning about the cobblestone street on which the pit had strewn stones and other debris in the immediate area. She also recalled a small knoll about ten feet tall formed next to the hole during its creation. To her estimates, it would be on the other side of the churning tar. If she was on the wrong side of the hole, she might very well fall off the knoll and into the unholy tar, and that would surely kill her. However, she had no choice but to continue. She was not only suffocating; she was drowning in her blood. She managed to regain her footing and leaped in the direction of the pit in a final effort to reach the tar.

She hit her face hard on some loose cobblestone and nearly blacked out. She stretched her arms out in front of her, reaching for the churning pit. Her fingers were only inches away from it when she felt the essence of the unholy place reach out to her and seep through her pores. She had made it! For a brief moment, she basked in the glory of her god. She had made it; she was indeed at the pit of Marnelphion. Her excitement was short lived, though, as the poison finally stilled her heart. Her eyes went wide, and there, alone in the gas, she died.

~

Heinsvick rose as the sun set. He stood and looked over his most precious bride, who shared his coffin. Emiline lay peacefully there, still fast asleep. She was so beautiful, and he stroked her cheek lovingly. It was almost night, and his harem would soon be ready to feast. He grabbed a handful of the soil in the coffin and held it up to his nose, smelling the rich, earthy fragrance. It was his burial soil from all those centuries ago, and it invigorated him. Just one whiff, and he felt more vital, more powerful, and ready to begin the hunt.

Emiline stirred and looked up at him with those big blue eyes. She smiled when she saw him, and it made him happy. The elven vampire was his prized possession, and he looked forward to the bloodlust that would overcome her this night. She would ravage whatever poor creature happened to be her prey. It felt so right because it contradicted everything she'd stood for in her previous life. He had changed her, and she was all the more beautiful for it, in his opinion.

She sat up and seemed to remember what was in store this night. She looked at her master excitedly and asked, "Time to feed?"

"Yes, tonight you will taste elf blood."

Emiline sat unblinking, cocking her head slightly to the right as if trying to understand the meaning of his words. His other brides started moving into his chamber then, filled with bloodlust and ready to hunt.

"My beautiful brides, tonight we feast. I want you all to go to the throne room for now and await my arrival. I will be taking you out five at a time, as we usually do. Prepare yourselves!"

They squealed with delight and hurried off. When the vampire lord was alone, the smile faded from his face. He turned toward Emiline and motioned for her to approach. She obeyed without question. "You will not need this tonight, my love," he said, removing the emerald necklace from her neck.

He had gifted her the necklace, which he had found in the bowels of the castle centuries before. It was one of the few remaining null stones in existence, and it negated all magics in its immediate radius. Emiline wore it because she thought it was beautiful; he allowed her to wear it to protect her. And because she was usually near him, he reaped the benefits of the jewel as well. However, he would need full use of his warlock powers this night, and therefore the necklace would have to stay hidden. He smiled at Emiline and hurried her on her way to the throne room, then buried the null stone in the dirt of his coffin. She did not know the power the stone held, and he liked to keep it that way. Once the stone was hidden, Heinsvick followed his brides to the throne room. Then it was time to hunt.

~

Matilda found herself in the dark. She wasn't sure of her surroundings because she couldn't see in the pitch black. The mighty priestess could also smell sulfur, and it continued to get stronger, almost to the point that it was overbearing, and she became terrified indeed. Her first thought was that she was dead. She no longer felt the pain in her lungs, and she no longer struggled to breathe. In truth, she didn't feel like she was breathing at all.

"Hello?" she managed to squeak out into the darkness. There was no response, so she tried to move, but she could not. Was she paralyzed? Was she dead? How had she gotten here? Suddenly, a small red dot glowed in the darkness, then began to grow. She focused on it, trying to understand the phenomenon. Then, to her horror, she realized that the dot was not increasing in size; she was moving toward it—no, floating toward it! The red dot gave some light as she got closer, and she could see that she was indeed standing, but her arms hung limply at her sides, and her legs did not move. There was no floor, and she just seemed to glide through the pitch black that surrounded her.

The red dot was now close, and she recognized it for what it was: a doorway lined with swirling fire. Heat and sulfur fumes emanated from it, making her uncomfortable, but she was still gliding toward the fiery door, unable to stop. Something was drawing her toward it, and she was powerless to stop it. But then she felt it—a presence unlike anything she had felt before. Being a disciple of Marnelphion, she had communed with many demons of hell and even summoned several lesser demons to her temple. The aura that such a creature gave off was unmistakably evil and unforgettable. She felt the presence of a demon—or something even more powerful than that.

"My lord?" she said, barely able to summon the courage to speak. Then she stopped gliding and hovered in front of the strange portal. She was close enough to hear the moans come from the depths of the glowing orb, and the terror of that sound humbled her. She was in the presence of her god or something nearly as powerful. "I am dead, then. I have failed you, my god!" she said.

A maw of razor-sharp teeth appeared over her left shoulder. Saliva dripped from the bared teeth and splattered on her blouse. The touch of it burned, and she could feel the terribleness of it seeping into her skin. "Not yet, my dear," the creature hissed, its breath warm on her face and more odorous than the sulfur-like smell that poured from the doorway. The voice sounded female, though the horrible face showed no gender.

"Who are you? Where am I?"

The maw disappeared back behind her, slipping into the darkness. Its voice then filled the very air around her. "Your mortal body was left crumpled on the pavement of Novafontera. Your journey to the afterlife has begun, and now your soul belongs to me!"

"No!" she screamed out in desperation. "I made it to the pit! I am the only mortal ever to do so!"

A barbed chain flew from behind her and wrapped around her neck tightly. It squeezed off her voice, cutting her breath and drawing blood. "Wrong, mortal! You failed!" replied the voice. "Now you are mine for eternity. I am Vasheba, your tormentor that Marnelphion himself has hand selected to make your afterlife most unpleasant."

"No!" Matilda said as she began to lose consciousness. She felt herself moving once more toward the doorway. How could this be happening? She had served her god well over the years. How could it end like this? "Please … my god, Marnelphion … I beg—"

Suddenly the chain was gone from her neck and she could breathe again! A quick thought passed briefly through her mind: How could she breathe if she was already dead? However, that thought immediately vanished as a supernatural force much more potent than Vasheba overshadowed the beast. Matilda could not see it, but she felt it all around her. If she had been standing, her knees would have buckled, and she would have prostrated herself in the presence of this, the raw essence of a supernatural being. Was it Marnelphion himself? She could not know, but she spoke to it as if it were, hoping he would have mercy on her soul.

"My god, have I failed you?" she asked, sounding weak and inferior. The presence was powerful. Matilda dared not look up, understanding that this was probably her god in all his unholy strength and that the mere sight would probably kill her.

Then Vasheba's voice filled her head with what felt like enough pressure to make it split open. Her arms worked then as she covered her ears and applied as much pressure as she could. The pain was intense, and the pressure was tremendous, but she understood her words and knew this was a blessing. "No, you have not failed … not yet, human of minimal worth. But, regrettably, you are going back by his command. Therefore our time together is temporarily delayed, for a special task is placed upon your shoulders—one that I am confident you will fail, and when you do, your soul will be mine for eternity!"

The mere mention of spending an eternity with Vasheba had her groveling. Finally, she openly wept. "Yes, anything you ask of me."

"It is not I that asks this of you, fool; I am but the messenger. Indeed you feel the force that surrounds us now. However, you are not prepared to witness the raw power that is Marnelphion, so I am the one to make your small mind understand the task.

"The 666th anniversary of the banishing is nearly upon us. You have two years and three scores' worth of days to prepare for the unholiest of events. During that time, you must collect 666 sacrificial subjects for the altar of Marnelphion. The 666th one must be a virgin and, more important, must be Kane, the lich god's offspring. At midnight on that special anniversary, you will begin the sacrificing. If successful, you will open a gate powerful enough for Marnelphion himself to walk through, and you will spend your days ruling the mortal world along his side.

"A human must do the task, and you are deemed worthy because of your desire to serve and your success at reaching the pit. Therefore he has chosen you. You have cheated death for now, and he has blessed you with this undertaking."

"Yes. I have achieved the rank of the high priestess, then?" she asked, weeping uncontrollably at the honor bestowed on her and the relief she felt, knowing she would not be going through the gates of hell.

"If the title pleases you, then call yourself what you will. Marnelphion does not care for titles, especially for those of such little worth. Prove to him that you are a reliable asset. The troublesome lich god hides its child from our eyes, and it will take a mortal to track the child down. The filthy thing is necessary to open the gate. The lich's arrogance will be his downfall, and his offspring will suffer for his defiance!"

Matilda listened but didn't fully understand who the lich god was or what he had done to invoke the wrath of her powerful demon god. She tried her best to remember the words Vasheba spoke, for she had to complete the task. She was not ready for an eternity with that awful creature.

"We have discerned a clue as to the child's whereabouts," Vasheba said. "The clue I speak of is a raven's feather. So solve the riddle, high priestess. Do not fail. You know the consequences."

"Yes, Vasheba, I will not fail you."

"I care not for your task! It is not I who asks this of you, foolish mortal! If it were up to me, you'd be in my chains already and I would be flaying the flesh from your bones!

"Also—and let me make this abundantly clear—you are not worthy enough to call me by my name. You do it again, and even Marnelphion will understand as I pluck the tongue from your mouth. Go back to your pathetic mortal body and begin the quest that is before you. Fail, and my chain will be quick to pull you back into the afterlife."

Matilda thought she could feel that awful chain rub against the back of her neck just then. She swallowed hard and tried to steel herself. Dealing with this powerful demon would not be easy. She found it challenging to be in its presence because of the power it exuded.

"Consider his message delivered. Return to your home and begin your preparations. Find the child of Kane. It is no more than eighteen years of age and still a virgin. However, if it loses its virginity before you find it, the great summoning will fail. Then your soul belongs to me."

Matilda then felt herself falling away from the fiery door. The heat, the smells, and, more important, the presence of Vasheba's power all subsided. She began to drift off to sleep. Faintly she heard the last command and remembered it.

"Start your search with Heinsvick, the vampire lord," Vasheba's fading voice echoed in her head. "He can guide you to the virgin child."

~

"Now we hunt!" Heinsvick exclaimed, holding his arms out wide as he entered the throne room. His brides ran to him and fell to their knees at his feet, rubbing and kissing him. He took five at a time that night, using a spell to teleport them to a safe place very far away, a site far from Novafontera. Those woods were familiar to him all those centuries ago, before he had become blessed with undeath. It was a place he'd often frequented as a young man. It was peaceful there and full of life—the life that would sate the bloodlust of his brides.

Once the teleportation sickness wore off, he sent them off on their hunt. He stood perfectly still and closed his eyes, establishing a mental link between himself and the lesser vampires. The only rule was to stay together, hunt together, and not kill a humanoid without asking him first. They hunted well that night, the first group killing a small herd of deer, the second group a pack of wolves, and the last group a small band of goblins, after his approval, of course.

After all his brides had fed and were brought back to the castle, they lay about the throne room bloated on fresh blood, their hunger temporarily satisfied. There was one still left to feed, and he had saved the best for last. He went to his room to find Emiline waiting patiently.

He took her hand and said, "It is time, my love." The excitement on her face and her beautiful smile made him happy. "Are you ready?"

"Yes!" she whispered.

He took her hands in his and looked into her bright eyes, then conjured the teleportation spell once more, but this time to a different location. This time he took his beloved Emiline to the woods where he had initially found her, just a few miles from an elven village. She recognized the place and soon frolicked in the understory, remembering the elf she used to be and enjoying her innocence once more. He watched her lose herself in the familiar woods for a bit but eventually left her there to begin the hunt. When he found the perfect prey a few hours later, he called to her mentally. It didn't take long for her to answer that call and come rushing to him. She skipped through the trees and into sight, now wearing several flowers in her hair. By all accounts, she was a fairy of the woods once more and seemed to have so quickly forgotten her true self. So he reminded her of why she'd come, and soon she remembered her thirst for blood.

Emiline looked at him with pure innocence, and he could feel that she was sorry to have forgotten such an important task. He kissed her on the forehead and smiled, making her relax, and she gave him a large genuine smile in return. He commanded her mentally, not wanting to speak this close to their prey. He commanded her to go deeper into the woods and wait for his call. She eagerly obliged, and he moved quickly back to the easy meal he had discovered.

He spotted two elves segregated from the rest of the village, one male and one female, and they were apparent lovers, he deduced from watching their interactions. They were on one side of a yawning river, at least a hundred yards wide, the village visible on the other side. A small boat sat on the remote sandy beach where the couple had intentionally strayed for some alone time. Their camp was neat, with a pot of something boiling over the fire, and the smell emanating from it repulsed him. He knew that he'd enjoyed cooked food when he was among the living, but now, in his state of undeath, the smell was dreadful.

The couple was perfectly content and happy frolicking around the camp, the male playing the harp while the female danced around him. Heinsvick had to use caution with the village so close. He wanted Emiline to feed at ease and without interruption, and to do so, he would need to separate them and capture them off guard. The couple spoke in elvish, and although he understood little of it, he wondered whether his beautiful bride remembered those words. He knew she was just a few dozen feet behind the camp, waiting and listening.

After waiting patiently for at least an hour, he got a break. The male was heading back to the village, which was still bustling with activity. The way the male elf was motioning with his hands, he would not be gone long. Heinsvick couldn't understand their language, but the elf's actions indicated he had forgotten something in the village and intended to fetch it. Heinsvick's opportunity was never more effortless as he watched the elf quickly paddle away. Once he was almost to the other side, the vampire lord made his move.

He approached the elf maiden, who had her head down, trying to play the harp her lover had left behind. She fiddled with the strings and began playing a song that didn't sound bad to his old ears. However, she wasn't perfect, and her concentration on the instrument allowed him to walk right up to her. She looked up at last when he was only several steps away. She dropped the device and was on her feet in an instant. That's what he remembered about the night he'd turned Emiline—she was quick, graceful, and not so easily charmed by his vampire persuasion.

The elf pulled a small knife out of her boot and raised it threateningly at him. She may have had some training with the weapon—he didn't know—but it wouldn't matter. He saw the terror in her eyes as she realized what he was. Her next move was all too predictable. She began to yell out toward the village, hoping against hope that someone would hear her and come to her aid. But what she'd intended to be a scream was a short single note stifled by a well-placed punch. He hit her hard in the mouth, knocking her from her feet and nearly striking her unconscious. Heinsvick kept the attack silent, and no elf from the village even bothered to look her way. He glanced over his shoulder to make sure no one had been alarmed.

He saw her male counterpart had just reached shore and was pulling the boat onto dry land. He pranced away in his merry elf-like way, not realizing his lover was about to die a horrible death. Heinsvick smiled and turned back to the elf maiden, who was regaining her feet and brandishing the knife. Blood dripped from her mouth, which only made him desire her death more. He attacked again, knowing he should not let her regain her senses. He feigned another punch but stopped short, predicting her use of the weapon. He allowed it to slash across just in front of his face, the momentum of the wild swing making her off-balance. He stepped in, forcing her to continue her spin so that her back was to him.

In that same instant, he hooked her arms around her back and quickly took the knife from her hand. Now he had her in a very compromising position, and she knew she was doomed. He held the blade up before her face, teasing her with it, spinning it. She struggled desperately to break free, trying all the tricks she knew. She stamped his foot, but he hardly registered the pain. She slammed her backside into him, trying to dislodge the hold with little effect. Finally, she threw her head back, and when it smashed his nose, his patience came to an end.

With blinding speed, he took her knife and stabbed it deep into her stomach. She stopped thrashing and let out a yell, loud enough to alert the village. He didn't care at that moment—he wanted his love to feed, and she would have plenty of time, even if every elf came to the maiden's rescue. "Come to me, Emiline. Come and feast!" he mentally called to her.

Within a few moments, Emiline appeared from the brush, right in front of the wounded elf. The maiden was wheezing, her breath coming in labored gasps. She spoke, but Heinsvick had no idea what she said. Emiline, however, knew. She stopped and tilted her head sideways, as she usually did when something did not make sense to her. Did she remember her life as an elf maiden, before Heinsvick had turned her? He didn't know, but he wanted her to feed, not reminisce. He suddenly heard music behind him, coming from the far side of the river. The elves were beginning some kind of group song. That was good because it meant no one had heard her screams and no one would pick up any sound coming from her in her weakened state.

"Feed, my love," he said.

Emiline stood there unmoving, despite having not eaten in days and having looked forward to the night's hunt. She was in turmoil, he could tell. His bride wanted to help the elf, who was now leaning heavily forward and would have indeed fallen to the ground if he weren't holding her up with his incredible strength. She still gurgled something unintelligible, perhaps pleading for Emiline to help her. Better yet, maybe she recognized Emiline's features and thought her a fellow elf who would save her. He chuckled at the thought. Emiline reached for the elf as if to calm her, but he refused to let her.

"Emiline! Obey me! Look at me!" he said, keeping his voice low but the inflections severe enough for her to understand him. She looked up at him with her big bright eyes. She looked so beautiful and innocent at that moment, and he loved her.

"Feed, my love. Taste her blood." He grabbed the elf by the hair with one hand, now that it took so little effort to keep her under control, and jerked her head back and to the side, exposing her neck. Knowing she was doomed, the elf maiden began to sob. Exposing her tender jugular had broken the barrier, and Emiline's demeanor changed. No longer concerned for the elf, she showed her fangs as her pupils dilated. Then, with an unnatural quickness, she lunged at her prey and bit hard into her neck. The elf made a small whimper, as she had little fight left in her. He let go at that point, and Emiline fell on her, sucking the last bit of life out of the maiden.

He watched his love feed, enjoying the perverted spectacle. He loved watching her feed on elves, killing her kind most cruelly. She had once been just like the female elf, peace loving and friendly in her old life. Now she was a murderer, and she could not help it. Yes, he had to coax it from her on occasion, but that made the scene all that more erotic for him.

As Emiline fed, he noticed the boat was on its way back, the male elf whistling a happy tune as he paddled. He would not be able to make out much until he got a little closer. Then there would be panic and screaming, as he would see the carnage of the small camp and the remains of his lover. That was good, Heinsvick thought. After all, he was hungry too.

~

Matilda awakened some time later, her fingers throbbing. It took her a few moments to register the pain and to take in her surroundings. She was lying facedown on a cobblestone street, and toxic gas was still whipping about, assaulting her senses. Then she remembered where she was—Novafontera! She remembered the messenger, Vasheba. How close had she come to death? The fear that the creature instilled in her made her unable to move for many moments. Was that her destiny—to be tortured for eternity by that nasty demon? Her heart sank at the thought, but then again, demons were notorious liars. Perhaps Vasheba had been trying to frighten her. All she knew was that the experience she'd just gone through had been authentic.

She tried to sit up, but her head throbbed, and something pulled at her hand, holding her down. She fell back to the pavement, and that's when she noticed her fingers wrapped in the sticky tar-like substance of the bubbling pit. The pit of Marnelphion. The thought both excited her and terrorized her as the pain in her fingers grew. It took all her strength to pull free of the substance, and she grasped her sore hand by the wrist. She sat up slowly this time and examined her injured fingers, the tar coating two of them. She watched in amazement as the tar quickly seeped into her pores and was gone.

She studied her hand, holding it out in front of her. The pain was gone, and she realized the gas was not affecting her for the first time. She looked around, but she could see very little; the gas was thick, and it was also night. She breathed deeply and felt no ill effects from the poison. He was protecting her. He had sent her back, and she was now a high priest of Marnelphion. More important, he blessed her now. Suddenly Vasheba meant little to her. She was alive and well and had a mission directly from her god, and she would not fail. After all, how could he send her to an eternity of torment if she successfully summoned him back to this world?

She stood slowly, her head still injured from the fall and the assault she had mentally endured from Vasheba. She took a second to get her bearings, as her legs felt weak and she was very dizzy. "So that's what a near-death experience feels like, then?" she mumbled to herself.

Then the pain hit her. It doubled her over, and she fell to her knees once again, hitting the cobblestone hard. She held her arms to her stomach as pain bubbled inside her.

The tar! she thought.

She felt it—felt him inside her. His very essence mixed with her life force. It was the most excruciating pain she had ever felt, and yet it was the most beautiful experience she could have known. She fell to her side, still clutching her stomach. She vomited on the street, but the act never registered with her. She became catatonic then as her mind became assaulted by the evil that now lived inside her. Her body fought the intrusion the best it could, and for the next several hours, she suffered unbearably, rolling around on the cobblestone. At some point, she passed out from the pain.

When she awakened, she felt renewed. She felt strong. There was no more pain, and her senses heightened to a godlike level. At that moment, she felt like she could conquer the world. She stood quickly and inhaled the delicious gas, taking it in as she would a breath of fresh air. Her eyes appeared darker than their normal almond brown, but she physically appeared the same, by all accounts. However, the tar had increased her powers substantially, and she was more powerful than she could have ever imagined. Powerful enough to meet a vampire lord.

She turned knowingly in the direction of the castle. She couldn't see it in the dark or through the gas, but she knew where it was. So she walked confidently toward it, and with an extra kick in her step, whistling a happy tune as she did, like she hadn't a care in the world.

~

Heinsvick was not pleased with being awakened from his slumber. The most pleasant dream of his beloved Emiline feasting on her brethren and Heinsvick tasting the innocent elves' blood had been most beautiful. It took him a moment to orient himself to his surroundings. When he did, he found Emiline was missing from his coffin. After their feast, he had ravaged her, and they had fallen asleep in each other's arms. She never left the coffin without him or his permission. Something was amiss.

He jumped out of the coffin in one fluid motion, landing softly and quietly on the floor. Something called to him then, something otherworldly and mysterious. He quickly checked the rest of his harem in the castle's large dungeon area that they shared as a bedroom. All the coffins were empty! He bounded up the steps quickly, making sure not to make any noise. The calling grew louder, and he stopped to listen. "Heinsvick of Novafontera, you are summoned to the throne room. Come to me."

It was a female voice—and one he didn't recognize. Was it another vampire invading his kingdom? He quickened his pace, mentally preparing his most potent spells. Whoever this intruder was, she was dangerous, and he had not felt threatened in many centuries. It was time to find the threat and end it. When he finally made it to the throne room, he forcefully swung open the massive doors that would have taken two stout men to open back in the glory days of the New Order. Heinsvick had the strength of a giant at that moment, and no door was going to slow him in his aroused state.

The throne room was massive, with a fifty-foot ceiling supported by four massive columns, and lined with large windows, which he and his brides had covered with thick black curtains to block the dangerous sun. He could see out of the corner of his eye that it was daylight. The curtains were blocking the light, but the light dimly filtered through them.

A blue-and-gold carpet ran the room's length, leading straight to the thrones at the far side of it. The throne room was once a gathering place for the New Order and their allies, with many feasting tables and large tapestries adorning the walls. But now it was just a shell of its former existence, which was just the way Heinsvick wanted it.

He was relieved to find his brides lined up alongside the carpet, opposite the wall with the windows. However, they looked sad and scared, and he knew something was very wrong. He took just a moment to take in the scene—then he saw the intruder. She appeared human and small in stature, reclining easily on his throne, her leg casually draped across one arm. That made his anger boil, but then he saw Emiline. She was kneeling beside the throne, facing him, and the intruder was casually stroking her hair.

Usually his brides would have destroyed anyone who entered the city, much less the castle. Why were they not taking action? Why were they so submissive and subdued? He reached out to them mentally to form the link that would allow him to communicate telepathically.

Something blocked his attempt; he could not reach them. He growled and made haste toward the throne. He would find his answers now!

He was within twenty feet when the intruder suddenly sprang to life, grabbing Emiline's hair and jerking her head back roughly. She then produced a symbol he had seen before, one of a deity he harbored much hatred toward. She held the small obsidian skull-like holy sign of Marnelphion, demon lord of the undead. She held it before Emiline, who whimpered in response. He stopped his approach and held his hands up in front of him to show the intruder he meant no harm.

The woman smiled. "The others told me she is your favorite. You care for her, don't you, Heinsvick, lord of Novafontera?"

He couldn't understand how a mere human had so easily invaded his castle and taken control of his harem while he slumbered away in his coffin. He tried to wrap his head around this new adversary and thought caution would be the best action to take until he knew more about her. "You know of me, but I am at a disadvantage here. Who are you who callously walks into my home and treats my family like this?" he asked, never taking his eyes off Emiline.

She released Emiline's hair but still held the skull in proximity to her face. Emiline looked terrified and sensed the awful power that the symbol possessed. "I can kill them all, you know, without much trouble at all," she said casually.

His anger grew. "I asked you a question, and you will answer me, woman! You are not undead; I can hear your heartbeat and smell your blood. Who are you? How can you resist the toxins of the gas?"

She smiled and began to pet Emiline once more. "I am either your enemy or an ally. It is your decision."

"My patience grows thin, priestess of Marnelphion. Never have I called one such as yourself an ally."

"Well, perhaps it is in your best interest to do so this time, vampire lord," she said.

Her confidence unnerved him a little. He hadn't survived for centuries without respecting things he did not understand. Nevertheless, this diminutive woman had him intrigued, and as long as she had Emiline that close, she made him nervous.

"My name is Matilda, and I am here to negotiate with the mighty and powerful Heinsvick of Novafontera," she said, standing from the throne and bowing.

He was not impressed. He wanted nothing more than to sink his fangs into the woman's neck and end her life immediately. The only thing stopping him was the null stone. Emiline wore it, which meant the power that kept the woman from being dissolved by the gas was natural and not magical. Also, the hint of this one's strength, as she blocked his communication with his brides, demanded respect. "Why have you come?" he asked.

"I have come in need of your services," she said as she began to walk toward him. She led Emiline behind her by the hand.

He noticed Emiline's expression still reflected fear, along with a sense of subjugation. She was utterly under the woman's power. He turned his attention to Matilda, who was walking seductively toward him. She was confident and sexy, and she walked right up to him, Emiline in tow, and stood, looking into his eyes. She was much shorter than he, and he towered over her menacingly. However, she did not flinch, and if she was scared, she did not show it.

Her face was pretty, but her eyes held some dark secret, as if he were looking into her soul and found nothing but pure evil there. She was powerful in a way that made him feel inferior. She could control his brides, but could she control him the same way? He reasoned that she must be able to, or she would not have walked straight up to him. "What do you request, priestess?"

"I will bring Marnelphion back to this world to rule once more!"

"Stupid woman!" he roared, which made her take a step back, and the fear on Emiline's face reminded him that he must stay under control—this situation was too volatile. He calmed himself and focused once more. "Why would you do such a thing?"

"To rule by his side, just as you will."

"Impossible, wench. He will destroy us both if you are stupid enough to summon him here."

She stuck out her bottom lip in a fake pout and reached up to rub his chest. "Tsk, tsk, Heinsvick. That is not the attitude I was hoping you would have."

He grabbed her wrist and squeezed it tightly, her grimace of pain pleasing him. "Do not touch me, foolish woman. If it happens again, you are dead!" he said and slung her arm down.

Matilda brought her arm up to her chest and cradled it there. He could hear her heart beating faster, and he could smell her blood. He prepared to lunge at her, but with surprising speed, she brought that injured hand out in front of her, and this time it held the skull symbol, its red eyes glowing brightly in the green fog. Emiline shrieked and fell to her knees, hiding her face from the horrible skull. Heinsvick hissed and backed away. The power contained there was undeniable. She possessed the power of destruction. He could feel it.

"Now suffer the consequences of your actions, vampire lord!" she said and laughed crazily. She turned toward the line of brides against the wall and held the skull toward the closest one.

"No!" Heinsvick pleaded, just as Matilda unleashed an invisible wave of destruction that hit his surprised bride, who screamed briefly before turning to a fine, powdery ash in a flash. The way she'd looked at Heinsvick as she died, her eyes pleading for help, boring straight to his heart, inflicted more pain than a sharp stake could ever have done. Junet was one of his oldest brides, one of the first he had turned all those centuries ago. They had shared so much time, and now she was a pile of ash. Just like that, she was gone. He stared at her remains, unable to move or even comprehend the devastation that Matilda was.

"Who's next?" she screamed at him. "Shall I destroy all of them?"

He turned back to her and knew by the wild look in her eyes that she meant what she said. He could tell she was losing control, and he feared if that happened, she would destroy all of them, himself included. "No more. I will hear you out. What is it that you want me to do?"

She was breathing hard, her heart beating fast, but his words calmed her. Finally, after a few moments, she collected herself. "That's more like it," she said with a smile, as if nothing unusual had happened. "As I was saying, I am going to summon Marnelphion so that he may rule the world once more, and you are going to help me."

"Why would I do that?" he said with a sigh.

"Because I will have collateral," she smirked, taking Emiline's hand and pulling her to her feet.

Tears streaked down Emiline's beautiful face. Even in her state of undeath, she had the heart of an elf and felt the sting of Junet's death as much as Heinsvick did. He could not lose her; she was precious to him. "No!" he screamed, realizing what the woman had in mind. "You may not take her!"

"Oh, but I will, vampire, and there is nothing you can do to stop me. You see, this will be the only way I can trust that you will perform the task. If you succeed, you get her back. If you fail, you lose your life, and I keep her as my plaything."

"I don't agree to that! She stays!"

Matilda smiled and turned her attention to Emiline, wiping her tears. "What was your name, child?"

"My name?" Emiline asked, tilting her head to the side as if she didn't understand the question.

"Yes, your name—when you were alive?"

"My name was and is Emiline."

Matilda turned back toward him. "Oh, she is a keeper. I see why you like this one, Heinsvick."

"You may not—"

She held up a hand. "Shut your mouth, vampire! Shall I destroy more of these filthy creatures you call family? Then will you agree with my proposal?"

"You will have to kill me if you want to take her!" he said through gritted teeth.

She took Emiline over to the closest two brides, who recoiled and fell to their knees. Heinsvick tensed, not knowing what to expect from the volatile woman. One thing he knew, however, was that he was not going to let the nasty priestess kidnap his favorite bride. He would die stopping her if he had to.

"Get up, you fools!" she said, and they quickly did. "Take Emiline to her coffin, nail it shut, and bring it back here to me, understand?" They nodded eagerly in the hopes of leaving her presence, if only for a few moments. So they took Emiline, one on each arm, and began to escort her away.

"Wait!" Heinsvick said.

The two vampires looked very confused at that moment, which gave him some satisfaction, knowing that his control over them remained. He sensed the panic in Matilda as well—perhaps she wasn't nearly as strong as she was hinting. He smiled, understanding it best for them to continue so that she would be safe and the null stone would no longer be able to negate his spells. Perhaps then he could kill this priestess of Marnelphion.

After a slight pause, he said, "Proceed, my lovelies. I will be there momentarily to assist you." He watched the three leave and noticed Emiline held his gaze until he could no longer see her. Once they had left the room and the giant doors closed, Heinsvick lunged at Matilda, or at least tried, but she was in his head.

"Stop, in the name of Marnelphion—I command you!" she screamed, holding her skull symbol toward him. The angry red eyes of the nasty thing glowed with power, and he felt her intrusion in his head, the skull modifying her ability.

He gritted his teeth and tried to resist, but the command was too powerful. He slowed and gradually stopped, just inches from the skull. He continued to fight, and Matilda's control was shaky at best. Her hand quivered, and her arm strained to hold the small symbol before her. He smiled, knowing that she could not keep it up for very long. He also saw his brides stirring behind her, her influence over them waning as her concentration was now entirely on him.

"I have a special gift for you, Heinsvick," she said.

"I want nothing from you other than your blood, woman," he hissed back, still struggling against the intrusion in his mind.

"A gift from the most powerful of gods! A seal of great power!" she said, her arm holding the skull and visibly shaking now.

His brides were inching closer, tentatively, knowing that if she turned on them, she could destroy them, but he saw the bloodlust returning to their eyes. They were ready to kill for him, to die to save him. Just as it had always been, just as it should be. He smiled, showing his fangs.

Matilda's face began to contort with pain, and her lips quivered as she said, "Give me your hand," and began to chant softly.

To his dismay, he began to raise his left hand toward her, following her command. He struggled to stop the motion, but he could not refuse her. The evil eyes of the skull bore into him, forcing her will on him.

"With this seal ... I thee slave!" she said with all her strength, grabbing his hand and covering the back of it with her palm.

He felt as if his hand were on fire as smoke wafted from the unison of their hands. The stench of burning flesh—his, no doubt—began to fill his nostrils. He felt the power of the seal surge in his hand and through his arm. When she finally stopped her chanting and removed her tiny hand from his, he could make out the symbol of a skull, the same as her holy symbol, on the back of his hand. He now carried the brand of Marnelphion.

Matilda sensed an attack from behind her and quickly turned, holding the skull out in front of her. "Back, you filth!" she screamed at them, falling to her knees in exhaustion.

Heinsvick's mobility returned immediately, she was out of his head, and now she would die. He grabbed her by the hair and bent her head back, exposing her neck and lifting her to a standing position in one motion. His other hand smacked the skull symbol from her grasp, and it flew across the room, hitting the far wall and rolling into a fog-filled corner. He had been in this same position just a few hours earlier when he had presented the elf maiden to Emiline. This time, he would perform the killing.

With the skull amulet gone, his brides were no longer afraid, and they eagerly crowded around, hissing and spitting at the small woman. She looked up at him, and he expected to see the terror in her eyes, as he had so many times before—the look someone gives when they know they're about to die a horrible death. But instead, he saw a calmness in her eyes. He didn't understand this one but knew he had to destroy her. He bared his fangs and prepared to plunge into her neck. That's when he felt the immense pain in his forearm. He looked down to see that his skin was split open and bone was visible from his wrist to his elbow.

He screamed in pain, releasing her as he held his injured arm in front of him. What had caused such an injury? Before he could figure out the mystery, his other arm split the same way, and as his blood spilled onto the floor, he dropped to his knees, swooning from the pain and nearly blacking out. He held his arms out before him and tried to conceive what was happening.

"Get back, or he dies!" Matilda screamed, switching places to now stand behind him.

He blinked several times, groggily, trying to grasp his surroundings. Finally, he noticed his harem as one; all stepped back to give them plenty of room. Matilda now held complete control of the situation once more.

She whispered in his ear, "Through the seal, I can tear the flesh from your bones with merely a thought. I am the one responsible for your pain. I am also the one who can soothe it. The seal binds us mentally and physically. I can reach out to you anywhere in this world at any time. Likewise, I can inflict grievous wounds on you. Do you understand?"

Heinsvick nodded, still holding his throbbing arms out in front of him.

"Do you require healing, vampire slave?"

Again he nodded, giving entirely to her will and paying no heed to the new title she bestowed on him.

"Good," she said.

She cast a healing spell, and he felt the soothing sensation in his arms and witnessed his torn flesh mend itself. The skin closed, and the bleeding stopped, proving to him that she could just as quickly kill him or keep him alive at her discretion. The wounds were still severe but were no longer life-threatening. After searching for a few moments, she retrieved her amulet, and he took that opportunity to stand and silently command his harem to their coffins. It was still daylight, and they needed rest. In truth, he just wanted them away from the crazy and powerful woman.

Matilda ignored the fleeing vampires and said, "Come, Heinsvick. Let us sit and discuss our plans," pointing toward the thrones and donning her skull symbol once more.

He lowered his wounded arms and followed her to the set of thrones, obediently taking his seat and feeling very much a slave in his own home.

"We have only a little over two years to prepare; we must act quickly," she said.

Heinsvick leaned back on the throne and closed his eyes, trying to ignore the pain that still throbbed in his arms and make sense of the events that were transpiring. Matilda sat on the queen's throne as if it had been designed for her all along. "What do you require of me?" he finally asked.

"It makes me so happy that you have changed your attitude toward me and that we can be allies," she said as if he were acting of his own free will.

He tried to control his anger, and he knew he had no choice because of the brand. But he also couldn't bear the thought of losing another of his precious brides. His eyes fixated on the pile of ash that remained of Junet, and his heart truly ached for the loss. After some time of silence, he said, "Yes, I will assist you to my fullest ability, and I ask that you keep Emiline here with me. She can assist me on whatever quest you desire."

"Hmm," Matilda said, tapping a finger to her cheek, looking at him but appearing deep in thought. Then, after a few moments, she said, "No. You are my slave, but you are also powerful enough that I need a safety net. Emiline will serve as that net. While I have her, I know that you will complete the quest."

"Understand, though, that she is everything to me. I will not be so willing to serve if anything should happen to her. Death would not even be such a bad thing."

"Understood and agreed. I will make sure nothing happens to your bride. All I want is to complete the summoning, and if that happens, not only will she be back in your arms, but you will have a special place in the rulership of the world."

He sighed and closed his eyes, not impressed by her visions of grandeur. "What is it that you require of me, then?"

"Your task is simple, my servant."

He squeezed his fists tightly on the throne's arms, causing searing pain to shoot down both arms. He grimaced and looked at her from the corner of his eye. She hadn't noticed the reaction, but the pretentious way she called him a servant made him angry enough to rip her limbs from their sockets. Such a thought made him happy, even if it meant it would cost him his life.

"As I said, I have much to do and only two years to do it. Therefore I only require one task from you. Complete it, and you will earn your freedom, bride, and dignity back."

"One task, and I will not fail you," he said.

She smiled. "Of course you won't. But considering your powers and knowledge of this old world, I have faith that you will complete this in less than a year. So your most important task is to find the offspring of Kane, the lich god."

He sat up with a start at the mention of the lich's name. He hadn't seen or even thought of the lich since the time of the banishing. Kane had been such a thorn in Marnelphion's side, refusing to recognize the demon lord as the master of undeath. Legends said that he'd even assisted the New Order in banishing the demon back to hell.

"Kane has offspring?"

"Yes, my sources say so. The child would still be young, perhaps less than twenty years. Our time grows short, however, because if the child loses its virginity, it will not properly serve as the 666th sacrifice and therefore will not open the gate."

"So I need to find this child and do what with him ... or her?"

"Simply secure it and keep it alive until I retrieve it from you. But, of course, I will expect you to guard its virginity as well. Contact me using our new telepathic powers to let me know you have succeeded. I will then trade Emiline for the child, and you will be free once more."

"Sounds easy enough. How will I know when I have found the one?"

"My sources don't have that answer yet. The only clue I have to find the chosen one is the vision of a raven's feather. Does this mean anything to you?"

Heinsvick rubbed his chin, grimacing away the pain the movement caused. "Not immediately, but I have access to many sources of information. I'll research and discover the meaning."

"Good. I hope that's enough for you to complete your most important of tasks. We still have several hours of daylight left. Once the sun is down, I'll take Emiline and leave this place. You may contact me any time you find information that's important to our cause; focus on the power of the brand to do so."

He shifted in his seat when she mentioned taking Emiline. He tried to think of a way to change her mind, but he knew the effort was hopeless.

"Tell me of those long-ago years, vampire lord. You were there ... at the time of Marnelphion. Tell me all about it, and leave out no details."

He didn't want to talk right then, and his mind worked hard trying to discover a way he could kill this one and save Emiline from her kidnapping. But alas, he spoke because he knew he had no choice. He told her of the terror Marnelphion had exerted over the world. Hope in those days had faded for humanity. He emphasized how the New Order had returned that hope and that Kane, the lich god, had assisted them in defeating the demon lord and sending him back to hell. Matilda's discomfort during those parts of the story pleased him, and he secretly enjoyed her pain as she took in the story of her god's defeat.

His stories lasted the rest of the evening and into the night. Once the moon was at its highest point, Matilda summoned two of his brides to bring her the casket of Emiline. She looked over the handiwork where they had crudely nailed it shut. She heard Emiline's muffled cries come from within and her pounding and clawing at the lid.

That's when Heinsvick cried out to his love, rushing to the coffin and putting an ear to the lid. "Do not be afraid, my love. We will see each other soon enough. Be strong, my dear." Hearing his voice seemed to calm her, but soon after, he could hear her gently weeping. The anger on his face was undeniable when he turned back on Matilda. "Do not harm her! I will cooperate only as long as she is safe."

A hint of anger flashed across the small woman's face, but instantly, a calm visage replaced it. She nodded. "She will be treasured by me, for she is my key to obtaining the child of Kane. So she is valuable to me, and I guarantee her safety. Now, if you'll excuse me, vampire lord, I have much work to do."

She commanded the two brides to carry the coffin to the docks, and Heinsvick followed closely behind, saying no word. They passed the bubbling pit on the way, and she felt its power, its pull on her, and the pure evil that it evoked. She thought about how that pit would boil over and cover more of the land once Marnelphion arrived. The thought made her giddy.

Once they reached the rotted docks, she motioned for the other two to put the casket down, and after they readily complied, she held her holy symbol up and whispered a command. It glowed brightly, and she held it out toward the sea. She couldn't see the sunken ships, but rotting masts loomed all around her, and she could sense the presence of many powerful ghosts haunting the dark waters.

She knew her crew would be nervous about coming back to the dock to pick her up, especially with three vampires there. She turned to Heinsvick to order him back to the castle, but he was gone. He and his brides had vanished, and all that remained was the fog of death. It reminded her of just how powerful he was. She smiled and looked down at the coffin. It didn't matter; she now had all the leverage she needed to keep that one in check.

She soon saw the lanterns of the small boat that paddled closer toward the dock. She could make out six men on it, with four more rowing. The most prominent figure was that of Cerus the Gray. She had been in the city for nearly two days, and he had not left her. He was as faithful as he was powerful, a solid and trustworthy ally. As they reached the dock, he jumped the remaining five feet and landed nimbly beside her. He looked immediately at the coffin with disgust.

"You brought the filthy vampire lord with you?"

"No, Cerus, the coffin contains something better—his favored bride," she said excitedly.

"You survived the test. So you're now a high priest?"

"Yes, and more, my dear Cerus. I have received a special blessing from Marnelphion and a most important mission. I am delighted to say that your army will soon find blood at the tips of their spears."

Cerus smiled. She knew nothing gave him pleasure as much as war. She pulled him near and whispered in his ear, "These few days have been a blessing to us, my dear Cerus. The world is nothing more than an oyster, and we are the pearls. Great things await us. Now let us start our successful journey home so that we may begin our quest."

"What quest do you speak of?"

"I'll tell you once we are on board."

"My men will not be happy about sailing home with a vampire."

"Your men should know their place. They will not only be happy about it, but they will load the precious cargo for us. Any more questions or concerns, General?"

Cerus found himself laughing out loud. "None that I recall! Your logic sounds reasonable to me!"

The crew had tied the small boat to the dock and were awaiting orders. They all appeared very nervous, looking around and holding out their lanterns into the foggy night. If they could have felt the ghosts' presence as surely as Matilda did, they would have fallen over from fright. They were thick there at the docks, and she knew that not one of them would show themselves. She was a high priest of Marnelphion now and blessed with powers beyond most mortals. The undead knew it, and therefore they shied away from her.

The men took in the carnage of the dock. The large ships long destroyed during Marnelphion's rule lurked in the haunted water, making the place incredibly eerie. Cerus ordered four men to carry the coffin onto the small boat, and they left as quickly as possible afterward, the crew all looking around anxiously. All except Cerus, Matilda noticed. He feared nothing, and that's why she'd picked him as the general of her army. Everything was going as planned. She was certain that if Heinsvick proved helpful and discovered Kane's child, the summoning would become a reality.

Once their cargo was secure on the small boat, they began rowing toward the ship. At that point, Matilda glanced at the docks and could vaguely make out the figure of Heinsvick there. She reached out to him telepathically, using the brand that now connected them. "Do not fail me, vampire lord. I'll be watching and waiting."

He stood frozen at the rotting dock, staring at the small boat as it rowed away. Matilda could sense his feelings and knew that he struggled not to attack their vessel. Even though he didn't answer, Matilda knew he'd heard her. She could feel the bond between them through the brand. The evil priestess closed her eyes and smiled. He would obey her, or he would die. Either way, she had her plans for Emiline.

"What is it, my lady?" Cerus asked, looking back to the docks and seeing nothing.

"Oh, nothing, my dear Cerus. Things are working out perfectly, as planned," she said and patted the coffin with a smile. The world was hers for the taking, and she meant to take it.

CHAPTER 5

TRIALS

Unis Rho had often dreamed of the dark man, and in truth, he'd haunted her sleep frequently in her final years. Each dream was the same: a dark, mysterious man would come to the orphanage to find the two Rho girls. Unis would hide, but he always found her, usually in the closet, trying to stifle the girls' sobs. He would then kill her and take the girls. She'd never told anyone about those dreams, but they were genuine to her, and she'd lived in fear that someone would take her twins from her one day.

Now it was Cassandra's turn to dream of the dark man. However, she saw him differently than Unis did. He was tall, handsomely rugged, and very mysterious. He had a well-trimmed goatee and dark hair. He didn't speak to her, but she could sense his desires by how he carried himself and even how he looked at her. She didn't feel threatened by him, but she also wasn't comfortable being in his presence.

She found herself in a cave in the dream, light pouring in from two holes in the far wall that served as windows. A small stone table stood in the center of the room, rays of sun shining brightly on it. The dark man stood on the other side of the small table and watched her intently. She could not look at him long because he unnerved her; something about him was familiar yet foreign at the same time.

He then pointed to the table, and her gaze followed to find a thin silver rod with a blue topaz gem the size of a small chicken egg adorning the tip. It shone brightly in the cascading sunlight and twinkled so much that it took her breath away. She walked up to the table and reached for the rod, but before she could touch it, it faded away.

After the beautiful rod vanished, she noticed words etched on the table's surface: "To find a king." She was confused by the message, so she looked to the dark man for answers. But instead, he motioned with his right hand to the windows letting in the light.

She tentatively made her way to them. The sun felt warm on her skin and the air dry and gritty as she moved closer. Once she reached them, she had to shield her eyes as the daylight overwhelmed her, and the hot air took her breath. Once her eyes adjusted, she could see that she was high above a desert terrain. There was sand as far as she could see, with rolling dunes in all directions. There was only one water source in view: a lazy river that flowed far below her position. Something about that river made her feel uneasy. It seemed out of place. The environment was far too harsh for a river to run right through it.

Then suddenly she was there, on the shore of the strange river. The foulest smell she could ever imagine invaded her senses, and she dry heaved into the sand for many moments. The river reeked of rotting flesh. She looked over her shoulder to where she had stood a moment before, and she could see a massive outcropping of rocks, and at the very top were the windows. They reminded her vaguely of a skull sitting atop the rock formation.

She could feel the dark man in there watching her. She covered her mouth with her arm to block the stench emanating from the foul river and turned back to investigate it. That's when she noticed that the river was not flowing at all. Instead, it seemed to move of its own accord, as if it were alive, but that wasn't exactly accurate either. As she looked on in amazement, she realized it was just a gathering of many, many birds and no water at all.

"Ravens?" she whispered into the hot, dry air.

At the sound of her voice, they took to flight all at once. There were thousands of them, and Cassandra's voice had startled them. They flew straight up, covering the sky and partially blocking the sun. They weren't ravens—they were vultures. She looked back at the river with wide eyes, and what she saw made her fall to her knees and retch once again. Thousands and thousands of bodies made up the river. The stench was the decay of the dead. There was no water, just a long burial plot full of decaying bodies.

~

Cassandra awoke from the dream with a splitting headache. She blinked away the horrible vision and tried to catch her breath. Her surroundings were unfamiliar, and not only did her head hurt, but her arms and mouth ached as well. She was lying in a strange bed. The small room had an open window to her left that let in the fresh air and sunlight, and a small door was to her right. Her bed was the only piece of furniture in the room. She tried to sit up, but she realized she couldn't because her arms were bound to the bedpost. She looked around in a panic, noticing both arms attached to the headboard with a thin rope. She tried to yell out, but she discovered that was impossible because another piece of rope was tied around her mouth, cutting off her ability to speak. It dug grooves into the corners of her mouth and was tied tightly behind her head.

The back of her head throbbed, so she laid her head down and tried to remember what had happened and exactly where she was. Her eyes went wide when she remembered those final moments before she blacked out. She had attacked Ronnis with her magic. She had killed him! Then something had hit her from behind, most likely the sheriff or one of his deputies. The memory made her head throb even more as she recognized the painful wound for what it was.

So she had killed someone and was arrested because of it, but she wasn't in any jail cell. So where was she? She closed her eyes and tried to calm herself. Surely someone would be in eventually to tell her what was going on. She kept her eyes closed because that made her head hurt a lot less, but she became more and more agitated as she lay there and pondered the situation. Were Kessi and Sera all right? Where was she? Why was no one there to provide answers? She started to struggle again, working herself into a panic, and for Cassandra's effort, the ropes dug deeper into her wrists. She needed to free herself from the bindings, she needed to speak, and, most of all, she needed answers.

She cried out during her fit, and that's when the door finally opened. Her cries gained the attention of a young man dressed in white robes. He couldn't have been much older than she, perhaps in his early twenties, and he stood there watching her squirm on the bed. When she noticed him, she stopped her struggles and pleaded for him to release her. Tears streamed down her face, and she knew he couldn't understand what she'd just asked of him. So she stopped struggling and tried to ask again, but the gag stifled her words.

"I … I … will be right back!" he said and ran out the door, and she could hear it lock behind him.

Perhaps she was in jail after all. She laid her head back down and closed her eyes, feeling the tears flow down her cheeks and pool in her ears. She tried to calm herself, hoping that the sheriff would show her mercy enough to untie her. A very long time passed before she heard the door open. The young man came into view and stood to the side as an older, more distinguished man came in wearing priestly robes. So she was in the temple, probably because of her head injury. That answered a lot, but it also meant that she was probably going to jail once she healed.

The elder turned to the younger man and said, "Go fetch the sheriff, John. Tell him his young prisoner has awakened."

The younger man bowed and left, shutting and locking the door once more. The older man came and sat gently on the bed next to Cassandra. He wiped the tears from her cheeks and smiled. "Don't you worry, young one. The sheriff will be here soon. I bet you're scared, huh?"

Cassandra nodded but kept calm, trying to suppress her anxiety over the fact that she was still tied and gagged.

"As well you should be. Half the town is after the sheriff to turn you over to them for justice." Cassandra's eyes went wide. Undoubtedly the town would be on her side, for she had killed a man, yes, but a rotten man. He was the bad guy, not her. He smiled at her discomfort and stroked her cheek gently. "Do not fear. As long as you are in the temple, you have immunity from the town's laws. I will keep you here as long as possible, in the hopes that the people will calm. Does that sound like a plan you are agreeable with?"

Cassandra nodded and gave him a muffled, "Thank you."

"You are quite welcome, child. My name is Barktuck Misol, the high priest of Meshlor. I have been given charge over you during your stay at the temple."

Then his pleasant, soft smile gave way to a scowl of pure anger. He squeezed Cassandra's cheeks hard and used the palm of his hand to cover her mouth. He pressed down forcefully, driving her wounded head deep into the pillow. With his other hand, he pinched her nose so she couldn't breathe. He leaned in close to her as she thrashed wildly, trying to move her head to the side so she could draw a breath.

"You listen to me, you little witch. Ronnis is a dear friend of mine, and if he had died at your hands, I would have already seen to your extermination. However, he is going to live, thanks in part to your sister. I am fond of her as well, and that fact has stayed my hand from killing you. Be warned, though, your life hangs in the balance, and rest assured—if the people of this town don't exact justice for your actions, I surely will."

His breath stunk of sour wine, and his hand tasted of sweat. Cassandra's head throbbed, and the pressure he applied made it much worse. Her lungs burned for air, and she was near passing out. But before she did, he released her, and she sucked in a big gulp of air. As she did, he quickly produced a tiny flask from his robe pocket and poured the contents in her mouth, then held it shut, tilting her head back as he did. The pain racked her head once more, and she involuntarily swallowed the odorless, tasteless liquid. The rope had absorbed a small amount, but he'd forced her to consume most of it. It happened so fast; she couldn't process his words correctly. Had he said that Ronnis lived? She tried to shake the cobwebs from her mind, to focus on his words, but she could not.

He eventually released her and stood, straightening his holy robes, putting a pleasant smile back on his face, and sticking the flask into his pocket just as the door opened. She saw the sheriff enter then, along with two deputies. She meant to scream out for help, but she just couldn't summon the energy, suddenly feeling very tired.

~

"So as you can see, dear sheriff, she is still suffering from the trauma your blow caused her," Barktuck said sadly, waving a hand at Cassandra's unresponsive form. "We should not have been so quick to summon you, for it appears her few moments of consciousness were in delirium and driven by her fever."

Sheriff Quinn looked over her and gently moved her head to feel the large bump at her skull base. She moaned softly, and he shook his head, gently removing his hand. "I don't understand; I didn't think I hit her that hard."

"Well, head injuries are quite the conundrum, Sheriff."

"I suppose. Are these restraints necessary? I mean, this seems a little excessive."

"Well, she is guilty of attempted murder … and witchcraft. And according to the stories I have heard, she made a gesture toward Lord Ronnis and mumbled a few words before her witchery decimated the poor man. Do you think it would be wise to release her bonds or ungag her?"

Quinn thought about that for a moment. The young woman didn't seem much of a threat, but he had witnessed the raw power of her magic. "No," he finally said. "Leave the witch bound until she is fully awake. Then summon me at once."

He moved to the window and observed the growing crowd below. Barktuck joined him and shook his head. "That mob may get out of hand, Sheriff. If they do, there could be dire consequences. But unfortunately we are priests, not warriors, and are not capable of stopping an angry mob should it come to that."

Quinn waved his hand at the priest and nodded. "My men will try to disperse the mob and at the least protect the temple from being stampeded. But if that does happen, you have my permission to let them take the child. Her blood will be on their hands, not ours."

"Yes," Barktuck said, "no sense in others risking injury or death just to save a criminal."

Quinn turned sharply toward the older priest, a scowl creasing his forehead. "She is young, barely an adult by our standards. Please remember that, Barktuck."

"Yes, of course … and that young woman removed half of Lord Ronnis's face," the priest said and smiled.

"I am aware," was all Quinn could manage to say about it, the weight of the world bearing down on his shoulders. He massaged his mustache, deep in thought. Then, after a few moments, he asked, "How is Lord Ronnis?"

"Very well, surprisingly, thanks to the other Rho girl. He may never see out of one eye, and food will never taste the same to him, but he will live."

Quinn nodded with a faint smile. "That's good news. Something rare in this town these days, I'm afraid. Carry on, then, dear priest, and alert me the moment she's coherent."

He started away, motioning for his deputies to follow him. He knocked on the door, and John, the young acolyte, stationed right outside, quickly unlocked it. Quinn turned to the elderly priest as the door swung open. "I'm going to announce a special town meeting tomorrow morning, just past dawn. I want to ease the tension of the townsfolk. I need you to be there, Barktuck. I need your testimony concerning Cassandra and Ronnis. Can you make it?"

"Of course. I wouldn't miss it," Barktuck said with a grand smile.

Quinn nodded and left the room. That night, Barktuck visited Ronnis, who was in a different temple level, recovering from his wounds. They discussed many things, including the sheriff, Lady Sera, and the angry mob outside the temple. But, of course, the first order of business was Ronnis's wounded pride and injured face.

Ronnis threw the handheld mirror across the room, shattering it against the far wall. Unlike Cassandra's sparse room in the temple, this one was luxurious, with a nice rug, tapestries, and several pieces of oak furniture. Barktuck expected as much as Ronnis saw his torn face for the first time.

"There is still much healing to do, Lord Ronnis. But it will look better in time," Barktuck said.

"She has ruined my looks! She has ruined me, Barktuck!" Ronnis cried.

The old priest agreed but offered hope. "I discussed this issue with the high priests of the temple. They were all in agreement, under the circumstances, that we offer something to help with your prosthetics."

"What do you speak of?"

Barktuck couldn't look at him for long; the wound showed his bottom right jawbone and a few teeth. There were also holes in his gums where two teeth had been. In addition, Barktuck could see Ronnis's tongue wag as he talked, making the wound even more repulsive. The torn cheek exposed his mouth, but the injury reached his right eye, which was swollen shut, and the priests feared that it would no longer function once the swelling subsided.

Unable to look him in the face, Barktuck said, "The temple stores contain a few artifacts of value. These are mostly trinkets that the temple has owned for many centuries. One in particular is an old porcelain mask that is worth its weight in gold. It was used in plays centuries ago and is a prized relic to many enthusiasts. The older priests have agreed to offer it to you as you go through your recovery."

Barktuck reached over to the vanity, picked up the silk bag there, and handed it to his friend. Ronnis looked at it hesitantly, then looked back to the priest.

"Go ahead, Ronnis. I think the mask is beautiful, and it will not only look distinguished on you, but it will only add to your lore, in my opinion. Imagine when the townsfolk start referring to you as the masked lord of the Oldorburg Orphanage!" Barktuck exclaimed excitedly with a wave of his hand.

Ronnis slowly took the bag and untied the drawstring. He reached in and removed the smooth porcelain mask, studying the ancient craftsmanship. It was solid white, with two eyeholes; a nose mold; and a perpetual smile, with a tiny opening through which the wearer could speak.

"It is in perfect condition, considering its age. Quite a generous gift from the priests of this most sacred place," Barktuck said with a bow.

Ronnis extended his hand, and they shook vigorously. "You are a good friend, Barktuck, and I will not forget your generosity."

"May it serve you well. Now try it on!" Barktuck said.

Ronnis sat up straighter in the bed and slipped the mask over his face. The leather strap in the back was adjustable, and it took him a few minutes to get it right. Once it was on, he asked through the mask, his voice slightly muffled, "How do I look?"

"I'd give you a mirror to see, but I'm afraid I can't seem to find it."

The two stared at each other for several moments, Ronnis in his formfitting new mask and Barktuck's face a rock showing no emotion. Ronnis finally ended the silence with a hearty laugh, and before long, they both roared with laughter. After they had calmed themselves, Barktuck confirmed how distinguished he looked with it on.

"You give off a presence that few can resist. You are a mystery that will demand respect. In other words, it looks exquisite on you!" Barktuck said.

Ronnis removed the mask and took his friend's hand. "I owe you for this, Barktuck. I will not forget the gesture. Tell the other priests that I have accepted their gift and will cherish it."

"I will, I will," Barktuck said. "But first, I have one more thing that you might be interested in."

Ronnis looked at him, puzzled. "What is it?"

"How about Cassandra Rho?"

Ronnis lit up and leaned in toward his friend, suddenly very serious. "Tell me more."

~

While Ronnis and Barktuck were making their sinister plans, Sheriff Quinn made his way to the orphanage. He came alone, with no guards escorting him this time. The hour was later than the sheriff had intended, but Quinn had to speak to Sera. He knocked on the door, and was led to a common room where Sera and Kessi were pouring over some books, which he assumed was homework for Kessi.

"Lady Sera," he said with a bow.

"Sheriff Quinn, please join us," she said, standing and extending her arm.

He nodded and entered, noticing right away that both of them looked exhausted. He assumed they had not slept much over the last two days since the incident.

"Please sit down, Sheriff," Sera said.

He grabbed a seat next to Kessi and smiled, even though his heart wasn't in it. Unfortunately she returned his smile with one that was somehow even more pathetic.

"We haven't heard from the temple, and they won't let us visit Cassandra. How is she?" Sera asked anxiously.

"I've just come from there, and she's doing better," he said.

Sera's look of relief confirmed that she was concerned for the girl's safety. "That's good. We've been worried that she wouldn't receive the kind of care that—well, let's say I'd rather Kessi be watching over her." She smiled and took Kessi's hand.

Kessi gripped her mother's hand so tight her knuckles turned white. Their connection was genuine, and their concern for Cassandra was real. Since the incident, the sheriff had slowly discovered the love the family of three shared and how that didn't seem to mesh with what Lord Ronnis believed.

The three sat there, unable to find the words to proceed, until Kessi said, "I am no longer welcomed in the temple … at least not until Cassandra leaves. I plan on not returning when that time comes. I question the values of the place." Then, on the verge of tears, she added with a whisper, "I could heal her, though."

They had both witnessed her healing powers on the night of the attack as she had saved Lord Ronnis's life. That gave credit to the young woman's claim, and both Sera and Quinn nodded.

"I hear that Ronnis is also in the temple and on the mend," Sera added quietly.

"Yes, I think he is," Quinn said and nodded.

"Do you think that's wise? Do you think Cassandra is safe?" Sera asked, tears filling her eyes.

"Yes, they are both in good hands, and the high priests will make sure nothing happens to her. I have faith they are doing all they can to help her," Quinn said, again not mentioning Cassandra's current treatment.

"Not Barktuck Misol," Kessi said softly, more to herself than anyone else.

Quinn's brow creased, and he looked at her with a deep curiosity. "What do you mean?"

"Is Barktuck Misol involved in her care?" she asked, her face a reflection of fear and anxiety.

"I believe he is, but—"

Tears streamed down her face, and she lowered her head. Her sobs were quiet, and large drops fell from her cheeks onto the table.

Sera hugged her. "What's wrong, dear?" she asked with a sniffle.

"He is not a good man," Kessi replied softly.

"He is a high priest—one who is trusted and one who runs the temple's affairs," Quinn replied.

"You're wrong, Sheriff," Kessi said, the tears still streaming down her face. "His god is evil. The other high priests are afraid of him. I've seen it. If she's in his care, she's doomed."

"Can you get her out of there?" Sera asked, her eyes reflecting sudden desperation.

"I can't. Cassandra is protected there, and the temple doesn't fall under the town laws. Therefore I have no jurisdiction to move her."

That seemed to crush Sera as she hugged Kessi close and kissed her head. Kessi's reaction to hearing that Barktuck was in charge of Cassandra gave credence to her fears. Sera and Quinn shared a glance as Sera wiped away a tear from her cheek. Quinn shook his head helplessly and gave a weak smile in return.

He finally said, "Sera, the town is in an uproar. They are angry and scared and want answers. I hoped we could have a quick trial for Cassandra, but her health will not allow that. So instead of letting this fester, I've decided to have a public meeting tomorrow morning. I announced this as I left the temple tonight. I had to disperse the crowd, and promising a meeting first thing tomorrow did the trick."

"What kind of hearing do you mean?" Sera asked.

"Well, it won't be an official trial, but it will be a gathering where the townspeople may ask questions. I can provide some answers, but it would be helpful if others could help answer their questions. Barktuck will be there, and I was hoping you would come as well."

Sera nodded. "Of course I'll be there if you think it'll help Cassandra."

"I can't guarantee that, but my thought is that it will help calm the townsfolk, which in turn will be good for Cassandra."

Sera smiled. "Very well, Sheriff. I will be at the courthouse when the sun rises. You can count on me."

"Thank you, Sera," he said, taking her hand and giving it a slight squeeze. "I'll be going now. I've bothered you far too long this evening."

"No, you have been no bother. You are a blessing to our family right now, Quinn, and we appreciate you."

He shared a smile with her and then looked at Kessi, who was no longer crying but still hugging Sera. Her face hinted at a bit of hope, and that made everything worth the effort.

He rose to leave, and Sera stopped him. "Sheriff?"

"Yes, Sera?"

"Please don't let them hurt Cassandra. She has been through enough."

He nodded and tried to smile, but with little success, his guilt evident on his face. They were worried for Cassandra's safety now, and that made smiling a problematic task. After Quinn left, Sera and Kessi quickly turned in, but sleep didn't come easy for them that night. Quinn's rest was the hardest to come by, as it became more and more evident that Lord Ronnis had tricked him into arresting Cassandra.

~

The following day, as the sun rose, the town hall was opened to the public. However, it soon moved outdoors, as the attendance exceeded the hall limits. It was a crisp autumn morning, with a bit of a nip in the air, but the rising sun soon produced enough warmth to keep the townsfolk comfortable. Quinn was on the front porch of the building, and with him was Magistrate Sams. Sera and Kessi were nearby so Quinn's deputies could keep an eye on them.

It started nice enough, as people commingled and chatted about the week's routines, such as what goods were selling and how much longer the weather would allow the merchants to sell outside. The mood was generally good, but a group showed up who could cause grief for the sheriff. Buster Agnew led the five leaders of the merchant's guild, the one entity that had the power to overrule his actions. Oldorburg's founders had formed the guild to have the merchants' interests at the center of the laws. Since merchants had built the town, the laws favored them. As a result, the guild's five leaders had always had the power to change specific rules, appeal the sheriff's decisions, or even strip the sheriff of his powers. Quinn rarely thought of such things, but when he saw Buster's worried expression, he promptly called the meeting to order and began as calmly and as cheerily as possible.

"Dear friends, thank you for attending this most urgent and important meeting. As you know, Cassandra Rho committed a crime a few days ago, and I have decided to hold this meeting in the hopes of answering any questions you might have about the event.

"I must tell you first, to clarify, that I am speaking of the attack that several people, including myself, witnessed. Cassandra Rho, an orphan at the Oldorburg Orphanage, attacked Lord Ronnis D'Breeth, the orphanage's administrator. In said attack, she blatantly used the powers of arcane magic to assault her victim, with what appeared to be the intent to kill.

"Unfortunately, she is still in the temple, receiving healing from the priests for the injuries sustained during the confrontation. Lord Ronnis is still in the temple receiving treatment as well. I am happy to say that his injuries are not life-threatening.

"So, at this point, the trial has been delayed simply because Miss Rho is not healthy enough to stand trial for her crimes. However, I want everyone to know that she is young and has never harmed anyone before this incident, and I do not feel the woman is a threat to anyone in this town. Cassandra is under heavy guard, and there is no chance of her harming anyone else. In reality, I don't think she would, even if she were walking the streets among us. I believe there is more to the story than just a blatant attack, and I want her to have her say in court and for us not to judge too quickly."

He looked around the gathering, and to his relief, his words seemed to have a calming effect on the gathered citizens. Then, continuing the meeting quickly before anyone could stir the crowd's emotions, he asked, "Are there any questions at this time?"

Luckily for the sheriff, there were only a few minor questions about the incident. He looked out among the faces and knew many of them. They were good people. His words seemed to have a positive effect on their mood, which would hopefully diffuse the situation. He could then focus on how to handle the trial that would follow. But unfortunately there would be little he could do to stop her execution if the people demanded it. The only hope he had was that because Cassandra was young, the people would show her mercy.

"I would like to invite Barktuck Misol, one of the high priests of the temple, to report on the health of both Ronnis and Cassandra," he said, motioning with an outstretched arm in the direction of the elderly priest.

Barktuck nodded and made his way to the porch to join Quinn and

Sams. He was wearing his ceremonial robes and looked overly dressed for the occasion. Quinn stole a glance at Kessi and could see the look of fear on her face as the flashy priest made his way to stand beside him.

"Dear people of Oldorburg, let me begin with a prayer to the most wonderful of gods, Meshlor!" Barktuck said. The people bowed and listened patiently as the priest rolled out many blessings and thanks to his god. But unfortunately the man was used to making a show and used this opportunity to promote his god. Quinn once again looked Kessi's way. The young woman sat defiantly, not bowing her head or participating in the prayer, her dislike for the man showing on her face.

When the prayer was over, the high priest said, "So the good sheriff has asked me to report on the health of the two people involved in the attack. First, I am happy to say that Lord Ronnis is doing much better. Indeed, his injuries are not life-threatening, but his scars are forever.

"Cassandra Rho is doing better but is still suffering from a fever. We expect her delirium to end in the next few days. At that time, we will turn her over to the sheriff so that she may stand trial."

There was some mumbling among the crowd, but the mood seemed to be primarily positive. No one seemed to be panicked, as Quinn had witnessed a few days earlier outside the temple. The people there were predominantly wealthy citizens concerned for their families. However, most of them were educated and understood the risk to the town and their families was minimal. The meeting had served its purpose, and now they could focus on the coming trial.

Quinn stood beside Barktuck and said, "So if there are no further questions, I suggest we all get back to our lives and go about our business as usual. I assure you: we do not have a monster among us."

The people nodded, and even Buster and the merchant guild members seemed happy with his explanation. People began to leave, until, seemingly out of nowhere, a masked man appeared at the back of the crowd. The stranger proceeded to make his way toward the sheriff. The white porcelain mask covered his entire face, and it wore a slight smile that seemed more creepy than pleasant. The sheriff signaled his men to become vigilant, and they took up their positions and trained their weapons on the unusual intruder.

The man walked confidently toward the porch, and Quinn placed his hand on the hilt of his weapon, noting a sword strapped to the man's side. The weapon's pommel was that of a black snake eating its tail. The townsfolk fell silent and parted to let the man through. He paid them no mind as he kept his sights on the sheriff. His gait was familiar to both Quinn and Sams, and as the man approached, it became clear who was behind the mask.

"Ronnis," Magistrate Sams whispered to Quinn.

"Why is he here, priest?" Quinn asked quickly.

Barktuck shrugged as if he didn't understand. "His healing has progressed better than I thought. A pleasant surprise that he has come."

Ronnis stopped short of the porch, and everyone grew quiet. A long moment of silence passed, the man in the mask sizing up the sheriff. Then, after many moments, the new arrival finally spoke. "Good sheriff, is there no justice left in this town?"

"What do you speak of, and whom am I addressing, good sir?" Quinn asked, although the answer was evident.

"You know me, Quinn. I am none other than the victim of this heinous crime!" He turned to the crowd and removed his mask. "I am Ronnis D'Breeth!"

The townsfolk gasped, including Sera and Kessi, who were sitting near the disfigured lord. Kessi looked at Sera, but her mother kept her frightened gaze on Ronnis. The right side of his face was red and swollen, his right eye still shut. His cheek on that side was completely missing, creating a hole in his face that stretched from his lower jaw to the corner of his eye. He was, by all accounts, hideous. After the townsfolk looked at him with a collective sigh, he turned back to the sheriff so the latter could see the wound. "What's the matter, Quinn? Does this bother you?" Ronnis asked.

"Not at all, Ronnis. I'm just surprised you're here," Quinn said.

"It's a good thing that I am. You feed these people false hope and make them believe that they are safe." Ronnis turned back to the gathered mass. "Look upon my face and understand that this could happen to any one of you or your family."

He began walking through the crowd again, and people gave way as if he were a leper. Finally, he approached Buster Agnew, leader of the guild, and stood before him, eyeing his reaction. "Buster, this could happen to one of your girls. Do you want this monster in our town?" Buster covered his mouth with his hand and shook his head slowly. "I thought not," Ronnis said.

He then slipped the mask on and walked back toward the sheriff and magistrate. "Do not be mistaken, good people of Oldorburg. Cassandra Rho is a sorceress witch and is extremely volatile. Anything could set her off!"

"Enough!" Quinn shouted. "This is not a trial! You will have your say at the hearing—as will Cassandra. The purpose of this meeting was to calm the good townsfolk and ensure them they are safe."

Ronnis chuckled at first, but his bluster grew until he laughed hard, bending over at the waist. Quinn stood motionless, his hand still on his sword hilt. He spied the look Sera had on her face, and he motioned for the guards to escort her and Kessi away. When Ronnis saw the guards approach them, he quickly regained his composure.

"Wrong, Quinn. The purpose of this meeting was to lie to these good people and fill them with false hope." He pointed to Sera. "You and that worm Sams have always had your eyes on my Sera, and now you think you can give her false hope about the little witch and that will somehow win her love? You have betrayed me as much as Cassandra Rho has. Do you intend to ruin my life completely for the sake of your lustful desires?" Ronnis said, his voice rising to echo down the still streets.

"Hold your tongue, Lord Ronnis. Your foul mouth spews forth lies!" Quinn said, his voice carrying as much as Ronnis's.

"And your badge is dishonored, I say! You are corrupt, Quinn. Admit it."

"I'll admit no such thing, and if your slanderous words do not cease, I shall have you arrested for contempt."

That produced another belly laugh from Ronnis. Finally, he turned with his arms outstretched before the crowd. "Now the sheriff would arrest me? Have I not been through enough? Am I not the victim? And as I stand here with my face torn and my future shrouded in doubt, he takes my love interest?"

That proclamation produced more whispers from the crowd and even some shouts of agreement, and Ronnis smiled behind his mask.

Sera shook her head and waved off the guards, refusing their escort. Finally, however, she insisted Kessi go with them, and the young woman reluctantly did after a few reassuring words from her mother.

Quinn said to the people, "Please return to your jobs and your homes. There is nothing else to discuss until the time comes for the trial. Everyone here is welcome to attend."

"Not so fast, Sheriff! I don't think you are worthy of running this trial. I think you have become blinded by your lust for Sera. Therefore I object to you being the sheriff when the trial begins!" Ronnis said, dramatically flailing his arms.

There were gasps from the gathered mass, then lots of mumbling. The encouraging talks had been going so well before Ronnis arrived, and now they were lost to the lord's antics. Finally, having heard enough, Quinn signaled two guards to come over and take Lord Ronnis into custody. Ronnis didn't resist but turned toward Buster for support. The guild master seemed to be caught off guard by the sudden turn of events.

The guards took Ronnis's sword, then began cuffing his hands behind his back. Ronnis said nothing and didn't resist but kept his cool glare on Buster. Finally, Buster cracked under the lord's gaze. "Hold! Leave this man be!" he said.

Ronnis's smile grew behind his mask.

"As the appointed leader of the merchant guild, I at this moment exercise the guild's right to revoke the badge of Sheriff Quinn … until after the trial of Cassandra Rho, which the guild shall oversee."

Quinn watched as his men released Ronnis and returned his weapon. Buster made his way to the porch then, and when he reached Quinn, he held out his hand. Quinn reluctantly unfastened his badge and handed it over. Sera was beside him then, no longer guarded.

"Come—let us retire, my dear," Ronnis said to Sera with an outstretched hand.

However, she did not move and only shook her head slowly. In the meantime, Buster was dispersing the crowd, assuring them of the justice at hand. Ronnis stood firm with his hand outstretched. "Come to me, Sera," he said through gritted teeth.

"Never, you beast!" she said, tears welling in her eyes.

"Don't make me come up there and get you."

"She said no, Ronnis. I may no longer be sheriff, but I promise you I'll run my blade through you if you move against this woman. You've done enough damage. Now leave," Quinn said.

"Sera! You have betrayed me twice now! First you made plans to leave the town without me, and now this. Consider our relationship severed. You have used up your usefulness. And that just made things a lot worse for Cassandra." Ronnis stormed off into the crowd, and Sera broke down crying. Kessi ran out of the town hall then and joined her mom, embracing her in a tight hug.

"Come, Sera and Kessi. You may stay at my place tonight. I somehow suspect you are no longer safe at the orphanage."

"Thank you, Quinn," Sera said, gathering her composure. "I am sorry you lost your job. What will you do now?"

"I don't know, but I'm leaving Oldorburg. There is little doubt of that. After the trial, of course."

The three of them walked off toward Quinn's small apartment in the center of town. None of the three noticed the stranger at the back of the disbanding crowd. Baxter, still dressed like a wealthy merchant, and blending in quite well, had witnessed the whole meeting and had a bad feeling that Cassandra wasn't safe. He had forgone his trip back to Pelesea after briefly meeting Cassandra and Kessi a few nights earlier. He had initially wanted to wait and see whether they would decide to leave the town, but then the arrest had complicated everything. The events of the meeting made things go from bad to worse. He left the gathering fearing Cassandra's safety, and he felt he might already be too late to help her.

~

Later that night, Barktuck and Ronnis met in Ronnis's room at the orphanage. Ronnis handed his mask over to Barktuck, who gave it to Andre, one of the temple's lesser priests. Andre had a stature similar to that of Ronnis and had just changed into Ronnis's clothing. He put the mask on and could have easily been mistaken for Ronnis at first glance.

"Well, how does Andre look?" Barktuck asked.

Ronnis smiled, which showed his wounded gums, making Andre

shift uncomfortably in his seat. "He looks just like me. How will you keep someone from speaking with him?"

"We will tell everyone that you are on a powerful healing concoction that makes you tired. Andre will feign sleeping for a few hours in plain view of all the guests. I will then explain how much you wanted to join in the festivities but the pain was too great and I had to administer the medication. They will not only see that you are at my little gathering, but they will also feel sorry for you to be in so much pain. After a few hours, I will take Andre upstairs and tell people I am tucking you in for the night. All the powerful people of the town, the merchants and nobles alike, will know without a doubt that you were at my gathering during Cassandra's assault."

"That sounds perfect! How long will I have to, well, teach the little witch a lesson?" Ronnis asked eagerly.

"Two hours—not a minute more."

"That's not enough time for all the things I've planned, but I'll manage."

"Good. Here is the key. I took this directly from the acolyte in charge of her room. I gave him the same mild poison I gave the Rho girl, so he should be indisposed for a few hours. However, if he awakens and finds you in the act, I will not be able to protect you. If that happens, you are on your own, and if you include me in your story, I will deny every bit of it. Go now, do what you must, then place the key back in the acolyte's pocket. He will be the one *sleeping* outside of her room. Understood?"

Ronnis smiled, and with a slight nod, he put the key in his pocket. He then put on his hooded cloak and pulled it tight to hide his face. He wore Andre's priestly garments, and with the hood pulled tight, he looked like a priest heading home to the temple. He moved quickly toward the building, trying not to gain any attention. And once the temple was in sight, he quickened his pace. He had looked forward to this moment for years now, but the fact that he would be able to pay Cassandra back for her vicious attack made him desire this special meeting even more. He thought of the awful things he would do to her and the related consequences. He would have an alibi, with Andre posing as him at Barktuck's social gathering. Besides, no one would care if something happened to an attempted murderer accused of witchcraft. Even if they did, he had enough people in high positions to get him off whatever charges Cassandra might bring against him. He hurried his pace in anticipation.

~

Quinn, Sera, and Kessi had just finished a meal together in Quinn's small apartment. Sera and Quinn washed the dishes, and Kessi dried them. As they did, Quinn sneaked a peek outside his second-story window and absently rolled his mustache with his fingers. Sera and Kessi were in relatively good spirits and even shared a few laughs. Therefore he didn't mention the guards he saw on the street below, watching his apartment.

"Thank you, ladies, for helping clean up," he said after the dishwashing. "I have arranged for you to use my bed this night, and I will sleep in my bedroll in the sitting room. Sorry the bed is so small, but I hope it will suffice for now."

"It's perfect, Quinn—thank you," Sera replied. "We'll need to return to the orphanage for our belongings tomorrow."

"I'll go with you … if you'd like for me to," Quinn said.

"That would be nice. At this point, I don't feel safe, and I know Kessi feels as I do. Ronnis has always been a bad person, but now he has changed. He has become dangerous."

"So you're no longer in love with him?"

Kessi laughed, obviously thinking the comment was hilarious, until she noticed them both looking at her, neither laughing. She stopped and blushed. "I'll prepare for bed now," she said and quickly made her way to the bedroom.

Sera shook her head. "Quinn, promise me that if anything should happen to me that you'll look after these girls. They're both extraordinary and never cease to amaze me with their perceptiveness."

"Yes, of course, but nothing will happen. To you, I mean," the flustered sheriff said.

"But you worry something will happen to Cassandra?"

He nodded, a serious look on his face. "I didn't want to say anything in front of Kessi, but she's in serious trouble. I know Cassandra doesn't care much for me, but as sheriff, I would have given her every chance to explain the situation and hopefully not pay for this mistake with her life.

"I know the laws better than anyone—well, except for Magistrate Sams. They call for death in this situation, as long as the victim wants to prosecute."

He stopped and studied Sera's face, letting the news sink in. "The gallows have been empty since I took over as sheriff, but I fear that these new people, these guild members, will be heavily influenced by Ronnis. If that's the case, I'm afraid they will show her no mercy."

"I know. I have known deep down that Cassandra has no hope, but I cannot give up on her. You don't know her, Quinn, but she is a good person—just misunderstood. Also, to answer your question, I never loved Ronnis. I slept with him only so he would leave Cassandra alone. Now that I can no longer protect her, I'll have nothing more to do with him."

"So you never wanted to be with the man?" Quinn asked.

"Never."

"That explains a lot—I mean, the two of you are a bit of an odd couple." They both laughed at that, and Quinn asked, "So Kessi knows this?"

"Oh yes, both girls have known all along." She looked over her shoulder to make sure Kessi wasn't listening and lowered her voice, saying, "He used to hurt me … physically. Kessi used to come into my room at night and heal my bruises. Cassandra would come with her. They don't know that I know about this. It means a lot to me that those two would go to all that trouble to make me feel better. I love those girls."

The tears came again at that point, and Quinn was there with a handkerchief.

"Tell me more, Sera, so that I may know these girls better. A few days ago, I wasn't impressed with Cassandra—too wrapped up in my job and feeling the pressure from Ronnis to investigate her. I didn't give her a fair chance, and now I feel that I've made a mistake. I feel that Ronnis tricked me into arresting her. I want to know these girls better so I may know who Cassandra is."

Sera nodded and began her story of when she first came to the orphanage, right after Unis Rho had perished, about the time the nursery rhyme about Cassandra had started circulating the orphanage. She told him everything she knew and how her love for the girls had only grown over the years. They stayed up most of the night talking and bonding.

At some point, Baxter came by to tell them his plan. He spotted the multitude of guards positioned around the small apartments and knew it was too risky. There was simply no way for him to relay his plan to them. Instead, he would have to proceed with it and send word to them later. And so he changed his course before the guards spotted him and made his way to the temple.

~

Barktuck's chateau, located near the temple, close to the center of Oldorburg, was the site for the evening's agenda. His vineyard had been blessed by Meshlor the previous summer, and the wine flowed freely. Only nobles of the town were invited, including all five members of the merchant's guild—except for Sir Garret, who was at home, sick with the flu. Nevertheless, almost all the invitees attended the event, to Barktuck's delight. As Andre "slept" on the plush couch in plain sight, it gave credit to the fact Ronnis was indeed unconscious and nowhere near the temple. Barktuck's plan was working even better than expected. On occasion, Andre would moan and turn over, but for the most part, he just tried to keep his masked face turned away from people.

"So he's in a lot of pain, then?" Buster Agnew asked Barktuck as they sipped the priest's delicious wine from ornate glasses.

"Oh, yes, that's why the healing potion I gave him has made him sleepy. We're worried that there may be an infection if we don't use the most aggressive treatment. And everyone knows you don't want an infection in the head as that could likely lead to death."

Buster seemed to be happy with that answer and appeared sympathetic. "He seemed very animate at the meeting today."

"Yes, and now he is paying for his exertion. Of course, I didn't want him anywhere near that meeting, but can you blame the poor soul? He only sought justice and didn't trust Sheriff Quinn to carry that out. I guess he panicked, but your quick decision to strip Quinn of his badge was well founded," Barktuck said.

The puffery made Buster beam with pride. "Yes, it seemed to me that the good sheriff had too much of an interest in Cassandra's mother. When did his unhealthy and quite inappropriate infatuation with the woman begin?"

"Oh, I think this has been going on for some time now. I have even heard rumors that they were sleeping together while Ronnis and Sera were courting!" Barktuck said, fueling the case to keep Quinn out of the office until the trial was over.

Buster's face turned red, and he shook his head. "Poor guy has been through a lot lately, hasn't he?"

"Yes, he has," Barktuck said, looking somber and letting the silence play on Buster's mood.

So the farce worked well, and after a few hours of Barktuck's sharing the same lies with other guests, the hour drew late, and people started to leave. That's when Barktuck boldly asked Buster to help him move Ronnis upstairs so he would be more comfortable. The guild master eagerly assisted and never once suspected that the man who had been the focus of his sympathy all night was not Ronnis D'Breeth but instead a simple acolyte from the temple.

Barktuck was anxious for Ronnis to return, and after everyone left, he poured himself another large glass of wine and sat on the plush couch. He laid his head back and relaxed, basking in the glow of a perfectly played lie. Ronnis had been instructed not to come to the chateau until all guests had left. They were now gone, so he would be along any minute to share the details of the various tortures he exacted on Cassandra Rho. The thoughts made Barktuck smile, and he couldn't help but chuckle to himself. "Well done, Barktuck, well done!"

~

Ronnis had easily entered the temple, as the massive doors remained unlocked to the public. He was in Andre's acolyte robes, the hood pulled tight and his head low, so no one questioned him as he made his way through the giant and gloriously decorated building. He didn't care about religion and paid it little mind, other than what Barktuck had told him about Meshlor. He was making his way toward the second-floor steps when a voice said, "Acolyte, come with me. There is a chore that cannot wait until morning."

Ronnis turned toward the voice and saw another high priest standing in the hall with his hands on his hips. Ronnis hadn't cared enough to learn the man's name, but he knew that he held some influence over the temple. So he decided to play along and hurried over to the older priest. "Yes, my lord, what is it that needs attending?"

The man looked at him inquisitively, and Ronnis thought the man might have recognized him for who he was, but after a few moments, the priest turned and walked down the massive hall. "Follow me," he said.

Ronnis complied and stayed right behind the man, who dressed in fancy garb. It wasn't religious—more like something one would wear to a social function. Ronnis could only assume that the man was going to Barktuck's social.

The man said as he walked, "We are holding morning mass at sunrise, and Andre has failed to replenish the candles this evening. There's a new case of them in the storeroom. I want you to bring them out here and replace all of them that have burned down to less than two inches tall," he said, stopping in one of the sanctuaries of the temple and pointing to the many candles on display near the altar.

Ronnis nodded and tried to open the oaken door near where the man was standing, but it would not open.

"No, son, in the storeroom—over there." The man pointed to a similar door across the room.

Ronnis nodded and followed the man's instructions, hurrying away to complete the task. The priest stayed and watched over Ronnis's work, making sure he correctly replaced the candles. After a few moments, the priest was satisfied and left Ronnis to his work. Ronnis made quick work of the candles, moving as quickly as possible. The chore had been an inconvenience that he could not afford, wasting nearly half an hour of his time. He threw the remaining candles into the storeroom, then made his way to the stairs. This time he was more careful in his movement and made sure no one else saw him.

~

Baxter found himself outside the temple just moments after Ronnis had made his entrance. He waited patiently for a temple member to exit the massive doors. Finally, an older gentleman dressed in fancy clothing left the temple. He wasn't sure whether the man was a priest or even someone with knowledge of the temple, but he couldn't keep waiting. He felt the time was running out for Cassandra. So he began casting the charm spell quickly and effectively. After all, he had become the school's master of charm spells.

The wave of invisible energy rolled from his hand and struck the man as he walked out the temple doors. The wave neither harmed nor hindered the man, and he had no idea that the surge of energy had targeted him. Baxter thought it ironic that he was a true wizard in the middle of these people who were so superstitious about magic. He was freely casting spells—something that could cost him his life.

"Troglodytes," Baxter whispered to himself, stepping out of the shadows. "Good night to you, sir!" he exclaimed.

"And good night to you, stranger," the man said and smiled.

Baxter could tell right away that his spell had delivered the maximum effect on the man. He would now be able to extract information from him carefully, and hopefully it would be information that would lead him to Cassandra. "May I ask a question, friend?"

"Of course! How may I be of assistance?" the man asked, stopping his brisk walk.

"Are you a priest of the temple?"

"But of course! Bartholomew Jost, a high priest of Meshlor, at your service," he said and bowed.

"Excellent! I've heard a lot of good things about Meshlor. Perhaps I can chat with you tomorrow about him?" Baxter said, trying to sweeten the man's mood even further.

"I would be delighted! Uh, what is your name again?"

"Baxter," he said, not thinking of a need to lie.

"Yes, Baxter, we have mass at dawn. So why don't you visit with me after service to discuss the wonders that are Meshlor!" he exclaimed, holding his arms out wide and looking up to the sky.

"That would be perfect, for, you see, I am but a humble merchant selling beautiful flowers in the town square. A few anonymous townsfolk are sympathetic to the Rho girl and wish to deliver her flowers tomorrow morning. Might I ask what room she is in so that I may grandly deliver them? Afterward, I will attend mass. Then perhaps we may have a counsel to discuss your amazing god."

"Ah yes, the Rho girl. Quite a shame that she will probably die at the end of a rope. For some reason, our methods are not healing the wounds she suffered during her arrest. But unfortunately Brother Barktuck is in charge of that one and is quite upset at the lack of progress. He feels we should be able to heal the woman, even if the result is a good hanging."

"So you don't know the room?"

"Oh, yes, all the high priests know. I'm not supposed to tell you, but since we've been friends for so long, I can't see why it would hurt!"

Baxter smiled and nodded. If this man was a high priest, that didn't say much about the temple. However, the charm was far more effective than he'd expected, and if he had the time, he could probably uncover many secrets about the temple from this man. Of course, he would love to know more about Ronnis D'Breeth himself, but that would have to wait for another time.

"So, Baxter, bring your freshly cut flowers tomorrow morning and deliver them to the third room on the right on the third floor. I'm afraid you'll have to leave them with the acolyte there. He will not let you in to see the girl. Then come to the east sanctuary for mass. I will be waiting there to enlighten you."

"Great! I'll see you then!"

The man hurried off then, excited to be on his way and whistling a happy tune as he did. Baxter watched him go, then, once he was out of sight, turned and surveyed the temple. It was three stories high, and he could easily guess which room was the third on the right—but from which direction was the man referring? Baxter would have to try one at a time because they would be on opposite sides of the building. He walked toward the temple, already casting his next spell.

~

Ronnis found Cassandra's room quickly enough, moving through the shadows and making sure no one saw him. He found the young acolyte whom Barktuck had referred to as John fast asleep outside the door, a pool of drool on the bench he lay on. Each room on this floor had an alcove to each entrance, marked with two soft benches on either side of the door to be used by grieving family and friends. Now it served as a bed for the dedicated young acolyte. Ronnis smiled and nodded to the young man. "Don't mind me; I'll be a few minutes. Keep up the good work," he whispered as he unlocked the door.

The room was completely dark, with only one stained glass window, which let in very little light. Ronnis shut the door and locked it quickly, allowing his eyes to adjust to the darkness. When they finally did, he spotted his prey. He could see the bed between himself and the window and Cassandra's prone form resting on it. There were no other furnishings in the room, and at first, he felt sorry for the young woman; Barktuck had made things miserable for her. Then he remembered why he was there. He touched the wound on his face, poking a finger into the hole to pick at his teeth. The little witch had done this to him, and now it was time for payback.

He made his way to the window and opened it, allowing the moonlight to enter the room. It fell perfectly on Cassandra's motionless form. He wanted to see the look on her face when he assaulted her but did not wish to light a lamp and bring attention to the room. The moonlight was perfect.

He withdrew his dagger and sat down gently on the bed. He could hear her shallow breathing and watched the rise and fall of her chest. Her hands were bound to the headboard tightly, and a similar rope gag dug into her mouth. Her lips appeared cracked and dry, and her hands were bruised and swollen. He liked knowing that she had suffered at the hands of his friend, a fitting beginning to the plethora of punishments he had in store for her.

He lowered his face close to hers and wiped the hair out of her eyes. She was a pretty woman now and would be lovely one day as she continued to mature, but none of that mattered now. She had been a thorn in his side since she was five years old, stubborn and annoying. Then, when he had been with Sera, he had grown to hate her. Something about her rubbed him the wrong way, and now it was time for some much-needed revenge. Lustful thoughts filled his head, and he knew from being around her and conversations with Sera that she was undoubtedly a virgin. After all, what young man would waste his time with a little witch like Cassandra?

His hand stroked the side of her cheek, but she made no response. He lowered it further and made his way inside the front of her shirt. He explored her breasts for a bit, becoming rougher as he did so, trying to elicit a response from the young woman. She moaned softly but was far too drugged to appreciate her surroundings. He kissed her neck, which was bittersweet. He felt as if he was kissing his sworn enemy, but his lust overrode any rational thinking. He kissed her neck harder, and his roaming hands squeezed and pinched her in places no man had ever touched. After a few minutes of this, he broke the kiss and smiled. It was time to take this punishment to the next level.

He forcefully tore open her shirt, exposing her breasts. He was reasonably impressed with what he saw and licked his lips in anticipation. She was still very young but was developing nicely into a woman. She looked delicious to him at that moment. He looked at her pretty face and knew that he needed to have her awake to enjoy this properly. He straddled her and sat down hard on her stomach, putting all his weight on her diaphragm. Her breathing became labored immediately, and she turned her head and moaned. He laid the dagger next to her head and then did something he had wanted to do for a very long time—he backhanded her hard across the cheek. It felt good, so he did it again. Her eyes fluttered open for a moment, and in that brief instant, she registered that Ronnis was there. The look in her eyes and the terror he saw made a wicked smile crease his deformed face.

~

Cassandra could feel the hands on her body but was too tired to react; she felt the unwanted kissing on her neck but could not push away. Her body would not respond until the weight on her stomach took her breath away and she slowly came out of the grogginess. Cassandra pleaded to the dark man, whom she had been dreaming about once again, but he just stood there with a look of disappointment on his face. Once more, she was in the cave with the table, the silver rod lying on it, calling to her.

Then there was an explosion of pain, and the dark man, the table, and the cave were gone, replaced by Lord Ronnis. Could it be? She blinked away the sleep and tried to focus on her surroundings, but the pain came again, and this time she could hear the smack and feel the strike to her cheek, which shot through her skull and reawakened the dull ache in the back of her head. She tried to open her eyes again, to focus—she had to wake up.

"Wake up, little witch." The unmistakable, grating voice of Lord Ronnis was in her ear.

Then his hands were around her neck, squeezing, stealing her breath. That was enough to bring her out of her stupor. Her eyes flew open in the sudden realization that he was attacking her. She had thought him dead!

~

Ronnis smiled when Cassandra's eyes finally opened wide with shock and fear. Her right cheek was already red and beginning to swell. She tried to speak and realized that was impossible through the gag. She tried to move, but her hands were tied tight. The fear he saw in her eyes was rewarding to him, and as the tears streamed down her face and she struggled to breathe, he applied more pressure to her throat.

The anger almost took him to the point of no return as her eyes rolled into the back of her head and she began to lose consciousness. It was only then that he realized she would die if he didn't stop. He didn't want her dead—not yet, anyway. He released his grip, and she sucked in the air with labored gasps. He took up his dagger and leaned down to her face, rolling the blade in front of her. It took her a moment to regain her senses, and when she saw the weapon's edge, her eyes went wide again.

He smiled. "Not so fast, little witch. I'm not done with you yet. You will die—I'll see to that—but for now, you are my plaything." He enjoyed her reaction, her eyes never leaving the blade, and the fear in them made her seem much more childlike than the brave young woman who had attacked him a few days ago.

"I'm going to cut this side of your face off, scarring you, just as you have done to me," he said, running the blade across her right cheek. "But first I'm going to cut this gag off you. Not because I want to hear your annoying voice, nor have I ever wanted to hear what comes out of that wicked little mouth of yours, but because I want to hear you scream as I torture you."

With that, he cut the gag swiftly and cleanly, making sure the blade cut ever so lightly into her cheek after it severed the rope. She tried to scream out, but his hand quickly covered her mouth, muffling the cry. He brought the blade up to her eyes again, still holding a clamp over her mouth. He could see the fear there as she looked from the weapon to Ronnis, then back to the blade. She was fully awake now and entirely at his mercy. That was just how he wanted her, helpless and at his disposal.

~

Cassandra tried to think of a way out of this mess. She had little hope of escaping this foul man's attack, and she knew he meant to rape and probably kill her. If her hands weren't bound, she could cast her magic, but as it was, she was helpless to defend herself. The thought of being at his mercy not only frightened her but disgusted her at a level she had never felt. No boy had ever touched her because she was not interested in such things and didn't find any boys at the orphanage especially attractive. However, to have this man take something so precious from her was beyond disgusting. She would rather die.

She tried to calm herself as his hands explored her once more. She tried to ignore his touch and, at the same time, deal with the pain from her various wounds. Most important, she tried to wake up. With her senses dulled, she couldn't think clearly. She tried to call to the birds as she had done all those years ago. She thought of the power she'd felt that fateful night in the woods and tried to summon the same energy to call the birds again. The window was open. All she needed to do was call them. She stopped struggling and closed her eyes.

~

Baxter took the live spider from the small pouch and quickly put it in his mouth. He hated to eat the tiny creature, especially since it was still living, but it was necessary to perform the spell properly. After Baxter chewed and swallowed it and said a few magical phrases, the effects took hold. He was standing at the great temple base near the third floor, where the recovery rooms loomed. The crafty wizard looked up and reached his hands out to the wall. They stuck instantly, and he began to climb the smooth surface, as a bug would, thanks to his freshly enacted spell.

He wasn't sure exactly where Cassandra's room would be, but he had a general idea that the rooms began on the east side of the building, and there were twelve sets of windows on each side of the building, a total of twenty-four rooms. He counted the third window on this side and climbed toward it. He hoped he would find her quickly. If anyone were paying attention, they would surely see him climbing the walls, and then he wouldn't have much time. Finally, he reached the window and carefully peered in. Unfortunately it was stained glass so that he couldn't see through it at all. There was also no way to open the window from the outside. He struggled to find a fingerhold in the small crack between the two panes of glass, but it was no use.

He cursed his bad luck, then decided to climb to the roof and rethink his options—and, more important, get out of plain sight. He quickly climbed the rest of the way up and walked freely around the roof. He checked on the rolled-up rug he had hidden there the day before. It was still tightly and neatly rolled up at the lip of the guttering on the north side. He decided to check the other side of the building to see whether he could find any clues there.

A set of windows were open, to his relief, and according to his count, they were precisely where her room would be, assuming he had chosen the right end from which to count. Then he saw something that made his heart jump: two ravens perched on the window ledge.

~

Ronnis kissed down Cassandra's neck as his hands mauled her perfect breasts. He bit her neck while his hands pinched and squeezed, hoping to get a response from the young woman. She moaned slightly, but she had closed her eyes and was being stubborn as usual. She was going to scream one way or another. He sat back up on her stomach and put the dagger next to her left side on the bed. He backhanded her hard once more, producing the desired response, as she moaned and then started to cry. She would not cry out loud, and only silent tears trickled down her face. Her stubbornness made him all the angrier, and he knew how to get the scream he wanted.

He made his way to the end of the bed, not noticing the two ravens that had landed on the sill as he passed the window. Cassandra was crying now, and that made him feel a little better, listening to her sniffling. Now he would take her virginity and make it a most unpleasant experience for the girl. He undid her belt and removed it from her pants. He unbuttoned the pants, then slid them down her legs, leaving her naked except for her underwear. She had put up no resistance at all, and he supposed she had just come to terms with what would happen to her.

He pulled her prone legs up so that her feet were flat on the bed, and then he spread her knees apart. He leaned forward to kiss her inner thigh, but as he did so, she suddenly brought her left knee up, cracking him in the nose. He saw stars for a moment and fought hard to remain conscious as he fell backward off the bed. He landed with a loud thump on his backside, and blood trickled down his nose—yet another wound caused by the little witch. He held his nose for a moment, just sitting on the floor, waiting for the shock to wear off. When he regained his senses, he was furious.

"I am going to beat you until …" he began, but then he discovered another person now in the room, brandishing his dagger. "Who … where?" Ronnis stammered.

"That is of no consequence. I will take this girl far away from here to a place you can no longer torment her."

"I am—"

"You are going to stand in the corner over there and shut up!" the intruder said. "Do you not understand the situation you are in?"

"What do you speak of?" Ronnis asked, still trying to figure out how this stranger had entered the room.

"This is Cassandra Rho—remember?"

"I know well who the brat is, you fool!"

"You've heard the nursery rhyme, haven't you, Lord Ronnis?"

The man stepped away from the window at that point, closer to Cassandra, revealing the two ravens. Ronnis's eyes went wide, and he backed into the corner. Ronnis looked at Cassandra, but she was catatonic. Her eyes were open, but she seemed unresponsive. The man kept one eye on Ronnis and cut her ropes from the headboard. The ravens moved around restlessly, cawing. Their movement became more agitated as the stranger tried to cover her up with her torn shirt. Finally he sat her up and tried to get a response from her. "Cassandra, can you hear me? I have come for you."

The only response he got was a weak slap to the face. The ravens moved to the bed's footboard and began their dance anew. Ronnis knew better than to move as the birds became agitated. He hoped that they would peck the man's eyes out for his intrusion so that he could finish what he'd started. Instead, the intruder dug around in his possessions and produced some smelling salts. He held them under Cassandra's nose, which had a two-pronged effect: her head snapped back, and she quickly slapped the salts from his hand.

"It is I, Baxter!" he shouted.

Her eyes were wild and glossed over, and Ronnis knew that she was heavily drugged. Nevertheless, his name did register with her, and she blinked away the fog and studied his face. "Baxter?"

"Yes, it's me. I have come to rescue you from this foul place."

"Baxter? You're the wizard from Pelesea!" Ronnis exclaimed.

Cassandra looked over Baxter's shoulder at Ronnis, and her eyes widened. Her face immediately reddened as she struggled to stand. Baxter helped, letting her lean on him heavily. She tried to make her way to Ronnis, but Baxter guided her to the window instead. "No—this way, Cassandra."

"I'll find you, Cassandra Rho! You can run, but you will never be at peace. I will have my revenge!" Ronnis screamed.

Cassandra was a tiny woman, just over five feet tall and barely over 120 pounds, but Baxter couldn't hold on to her in that moment of rage. With the last bit of energy she had, she stood and pointed at Ronnis. "If ever we see each other again, I will finish what I started. And beware, Ronnis D'Breeth—I will kill you!"

With that, the two ravens screeched and flew straight at Ronnis, following the path of Cassandra's pointing finger. They raked and pecked at his already torn face, and he covered it with his arms and screamed, falling back into the corner.

Cassandra collapsed from the exertion, but Baxter was there to catch her. The birds provided the perfect distraction for her escape. While Ronnis fought with the birds, Baxter lowered her to the floor. He then tied the ropes together, binding her hands in front of her. "Hey!" she yelled as her groggy mind suddenly realized what he was doing.

"Trust me, Cassandra—this is so you won't fall. We must escape while the birds have him distracted," Baxter said.

Ronnis caught one of the hateful birds in one hand and began smashing it over and over again on the floor. The creature was dead, its neck snapped, but he continued to beat it, taking his anger out on the bird. The lone raven continued its assault, but Ronnis paid it no heed and instead focused on the duo preparing to climb out the window. That was something he could not allow. Once Cassandra's hands were bound, the wizard took out what looked like a bug and ate it, casting some kind of spell.

Ronnis watched as Baxter stood Cassandra up and put her bound hands around his neck. They were face-to-face, and Ronnis noticed Baxter stop and stare at the woman as a lovestruck child might. She, too, just stared, still not fully aware of her surroundings but aware enough to whisper, "Gross … you ate a bug."

Her words seemed to break the wizard from his trance, and a dumb smile widened on his face. He gently made his way to the windowsill and grabbed hold of the outside wall. He went out back side-first, ready to steal Cassandra away from him. Enraged, Ronnis grabbed the lone raven that pecked at his face and wrung its neck, then tossed it aside. His anger would not allow this wizard from Pelesea to take his prized possession. He regained his footing with the intent of lunging at the two but immediately fell back against the wall, dizzy from his various wounds. Baxter saw this and moved quickly, pulling himself out the window and Cassandra with him.

"No!" Ronnis yelled defiantly, then staggered to the window. He poked his head out and looked up just in time to see the two go over the guttering and onto the roof. "I will find you, little witch, and I will personally burn you at the stake!" he shouted. "Also, Sera and Kessi are mine! You abandon them to their doom! They will pay for your crimes, witch!"

On the roof, Cassandra's eyes went wide at the threat. "We can't leave them. We must get my mother and sister."

Baxter lowered her to the roof and made her as comfortable as possible. He knew that Ronnis's screaming had probably alerted the priests, and he didn't want to wait around to face their spells. So he worked fast, unrolling the red rug that Victoria had let him borrow. A carpet of tremendous power—one that could fly.

"Cassandra, we must leave this place," he said.

"No, I will not leave them!" she said, struggling to sit up.

He sat on the carpet near the center and pulled her into a sitting position in front of him. She was barely clothed, and the ride would be cold for her, but he had no choice but to put her facing forward, as she was too dizzy to sit behind him and might fall off doing so.

"I'll come back for them. I promise," he said.

She lay fully back on him, and he wrapped his arms around her. His heart raced at being so close to her, fully aware of her near nakedness. He had developed some strange physical attraction to her over a short time, which felt good but worried him as well. Ronnis was still screaming from below when Baxter activated the magic rug with a simple command word. The carpet hovered about five feet off the roof, then proceeded to fly north, out of the town. It was slow at first but picked up speed quickly. Before Ronnis could alert anyone that Cassandra was on the roof, trying to escape, she and Baxter were miles out of town. Cassandra mumbled one thing before falling fast asleep as they began their journey. "Kessi."

It was a bittersweet journey home for Baxter. He held Cassandra tightly to him and wrapped her up as best he could. He even had a minor spell of warmth available, which he cast on her. She dozed the entire way, still fighting the poison, and he held her securely so she wouldn't fall. His eyes drank in her nakedness as often as possible, and he fell entirely in love with the woman during the trip. Finally, he made a silent vow to help the young woman bring Sera and Kessi to Pelesea.

Chapter 6

Pelesea

Kringus's long dark hair stuck to his face and shoulders, matted to his skin from the sweat of combat. He was a large man, standing nearly six and a half feet tall, his muscles toned from many combat years. His neck, chest, and shoulders reflected burn scars of a previous battle, but they in no way hindered him. His breath showed in puffs on this unusually cool autumn morning, his chest and arms glistening with sweat in the rising sun. He had been in this battle for over an hour now and refused to tire or surrender. His longsword cut smoothly through the air with a precision unmatched in all the lands—his current opponent possibly being the only exception. His small buckler had been a family heirloom and fit easily and familiarly on his left forearm. Melee combat was Kringus at his best, a true warrior in every sense of the word.

Where Kringus fought with power and strength, his opponent fought with speed and precision. Kringus was a large man, even by human standards, and he towered over his half-elven female opponent. On the other hand, Penelope was small, with fiery red hair and beauty that few could contest. Her green eyes sparkled with intensity and concentration as she easily deflected his attacks, knocking his sword aside with her slender blade moments before a strike could land. She was a blur of grace, and Kringus, although much slower, knew her moves well and was always ready to counter.

And so the battle continued, with neither landing a clean strike, the killing blow remaining elusive. It was mesmerizing to those viewing the fight, almost as if they were dancing, not fighting. The breathtaking garden of exotic flowers and rare trees where they fought only added to the scenario's beauty.

Finally, with his stamina wearing down and Penelope barely out of breath, Kringus made a slightly unpredictable move; he jumped backward after a clean parry and landed at the edge of a large plant with white blooms. Even with the onset of autumn, the hardy plant was still thriving, and the large white petals were a thing of beauty. His sword was at the central stalk, resting against the large stem. He looked back at Penelope, a look of triumph on his sweaty face.

"You wouldn't dare!" Penelope said, her sword tip lowered to the ground.

"Only one way to find out. You either drop your weapon, or the plant gets it!" he said, giant puffs of cooling breath visible as he spoke.

"There are only three of those in existence, Kringus! Don't you dare!" she said and advanced a step, readying her sword once more.

With a flick of his wrist, he severed one of the blooms cleanly, flipping it up in the air, where he quickly caught it with his other hand. He sniffed in the fragrance of the bloom as he moved his sword quickly back to the stem for a killing blow. "You know, it does smell nice," he said after breathing in the aroma.

"Kringus, I surrender—do not harm the plant!" Penelope said in a panic, her green eyes suddenly filled with worry.

"Throw your weapon away."

She did as he instructed and raised her hands in the air.

"On your knees."

She obliged.

"And now, dear Penelope, I will collect my winnings," he said, approaching her and then placing his sword on the side of her neck.

"You cheated," she said.

"There is no cheating in combat; there is simply winning or dying. I won."

"And yet your sword hand stays. Is it because my beauty has intrigued you?"

Kringus thought of it for a moment and studied his new prisoner. She was far more beautiful than any woman he had ever known, and if this opponent had been an enemy, then indeed, he would have ended her life by now. Not Penelope, though. She was a real prize worth savoring. "Yes, that is true—I must admit."

"Then your lust has killed you," she replied, swiftly taking a knife from her boot and holding it to his ribs.

He nodded. "Yes, but you cheated."

"There is no cheating in combat."

Kringus began to chuckle, and Penelope already wore a smile on her beautiful face. They discarded their weapons simultaneously and embraced with a passionate kiss. The two fell over each other, ripping off what little clothing they wore as they fell to the ground. A typical routine the king and queen of Pelesea often shared, which always resulted in very intense lovemaking. This morning was no different as Kringus and Penelope Brahmore made love in their wonderful garden right outside the castle itself.

Arrin Malik was positioned strategically in the garden, watching his king and queen, along with three other heavily armored men he had personally selected from the king's knights. These were some of his best warriors, loyal and hardy men who would die for their king. They felt it an honor to accompany Arrin to the garden on those particular mornings. Arrin was the captain of the king's army, tried and true, and, more important, a good friend to Kringus and Penelope.

Arrin and his men provided security as both the king and the queen put everything into their sparring and were usually oblivious to their surroundings. Also, occasionally, one of the combatants would be wounded, with Kringus usually on the receiving end of those accidental strikes. Arrin was always ready with the healing potions if required.

As the fight came to its usual conclusion, Arrin smiled and pointed a finger to the sky and made a circling motion with it, the signal for the other three to turn around. He turned around himself, giving his king and queen their privacy. The captain looked up at the bright blue sky and breathed deeply. Today was going to be a good day.

~

Cassandra awakened to a beautifully furnished room, complete with a chest of drawers and a nightstand, which had a pitcher of water on it. An open set of doors to her left led to a balcony, and the breeze smelled like the ocean. Sun poured into the room, and she could hear the sounds of a busy city outside, along with the lapping of water from a nearby shore. She blinked away the sleepiness and sat up. She felt much better but still had a dull throb in the back of her head.

She eyed the pitcher of water and licked her dry lips, realizing how incredibly thirsty she was. She swung her legs over the edge of the bed and noticed then that she wore a beautiful gown of white. She didn't remember dressing and wondered who'd performed the task. Her thirst got the better of her, and she dismissed the thought. She poured herself some water and drank it thirstily.

She poured another, but before chugging it down, she heard a voice behind her call, "Don't drink too much so fast, or it'll make you sick."

Startled by the voice, she nearly dropped the glass, spilling some of it onto the floor as she turned around. There stood a familiar figure on the balcony, a face she felt she should know. She thought back, trying to recall what had happened to her. At first, she did not know where she was and who this man might be. But then, it came back to her quickly. "Baxter?"

"At your service, young lady," he said with a smile and a bow.

He stood on the balcony, the sun framing his figure, giving him a holy appearance. She remembered little of the escape but understood that she owed this man her life. She couldn't recall exactly how, but she knew he had saved her. She smiled back, but then, as her thoughts came together and she remembered more of her situation, her smile faded. She urgently asked him, "Kessi? Sera? Where are they?"

Baxter entered the room, a serious look on his face. "We will find them and bring them here. I promise."

"Where is here?"

"Pelesea, none other."

"They're still in Oldorburg?"

"As far as I know."

"We must find them, Baxter. We must bring them here. They're in danger!"

Baxter held up a finger, indicating that he would answer her in a moment, and then moved to the small door at the end of her room and opened it, telling a young acolyte that Cassandra had awakened. The young boy ran off to fetch a priest. Soon after, a priestess walked in wearing a bright white gown, her blond hair tied back in a ponytail.

"I am Alleah, priestess of Sinnis. You are in my care until you are well enough to leave," she said. The young woman appeared to be in her early twenties and was stunning. "Let's have a look at your wounds, if you don't mind," she said and smiled.

Cassandra allowed her to feel the back of her head and softly rub her cheeks. Afterward, she examined her wrists and looked at Cassandra with her pretty blue eyes. "You have healed remarkably, with hardly a trace of any wounds!"

"Thank you for healing me, then, Alleah," Cassandra said.

"I wish I could take the credit, but this is the fastest I've ever seen my healing work!"

"Then I must be a fast healer. Baxter, we must talk," Cassandra said, turning her attention back to the wizard.

"Excuse us, dear priestess, but we have a private matter to discuss. May we stay in the room for just a bit longer?" Baxter asked.

"Yes, of course. I will inform the other high priests that she is well enough to leave, and you may leave the temple at your leisure. Luckily, we have no demand for this room at the moment."

As she left, Baxter motioned for Cassandra to join him on the balcony. She strolled over to join him but stopped just short of the doors and turned back toward Alleah, who was exiting the room. "Alleah?" she called.

The young priestess turned her head back into the room. "Yes?"

"I do feel much better, so thank you," Cassandra said and smiled.

That seemed to make her day, as she smiled back and nodded. She then closed the door softly, leaving Baxter and Cassandra alone in the room.

"Behold Pelesea," Baxter said as they made their way onto the balcony. The sun warmed her, and the smell of the sea air was refreshing. They were on the fifth floor of the temple, so her view of the city was grand indeed. The buildings were of a mysterious architecture to her, old and with a large amount of elven influence, which she had never seen before. She found the designs both beautiful and elegant. The cobblestone roads led this way and that, winding through the big city's many buildings and shops. It was a lot to take in for someone from such a small town as Oldorburg.

Fountains popped up at various points in the city, and Cassandra could see four of them from just this one vantage point. Giant trees grew among the buildings and made the city appear as if it were right in the middle of a forest. The smells of a nearby bakery had her stomach growling, making her realize she had not eaten anything for a very long time.

Then there was the magnificent shipyard. The temple was less than a hundred yards away from the massive docks, and the giant ships anchored there were a real sight for her. She had never seen boats that large up close before, and she was amazed at their size and the many men bustling around the docks, loading and unloading them. She was left speechless by her first sight of Pelesea. "Wow," was all she managed to whisper.

Baxter smiled as he watched her take in the sights. Pelesea was a fantastic city and one that he had called home for many years. Cassandra fit in nicely, and if they could find her family and bring them there, the young woman might find a good home in Pelesea.

"Kessi would love this, Baxter," she said, but then her smile changed quickly to a frown as she recalled her family's predicament. Finally, she looked up at him and sternly said, "We must go at once and save her and my mother. Where are my belongings? I can be ready in just a few minutes."

"Cassandra, you have no belongings. Besides, there are things that we must do here before making a rescue attempt, and you shouldn't go back to that place. Let Kringus and Penelope see to it that your family arrives here safely."

"What do you mean, things to do? And who are Kringus and Penelope?"

"They are the king and queen of Pelesea, both just and honorable. Once we tell them your story, they will send for your mother and sister."

"Let's go to them now. Time is of the essence," Cassandra said, walking toward the door.

"Wait, Cassandra! We have a meeting lined up with them in the morning."

"The morning!" she exclaimed, turning to address him, one hand already on the doorknob. "We can't wait that long!"

"Yes, we can. You've been asleep for three days; another day won't change things."

The news hit Cassandra hard, and she couldn't hide the surprised and panicked look on her face. Her eyes darted around as she tried to register the information. "Three days? How?"

"The priests feel that the leaders of Oldorburg had you poisoned. It was a nonlethal poison—one that makes you sleep. The dosage was heavy and the poison itself very potent. Alleah could do nothing for you other than let you sleep it off."

Cassandra walked back to the bed and sat down, still in a daze.

"Lady Victoria has asked for an audience with the king and queen, which they granted for tomorrow morning. So, at the very least, Kringus will send someone tomorrow to Oldorburg and determine the status of your family," Baxter said.

She looked up at him, still in shock. "Why didn't you go back and get them?"

"I was here, with you, watching you. Besides, I took a risk rescuing you from that place. I broke many of their laws, and Kringus would disapprove of me returning."

Cassandra looked back out among the city proper. She was overwhelmed with its beauty and didn't understand Baxter's kindness. But she wouldn't be pleased until Sera and Kessi were with her once more. She wanted them to experience this place beside her.

"So you stayed with me?" she asked.

"The entire time. I slept there." Baxter pointed to the corner of the balcony to a makeshift bed pieced together out of several plush pillows.

"You slept outside?"

"Dear Cassandra, the elements are nothing the powers of a wizard cannot handle!" he exclaimed, holding out his arms for dramatic effect. "Besides, this autumn weather is perfect for clearing out my sinuses!"

Cassandra smiled, and he looked at her with that same silly look she had vaguely noticed in Oldorburg. It was confusing to her because no other person had ever looked at her like that. It made her feel uncomfortable, so she walked into her room to break the awkward gaze.

~

Later that evening, after Alleah had checked Cassandra's wounds one last time before leaving the temple, Baxter walked her down the main streets of the beautiful city. She was in awe of the sights and sounds, and the people they passed seemed more polite to her than the townsfolk of Oldorburg. The way they looked at her and the occasional friendly smile made her feel welcomed. But, more important, for the first time in her life, she didn't feel like an outcast.

She marveled at the fantastic architecture and the great water fountains and marble statues that decorated the city. Even the smells were more pleasant. She immediately liked Pelesea and the people there, but she wished that her family were with her to experience it. Unfortunately, their absence created a void that didn't allow her to enjoy the grand city as fully as if they had been there.

She stopped at one particular fountain, which was fashioned into a stone tree of some type that she didn't recognize. Sitting atop the low-hanging branches were birds of various species. Each one had its mouth open with water pouring from it, refilling the fountain. She looked at them in a daze, lost in the beauty. Eventually, Baxter interrupted her thoughts. "Do you like it?"

She looked up at him and saw that he looked at the tree, not at her, awaiting her reply. "Yes," she said.

"It's elvish made, and the gnomish city folk helped engineer the pump system that allows the water to flow continuously. It's one of my favorites in the city."

Cassandra nodded and began walking again, and Baxter moved along beside her. She explored the city and took in their surroundings as they walked, and he was there to answer her questions as they arose. He was her tour guide and seemed excited to share the wonderful city with her.

"Whose clothes am I wearing?" she asked, not looking at them but keeping her gaze on the street ahead of her.

"They are Alleah's. She wanted you to have them."

Cassandra nodded. "They're nice. They fit well."

"I agree."

Baxter's face turned red immediately as she gave him a curious glance. Why had he said that? Was he flirting with her? He was far too old for her, so she hoped not. Besides, romance had never been one of her interests, especially now with her family's status unknown. However, since they had left the temple, and she had changed into more appropriate clothing for sightseeing, she had caught him several times admiring the tight pants and lacy shirt that she now wore. He didn't look at her but seemed to change the subject as best he could. "There it is!" he said excitedly, pointing ahead.

"There is what?" she asked, following his gaze.

"The school where you will spend the next four years of your life … I hope. Cassandra Rho, that magnificent structure is Victoria's School of Magic!"

She stopped walking, and her jaw dropped. They were very far away from it, maybe a dozen blocks, but it stood out as one of the most impressive structures in the city, even at this distance. It seemed to be made entirely of silver, and the evening sun glistened off it, creating a rainbow hue around the entire school.

"Do you like it?" Baxter asked.

"It's … beautiful," she whispered.

"It is. And there's the castle of Pelesea, just beyond the school."

He pointed to an equally impressive structure, with many towers and a great wall surrounding the majestic castle. The wall had bas-relief carvings on the outside surface, and red banners with white angel wings emblazoned on them hung from the parapets. The castle itself was beautifully designed, with a structure unlike anything she had ever seen. It seemed delicate yet sturdy all at the same time. "It's of old elvish design," Baxter said, still looking at the castle.

Cassandra didn't respond but instead kept her gaze on the school. Her heart raced with the thought of learning magic. It was something she'd always wanted, but she had no genuine interest in it at the moment. She couldn't focus on schooling until she once again had her family beside her. She finally whispered, "I can't stay, Baxter." She turned toward him with a sad look on her face. "I must get my family out of Oldorburg.

I can't start a life here without them. No matter what the king and queen have to say tomorrow, Sera and Kessi are my main objectives."

Baxter nodded. "I do understand, Cassandra. I vow to help you, with or without the king's blessing. Try not to think of it too much until tomorrow."

She smiled faintly. "It's all I think about."

Baxter nodded and then slowly turned toward the school. "We should go to the school now. They are already preparing a room for you. I will see that it's fully furnished and stocked with proper clothing."

"Thank you, Baxter. I don't know you well, but you have been very good to me. That's something I'm not used to, and I appreciate your kindness."

"I hope you can think of me as a friend, Cassandra, because I will give you whatever I have to make sure your life is happy going forward. I know that means delivering your family from the clutches of Oldorburg. I will do everything in my power to see that it comes to be."

He stopped and stared at her once again, and she noticed him swallow hard. It was almost as if he needed to tell her something but hadn't the courage to do so. She wrinkled her brow in confusion and asked, "What is it?"

Baxter caught himself and broke his trance, his face turning red yet again. "Oh, nothing," he said, a bit more flustered. "You have a meeting to attend is all."

His thinly veiled fib didn't convince her, but she played along, understanding he was trying to change the subject. "No, I don't have the energy to meet more people."

Baxter smiled. "You'll want to meet this person. Lady Victoria herself wants to chat with you. She is a delightful woman, and I think spending time with her will serve you well."

"She's interviewing me about attending the school, isn't she?"

Her perception seemed to surprise him. "Yes, in a way, but she also wants to learn more about you. I have told her about your uncanny abilities with magic and your control over the birds."

That comment conjured memories both sad and terrifying. Baxter noticed her discomfort and said, "Just be yourself, and you will learn far more from her than she will of you during that meeting."

She forced a smile, not wanting to meet Victoria at the moment but understanding that it was essential to Baxter somehow. She owed him the effort, but her thoughts remained on the problem at hand. Her family was in trouble, and she was unconvinced that anyone would do anything about it. She followed him toward the school, her heart not in it.

~

It was almost nightfall by the time they found themselves at the base of Victoria's tower. It rose ten stories into the evening sky and seemed to glow with a magical radiance. The structure seemed to be made of solid silver, with no windows or doors visible. It was standing in the middle of one of the four gardens of the school. This garden in particular grew many rare flowers and trees that would produce hard-to-find seeds and leaves for certain magical spells and potions. The colors of the garden were mesmerizing, even in the dim lighting of dusk.

"So this is Lady Victoria's tower," Baxter said to Cassandra, whose eyes were as big as saucers. "I know you haven't eaten since we left the temple. She will have a meal prepared; she is expecting you."

Cassandra didn't acknowledge him as her mind tried to wrap itself around the structure. She marveled at the smooth silvery stone, which resembled marble, as it seemed to thrum with magical vibrations. She could see some of the images she used to draw wrap themselves up in the magical energy that seemed to give the tower life. The whole place was intoxicating to her.

"So I will leave you now, Cassandra, to see to your room. Good luck with your meeting. I'll speak with you again in the morning."

"Wait," she said, putting a hand on his arm as he began to turn away.

He turned to her, and she could barely see him in the dark, but the glow from the tower produced enough light that she could make out that silly look once again on his face. He seemed to shift uncomfortably from foot to foot. "Yes?" he finally asked.

"I can't get in. There's no door."

"You will find the way—do not doubt. Victoria will show it to you."

She nodded, and he smiled weakly, seemingly unsure of what to do next. He eventually turned and took two steps away.

"Wait," she said again.

He stopped and turned once more. "Yes?"

She moved quickly beside him and gave him a peck on the cheek, which flushed immediately, and it looked to Cassandra as if he would faint. She found both humor and flattery in his reaction. "Thank you, Baxter. I owe you my life. I consider you a friend, and if you knew me well enough, you would know that is rare indeed."

"I—"

"No need to say anything. I'll see you tomorrow—remember?"

He left the tower garden with a giddy smile, turning and whistling a happy tune. Cassandra shook her head and watched him go. She truly believed that if she weren't watching him, he would have skipped away. That brought a smile to her face. She liked Baxter and trusted him as well. She would get used to his silly daydreamy looks because she knew she could trust him.

~

After Baxter had gone, Cassandra wandered the garden for a bit, a little apprehensive about meeting Victoria and even being there in the first place. The last few days had seemed like a whirlwind, especially with the drugging she had endured at the hands of Barktuck Misol. Nevertheless, her untrusting nature tried to accept that this city was safe. These were feelings she had never had in her short life, except as a very young child, before Unis had died. Had she ever really felt at home in Oldorburg? Not in recent years, and maybe not ever.

She finally approached the silver tower. The sky was dark now, and the structure itself glowed a light blue. She could sense the powerful magic within the walls. She reached out to touch it and felt the vibrations as the energy coursed through her. She closed her eyes and focused on it, seeing those familiar images in her mind. She knew it to be more powerful than she could comprehend, but Cassandra also knew that deciphering those symbols could produce powerful magic. For just a moment, she was excited, her eyes wide as she imagined the possibilities. Thoughts of her family filled her head then, and tears formed in her eyes. She lowered her gaze to the ground, never removing her hand from the tower.

"Lesson one: be mindful of magical wards," came a voice from beside her. She looked over, and a tall red-haired woman stood there, seeming to appear out of nowhere. She wore plain clothing but was holding a wand.

"Lesson two: you shouldn't sneak up on people," Cassandra said without thinking.

The woman approached her, and Cassandra turned to meet her, reluctantly removing her hand from the tower, disconnecting herself from the mysterious flow of power.

"Fair enough, Cassandra Rho. I am Lady Victoria, and I welcome you to my home."

Cassandra wasn't shocked that this was Victoria—she had guessed as much. However, nothing she wore gave a clue that she was a powerful wizard. Instead, the plain clothing, worn shoes, and slightly unkempt hair led her to believe that the wizard didn't care about her looks. She was a beautiful woman, but one who didn't care whether she made an impression. Cassandra could relate to that. "You don't look like a grand and powerful wizard," was all she could think to say—and in a harsher tone than she'd intended.

"And neither do you, but I know better. Besides, there is nothing grand about me. I am just a person who loves magic, just like you, Cassandra."

They both stood there, sizing each other up, and neither spoke for quite some time. Cassandra liked the woman right away. She had almost the same sense of humor and quick wit as she did.

"As I was saying, protective magic can kill you if you aren't careful." Victoria waved her wand at the tower and said, "Directus En Portus."

The outline of a door slowly came into view, which, ironically, was where Cassandra's hand had been. The door opened, and it was pitch black inside. The powerful wizard uttered another word under her breath, and light appeared within as several torches came to life, lighting up a foyer and a flight of marble stairs leading upward. She stepped to the side and extended a hand toward the door. "Please—will you come inside? We have much to discuss, and I have dinner waiting for you in my chambers."

Cassandra nodded eagerly and stepped through the portal, as she was famished. The inside seemed impossibly deeper than the outside dimensions would have allowed. She knew at once why she had sensed such powerful magic radiating from the tower. The torches' soft glow ran the length of stairs that seemed to climb only a couple of stories before leveling out to a large balcony. The foyer had a beautiful rug that reminded Cassandra of the one Baxter had used to rescue her. There were also several portraits of important-looking wizards hanging on the walls.

"Are you hungry?" Victoria asked as she began to climb the stairs.

Cassandra hesitated before following. "Yes."

"Did Baxter show you much of the city today?"

"No, we had little time, but what I saw was breathtaking."

They moved side by side up the stairs, not saying much. Cassandra knew she should be trying to impress her, but her heart just wasn't in it.

"Do you think you could call Pelesea home?" Victoria asked.

"Home is where my family is."

"Oldorburg was your home?"

"Never."

"Then your statement confuses me, Cassandra. Your family is still there, no?"

Cassandra stopped just short of the landing and turned toward Victoria. "Oldorburg never was home to me, but I can't call this place home without my mother and sister here. Does that clarify things, Lady Victoria?"

The powerful wizard smiled. "Yes, I understand, and I will do everything in my power to rejoin you with your family."

Cassandra looked around the landing, which was much larger than she'd expected and easily exceeded the tower's boundaries. A long hallway stretched out in front of her, lined with doors on both sides. Each entry looked identical, white with marble doorknobs.

"What is this place?" Cassandra whispered.

"Do you like it?"

Cassandra could only nod as she climbed the final step and found herself looking down a hallway that seemed never to end. She turned and saw a railing on the other side of the landing, creating a balcony that looked out over the other half of the tower. The foyer was visible several stories below. The rug and the paintings were still there but appeared much smaller now. Then she saw the mural on the tower's east wall, above the tower door. She hadn't seen it when she'd first entered and even now had to crane her head up to regard it. It was magnificent! The mural stretched across the entire east wall and depicted a fantastic scene where an army of men and angels battled demons. In the center, the horrible image of Marnelphion dominated, fighting the New Order's leader, Spring Goodwright. Constructed by angels after the battle with Marnelphion, the painting held magic greater than Cassandra could ever know.

All who witnessed the scene were amazed by it, and just a few could see the images move. The magic used to create the mural would allow anyone proficient or entuned with magic to watch the scene unfold. Unbeknownst to Cassandra, Victoria hand selected people to her tower to gaze at the painting. Cassandra studied it for many minutes, taking in the entirety of it. Then she turned to Victoria and asked, "So what is this about, and how do you make the images move?"

Victoria smiled. "It's a painting of the final battle of the New Order. It took place deep in the bowels of hell as they chased down the demon lord Marnelphion. All members of the New Order died in that battle but saved humanity by doing so."

"Who is the New Order?"

"They were a group of heroes, led by the half-elven king of Novafontera, Spring Goodwright. He's the one in the center, battling Marnelphion."

Cassandra turned toward Victoria at the mention of Novafontera. "Novafontera? Isn't that a city not too far from here?"

"Yes, between here and Oldorburg. You would have seen it from Baxter's flying rug had you been conscious."

She nodded and trained her eyes back on the mural, taking it all in.

"Some of the angels depicted in the painting constructed this tower right after the battle and painted the scene. So the magic is not of this world, and I cannot tell you how it works," Victoria said. "It is well before my time."

Then, seeming to surprise Victoria, Cassandra asked, "Who is the dark man near Spring?"

Victoria frowned and focused on the scene near Spring. "I see no dark man."

"Then why do I?"

"That is an excellent question."

"I've seen him before, in my dreams … very recently."

Victoria studied Cassandra's face as if looking for the hint of a lie, but Cassandra matched her gaze, sincerely wanting an answer to her question. The dark man had haunted her long enough, and perhaps this wizard could help her decipher her dreams. After a few moments, Victoria placed a hand on her shoulder and said, "Come. Let us retire to my chambers so that we may discuss the school."

Cassandra nodded, and they walked down the hall, away from the mural. Cassandra noticed that the wizard looked back at the painting as they walked. She could only assume that Victoria really couldn't see the dark man. Cassandra wondered what that meant precisely, but Victoria changed the subject by discussing the actual location of her room. Victoria cautioned her that the site of her room magically changed within the tower each day; each fake room warded against intruders, except for the real one. She reiterated what she had said earlier about how protective magic could kill those not prepared for it. Cassandra wasn't listening, though; she was thinking of the dark man. Why did Victoria not see him? Who was he? She hadn't told her everything about the painting. As it had moved and played out the battle, the dark man tried to give something to Spring: a silver rod with a topaz gem at the tip, the same rod from her recent dreams.

Victoria finally opened one of the doors with a crystal key after they had walked what seemed like an eternity, breaking all the laws of space that made the tower look tall on the outside and not so long. It was an unmarked door, exactly as all the others, but Victoria somehow knew which one led to her private chambers. They entered the room, and the aroma made Cassandra's stomach growl.

It was large and plushly furnished, with several couches, carpeting, and many pictures adorning the walls. Several lanterns hung there as well, already burning when they entered. There was a marble table and steaming-hot food on it, as well as a pitcher of cool water. She ate hungrily, listening to the wizard describe the school and how she had gained the position of head wizard years earlier. Cassandra only half listened, more intrigued by the decorative but dull room. There were no wizardly items like spell books, scrolls, potions, components, or tomes of magical writings. It was not at all what she had expected.

She turned back to Victoria, midsentence. "And after four years, you will graduate to apprentice. You may work under me then and begin your career as a powerful wizard. So what do you say?"

Cassandra thought about it for a few moments and stared at Victoria, who never broke eye contact with her. Then, with a shrug, she finally said, "Well, I like it here; the city and your school are intriguing to me. Once my problems with Oldorburg are resolved, I would like nothing more than to attend your school."

"You have less than two weeks before classes begin, so get your affairs in order and report back to the dorms by then. I want you to be serious about this, Cassandra, because I see great potential in you."

Cassandra smiled, and it was the first time she had done so since they had met. "Thank you, Lady Victoria. I would normally be so excited right now about attending your most wonderful school! It's everything I've dreamed of, but not with the stress I have on my shoulders."

"I understand. Come and sit on my couch. It's very comfortable, and now that you've eaten your fill, it would be good for you to relax."

Cassandra hesitantly made her way to the couch, feeling its softness with her hand before settling on it.

"There's a meeting in the morning that I'm sure Baxter mentioned. I hope that it goes well, and I'll put a good word in for your cause. I believe the king and queen will aid you," Victoria said.

That potential eased Cassandra's mind, and the stress melted away at Victoria's reassuring words. She became very comfortable on that plush couch, as Victoria had predicted she would, and soon she found her eyelids very heavy. Victoria discussed some of the school's opportunities, and she listened as long as she could. However, sleep eventually won, and Cassandra slipped into a profound and peaceful slumber. The following day, she awakened refreshed in her dorm room bed, the meeting with the king and queen already underway.

~

Kringus and Penelope Brahmore held the meeting in the castle's banquet hall and skipped all the formalities that came with their position. There were no guards posted in the room because none were needed. The friends required none; each trusted the others with their lives. Although the meeting had bitter undertones, the mood was light, and all shared casual stories. The gathering was the first in almost a year, and there were many such stories to tell. The group of friends had taken the moniker the New Order a few years earlier in honor of the original group of heroes. However, this New Order had no legal power—nor was it recognized by any other city. When needed, this group performed services for neighboring cities, bringing justice to the lands, but nothing as powerful or impressive as the original New Order had accomplished. Their purpose was simple: help those who are oppressed and stand against evil.

Neither Kringus nor Penelope wore a crown, insisting on keeping the meeting as informal as possible. Instead, Kringus wore a plain shirt, which strained against his massive arms and chest, and ordinary pants, while Penelope wore a simple dress. Other than the king and queen, the others in attendance included Arrin Malik, captain of the king's army; Lady Victoria, head of the school of magic; Von and Lenore Arandur, elven brothers, cousins to the queen, and two of the best archers around; Alleah Mansuell, high priestess of Sinnis; and Daro the Keeper, a ranger of the dell east of Novafontera.

Two servants delivered trays of food and pitchers of the castle's best ale. The servants were at ease and smiled as they worked because they were treated as family and felt comfortable serving the honored guests. The grand hall, adorned with many large windows, was flooded with the morning sunlight. The mood was pleasant, and small talk filled the room for almost an hour before Kringus called the meeting to order. He stood and took a couple of grapes from the nearest tray and began to walk around the table.

"I hope everyone rested well last night and that the road was good to those few of you who do not live in Pelesea," he said, clapping Daro on the shoulder as he passed and popping a grape in his mouth.

"Your large bed made up for any trouble I encountered on the road here, dear Kringus," Daro replied, as always with a wit uncontested.

Kringus made his way to one of the windows and looked out over the large city, adding a second grape to the first one and smiling. "We have plenty of room here for you, ranger, if ever you should grow tired of sleeping on the forest understory."

"I note your offer, good king, and you'll be the first to know if I desire your governance."

Kringus laughed and turned back toward the table, his mirth contagious among the friends. After the laughter had settled down and Kringus returned to his seat, his expression turned serious. "We have important topics to discuss this day, my friends, so let us begin. The first order of business begins with our elven friends up north. Von and Lenore, we are delighted to see you today, and how goes the white elves of Nessor?"

"The elves are ever demanding of border restrictions with their neighbors, but their fussiness is tolerable. The trade negotiations will continue once the borders are secure and King Rowlan is happy with its parameters," Lenore said.

Nessor was locked in a heated debate with the men of Whitewood, a human settlement a few miles outside Nessor's borders. The men of Whitewood had taken liberties of the game found on the elvish land, and King Rowlan was none too happy about it.

"Hopefully King Rowlan will make peace with the hardy men of the north and our negotiations will continue," Kringus said. "We have fine silken goods, pearls, and such that we are willing to exchange for the fine elven lager made in the snowcaps of Nessor."

"Yes, we have relayed this offer to the king, and he seems interested. We'll let you know when this issue has become a priority to him once more," Lenore said.

Kringus nodded. Von and Lenore split a lot of their time between the two cities, and if anyone could work out a trade deal with the stubborn king, these two could. "Your assistance in maintaining the peace between the elves and the humans is immeasurable," Kringus said. "I will trust in your judgment on this matter and will table it until the elves are ready to negotiate."

"I have a matter far more serious than a trade agreement, Kringus," Daro said sourly.

All eyes turned toward the unusually pessimistic ranger.

"There is movement in Novafontera once again," he continued.

"Explain," Penelope said before her husband could utter the words.

"I can't give specifics, but something stirs in the great city. The animals sense it and keep clear of the place. I sense it, as if the city itself is a living, breathing entity," the ranger said.

"This is a grave matter indeed, Daro," Kringus said. "One that we will have to investigate to give credence to your words. As the New Order, we must ensure the old city never falls into the hands of evil. That was part of the vow we took."

The others all nodded, but none had an answer to the problem, so their expressions were solemn.

"If what Daro senses is true, then there can only be two possibilities, in my opinion: undead or demonic inhabitants," Victoria said. "Those are the only two things that could withstand that poisonous cloud."

"I agree with the beautiful wizard," Daro said. "Nothing of this world can live there. But if the demons are rising again, we must prepare Pelesea and all the neighboring cities. But how do we search the city with that horrible curse still in effect?" Daro sat back in his seat and puffed out a breath of air in resignation.

"Victoria, is there some magical means to do this?" Kringus asked.

"None that I possess, my king."

"Then we can only monitor the city as Daro has done and report changes as they occur. This group must undertake this task, and I ask you, Daro, since the queen and I are hard-pressed to leave our positions here in the city, if you are willing to keep a watchful eye on Novafontera. I'll also ask Arrin to join you in this task for the next three months. The two of you watch and document any changes. Then, after autumn has passed and winter begins to set in, both of you return and report your findings."

Arrin nodded. "I serve you, Kringus, as both my king and the leader of the New Order. Your wish is my command."

"Thank you, Arrin. You are a true and loyal friend, and I always know I can count on you."

"I don't have the … luxuries that you are accustomed to," Daro said and frowned.

"I don't need them. I'll bring my bedroll. It'll be an easy three months, I assure you, ranger," Arrin said.

"Very well. We agree, then. We will discuss the monitoring of Novafontera when next we meet," Kringus said.

"Why the long face, Alleah?" Penelope suddenly said, gaining everyone's attention.

Alleah jumped at the mention of her name and looked wide eyed around the table at the curious faces of her seven friends. The beautiful priestess of Sinnis blushed, as she did in social situations. Any man would agree that she was one of the most attractive women in the city—even most women would attest to that—but her faith was her life. She shared intimacy only with Sinnis, so gatherings of people, even her dearest friends, were difficult for the shy priestess. She had her long blond hair pulled back in a braided ponytail, and her priestly robes covered her shapely figure. Again she blushed as she became the center of the conversation.

Sitting next to her, Arrin put his arm around her and said, "You are among friends, dearest Alleah. Please don't be shy."

She smiled and patted his hand. Arrin was one of the few males allowed to touch her, as they'd grown up in Pelesea together. However, Arrin respectfully removed his arm once she gathered the courage to speak. "I'm sorry to interrupt, but there's a topic I'd like to discuss if the time is right."

"Yes, of course," Penelope said.

"There are reports from my sisters of the faith, who travel by ship through our city. They say that Gorl is forming an army on the faraway lands across the ocean."

"Without disrespecting your religion, may I ask how that affects us directly?" Kringus asked.

"Well, perhaps it doesn't ... for now. However, the worshippers of Gorl are warmongers and evildoers. Priestesses of Sinnis keep a watchful eye on such things, always on the lookout for just such an atrocity. If the reports are true, then you can rest assured that this will be no minor skirmish. These men want to destroy everything in their path. Conquering lands to rule people is not their main objective; killing and torturing are."

"What proof do we have that an army is forming, other than what you've heard from travelers?" Kringus asked.

"We have none. But …" She gently grabbed the holy symbol hanging from her neck.

"Go on. You are with friends," Penelope said.

"I'm willing to travel there to get a firsthand look at this army and determine if it exists."

"Across the ocean. To the west?" Kringus asked.

She smiled and nodded, and a sour look crossed the king's face. To the west, over a thousand miles across the ocean, were two continents. The closest, Illid, was civilized and contained many cultures and cities, just like the continent of Torlia, where Pelesea resided. However, these two continents were far enough apart to interact only rarely, aside from occasional trades. Those trades were few and far between, and for the most part, inhabitants from each landmass interacted with the other sparingly. It was almost as if two solid and peaceful cultures coexisted, but rarely together, and they were deemed safe for traveling.

However, Varish, the sister continent to Illid, was a wild and dangerous place where few settlements existed. The land was just as chaotic as those who lived there. The lack of law and order was abundantly clear to any who visited the wicked place, but few ever lived to warn others about it. Kringus hailed from Varish, having ruled a large city there as a young man.

"To Varish?" he asked.

Alleah made eye contact with him and nodded. He sat back and took another handful of grapes. He ate them slowly as the others waited for him to respond. He looked briefly at his lovely wife, and she raised her eyebrows at him, which meant she supported whatever decision he made.

He sat back up and looked at Alleah sternly, which made her wilt a bit under his gaze. "As your friend, I say go where you desire; your goddess will protect you. But as your ally and comember of the New Order, I commend you on your courage and selflessness. And as your king, I strictly forbid you to go."

Seeming to have expected the rejection, she turned her gaze to the table and nodded. Her knuckles whitened as she grasped her holy symbol even harder. The king and queen shared a knowing glance— they would need to discuss this further with the priestess privately.

Seeing her distress, Penelope added, "Perhaps you can still use the sisters of your faith to keep informed of the situation. If you learn that the threat is real and grows closer to home, please let us know."

"Yes, I think that would be wise," Alleah said with a half smile.

"So what else do we need to discuss today? Our time together always seems to run short, and I would like for us to address as much business as possible while assembled," Kringus said.

After no one else spoke up, Victoria said, "I have a matter of importance."

"Sure. What do you have for us today, dear lady of magic?" Kringus asked and smiled.

"I have an unusual problem centered around a young woman."

"Cassandra?" Alleah asked before she could stop the words. She looked at Kringus apologetically.

"You know her, Alleah?" the king asked.

"Yes, she came to the temple a few days ago," she began, then looked to Victoria for permission to proceed. Victoria nodded, so Alleah added, "She was injured and poisoned."

"How young is she?" Penelope asked as both she and Kringus sat up in their seats at the mention of it.

"She can't be more than seventeen or eighteen years in this world, so not much younger than me. The poison was real, but not the kind one uses to kill someone. It was strong but designed only to make one sleep. She'd consumed quite a bit, as far as I could tell."

"You treated her?" Kringus asked.

"Yes, and her wounds healed very quickly. I gave her permission to leave the temple yesterday, having almost fully recovered from her injuries." Alleah turned to Victoria. "I do hope she's feeling well and enjoying her stay."

"She is doing very well, Alleah. Thank you for nursing her back to health," Victoria said and smiled.

Alleah smiled back and nodded.

"Who would have done this to her, Victoria?" Kringus asked.

"A man named Ronnis D'Breeth. He is a lord of some power and reputation from Oldorburg, roughly eight hundred miles south of here."

"What is the girl's full name?" Daro asked.

"Cassandra Rho."

"The little girl who kills wolves," Daro said. The rest of the friends looked at one another, confused by the response. Finally, Daro noticed the eyes on him, and he shrugged. "It's a common nursery rhyme in the parts south of here. Supposedly this little girl was attacked by wolves in the woods and she summoned ravens to kill them. The little girl of legend is none other than Cassandra Rho."

"Is the story true, Victoria?" Kringus asked.

"From what little time I spent with her last evening, I would say it is. She's an extraordinary person, and I think she would be capable of doing such an amazing thing."

"So why is she a topic for the New Order to discuss?"

"Because she fled Oldorburg, and namely Ronnis, to come here."

"Why here?"

"I invited her to attend the school, and I've watched her since the rise of the nursery rhyme. She is more powerful than anyone knows. I feel I can make her realize her potential."

"So you now have a gifted student for the school? I see no problem yet," Kringus said.

"There's more to the story, I'm afraid. Cassandra is wanted for two crimes in Oldorburg." She paused, seeming to collect her thoughts.

"And they are?" Kringus asked impatiently.

"Attempted murder and witchcraft."

His face wrinkled up in confusion. "Wait—this young woman who you claim is so very gifted is wanted for attempted murder?"

"And witchcraft?" Penelope said, just as confused.

"Yes, from what Baxter told me, Lord Ronnis is very corrupt and has abused her and her mother for years. It seems she finally snapped and used her magic to attack the lord. He survived but now wants to exact the harshest punishment the law allows on her—and possibly her family."

"And what might that be?" Kringus asked, a concerned look on his face.

"Death."

"I see," Kringus said, sitting back in his chair and rubbing his chin. He glanced at his wife, who wore a perplexed look.

"Furthermore, Ronnis spotted Baxter during his rescue attempt and knows that he hails from Pelesea. Emissaries from Oldorburg are sure to follow."

"Wait, what rescue attempt?" Kringus asked.

"She was being restrained and drugged, as Alleah pointed out, at the corrupt temple there. Baxter found her and freed her. He brought her here."

"So now our city harbors criminals?" His neck muscles constantly flexed when he was upset. They were doing so now, and Victoria knew that wasn't a good sign.

"No, of course not, but Baxter believes that Ronnis is evil and has the town officials in his back pocket. He believes that she would have been executed without a fair trial if he'd left her there. They've already dismissed the sheriff."

"Still, it's not our place to interfere with another town's laws."

"Even if those laws are unjust? I thought that was the whole point of the New Order," Victoria said.

Kringus sat back and soaked in her words for a few moments, then asked, "So you have a gifted young wizard who has already attempted to kill a man at only eighteen years of age? Will you still allow her to attend your school, knowing Oldorburg didn't try her for her crimes?"

"Yes."

"Knowing that she could do this again?"

"Yes."

"I don't understand this, Victoria. Why are you determined to help this girl?"

"Because she's special. She has powers that I've never seen in another wizard."

"Like summoning ravens?" Daro asked.

"Yes. Plus much more. Cassandra saw the image in the tower."

"You mean the ever-moving image created by the angels?" Penelope asked.

"Yes. In the ten years I've run the school, I've only had four students who saw the image move. The other three went on to become great wizards."

"So she *is* special," Kringus said.

"But there's more," Victoria said. "She saw images in the painting that I could not. Never has this happened before."

Kringus sat back then and rubbed his chin again, deep in thought, but before he could respond, Victoria said, "There's more yet—the real reason I'm here among my friends this morning. Her mother and sister are still there in Oldorburg, and she fears for their safety. She was hoping you would assist her in bringing them here."

Kringus sighed and, after some thought, said, "So here is what I propose: She is welcome to stay here, but only if she agrees to remain on the school grounds. I will have her watched, and if she breaks this rule, I will have her arrested and personally send her back to Oldorburg.

"I will furthermore go to this town, along with some of my best knights, and visit with the authorities. Then I will propose to try the girl in Pelesea for her crimes, explaining that she does not feel a fair trial is coming by the leaders of Oldorburg. If we find her guilty, she will be sent back to Oldorburg for punishment as they see fit. While there, I will also visit her family and offer to escort them here if they desire to come.

"This is the best I can do, Victoria, and I hope she agrees to these stipulations. If not, she must leave the city immediately. Your thoughts?"

It was Victoria's turn to sigh as she nodded. "You are a good friend and a wise king. I accept your decision and will relay it to Cassandra immediately."

Victoria stood to leave, officially ending the business part of the meeting. The other seven stayed a bit longer, sharing more stories and reminiscing about the old days when they'd traveled the world, looking for adventure. Their time was joyous and well spent, but the news of Cassandra burdened the royal couple. Her presence in the city could cause a lot of grief for the king and queen. Being royalty was exhausting.

CHAPTER 7

THE SEARCH BEGINS

"WHAT HAVE YOU DISCOVERED, HEINSVICK?" CAME THE telepathic intrusion.

"Nothing as of yet," was the curt response.

"Just like our time, my patience is running out. I want results from you if you want to see your precious Emiline again."

"Return her to me, and perhaps I will be more motivated to serve."

After a long pause, Matilda answered his request with such finality that it stole the vampire's mounting courage. "I grow tired of your unwillingness to serve. If you do not deliver solid evidence that you have found the child of Kane within thirty moons, I will rip the flesh from your skin and Emiline will burn in the morning sun!"

With that, she severed the link.

"Matilda … Matilda!" he thought, trying to reach her.

"Matilda!" he finally screamed, sending his brides scurrying into the shadows of the throne room.

He clutched the arms of the throne tightly and looked around the room, trying to reorient himself. The hateful woman had severed the mental connection, and he felt like finding her and ripping her throat out. Instead, he promised himself to do just that if the opportunity arose. The pile of ash that had once been his beautiful bride Junet was still lying on the floor, reminding him of the sheer power of Matilda. He had left her there as a reminder of this potent adversary. Matilda had taken much from him during that ill-fated visit.

Since she had left, he had sat on his throne and moped. Several weeks had passed, and this was the first time the evil priestess had contacted him. He didn't care about completing the task; he would take whatever punishment she offered. Even the burning sun was acceptable to him because he could not live without his Emiline. No, he would sit and let the priestess kill him through the slave brand he now wore before he would help her. He was nobody's slave!

That was his plan, anyway, originally. However, Matilda had threatened to harm Emiline again, and he couldn't let that happen. So he decided to either complete the task or find Emiline and bring her home. The proud vampire lord could not sit and pout any longer; Matilda was too dangerous. He watched as his brides tentatively crept back from the shadows, crawling toward his feet, careful to avoid the pile of ashes. They were hungry, but they hadn't complained. They knew he was hurting; they knew something was wrong. They lay at his feet, all trying to touch his shoes or legs, gently stroking them, and remind him that they needed him. He had neglected them since Matilda had come into their lives.

"Allustria," he said to a tall redheaded bride, his oldest now that Junet was no more.

"Yes, my master?" she said, raising her pretty face to meet his gaze.

He saw a glimmer of hope in her eyes—perhaps she thought he'd feed them. But that look of hopefulness quickly turned to fear when he said, "I'm leaving."

"No, you can't!" she cried in desperation, which triggered the other brides to wail and plead with him to stay. They quickly worked themselves into a frenzy, crying and pawing at his legs.

"Enough!" he screamed and stood to regain his control. His brides scampered away once more. "Allustria, come to me!" he demanded, motioning for her to come back to him with the repeated curling of his finger.

She reluctantly walked toward him, the others close behind her. They were scared, and they had good reason to be. He wasn't sure how long he would be gone, but he was determined to rid himself of the curse that was Matilda. He would hunt her down and kill her and hopefully save Emiline in the process.

"I'm leaving, my lovely brides. I would take you with me if only I could. My road is one filled with danger, so I must travel it alone. Allustria is in charge until I return, and if I never return, you must stay here together as a family. Protect each other, and defend this city from all intruders. If the demons come, flee."

"What shall we do for food, master?" Allustria asked.

"Hunt in the neighboring woods. Kill sparingly and always in different parts of the woods. Let no one see you enter or exit the city."

He looked at his frightened harem and understood that he was leaving them vulnerable without him. He realized he might never see them again, which concerned him immensely. This collection of timeless beauties he had spent centuries gathering may be lost to him—just another casualty in his dealings with Matilda. He stroked Allustria's face and kissed her forehead. "Goodbye, my loves! I hope to see you again one day!"

He quickly cast the teleportation spell that took him to the elven village where he'd first met Emiline and where the two had feasted just a few weeks earlier. He would find a temporary replacement for Emiline. He missed her too much, and he could travel with one bride as he hunted down and killed Matilda. As the teleportation spell faded and the woods came into focus around him near the elven campsite, his emotions got the best of him. His anguish overcame him, and he fell to his knees and began to wail.

~

As Victoria left the meeting with the New Order, she met Baxter in the large and comfortable foyer, where he had waited impatiently. They quickly exited the magnificent castle and made their way to the school of magic, where they knew the New Order's decision would not sit well with Cassandra.

"So what will be her reaction, Baxter? You seem to know her better than anyone."

"It won't be positive. Perhaps I should offer to go and retrieve Cassandra's family before something does happen to them."

"No, you will stay at the school and prepare your curriculum for the fall classes. This Ronnis fellow already has seen you and will have the town guards looking out for you—don't doubt. Also, Kringus assured me that he would take care of it."

"Yes, I understand that, but does Kringus understand the urgency of this matter? If we act too late and something happens to her family, she will not handle it well. We have already delayed too long, in her eyes, and she will not easily forgive failure where her family is concerned."

Victoria stopped her brisk walk and turned to her most trusted instructor. They were now out of the castle grounds and into the city proper. The day was bustling with business as fishing ships unloaded their catches from the early-morning run. Seagulls were calling and watching the process, grabbing dropped fish as the opportunity presented itself.

"We will tell her the truth," Victoria said. "We will tell her what the New Order decided. It's up to her to understand. She has raw powers—beyond anything I've seen before. I would love nothing more than to take her under my wing and shape those powers into something special. However, I can't worry about her reaction to this or what she might do after hearing it. If she leaves, there is nothing I can do to stop her. If that happens, I will move on to the next prodigy."

Baxter shuffled his feet as if he wanted to say something.

"What is it, Baxter? We've known each other for a long time, and we can trust each other with our lives. So if there's something you want to say, please do it," Victoria said.

"I wish it were that easy," he said, looking at his feet, his cheeks turning red.

Victoria's eyes went wide, and she grabbed him by the shoulders. "You're becoming emotionally involved with her! That cannot happen—you know this! An instructor must not become involved with any student in any capacity other than a mentor."

"Yes, I'm aware," he said, his voice a little higher than usual. He looked around, making sure none of the busy citizens had heard him. "I have only known her for a few days, my lady, and I have feelings for her that I can't explain. It's unintentional, I assure you, but I can't help how I feel."

Victoria began walking again, letting out an audible sigh. Baxter followed with his head down, watching his feet. They walked the rest of the way to the school without saying another word. Once they reached the school dorms, she turned to Baxter and laid a hand on his shoulder. He stopped and looked into her eyes.

"Why don't I tell her the news? You're too emotionally involved to remain objective. Why don't you go to the alchemist shop and get your mind off this? Focus on the fall semester and how many other students you'll help. I'll deal with Cassandra for now," Victoria said sternly but with a smile.

"As you wish," Baxter sighed and turned to leave.

"Baxter?"

"Yes?" he answered, stopping and turning.

"I mean permanently, at least until I resolve this."

"What do you mean?"

"I mean that you should keep your distance from her. I'll fill you in later on how she took the news. But for everyone's sake, just stay clear of her until she decides to enroll or not. Agreed?"

He sighed again and gave her a slight nod. "Agreed."

With that, he turned and walked away, leaving Victoria with the dirty work of delivering the information to Cassandra. Perhaps having Cassandra Rho as a student wasn't such a good idea anymore. With a shake of her head, Victoria turned to enter the dorms.

~

"Emiline, can you hear me?" Matilda whispered through the coffin.

"Yes," came the meek reply.

"It has been a long voyage, but you are home now. Would you like to come out?"

"Yes."

Matilda straightened and smiled, but Cerus did not reciprocate. They had just docked their ship the day before at Port Racip, spending nearly three weeks at sea, carrying the vampire in the hold of the vessel. Then they had made their way from Racip to the fortress that Cerus's men were currently constructing. They had cut deep into the caves of Nesin and had established a heavily fortified stronghold that served as their headquarters. Originally Cerus had joined Matilda with the promise of war thick on her lips, but thus far, his men had only been used as slave labor to work the caves into a fortified base of operations. Naturally Cerus was not pleased with this, and now the objective had changed once more to prepare for the great summoning.

"The thing spooks my men, Matilda. Let's destroy the abomination!" Cerus said.

Matilda shook her head. "Your men will have to get used to the undead being around. Once he has come, it will be commonplace to have them walking among the living."

"What are your plans for her, then?" Cerus asked.

"For now, she's collateral, but she could be more valuable than that. I feel that she's special, almost gifted, for a vampire. I wish I had more time to study her."

"It's a nasty creature that has no place here. We should have thrown it overboard when we had the chance."

"Open it," she said to Cerus's two soldiers, pointing to the sealed coffin.

The soldiers looked at each other nervously. They were in Matilda's quarters, where few were allowed. It was a spacious cave with a natural spring that formed a pool in the room's middle. She used it for bathing but also for relaxing, as the spring was naturally heated. The room consisted of softly glowing lanterns, which gave a peaceful yet mysterious ambiance to it. Tapestries hung from the cave walls, depicting war scenes or nude women pleasuring demons or, just as commonly, being devoured by them. Since rarely did anyone other than Matilda and Cerus enter that particular room, the two men were nervous even to be there. They worked quickly to unseal the coffin so that they could take their leave.

Once they partially unnailed it, the lid flew open, knocking both men to the floor. Both came up quickly with weapons in hand as Cerus stepped back and put one hand on his massive spear. Emiline jumped out quickly, showing her fangs at the nearest soldier and hissing like a wild animal. The man stepped back, his eyes wide in terror.

Matilda stepped between her and the soldier. "Now, Emiline, that is no way to act. Why do you show aggression to these two men who have freed you?"

"Freed?" the vampire asked, obviously confused.

"Yes, Heinsvick had you nailed in the coffin, but we have freed you."

"Heinsvick?" Emiline asked sadly.

"Yes, he gave you to us. He said that he no longer wants you and that we could keep you," Matilda said.

"Why?" Emiline asked, her eyes tearing up.

"Because he no longer loves you. How does that make you feel?"

Emiline started to cry. "Sad," she mumbled.

Matilda glanced at Cerus, who looked on suspiciously, his hand still grasping his spear. "But we love you and will accept you here. Would you like to stay with us?" Matilda said.

"Yes, please," Emiline whimpered, fighting back more tears.

"Good. Then you need to do as I tell you—do you understand?" Matilda said, gently cradling Emiline's chin in her hand.

Emiline's bright blue, tear-filled eyes showed how much Matilda's words had stung her. She was not some vicious, undead, unthinking thing; she showed genuine emotions. Matilda smiled and flatly said, "Undress, Emiline."

The vampire tilted her head, which seemed to be her response anytime something confused her. Matilda stepped away from the vampire and motioned to the two soldiers. "You will reward these two men for freeing you. You will do so with your body. Do you understand?"

Emiline nodded somberly and just stood there, her arms at her sides, looking at Matilda as if awaiting her command. The soldiers looked at each other, hesitant to go anywhere near the undead thing. Emiline was attractive, even in the afterlife, but beyond that was the fact that she was a vampire, one of the most powerful undead creatures known to man. Unsure of what to do next, the two soldiers looked toward Cerus for confirmation, and he nodded his approval for them to proceed.

"Then you need to say so and address me as your mistress," Matilda said, seemingly oblivious to Cerus's interaction with the two soldiers.

Emiline nodded and began unbuttoning her blouse. "Yes, mistress."

Matilda looked at the two men, who just stood there gawking at the vampire. "Well, why are you two hesitating? Ravage her!"

They looked to Cerus once more for confirmation. He finally released the grip on his spear, and an evil smile spread across his face. He said, "Follow your orders, men."

Both men knew they could not disobey, so they slowly undressed, but neither approached Emiline. She stood in only her underwear, her head down, waiting for them to come to her.

"Go to her, boys, and do not be gentle," Matilda said. She stepped back with Cerus as the two men, tentatively at first, moved to surround Emiline. Cerus had trained these men for battle, and they were afraid of neither pain nor death, but for them to be intimate with this creature at a moment's notice would be an actual test of their allegiance. The vampire was attractive, but it was still an undead thing and dangerous on top of that. His men prevailed, swallowing their fears, and moved to dominate her. They were awkward at first and somewhat gentle, testing how the creature would react to their touch. She let them handle her without complaint, and soon their confidence grew.

Before it was over, they had switched positions several times, manipulating Emiline in ways that would satisfy their lust. The things they did to her were very filthy indeed. And their willingness to ravage the vampire pleased Matilda. Emiline remained submissive to them, just as Matilda had instructed, no matter what they did to her. Shame filled the vampire's eyes as the two men spent themselves and moved slowly away. It was such an erotic scene that Matilda almost joined in, lost in her state of lustfulness. Cerus's firm hand on her shoulder was the only thing that kept her from doing so.

"Do you see, Cerus? She is completely under my control. She doesn't possess the savagery seen in most vampires and is willing to be completely submissive to me. Quite a gift we've received—don't you think?" Matilda asked.

"Yes, but why does this matter? Can't your God-given powers keep her under control?"

"Of course. I could destroy her with but a thought. But she's an ally as long as she believes she's freethinking. And from the looks of things, she is a very sexual creature and could be handy in the bedroom."

Cerus had seen many battles and had looked death in the face many times, but this had him back on his heels a bit. Since joining forces with the unpredictable woman, he had discovered what a sexual being Matilda indeed was. Her exploits rarely kept her satisfied for any length of time. She could play with the vampire all she wanted, and she would become bored with it soon enough. However, Matilda's sexual escapades continued to become more extreme.

"Don't act so surprised, Cerus. You know I like to try new things," she said with a wicked smile.

He had no response and watched as his men slowly dressed and shared whispers of their recent good fortune. Emiline obediently waited for Matilda's following command. One of the men, gaining courage after the despicable deed, smacked her hard on the backside and then clasped the shoulder of the other man. Their smiles quickly faded as they saw the look on Matilda's face.

"Emiline, are you hungry? You have slept for so very long." Emiline's eyes grew wide, and she nodded with excitement. The soldiers had a pretty good idea of what was coming next, and they moved for their weapons, both in various stages of undress.

"Feed, my pet!" Matilda screamed just as the men reached their spears and brought them to bear. Emiline was on the first one before he could move to defend, backhanding him across the face with such force that he flew against the cave wall, hitting his head hard and dropping his spear. She quickly turned to face the other man, the gentle look that she had worn only moments before now replaced with a hatred that startled the seasoned warrior. Her beautiful face contorted in rage, fangs showing, and an animal growl generated from somewhere deep within her.

He immediately lost his calm and took a step back, toward the center of the room. Emiline looked at him, her expression slowly changing back to her natural demeanor. She tilted her head, and her growling stopped. She gently made her way to him, and he began to calm.

"You have already lost control, Matilda—" Cerus began, but Matilda held up a hand, motioning for him to watch. Then, not wanting to lose two of his men to one of Matilda's displays of power, he said, "Destroy her, soldier!"

The soldier did not move, and Emiline continued to approach him. Cerus grabbed his spear, ready to assist the young warrior, but Matilda stopped him. "He is under her spell and can't hear you. Do you not see, my dear Cerus? She is hunting, and she is a brilliant hunter."

Soon the soldier lowered and even dropped his spear. It clanged to the floor, and he stood there, nearly naked, defenseless, his wide eyes staring blankly into hers. Then, as she advanced, he closed his eyes and turned his neck to expose his jugular to her. She closed quickly at that point but did not bite him. Instead, she used her strength to take his head in her hands and twist it hard to the right. The sickening sound of the man's neck breaking echoed through the room, and he fell dead at her feet.

She immediately turned and moved too quickly for any human to react, so that she was beside the first man who had hit the wall. He was on one knee and trying to shake the cobwebs from his head. She knelt with him, grabbed his head by the hair, and pulled back, exposing his neck. Then she fed, biting deeply into his neck. The man's screams were short lived as the creature quickly drained the lifeblood from his body.

Matilda seemed very pleased with this and allowed Emiline to feed on the second soldier after finishing the first one. Once the vampire had fed, Matilda took her to the pool and cleaned her up. Cerus called for two servants to come and remove the corpses from the room. He then left quickly to go to the barracks. After that display, he needed something to distract him from the image of her feeding on his soldiers. So he went to the barracks with news for his men that would make things normal for him again: the possibility of battle.

~

Heinsvick moved around the remains of the elven village, taking in the chaos that remained. Elven belongings were scattered throughout the place and into the surrounding woods. Bloodstained spots on the ground and in the high grass where bodies had once lain were abundant. Something—or, more likely, many things—had attacked the elves. He found signs of the elven fight that they'd put up, arrows stuck in trees, or broken and lying on the ground at various spots. The elves had defended themselves and probably killed many of the attackers. However, there was no surviving elf to inform him of the events and no bodies left behind.

He had seen this before, brutal and total. In all his long years of undeath, the only thing he had witnessed remotely close to this was a werewolf attack. His old acquaintance Logan had invaded a similarly sized human settlement with the same results. He confessed that his family of shapechangers became much more aggressive and reckless during a full moon, sometimes attacking settlements to store food for the winter or procuring slaves for entertainment during those cold months.

The moon was full this night, and the early onset of fall was upon the woods. He smiled at the thought of seeing the volatile creature again. Logan was wise beyond his years, especially for a werewolf, and Heinsvick wanted nothing more than to discuss the hateful Matilda with him. Perhaps the two of them together could find her and put an end to her reckless ideas and save his beloved Emiline from her clutches. If these clues were genuinely going to lead him to the old werewolf, he might have found the first step in freeing Emiline.

He hunted in these woods only with Emiline, and this place was hundreds of miles away from Novafontera. Judging by the moon's position, he had several hours left before the dreaded sunrise. If he found the attackers and it did end up being Logan and his clan, he could find shelter within their lair. Otherwise, he would use his teleporting spell to take himself back home to his rejuvenating coffin. He changed his form then, effortlessly contorting his body into that of a giant bat. He took flight in the hopes of finding an ally in his battle against the nasty priestess.

~

Cassandra's face was expressionless, but her cheeks quickly grew red after Victoria told her of Kringus's decision.

"So I'm your prisoner now instead of Ronnis's?"

"It's not like that, Cassandra."

"No, it's exactly like that," Cassandra said, her temperament changing and her face becoming redder by the second. "I'm your prisoner, and then I have to stand trial? For what—defending myself?"

"You will stand trial for the charges brought against you. It's only right," Victoria said calmly.

Cassandra disagreed with the woman's reasoning. Baxter had rescued her from the vile Ronnis D'Breeth only for her to be made a prisoner to the new jailor, Kringus Brahmore? How could this wizard, an intelligent being, not see this?

"Look at it this way," Victoria said. "If you joined the school, you would be on campus most of the time anyway. So you can focus on your studies and let Kringus bring your family to you. Once they're here, I'm sure you'll feel better."

Tears filled Cassandra's eyes, and she stared blankly at the wizard. A lone tear made its way down her cheek, but she didn't bother to wipe it away. Instead, she somberly looked at Victoria and said, "I don't deserve this. I'm tired of paying for the evil of others."

"What do you mean?"

"I mean that if Kringus doesn't rescue my family from that beast, Ronnis, then I will. This time, however, I will not fail at killing him. Someone has to put a stop to his evildoing. And I will not stand trial for any of it—that much I promise. Trials are for bad people. I'm a good person trying to make things right. Why would I stand trial for that?"

Victoria nodded and sighed, unable to respond. Cassandra liked her but couldn't fully commit to being a student while her family remained in danger. But she knew in her heart that it was too late. Cassandra wanted to put her faith in the people of Pelesea, but they had taken too long. Perhaps she could persuade Baxter to take her back on the carpet. Indeed, the two of them could do the job faster than a contingent of men on horseback. Then, before Kringus even reached Oldorburg, she and Baxter would be back, her family safe. She figured Baxter would probably agree to it if she asked him nicely. She felt he was smitten with her, evidenced by the stupid looks he always gave her. Suddenly, Victoria interrupted her thoughts.

"I have something for you—something to keep your mind off things," the wizard said, reaching into a pouch on her belt. The small bag was magical and held more than its dimensions should allow—similar to Victoria's tower. She reached her arm in and fished around, and Cassandra watched in amazement as the wizard brought forth a new spell book from the small bag. "I know you've lost your other book, and I figured this one could serve as a replacement. After all, you'll have to repen the spells you know before you learn any others. If you decide to stay, you'll have time to do so as you wait for your family. Name the spells that you know, and I'll send them to you in a scroll so that you may recopy them into your spell book."

Victoria offered her the book, which Cassandra took in shaking hands. Few had done anything that nice for her, and she was confused by the kind act. Her silent tears continued, occasionally splashing on the leather-bound book. Finally, she sat down gently on her bed and ran a finger over the cover, soaking in the thoughtful gesture.

Victoria produced a fresh bottle of ink and a new quill and set them on the room's small desk. "All I ask, Cassandra, is that you give me an answer by morning on whether you agree to stay at the school until the trial or if you wish to leave the city. I hope you will stay with us. Also, I'll need to know by week's end whether you wish to attend this fall."

Cassandra didn't answer but hugged the book to her chest, staring at the floor. Victoria smiled slightly and walked to the door.

Before Victoria could leave, Cassandra said, "Thank you."

Victoria turned and smiled. "Of course. I believe in you. You'll get through this."

Cassandra nodded and tried to smile. "You and Baxter have been very kind. You are true friends—the first I've ever had, other than my sister. I will always remember you for that."

Victoria nodded and smiled, then exited the room, gently shutting the door behind her. Cassandra stared at the door for a very long time, still hugging the book to her chest. Perhaps she should give Pelesea a chance; maybe Kringus would be fast enough and strong enough to rescue her family. Cassandra took her book to the desk and opened the new bottle of ink, dipping her quill. She began penning the spells from memory, not needing any silly scroll to do so. Soon the aspiring wizard forgot her troubles and it felt like that night when she and Sera had come home from Ronnis's office. Cassandra tried to rediscover the excitement she'd felt that night back in Oldorburg. After all, she was in a school now that would help her learn the craft. She quickly became lost in her work and put her immediate worries aside, at least for a little while.

~

The following day, all of Fortress Nesin's men and women gathered at the cave entrance to see off the war party marching into battle. Matilda was going over final instructions with one of her acolytes, specifically how to treat Emiline while she was gone. She had moved her coffin to the caves' lower reaches, in the prisoners' cells. The place served perfectly as the vampire's new home. However, Cerus disagreed with the arrangement because he didn't want the creature in the fortress. In the end, Matilda got what she wanted.

"So leave her in her cell, do not disturb her, and do not let her out. I have instructed her to wait there for me, and she will as long as she is not disturbed. Do you understand, Borin?" Matilda asked.

"Yes, my lady," the beady-eyed acolyte said with a smile.

While Matilda finished the details, Cerus addressed his men, preparing them for a short march to Attins, a small town located a few hundred miles away. They had agreed that the small town was the perfect place to start their conquest. Cerus's men had waited long enough, and although not much of a challenge, Attins would sate their bloodlust at least temporarily. The men needed this; they needed war. "Soon we march to our first destination in a long line of battles as we begin our quest to conquer this part of the world!" Cerus exclaimed, and his men cheered, raising their spears in the air as a salute.

The party consisted of five hundred of Cerus's trained and seasoned warriors ready for battle and six of Matilda's most powerful priests. Finally, after months of the group's laboring to establish their base within the mountain, the task was complete. The cave was fortified and fully operational. The only construction remaining was in the prison area, and if the sacrificing required 666 subjects, they would need a lot more room. Cerus and Matilda agreed that the slaves they captured in Attins would be used to make those expansions. There could be no delay, for not only did they need to find the virgin child of Kane, but they needed 665 other sacrifices for the conjuring. Time was suddenly of the essence, and Matilda felt the stress of that fact every waking moment.

"Matilda and her priests will go into the town first for reconnaissance, reporting back to us on what they find—the size of their militia, their strengths and weaknesses. Then we will slaughter them like sheep!" Cerus said, punching his fist in the air to emphasize the last part of his instructions.

His speech elicited more cheers, and Matilda looked on as Cerus basked in the growing joy of his army. He was the son of Gorl, the god of war, and to see his men so happy and eager for action made him proud, she knew. He would stain the lands with much blood in the coming months, making his father proud and proving what an asset he was to her.

Soon the tiny caravan was moving toward their destination, led by Cerus and Matilda and the other six priests, all on horseback. After that procession came two horse-drawn caged wagons, each capable of holding forty slaves. Then, behind the two wagons, marched the proud men of Gorl, adorned in chain mail and brandishing large spears, the favored weapon of their god. And so their march began that morning with the hopes of spreading war across the lands.

"I fear we have little hope in our quest. To find the child of Kane is difficult enough, but to find it with its virginity intact will be nearly impossible. I wish we had begun our search years ago," Matilda said to Cerus as they rode.

"Perhaps if you'd visited Novafontera sooner, my dear, then you would've had advanced notice," Cerus replied with a smirk.

The look that Matilda gave him erased his half smile. "Perhaps it's just a test," he added, "but I'm sure you will accomplish your goal. Didn't the demon in your vision tell you to start with the vampire lord?"

She nodded, satisfied with that response. "Heinsvick has been more than useless to me. As of yet, he has produced no leads and only whines about his missing bride whenever I contact him. I'll have to destroy him eventually."

"What about the spies you sent out a few days ago? Do you hold any hope in them?"

"Not much, but it's too early to tell. We must keep our ears and eyes open, dear Cerus."

Cerus nodded, but she knew he disagreed. He wasn't in this for the summoning; he was in it for the many battles he would enjoy. Moreover, he would probably prefer the summoning to fail because she had yet to convince him the world would be a better place with a demon lord in it.

~

The giant bat landed softly in the middle of the werewolf lair, in a clearing at the mouth of a large cave, surrounded by very thick woods and vegetation. The bat changed quickly to that of Heinsvick, the vampire lord. He settled down between two werewolves that were just completing the torturing of a male elf. One creature was eating the throat out of the fresh corpse, while the second one was feasting on the freshly spilled entrails. It was the screams of this doomed elf that had drawn Heinsvick to the encampment.

The creatures stopped immediately and turned to regard the new arrival. They rose slowly, not understanding the nature of this unknown intruder, but both seemed to be on guard, and Heinsvick could see their nostrils flaring as both creatures tried to determine whether he would make a good meal. Unfortunately neither recognized his strange scent. One was tall, close to seven feet, and his muzzle was bright red from the fresh kill. He approached the vampire lord threateningly, baring his massive teeth and producing a deep guttural growl.

"Careful, fool—I am Heinsvick the vampire warlock, and I am no enemy to the wolves of Logan."

The creature kept approaching, and Heinsvick could see others coming from the woods to surround him. "I will say it once more: I am a friend of the werewolves and have business with—"

Before he could finish, the giant werewolf lunged, and at the same time, the other half dozen or so creatures that had slowly surrounded him followed suit. The beast struck first and struck hard, meaning to grab him by the shoulders and clamp his fanged muzzle around his throat. The creature thought it an easy kill and was ready to jerk its head back and forth to rip out his throat. However, the initial contact did nothing as the creature passed through the insubstantial image, nearly falling as it ran utterly through it.

Before it even registered with the vicious creature that the image had been an illusion all along, the camp lit up temporarily as a large streak of sizzling white lightning shot forth from the nearby woods. It struck the off-balanced creature, throwing it to the side. The lifeless body lay motionless, smoking in the tall weeds. The others cautiously looked around, trying to determine what had happened, blinking away the temporary blindness caused by the sudden bright light. Then another image of Heinsvick walked out of the woods with an easy way about him, his fingers smoking from the discharged lightning bolt.

"Would anyone else care to test my powers?" Heinsvick asked, holding his hands out to the sides, inviting any who might be willing to challenge him. The werewolves growled and circled him but kept a safe distance, none of them getting too close. "No one? Then would you be so kind as to fetch Logan?" he said with a smile, hoping the word *fetch* was insulting enough to elicit a response but not so insulting as to provoke an attack during which he'd have to kill another one of the wild creatures.

None of them acknowledged him, and if they were indeed part of Logan's pack, they didn't indicate it. He let out a sigh and decided it would probably be best to leave the foul creatures to their own business. He didn't know why he'd bothered tracking them down anyway. What benefit was it to him to find Logan? Maybe negotiate an elf maiden from his clutches to serve as a companion until he could reunite with Emiline? The absurdity of it all had him second-guessing his decision to go there.

Suddenly a loud and powerful voice echoed from the mouth of the cave: "Heinsvick of Novafontera! State the purpose of your visit and the reason for the attack on my brethren!" Emerging from the cave was a considerable werewolf, standing over seven feet tall, his fur showing hints of gray but his physique nothing short of intimidating. Drool fell from his powerful jaws as he spoke, and his red eyes glowed in the firelight. He stopped temporarily at the cave entrance, and the other werewolves parted to make a path straight to Heinsvick. There was no mistaking this was his old acquaintance but never someone he'd honestly considered a friend.

The creature growled as it looked at the dead, smoldering figure lying in the tall weeds just outside the camp. "You shouldn't have killed Bron. He was a good and faithful wolf."

"He initiated the engagement after I stated the desire for peace, Logan. Truly I must be allowed to defend myself."

Logan walked right up to him, and the other creatures crowded around, finding their courage once more behind their fearless leader. Heinsvick didn't flinch but had a spell ready if needed. The volatile werewolves could very well attack, and they would be sorry if they did.

Then Logan began to change, transforming back into his natural shape—that of a large muscled human. The popping of bones, followed by the skin and hair reduction, was painful, and few nonwerewolves witnessed such a display and lived to tell about it. Heinsvick considered it a good sign that the leader was willing to be so vulnerable in front of him. The man grimaced and moaned as the transformation took its toll on him. Then, with the metamorphosis finally complete, the man he knew as Logan rose, now about a foot shorter after the change but heavily muscled and no less intimidating in his naked human form.

The man leaned in close, the threat on his face very clear. "I see your knack for a grand entrance has not changed."

"And I see that your men are as intolerant of visitors as ever they were," Heinsvick said.

Both men stared each other down, their faces only inches apart. The werewolves closed in, expecting a confrontation, but did not dare move against the intruder until their leader gave the word. Then, finally, after what seemed an eternity, Logan smiled. "And so we have a guest—Heinsvick of Novafontera! It would be best if you treated him as such and did not harm him in any way. Those who do not obey this command will answer to me!" Logan said to the gathering pack of werewolves. Some of them growled softly, but all of them immediately stepped back and went about their business, leaving the two of them alone.

The two were inside the cave a few moments later, using the solid oak furniture that Logan's pack had liberated from the elvish village. Logan was still naked from the waist up but had at least donned some breeches after his transformation. They sat just inside the cave, giving themselves a clear view of the full moon. Heinsvick noticed several packs of werewolves coming and going through the camp and into or out of the dark woods, their maws stained with fresh blood. All of them noticed him and indeed wanted to kill him—of that he was sure. However, none of them even made the slightest move toward him, showing the respect they had for Logan, now in his fifth decade.

Grabbing a delicately sculpted flask of wine from a nearby shelf, Logan asked, "So why have you come on such a glorious night?" and then downed half the drink before Heinsvick could answer.

"I followed your trail from the elven village."

Logan stopped drinking then, spilling a large amount down his chin and onto his hairy chest, and a giant smile appeared on his face. "The elves are mine. I have none to spare."

"I need none and want none."

Logan handed the flask to him, and when Heinsvick declined, the great werewolf laughed deeply, finding the notion hysterical. He slammed the flask down, nearly breaking it. "The elves make a fine wine, Heinsvick. It's too bad you can't sample it."

"Who says I can't? I simply don't desire the stuff."

Logan leaned close, the remnants of the elvish wine dripping from his sharp chin. "I know what you do desire, my friend." The werewolf leader stood and pointed to a much younger werewolf. "You! Bring our guest a refreshment!"

The smaller werewolf stopped what it was doing and looked at him stupidly, not understanding the demand. Logan threw the flask of wine at him, barely missing his head, and it smashed against the cave wall. The creature took a look at the shattered flask and wine-soaked wall, then turned nervously back to his leader. Logan smiled a wicked smile and said, "Fetch an elf maiden."

The creature understood that command, so he nodded and quickly scampered deep into the cave. The elder werewolf turned and flashed a smile toward Heinsvick, who understood the show was mainly for the benefit of the watchful pack. However, Heinsvick knew enough about the chaotic creatures to realize that Logan continuously had to exert his dominance. Logan grabbed another flask and reclaimed his seat next to Heinsvick.

"I thought I made it clear: I don't want an elf."

"Good, because I'm not giving you one … just a taste."

Heinsvick nodded and sat back in his seat, his thoughts lost on Emiline. Logan took another large gulp from the new flask, then looked thoughtfully at the old vampire. "So what troubles you? I have known you for a long time and have never seen you this—well, *sad*, for lack of a better word."

Heinsvick slowly shook his head and lifted his hand, showing Logan the brand. Logan grabbed his wrist and brought it up to his face, studying it. "A brand?"

"From a human priestess."

"Explain."

"A powerful female priest placed this on my hand. It is magical and binds me to her. Through the brand, she controls me. I must do her bidding, or she can destroy me from afar."

"And so you now do her bidding?"

"No," Heinsvick said, shaking his head. "Now I aim to kill her."

Logan smiled his big toothy grin, then stood and howled at the moon. All the other creatures in the camp followed suit, howling and growling in the night. It was a terrifying sound, and it had a devastating effect on the small elf maiden who was being led out of the cave by a leash just at that moment. The terrified expression on her face said it all as she lagged behind the young werewolf tugging the leash. She was so small, even compared to the juvenile werewolf, who pulled her roughly along. She struggled against the pull, both her tiny hands on the leather strap that fastened tightly around her neck. A small pack of bloodthirsty creatures followed the spectacle, anticipating a kill.

Logan stood and waved the pack over to him. He took the leather strap, and the others gathered around to watch what their volatile leader might do with the wretched elf. He pulled the strap hard, making her fall to the ground, and with his brute strength continued to drag her across the rough cave floor until she was at his feet. She managed to look up to her captor, her hands up in front of her and shaking.

Logan grabbed her by the hair and pulled her into a standing position. He towered over her, and her eyes bulged in terror, as she didn't know what to expect but understood her death was imminent.

"Bring me a knife and a goblet," Logan said, and the younger werewolf quickly obliged, grabbing the items from a nearby shelf. Heinsvick couldn't help but notice the wicked blade, which was jagged and covered in dry blood. He could only imagine what horrific tortures that evil weapon had recently inflicted. The elf recognized it as well, her eyes somehow going wider.

"Das merin," she said softly.

"What?" Logan asked, lifting her by the leash and flashing the wicked blade in front of her face.

The elf maiden panicked at the display of the knife, and she quickly said, "Das merin! Das merin! Das merin!"

Heinsvick watched the pack work themselves into a frenzy at the apparent kill at hand. The weaker the prey, the more excited they became; that was the werewolf's way. The elf kept pleading with Logan, but her words fell on deaf ears, and she got a good shake for her efforts. Logan's actions only made her scream all the louder, "Das merin! Das merin! Das merin!"

Heinsvick was lost in thought, the elf reminding him so much of Emiline. His heart ached for his love, and this pointless torture only made matters worse. He wasn't enjoying the spectacle nearly as much as the bloodthirsty werewolves were. "Have mercy," Heinsvick finally said.

Logan turned a curious glance to his friend, still holding the leash now in a way that choked the elf. "What did you say?"

"Have mercy," Heinsvick repeated.

"Explain," Logan said.

Heinsvick, not the least bit intimidated, said, "She is saying, 'Have mercy' … in elvish."

"You speak the language of fairies?"

"No," Heinsvick said, shaking his head. "I only know a few words from my time with Emiline. She said the same thing to me the first time we met."

Logan howled again, and the others followed his lead, working themselves further into a feeding frenzy. Finally, he released the leash, allowing the elf to draw breath once more, and as she gasped for air, he forcefully pulled her arm straight out, exposing her tiny appendage. At the same time, he put the filthy blade in his mouth, holding it with his suddenly elongated teeth. He was caught up in the moment and was beginning to shape-change once again because of it. His bones popped and grew, and his hair, nails, and teeth elongated, making him a weird mix of man and wolf as he grabbed the goblet with one clawed hand and instructed another nearby werewolf to grab her frail-looking wrist. Her screams became louder and more desperate as the pack closed in. Logan took the blade from his mouth and ran it slowly across her wrist. She screamed in pain, and blood gushed from her wound. The pack howled and snarled as Logan caught the lifeblood in the goblet, filling it quickly to the top, then handing it to Heinsvick.

Heinsvick took the goblet as all looked on, and the elf maiden cried in fear and pain, cradling her wounded arm to her chest. He toasted his friend, then drank the blood, just a sip at first, but once he had a taste, he drank it down, finishing the goblet quickly and nodding his approval to Logan.

His actions made the werewolf leader howl once more, and he took up the leather leash again. He pointed to six random men, including the young one who had fetched the maiden. Those six quickly gathered near the fire at the campsite as the others backed away.

The elf was on her knees, crying and holding her wrist, trying to stem the flow of blood. It took all of the vampire's strength for him not to feast on her wound, but Heinsvick remained in control and watched the spectacle unfold before him. Logan ripped the leash from her neck with such force that she fell on her back. He stood over her menacingly and pointed to the dark woods. He growled a deep guttural noise, and the elf didn't need to speak the same language to understand what was transpiring. She climbed shakily to her feet, her injured arm still spilling blood, and slowly walked toward the woods.

When none of the terrifying creatures moved to stop her, she picked up her pace, and soon she was running away from the camp with all speed. The werewolves just stood watching, and the six that gathered in the middle of camp paced restlessly, waiting for Logan's command. Finally, after what seemed like an eternity, he howled at the moon, and the others joined. After many moments of this, the chase was on. The six hand-selected werewolves took up the pursuit of the doomed elf.

Logan sat down again next to Heinsvick, his hybrid werewolf shape slowly changing once more back to that of a human. Heinsvick watched as Logan went through his strange metamorphosis; then, the werewolf leader took several large gulps from the flask of wine. Once drained, he threw that flask against the cave wall, shattering it, just as he had done with the last one.

"I wish I could join them in their fun," he finally said with a sigh.

"Why don't you?"

"I could, I guess, but it's good for morale to let the boys do the hunting."

"You mean by letting them score the kill, you gain favor so that you solidify your leadership here?"

Logan smiled and nodded. "You always were too perceptive for my liking, vampire lord."

A sharp scream echoing from deep within the woods interrupted their conversation. The cry elicited howls from many of the werewolves in the camp. Returning howls echoed back from the six hunters from somewhere in the woods.

"And so she dies?" Heinsvick asked.

"No." Logan shook his head, staring dreamily in the direction of the scream. "That was the first attack."

"First attack?"

"Of course—to maim her."

"To toy with her, then?"

"Yes, and, more important, to give her hope. You see, dear Heinsvick, the meat tastes better when the victim fights and feels there is a chance for survival. Especially with elf meat."

"She has no chance. Even the elf knows this."

Logan turned to his guest and leaned toward him in his chair, his eyes wide with excitement as he told of the werewolves' tactics in hunting harmless prey. "But her instinct to survive kicks in. You see, the first attack always cuts the hamstring or injures the leg at least. Now she is slower and the wolves will circle her. Soon they will surround her and toy with her as each takes a nonlethal hit. Finally, when she has tired and succumbed to the fact that she will die a horrible death, they will pounce. And she will die that horrible death—make no mistake about it."

Heinsvick sat back in his chair and stared at the bloodstained goblet in his hand. He pitied the elf maiden but in reality didn't care whether she lived or died. In another life, when he walked among the living, he would have thought differently, maybe. Tonight, all she was to him was a cool, refreshing drink. He had business to take care of, and this petty hunting game bored him. Another scream, this one much farther away, broke him from his thoughts. She was trying to live. She had made a great distance from the camp, but now the evil creatures would kill her.

"Ah, elf meat—there is not much better in all these lands," Logan said, staring dreamily at the moon.

Heinsvick didn't respond but noticed that the moon was lower in the sky. He had only about an hour of night left. After that, he would need to find shelter to rest out the coming day. Then he would begin his quest to rid himself of the troublesome Matilda and reunite with his dear Emiline. He gently tapped his finger against the goblet, staring aimlessly into the woods, listening to the sounds of the elf slaughter.

"The only thing I like better than elf meat is raven," Logan said absently, still studying the moon.

The words rolled through Heinsvick harder than a direct hit from a bolt of lightning ever could. Raven? Wasn't that a clue associated with the child of Kane? Matilda had told him something about a raven on that horrible night she had enslaved him. "Wait. What did you just say? You eat raven?"

Logan looked at him, his brow furrowed in anger. "Of course. Ravenkin have the most delicate meat on their frail bones. You should drink their blood—I assure you it's tasty."

Heinsvick tried to remember the conversation he'd had with Matilda those weeks earlier. But unfortunately he remembered little of it, other than she had tasked him with finding the child of Kane. He did remember something about a raven, though. He rubbed his temple and tried to recall what she had said about the ravens but couldn't.

Logan noticed his struggle. "What troubles you?"

"The human I told you about—she gave me some kind of clue. When she tried to search out the child of Kane, all she discovered was a vision of a raven," he said, the memory returning.

"She searches for a child?"

Heinsvick ignored the question, now too excited, trying to piece the puzzle together. It made much more sense now. A ravenkin could be the answer to this riddle. Had Logan accidentally given him a clue that he needed to solve the mystery?

"What are ravenkin, and are there any in the area?"

Logan laughed at his desperate question. "No, we took care of the only settlement we ever came across nearly twenty years ago. I'm sure there are more, somewhere in the wide world, if you search hard enough, though! They are nothing more than human gypsies who have a connection with the foul birds. It's hard to say how that supernatural relationship started, but they are known to be very proficient in the art of magic."

Heinsvick sank back in his seat, his excitement diminishing and his hope fading as quickly as it had formed after hearing Logan's words.

"However," Logan said, "there was an instance about a dozen years ago that you might find interesting. We took in a couple of strays from a pack that had been hunted and killed by vengeful humans. One was a big fellow, who passed a few years ago, but the other one, Sebastian, still lives among us. He was young at the time and has grown into a grand hunter. He came across what he believes to be a raven mother."

"Raven mother? What is that?"

"A raven mother is believed to be the most powerful of all the ravenkin, and one is born every one hundred years, or so the legend goes. However, I don't believe they exist because I have never met one in my long life—nor do I know of anyone who has, except for possibly Sebastian."

"So what does a raven mother do?"

"Legends say that she can control ravens, even summon them, and that she unites the ravenkin, enhancing their magical powers."

"Where did he see this raven mother?"

"I would love to eat a raven mother. I imagine she would be quite juicy," Logan said, his voice husky and his eyes filling with bloodlust.

"Logan, where did Sebastian see this … raven mother?" Heinsvick asked, trying to keep the werewolf focused long enough to gather the information he needed.

Just then, the hunting party reentered the campsite, most covered in the blood of the dead elf and a few even carrying pieces of the dismembered creature. One held a severed arm, waving it around and howling into the night. The other werewolves greeted them and howled as they paraded the remains of their kill. One larger one eventually challenged the one with the arm.

"That's Sebastian," Logan said excitedly, pointing to the challenger.

Heinsvick knew from previous encounters with this group of lycanthropes that those challenges were not uncommon and were encouraged among the volatile creatures. The two squared off as the whole pack gathered around to witness the confrontation. There was plenty of growling and insults thrown between the two, and finally, they engaged in what he would consider a fight similar to that between two rabid dogs. They bit, punched, and kicked each other mercilessly. Sebastian was much bigger, and even though he was not a full member of the pack, he earned their respect. He soon inflicted a nasty wound to his opponent's shoulder, having bitten deeply, tearing a chunk of flesh from it. The smaller werewolf yelped in pain and dropped the severed elf's arm, falling to one knee. Sebastian, quick for his size, scooped up his opponent and quickly lifted him over his head. He held him there for a moment, and the others backed away. He then heaved the smaller werewolf into the woods, where he struck a tree and fell unconscious to the ground.

Sebastian looked around, showing his teeth to each gathered werewolf, inviting others to a fight. He bent and picked up the arm when none took his challenge, then walked toward the cave, munching on his new prize. When the volatile creature reached the entrance, Logan called him over. He walked right up to the leader and stood, still biting large chunks from the tiny arm. "I won it. I will not give it up," he said defiantly.

"First, if I wanted it, I would take it. Second, if I told you to put it down, you would. Fortunately for you, Sebastian, the arm means nothing to me, and I'm going to let the insult slide," Logan said.

The creature relaxed a bit, but Heinsvick knew that such a confrontation could not go unpunished in front of the camp. As soon as he saw the beast relax, Logan struck impossibly fast, jumping from his seat and punching him in the mouth. Sebastian was stunned as Logan stood toe to toe with him, muscles corded in his neck and chest puffed out.

"Stand down, Sebastian, or things will go badly for you," Logan said.

Sebastian looked around the camp and saw most of the pack waiting for his next move. The scene stole his bravado, and to symbolize to everyone observing that he was obedient to the werewolf leader, he got on one knee and held up the half-mauled arm to Logan.

"Good. Rise, my loyal hunter," Logan said, reclaiming his seat and dismissing the offering with a wave of his hand.

Sebastian, shocked at his good fortune, took another large bite from the arm, this time with a piece of bone, which he crunched and rolled around in his mouth. Logan sat and watched, waiting for the right time to speak. His silence seemed to make Sebastian more uncomfortable as the minutes passed. Finally, he said, "So you do not want the arm, my lord. What is it that you desire of me?"

"Tell my honored guest of the time you saw the raven mother."

Sebastian regarded Heinsvick for the first time, so wrapped up in the confrontation with Logan that he hadn't even noticed him. His nostrils flared, and he leaned in to better smell the guest. "You smell of death, yet your flesh doesn't rot," he growled in disgust.

"Relax, Sebastian. This one is beyond you, and you would do well just to answer the question."

"What sort is he?"

"A vampire lord—and quite powerful. Now tell us of the raven mother."

Sebastian seemed to come to his senses then, and Heinsvick even picked up a touch of fear in his voice when he spoke. Nevertheless, he remained in his werewolf form, as were all the others, except Logan. Their appearance didn't bother the vampire, as he could decipher the words quickly enough between the snarls and growls.

"The child was a raven mother. Do not doubt my words."

"Wait—a child? How can this be, if she was a raven mother?" Heinsvick asked in confusion.

"A raven mother is born a raven mother. It is only a term given to the most powerful ravenkin and does not imply that she is an actual mother or even of adult age," Logan said. "Continue, Sebastian."

The creature took a step toward Heinsvick and seemed to look off into space, the half-eaten arm dropped to the ground, and his arms hung limply beside him as he recalled the event. "Boris, my brother, and I were hunting near a human settlement. There were young ones about, which offered fresh meat for the taking. We decided a late-evening snack was just what we needed to start the night of hunting. So we stalked in, taking the shape of wolves as we did. We saw two children and an old, dried-up woman—all three unprotected.

"We made our way to them, but something was wrong with one of the juveniles; she was not afraid. Boris wouldn't listen to me to turn back and leave them be. He paid the price, as the child summoned an unkindness of ravens as I have ever seen. I watched as they pecked away Boris's flesh, starting with his eyes. I dragged the old one away, but I'll never forget the look on the raven mother's face. She was not afraid, and Boris was dead!"

"How old was the girl?" Heinsvick asked excitedly.

"How would I know?"

"Your best guess."

"A few years, maybe."

"How many years ago did this encounter occur?" Heinsvick asked eagerly.

"Maybe a dozen."

"So it's reasonable to believe that the child is less than twenty years of age!" Heinsvick said, more to himself than to anyone else.

"I don't know, and I don't care. But mark my word, vampire: she is a raven mother. So I'll take my leave now, my lord?" Sebastian asked Logan, obviously hoping business with the vampire was at its end.

Logan looked at Heinsvick, who nodded and waved his hand at Sebastian. Logan in turn nodded to the creature, dismissing him. Sebastian issued one final low growl to the vampire, picked up his elf arm, and walked away, deep into the cave.

"So did that answer your questions?" Logan asked him.

"Where did this occur?"

"Near a small settlement, very close to your home of Novafontera—a human town called Oldorburg. I made sure to study that place and mark it well. None of my pack are allowed to go anywhere near it, assuming we ever find ourselves in that part of the world again."

"Yes, I know of this place—a small town, by all accounts! If this girl ends up being the prize the priestess wants, then I will have my Emiline once more, and I will pay you well for the information, old friend."

Both men stood then and said their goodbyes. What started as a trip to find and slay the nasty Matilda had suddenly turned into one of hope. There now was a strong possibility that he could locate the offspring of Kane. If so, Heinsvick would soon have his Emiline back. He left the werewolf camp in a hurry; he had much work to do.

CHAPTER 8

TEST OF FAITH

Greyson Kavince sat in Berro's quarters, high in the temple of Plath. The older priest discussed the coming journey Greyson would take, the trip that Plath required of him. He had been preparing for this adventure for the last six years, ever since his ordeal in the holy caves. In two weeks, his wanderlust would begin with his friend Darian, and they would live the rest of their lives traveling the world. His mind was on those coming sights and experiences, so as Berro told him of the importance of experiencing his life fully, he was thinking about the exotic women he would meet and court.

Various religious artifacts filled the room, from sculptures to tomes, tapestries, and parchments. Berro, the oldest of the high priests and probably the wisest, had summoned Greyson to his quarters as a formality. Greyson knew that it was a religious ritual that all young priests went through more than an informative meeting. It was supposed to enlighten him about what Plath expected from his journeys, but ever since his experience in the caves, Greyson felt he had a firm grasp of what his god desired of him.

So instead of listening to the old priest, he daydreamed of things to come and of a particular woman he would see later that evening. At only eighteen years of age, he had already developed quite a reputation as an excellent lover. He'd slept with eight different women over the last year—four of them married. His conscience weighed on him a little over that minor betrayal, but he felt that Plath wanted him to share his gift with as many women as possible, and he planned to. So as Berro spoke, his mind wandered.

"… and so, my son, the time has come for the prodigy to leave Tara," the old priest said, his words falling on deaf ears.

Karla would be waiting at their usual rendezvous spot between Tara and Attins, in the old abandoned barn.

"As you explore the world and …"

She would probably be wearing the mostly transparent white dress that he loved so much.

"… don't forget to recruit new members to the order …"

Her long dark hair would be down around her shoulders, her blue eyes reflecting the raw lust of her thoughts.

"Oh yeah," Greyson whispered huskily, his thoughts betraying him.

Berro looked up from the Tome of Plath, his spectacles hanging on the bridge of his overly large nose. Berro stared knowingly at him, and Greyson knew his daydreaming would now land him in trouble. His cheeks flushed, and he squirmed in his seat under that stern gaze. Berro closed the holiest of books and sat back in his chair. He reached up and removed the tiny glasses and smiled. "Greyson, you are one of a kind, son, and I want you to have an incredible journey. I know all these formalities bore you, and I will spare you from any further readings."

"Thank you, master Berro," Greyson said and nodded, trying to regain some dignity.

"I have watched you grow into a young man, and I think it's time that you lost your virginity. That's the first step, after all, to become a complete servant of Plath."

Greyson held back the chuckle as best he could, not wanting to insult the old priest. He had lost his virginity almost a year ago. But if Berro was going along this train of thought, Greyson wanted to know what he had in mind. "Yes, I think that would be a wise first step. How may this be accomplished?"

"I have already worked out the details of this most sacred ritual. You and Darian will travel to Attins to join the Festival of Harvests, an annual celebration of the fall crops, in seven more nights. There will be many available women there for you to choose from. Let Darian's wisdom guide you to the right one. I simply ask that you don't develop feelings for whomever you choose. It's easy to do the first time, but it's a burden that you and Darian can't afford. It's difficult to travel with a wife."

Again stifling a smile, Greyson nodded. So the temple's highest-ranking priest had no idea that Greyson had lost his virginity months earlier? Perhaps his secret was safe, then, and the affairs wouldn't come to haunt him before he left Tara.

"Greyson, in two weeks, you will leave our little community and travel the world." Berro sat back and sighed, deep in thought. "I remember the day I began my travels, and I assure you it will be a wonderful time in your life. It was bittersweet because I never saw my parents again. That's the trade-off for worshipping the most powerful of gods; you simply leave home, never to return."

Greyson had never considered that before. Berro and the other elders of the temple were most likely in their last decade of life, and it dawned on him that he would never see any of them again once he left. He sat up, suddenly understanding the reason for this meeting. It wasn't crucial to Greyson or Plath; it was essential to Berro, who was trying to say goodbye. Greyson cursed himself for not recognizing that up-front. He loved the man, and he had been the closest thing to a father he had ever known. In two weeks, he would say goodbye forever.

"I'll miss you, Berro. You've been like a father to me."

Berro smiled, his eyes watering up. "I want you to have something." He reached into his pocket and produced in the palm of his hand what appeared to be a tiny metal charm. He extended his arm to Greyson, revealing a small piece of silver in the shape of a tree. Greyson looked at it, confused, not understanding its significance.

"It's a good luck charm, my son," Berro said. "This little trinket was given to me when I first started my life's journey. It has brought me tremendous luck, and I want to bestow that good fortune on you."

Greyson took the tiny tree charm and held it up in the morning sun, where it reflected the golden rays like a small beacon from his god. He smiled and put it in his pocket. "Thank you, Berro. I appreciate the gesture, and I will treasure it forever."

"Good, but you should know that it's magical in nature."

Suddenly more interested, Greyson asked, "How so?"

"With a simple command word, that little trinket will become a giant oak, fully fifty feet tall! This activation works once and only once."

Confused, Greyson asked, "You mean it can become a tree permanently?"

Berro, understanding his confusion, chuckled and said, "Yes, I suppose it's a useless magical item, for I have never found the need to summon a giant tree! However, I do think it has given me a blessed and bountiful life, and I'm passing that on to you."

"Thank you, Berro."

"By the way, the magical phrase is Arbos."

"I'll remember," Greyson said with a smile, standing, assuming the meeting was at its end.

Berro stood, and they embraced for many moments, both fighting back tears. Greyson was ready to experience the world but would miss his old mentor. He would miss all of them. And in turn, the high priests would miss him sorely.

Greyson broke the embrace and held Berro at arm's length with a tearful smile. "I will say goodbye before I leave … to you and the other elders—do not doubt. I will never forget your instructions."

"Good. I will look forward to and at the same time dread that goodbye."

Greyson nodded, but before he left Berro's office, he had to ask one final question. "Father, may I ask something that I have always wondered about since I was young?"

"Of course. What it is, Greyson?"

"Well, your office has many scrolls, books, and other tomes, and you have shared most of those with me. However, that one scroll on top of your bookshelf has always remained in its protective glass case. You have never once spoken of it."

Berro seemed to know which scroll he referred to without even turning to regard it. The dusty case confirmed that the scroll had remained untouched for many years. "It is a scroll of returning. I will probably use it once you leave us because the purpose of my ministry will come to an end at that point."

"A scroll of returning?" Greyson asked, not recognizing the name.

"Yes, once read, it will take me, and only me, to a designated place halfway around the world. It will take me home."

"Only you?"

"Yes, or whoever reads it. I have been saving it for the day I would return home and live out my final years. I look forward to returning; it has been a very long time."

Greyson smiled and nodded once more, satisfied with the tale of the mysterious scroll. He quickly left Berro's office, and his hand went to his pocket and fingered the tiny tree token. He was excited to begin his journey, but realizing that he was leaving home for good made him feel a deep sadness. Thoughts of sexy Karla soon cured that.

~

The small town of Attins was decorated with banners and littered with carts full of harvest goods as tents and vendors crammed the streets. Performers abounded, from jugglers to magicians to musicians, and the spirits of the townsfolk soared as they celebrated their fall harvest. It was an annual celebration the small town enjoyed and was the sight that met Matilda when she entered the small community seven days after leaving Nesin.

Garyn, the high priest, second only to Matilda, accompanied her this very evening. As with all the priests of Marnelphion, Garyn was very eccentric and purely evil, but no one suspected a thing as they walked right into the town and blended in with the gathering mass. Matilda wore her brown locks down, and her almond eyes showed nothing but an innocent woman who'd come to enjoy the festival with her rather odd-looking but harmless boyfriend. They found a lady selling flowers, and Garyn bought one for Matilda and put it in her hair. The couple held hands and made their way through the vendors, seemingly to enjoy the festival. It was all an illusion, for their true intentions were to measure the small town's military prowess. Cerus's small army remained a mile north, awaiting their word.

As the sun set, they found themselves in a small tavern, enjoying a meal and drink. The two pseudolovers sat at a table near the window, watching the celebration as the night began to take hold. Lanterns and several braziers lit up as the festival crept into the night.

"This is a perfect start to our world domination. These people are defenseless," Matilda whispered.

Garyn smiled wickedly, nodding in agreement. "I can't wait to show the world our power, starting with this pathetic speck on the map."

Matilda nodded and quickly became lost in thoughts of all the wondrous glories Marnelphion would bestow on them. This small town was only the beginning, just a tiny step in a journey that would lead to her ruling the world next to him. She smiled as she gazed out the window at the fools who were just hours away from being destroyed. They were ignorant of the immediate danger, and if they knew what tortures awaited them, they would all flee in terror.

Then something caught her eye. Outside on the street, a gathering of rather giddy young women started to form near one of the tents. These women all looked young, probably under twenty years of age, and it would be correct to call them girls instead of women, Matilda thought to herself. They wore summer dresses reflecting the fall colors—orange, brown, and red—and wore crowns of flowers in their hair. Moreover, they had their faces painted in a way that might attract a suitor—almost whorish, she thought. It was quite a sight, and Matilda quickly became very interested in the spectacle. "That gathering of young women—what do you make of it, Garyn?"

"Looks like a group of young whores to me, my lady."

Matilda shook the simple observation away. "No, they're gathering for something special. We need to investigate the matter; we must be ever watchful for Kane's child to fall into our lap. All of them are in the appropriate age range."

Suddenly realizing what she was getting at, he quickly stood and said, "I'll find the nature of this gathering. Do not doubt, my lady." With that, he made his way to the door and exited the tavern, and she lost sight of him soon after that. She turned her attention back to the girls and studied their movements as their number soon doubled to about a dozen. They grew more excited as they gathered and peered off into the distance. She craned her neck to see where they were looking, but all she could see was the dark side of the mountain and the rolling hills that led into the town. Were they waiting on something to happen or perhaps waiting on a person?

She became more intrigued by the minute, and when she saw Garyn come back in, he had an older woman escorting him to the table. She was probably in her sixties, with long silver hair, dressed in clothing similar to that of the young women gathering outside the window. "This is my new friend Ruthie," Garyn said with a wicked smile.

Matilda knew by his look that he had used his charming spell to befriend the old lady that quickly. "Hello. Please sit down," Matilda said in her softest, friendliest voice.

"Thank you, young lady," Ruthie replied, taking one of the two unoccupied chairs at the table. Garyn sat down in the other one.

"Would you like something to drink?" Matilda asked.

"That's very sweet of you, but I can't drink this night. I'm in charge of the girls," she said, nodding toward the gathering of young women.

"I'm sorry—we're new here. My love and I are thinking of moving to Attins to start a family," Matilda said, reaching across the table to take Garyn's hand. "Can you please tell me what these young women are doing?"

"Oh, you two are quite precious, aren't you?" Ruthie giggled.

Garyn and Matilda looked into each other's eyes, playing the role of two lovers very well, feeding the lie.

"The girls are preparing for tonight—the first night of the harvest festival, of course," Ruthie answered. Then, as if remembering that she should be out there, orchestrating the gathering, she got up to leave, a confused and panicked look suddenly on her face.

"Wait!" Matilda said. "Just a few more questions. Then we'll let you get back to your work."

Ruthie stared at her, confounded by the demand, until Garyn said, "Ruthie, please sit back down. We're all friends here."

Ruthie looked at the evil priest, and she smiled as she seemed to recognize him for the wonderful friend he was. "Of course, of course, how thoughtless of me. Now what is it that you asked, young lady?"

"What are you doing with these young girls?"

"Oh, it's wonderful, and I'm so glad the two of you get to experience this night with me. You see, on the first night of the harvest festival, the daughters who wish to become pregnant gather at this tent. There, they will entertain suitors and offer themselves to any well-bred young man, with their parent's permission, of course. Also, it's considered very lucky to conceive on this night, and doing so not only blesses the town but blesses the family for the coming year."

"So parents give up their daughters for this ritual?" Matilda asked, amused at the whole thing.

"Oh yes. As I said, the gods smile upon those who conceive this night. Parents will readily give up their daughters for such a blessing."

"Sounds perfectly perverted," Garyn said with a smirk.

"Oh, no, it's quite honorable—you'll see!" Ruthie said.

"So why do the girls keep looking to the east, toward that mountain?" Matilda asked.

Ruthie followed the direction of Matilda's pointing finger, then smiled once more. "That's in the direction of Tara, where the priests live."

"Priests?"

"Yes, young lady, there's a small community of priests up that mountain, and their prodigy is coming this night to celebrate with the young women."

"What do you mean, prodigy?" Matilda asked.

"The young priest of Tara. His name is Kavince, and he's supposed to be the most powerful of the young priests. Tara announced he would come and would help any young woman try to conceive this very night as he takes his first steps into manhood."

Garyn laughed. "I'll assist with that as well!"

"Oh, no, you're in love with this lovely woman—remember?" Ruthie asked, almost in a panic.

"Oh, yes, of course. I was simply joking," he answered, trying to recover from the accidental slip. Matilda gave him a sour look, and he glanced down in shame.

"Besides, being impregnated by a priest of Tara is a blessing in itself! Their god encourages sexual activity among his priests, and to mate with one and have a child is a special blessing indeed. Especially if that priest is a prodigy!" Ruthie stood again, realizing she should be outside. "I must go. I'm sorry, but I'm needed!"

Matilda glanced outside, and now about twenty young women gathered, but one stood out to her, dressed in solid white, unlike all the other girls. "Wait, Ruthie! One more question!" Matilda said louder than she'd meant to.

"Yes, dear. Spit it out. Come, come!" the old lady said.

"The girl in the white—why is she dressed differently?"

Ruthie leaned over the table, looking through the window, studying the gathered mass of girls. "Well, solid white means she's a virgin. Oh, yes, that's the new girl. Just came into town last week."

"Are her parents here?"

The older lady suddenly looked very sad and shook her head slowly. "No, I'm afraid she's orphaned. An ogre attack killed her parents years ago."

"She can celebrate this night even though her parents aren't here to bless the joining?"

"Of course. She has the free will to participate if she's an orphan. She needs the blessing more than the others, I would think. Well, I must be off. Have a most wonderful night!" With that, she hurried away. Garyn was about to stop her, but Matilda shook her head, not seeing any point in further questions.

"This is perfect, Garyn! I want you to go to Cerus and inform him to invade at dawn. Tell him there's no resistance, plenty of slave potentials, and a good number of sacrificial candidates for the offering. There are also food stocks for this winter. Attins is a gold mine of riches for us."

Garyn got up to leave, but Matilda grabbed his arm. "Also, make sure he invades the community of priests up the mountain. Advise him to strike there first because they'll be the bigger threat. Leave none of the priests alive. Then Attins will be easily taken."

"Yes, my lady. I'll leave at once," Garyn said and turned to leave.

"Wait!" Matilda said, standing from the table, and Garyn turned to regard her.

"The virgin," she said with a nod toward the gathered girls.

"Yes, what of her?"

"I want you to take her, unharmed, to Cerus. She could be the child of Kane, and we'll gather all potential sacrifices as we travel. I'll seek this prodigy of Tara out to see if he is a candidate as well." She looked back toward the girls and saw the nervousness creeping across the virgin's face. "She is roughly my size. Before you leave, bring her to me, deep into the woods, behind this very building. I need her dress."

Garyn smiled evilly, catching on to what Matilda had in mind.

~

Greyson and Darian made their way from Tara to Attins just after sunset. Greyson had used his powers from Plath to light his holy symbol, wearing it comfortably around his neck. The light from it provided more than enough light for the two to see, and they sang a song to their god as they made their merry trip from high up on the mountain. They could hear the town's bustle and see the festival's lights even as they left their home. Soon the smell of pies and bread filled their nostrils, urging them on at a faster pace. Neither carried a weapon or a care in the world.

Darian draped an arm around Greyson's shoulder and said, "This is a night you'll never forget, my young friend! The sights, the sounds, the memories, the ladies! You'll become a man after this very night, my young prodigy!"

Greyson laughed but couldn't deny that he was very excited about the possibilities of this night. "You know I'm no virgin, right?"

"Shhh, you don't want Berro to learn of your indiscretions, do you?" Darian said, looking over his shoulder to make sure no one was close enough to hear.

Greyson laughed once more. "I haven't disappointed him yet, and I don't plan to. As far as he knows, I'm a virgin for the next hour or so."

The two kept up their comfortable pace, and soon the town's festivities, many lights, and sounds came into focus. Greyson and Darian were still a good half mile up on the mountainside, but the trees thinned there so they could view the town unhindered. Jugglers and musicians filled the streets, and the vendors with their baked goods and raw vegetables were abundant.

"I think I could use a nice slice of apple pie as we evaluate who you'll lose your virginity to," Darian said, rubbing his belly.

"I'd rather just begin courting, if it's all the same. I want to see how many women I can *enlighten* before the night is through."

"Relax, my friend. The last time I attended the festival, I was with five women in one night. They are all begging to sleep with us because they feel it's lucky to become pregnant this night."

"So you're a father?" Greyson asked.

Darian stopped at that point, his eyes wide. He stood there for a few moments, looking into the distance. Then he finally said, "I … don't … know."

He turned his head slowly to Greyson, his eyes still wide with wonder. At that point, they both started laughing so hard that Greyson doubled over, holding his stomach, and Darian soon had tears rolling down his cheeks. After they composed themselves, they turned back toward the town to begin their journey once more. However, they both stopped at the sight of a woman dressed in a see-through white dress only twenty feet in front of them. She was beautiful, by all accounts, and was slowly walking toward them. Oddly enough, neither had heard her approach.

"How did she sneak up on us so easily?" Greyson whispered.

"I don't know, but luck is with you," Darian whispered back.

"What do you mean?"

"She's wearing white, so she's a virgin."

Greyson smiled and put a hand on his friend's shoulder. "Stay here, my friend. I'll handle this."

Greyson made his way toward the woman, and Darian could only smile and watch the spectacle. At only eighteen years of age, Greyson was already one of the most fantastic lovers Tara had ever generated. He loved the art of seduction and had become quite proficient over the last year.

As Greyson approached, he could see the woman's breasts through the dress, and he knew that this one would be his first of the night. She was beautiful, with brown curly hair and large brown eyes. Her features were delicate, and she appeared timid. The only thing he found strange was the fact that she appeared older, almost middle aged. He didn't question his good fortune, though, and walked right up to her with a welcoming smile. "Good evening, my lady," he said with a bow.

"Hello, good sir," she replied with a slight curtsy.

He extended his hand, and she gingerly took it. He kissed her hand and gave her a quick look as he did. He couldn't help but notice the red in her cheeks. She was shy. Perfect. "I am Greyson Kavince, a follower of Plath."

Her eyes went wide at the mention of his name. "You're the prodigy of Tara?"

He smiled. "You've heard of me?"

"Oh yes," she said. "Your reputation precedes you, Greyson Kavince."

Greyson looked around curiously. "So why are you out here on the side of this mountain, all alone?"

"I have come to meet you … to have a chance—I mean, before you meet the other girls," she stammered, her face turning bright red.

Greyson smiled. "You will be rewarded for your cunning. What is your name, my lady?"

"I am Matilda … of Attins."

He gently took her hand and led her to Darian, sitting on a stump, waiting patiently. "Darian, this is the beautiful Matilda, and she has come to greet us as an emissary of Attins."

Darian stood and bowed. "Greetings, Matilda."

"We have some things to discuss," Greyson said to him. "Perhaps you can make your way into town and I'll meet you there soon?"

Darian winked at his friend. "Of course. I hope your meeting is productive, young Greyson Kavince!" Darian began singing as he started away to Plath once more, and soon his holy symbol lit up, spilling a soft light all around him as he made his way down the mountainside.

Once he was gone, Greyson turned to Matilda and said, "Come with me. There's a barn not too far from here."

"A barn with animals?"

"No, a barn deserted for ages. I have a special place there where we can get to know each other." He took her hand and began to make his way to the old barn that he and Karla had used just the night before. It was the perfect place, especially to take a virgin. Of course, he still thought she was a little old for a virgin, but he wasn't questioning his good luck.

"You have a place?" she asked, trying to keep up with his pace.

"Of course."

"So you've done this before?"

He stopped and smiled, turning toward her. He grabbed her shoulders and pulled her close. "Many times," he whispered only inches from her face. "I will be gentle. I promise."

He smiled once more and then started walking again. Matilda tried to keep up with him, but he was practically dragging her. If he had paid attention and seen her face at that moment, he would have realized the woman was puzzled. However, with his mind focused on finding the barn and bedding her, Greyson never noticed her budding anger. "There it is!" he exclaimed, looking at an old run-down building roughly fifty yards ahead of them.

"Come," he said, taking her hand once more and walking briskly to his goal. Once there, he opened the large barn door and ushered her in. He looked back to make sure no one had followed them, and once he was satisfied they were alone, he shut the door and reached to bar it from the inside.

Matilda stood watching, her arms over her chest. "You are but a child," she finally said.

Her words caught him off guard as he eased the locking bar into place. As he made his way to her, confusion crossed his face, and he gave her a suspicious look. He walked around her, admiring her body through the transparent dress. She stood with her arms crossed over her chest, an equally dubious look on her face.

"I am no child—I assure you. So why does my age matter to you? I think you're too old to be a virgin, yet I don't question you."

Her eyes went wide, and her face soured. "What do you mean, too old? And who said I was a virgin?"

"Your dress … all white means you're a virgin. I'm familiar with your customs. You're not too old for me, but I don't believe you to be a virgin."

"Well—" she began, but his mouth muffled her words as he kissed her deeply. She tried to push away, but he was forceful when he realized she wasn't fully committed to the struggle. Finally, she slowly gave in and began kissing him back. After sharing the passionate kiss, he broke away from her and took a step back, studying her face. "You are beautiful, and I will make love to you as you have never experienced before."

"I—" she began once more, but before she could finish, he was pulling her toward a ladder that led to the barn's loft.

A million thoughts entered his head at that point. Her kiss had been different; it intrigued him. The potential passion this woman promised sparked a fire deep in his stomach. He was very sexual, and he knew a kiss like that promised a night of delights. So he followed her up the ladder and had a good look up her dress as he did so. She was older, maybe, but her body had aged nicely. He was excited to have a closer look.

Once at the top, he escorted her to a soft bed with blankets that he and Karla had recently used. Greyson took one of the blankets, wrapped his holy symbol in it, and placed it near the bed. The covered medallion created a soft dull light that seemed very inviting. Matilda complied by slowly undressing, and Greyson did the same. Neither spoke as they did, lost in each other's eyes. Soon they fell into the bed together in a passionate embrace. He soon learned that Matilda was a bit of a masochist, enjoying a certain amount of pain with her lovemaking. He was happy to oblige.

He felt as if he knew what she wanted from him, almost as if she were a dance partner and he knew her moves. It felt as if he were looking into her soul. He had never experienced anything like that before, and she seemed to embrace the ecstasy as he ravished her. He wasn't rough initially, but as she became more submissive, he took the liberties she appeared to desire. Their lovemaking was genuine and authentic, and the connection for both of them was impossible to ignore. In total, they made love for five hours, exhausting themselves.

Greyson never made it into town that night, as he and Matilda finally collapsed into each other's arms and drifted to sleep in the early-morning hours. The last thought he had before rest took him was that this woman was someone he could cherish, that Plath had intended on him finding her. He decided then that he would ask her to come with him when he and Darian began their journey in a week. Matilda was a keeper, his soul mate, and he would make that offer, despite Berro's warning.

~

He awoke to her scent and, as he slowly opened his eyes, found himself nestled in the scruff of her neck. She was still sound asleep as the rays of the early-morning sun began to creep into the barn. There was a slight chill in the air, but the heavy blankets kept the lovers warm. He snuggled closer to her, and his hands began to explore, ready for round two of their lovemaking. She stirred slightly and accepted his advances, reaching her hand back to play with his hair. The thought popped back into his head immediately: *This one's a keeper!* He thought of the advice Berro had given him about how he shouldn't get attached to the first woman he seduced. He found it ironic that he had done just that, even though Matilda wasn't technically his first. Perhaps that was Plath's way of warning him, but he quickly dismissed the thought and moved into a position on top of her.

He looked into her eyes as she blinked the sleep away and found his heart racing. The chemistry they shared left little doubt that they should be a couple, but looking at her now in the morning light, he realized just how beautiful she was. Her look was simple and innocent, and he found himself lost in her almond eyes. He knew in his heart that she would come with him if he asked and that he could also convert her to a disciple of Plath. The possibilities swarmed his head as they began their lovemaking again, gentle at first but after a few moments very rough, just like the previous night. She enjoyed her lovemaking rough, and if that made her happy, he was willing to oblige. Everyone had a vice, and hers was just a little stranger than most. He would grow to like it, though—he had no doubt.

As they became entwined, there was a knock on the barn door, followed by a faint voice. "Greyson! Greyson! Are you in there?"

It was Darian. Greyson tried to rise, but Matilda pulled him down and climbed on top of him, holding him down and putting her weight entirely on him. She smiled at him as she continued her assault on his body. "You must satisfy me first," she said, a look of ecstasy on her face.

"It's Darian," Greyson said. "Something is wrong! I can tell it in his voice."

Again the cry came louder as Darian moved from the barred door to the open loft door near their bed. Of course, this door was on the second floor, and he couldn't enter or even look in, but his voice was more evident now as he stood right below it. "Greyson, wake up! There is trouble at Tara! Are you there?"

Greyson's eyes went wide, and he tried to move, but again she stopped him, a sexy look on her face as she neared the end of their lovemaking. He could have pushed her off him, and for a moment, he thought that was what she wanted, for him to be rough with her. He thought better of it, though, and decided to let her finish. He recommitted to the process and soon had her to a screaming orgasm.

Darian's calls continued, and Greyson called back. "Just a minute, Darian! Let me get dressed. I'll meet you at the door in a moment!"

"Tara doesn't have a moment. We must go now!"

Matilda slumped over on him, pinning him to the bed. At this point, he forced himself up. However, she still resisted, making it a difficult task for him. She didn't want him to go, and the pout on her face made that clear as he gently but forcefully moved her off him. Finally, he gathered his clothes and threw them on as Matilda wrapped the sheets around her and sat up.

"Stay with me. I need more," Matilda said and licked her lips.

She was insatiable, and he loved it. He paused while tying his boot and considered climbing back into bed with her. She was so sexy—unlike any woman he'd ever met. Was this how all women were outside Tara, or was she unique? She ran her fingers through her hair with one hand and beckoned him with a curled finger with the other. He began unlacing his boot to rejoin her, suddenly unable to resist the temptation, but when the sound of screams started drifting from Tara, he snapped out of the trance. He shook his head, berating himself for delaying, and hastily laced up his boots.

"Matilda, I have to go! Something is wrong at home!" He had his breeches and boots on and his shirt in hand as he started down the ladder. "Stay here, and—" he began, but his thoughts became moot as she was already out of bed, slipping on her see-through dress.

"I'm coming," she said with finality.

He didn't question it, having no time to argue with her. He nodded and quickly descended the ladder and threw the heavy bar off the door. He opened it expecting to find Darian waiting for him. But as he put his shirt on, he realized his friend had already left and was halfway up the steep hill to Tara. Then Greyson saw Tara burning. "Oh no!" he cried, the severity of the situation finally sinking in.

"I must go!" he yelled, but he turned to find Matilda next to him. "Stay here, please!" he demanded as he saw how delicate she looked in that dress and his concern for her safety came to the forefront of his thoughts.

She reluctantly stayed, a worried look on her pretty face. Greyson didn't have time to tell her goodbye or even consider that perhaps this would be the last time he'd ever see her. He pushed those thoughts to the far recesses of his mind as he turned and ran up the hill behind his friend. He could no longer see Darian or Tara but could still see the smoke billowing into the sky. His mind raced as the screams grew nearer. It was no simple fire; Tara was under attack! He considered the fact that he had no weapons, no armor, and hadn't prayed this morning to Plath. How effective would his minimal powers be if he hadn't even prayed during the sunrise?

He finally crested the ridge that leveled out to the flat part of the mountainside where Tara sat, nestled between the thick pines common to the area. Nothing could have prepared him for the sight that awaited him there. All the homes and buildings were on fire except the large temple, which remained intact. He considered this a strange fact, but he couldn't process the information at the moment. There was too much there that his young mind would never forget. The carnage would become a permanent fixture in his memories.

To Greyson's horror, an invading army was slaughtering Tara's people, who fought bravely against the attack. The small community had no enemies, and he couldn't determine a reason for such an attack. The invaders were dressed in dark chain mail and brandished large spears. He couldn't fully see the temple from his location because of the thick vegetation and full pines that partially blocked the view, but he decided to make his way there. That way, he could find the high priests and perhaps together they could quickly form a defense.

He made his way through the thick vegetation, catching glimpses of the giant temple. There was no smoke coming from that area, to his relief. His mind wandered back to Matilda, and he hoped that she'd stayed back at the barn. He already felt a connection there and didn't want anything to happen to her. He also worried about being spotted by the invaders. He had no way to defend himself. He stopped at the edge of the tree line, still out of sight, but could see the temple now. There was absolutely no activity coming from the place, which made no sense to him. Where were the high priests? He turned briefly toward the center of the community, where the buildings and homes burned. That seemed to be the focal point of the attack. Smoked rolled in from the burning buildings, reducing his vision. He could still see people fighting to defend their homes, people he had grown up with, friends, family, and even lovers. All of them fell to the cruel men with the spears. He had to do something.

He couldn't tell how many invaders there were because of the thick smoke, but he could tell that Tara quickly fell to those vicious men. The sounds of the wounded and dying were as thick in the air as the smoke itself. He decided he would continue on to the temple and find help. So he made a run for it, or at least began to, until he saw the awful vision that brought him to his knees. The temple grounds held a large orchard of apple trees. These were the trees he used to climb as a child, the same trees that he'd harvested many apples from over the years, the same trees he'd sat under many times, listening to Berro and the other elders teaching him the ways of Plath.

Now the scene was one of horror as all the pleasant memories of those trees quickly faded. Greyson's knees hit the ground, his eyes low, staring at the frosty grass. It took him a very long time to slowly raise his head and look at the carnage once again. He hoped that if he took his time, somehow it wouldn't be there—that perhaps what he'd first seen was an illusion. But he sadly discovered that was a false hope as his eyes took in the most horrific scene he could have possibly imagined.

Now those wonderful apple trees served as gallows for the priests of Plath. Dozens of them hung from the branches, their hands bound behind their backs and their faces bloated, eyes frozen in terror and pain, as thick ropes cut deep into their necks. Their bellies were cut wide, their entrails spilling out onto the ground. Greyson's whole life flipped upside down at that moment. His eyes absorbed the terrible nightmare, studying the faces of each of his brethren. So he had been wrong. Tara's buildings hadn't been the focal point of the attack; the temple had. The high priests were all dead. All he had ever known was lost.

Greyson was vaguely aware of enemies approaching him, but his attention was on the trees only. He was paralyzed with grief, knowing that his entire family was gone, their extraordinary and blessed lives having ended in horrible murders. Who were these men, and why had they done this? His eyes eventually found Berro and the other elders, Sebe, Jak, and Talis, their faces contorted in fear and pain. His heart broke, and tears came to his eyes as he tried to register the scene before him. A sudden rustling from behind brought him back to the moment, and he turned just in time to see the blunt end of a spear as it cracked the side of his head. He saw white as the pain shot through his temple, and he briefly felt himself falling backward. His world went black before he ever hit the ground, and he knew no more.

~

Greyson awakened to the sensation of being dragged across the hard ground. Someone had his feet and was pulling him roughly along. He squinted open his eyes, and the morning sun blinded him. He could vaguely see the hanging priests on the apple trees, and his mind recalled the terrible truth of the matter. He tried to blink away the sun and the pain shooting through his head but failed miserably. Finally, he closed his eyes and just relaxed, letting the person at his feet drag him across the temple lawn like a limp doll.

"We have another one, General Cerus," came the call from the man at his feet.

"Excellent work, soldier. Guard him as I deal with this other new arrival," was the response from a gruffer, somehow more evil-sounding voice.

His feet were dropped hard to the ground, rattling his body and sending shooting waves of pain through his head. He tried to regain his senses because he knew enemies surrounded him and knew that one of his brethren was in trouble. His life was at stake—he had to wake up!

Once more, Greyson slowly opened his eyes and saw the eerie trees, the priestly ornaments swaying from their branches. He looked at his feet, where two soldiers now stood, each witnessing the spectacle and wearing a sinister smile. Greyson followed their gaze and saw Darian. He was kneeling under a large branch, a rope tied tightly around his neck, the other end draped over the large tree branch and held by two other soldiers. A much larger man stood before him brandishing some kind of serrated dagger.

Greyson tried to sit up but found a boot on his chest and a spear leveled at his face by one of the wicked men at his feet, quite possibly the one who'd hit him with the blunt end of his spear. "Don't move, or I'll gut you, priest," the man said.

Greyson looked over toward Darian and briefly made eye contact with him. That one glance told him everything he needed to know about the situation. The look on his friend's face, knowing he was about to die, said it all. His life was forfeit, and he knew it; he was about to meet Plath. The look was not one of sadness but one of finality. He nodded slightly, his way of saying goodbye. Greyson returned the nod as best he could, but the effort made the pain in his head sear back to life.

The man with the blade stabbed it home straight through Darian's abdomen. Darian's eyes filled with tears, and his mouth contorted as he tried to cry out. The rope, tight around his neck, was already suffocating him, and he made no sound. As the dagger plunged home, Greyson yelled, "Noooo!" and began to sob, knowing that his friend was being murdered right in front of him. The large man who'd stabbed Darian, the one they'd referred to as Cerus, turned toward him with a smile, and he and the other two men shared an evil chuckle.

"Raise him!" Cerus ordered, and the men with the rope began to pull, raising Darian to his feet first, then completely off the ground. Cerus ripped the blade from the wound as Darian's feet left the grass, taking most of his entrails with it. They fell to the ground, and the priest became a dying ornament like all the others. Cerus had gutted all of them.

Greyson locked his eyes with Darian's for just a moment, long enough to watch the light fade from them. His friend was gone to be with Plath in the afterlife, and Greyson suddenly felt very alone. Darian was supposed to be his travel partner for life. They would have shared so many experiences, and would have lived a great and fruitful life together. Now there was nothing; his best friend was dead before the adventures had ever begun. This thought tore at Greyson's heart the most as the shocking scene continued to devastate him.

"Prepare him," Cerus said to the two guarding him as the rope wielders tied off the rope that secured the newest corpse to the trees.

The two men standing guard around him stuck their spears into the ground, and one lifted Greyson roughly to a kneeling position while the other fished around his backpack for a length of rope. Greyson swooned from the pain in his head and did his best to keep his balance. He noticed for the first time that he was more injured than he'd realized as blood trickled from his forehead and into one of his eyes. The crack with the spear had hurt him more than he'd thought. He fought the dizziness as Cerus approached him.

The giant warrior stood near seven feet tall, and his legs looked more like tree trunks to Greyson. The large man grabbed him by the hair and pulled hard, making Greyson look him in the face and making the pain in his head flare an angry white. "You are the last one, priest, and also appear to be the youngest. Are you ready to meet your pathetic god?"

Greyson looked him in the eye and tightened his lips. He wouldn't give the evil man the satisfaction of a response.

His stubbornness made Cerus laugh. "Have it your way, mighty priest! Bind him!" he said, moving a step back so his men could bind his prisoner's hands.

They'd cut a three-foot piece off the long rope, and one moved behind Greyson to tie his hands behind his back. The other one took Cerus's spot in front of him and quickly finished a tight noose. Greyson looked up at Darian one last time, feeling an overwhelming sadness for his friend. In just another week, they would have traveled the world together. They had planned to die in a temple somewhere on the other side of the world, surrounded by young priests, many years from now. They would have shared their stories of adventures and the many women they had experienced, and their stories would have been grand indeed! Now Darian was dead, and soon Greyson would follow. He tried to prepare his mind for death, tried to think of it as a positive thing somehow, for he would soon be with Plath—he had no doubt.

He thought of the caves during his trials a few years earlier as they pulled his hands roughly behind his back and placed the noose around his neck. The ordeal in those caves seemed like such a long time ago now. He had passed the tests of that holiest place and had believed he was indeed a prodigy of Plath. Now it all just seemed like a lie. He would end up hanging from a tree like all the other disciples of Plath. He was no prodigy; he had not saved the people of Tara—Plath's people.

The man behind him began to tie his hands together when a familiar voice broke the evil deed: "Stop!"

It was Matilda, and Greyson's heart sank. She hadn't listened to him. She'd followed him up the hillside and to her death. He thought of how protective he was over her already after just one lust-filled night together. She was vital to him, and now she would die with him. Thoughts of the two of them joining Plath in the heavens flashed briefly in his mind. It didn't seem such a bad fate. He opened his tired eyes and saw her walk right up to Cerus. None of the five men made a move, and the ones binding him stepped away. She moved down to him, took the noose, and removed the loose ropes from his hands. She stood in front of him and looked down, still wearing the see-through dress. She looked stunning, and he could still smell her sex.

"What is the meaning of this, Matilda? Exterminating the priests is my responsibility," Cerus said.

"Yes, and you've had your fun, I see," she said, looking at the many priests hanging from the trees.

Greyson's mind tried to register the turn of events. Did she know these men, and, worse, were they listening to her? Was she leading them? Cerus, the evilest of all, seemed to give her a lot of respect. Greyson slowly came to terms with the fact that she was part of the invasion. His heart raced as he tried to deny the truth, but his mind told him differently: She was evil. Their time together had been a farce.

Cerus seemed to grow impatient but allowed Matilda to take over the command of the cruel men. "You two, fetch some oil and a torch. Also, find Garyn and bring him here. I have a most special task for him," she said to the two soldiers who'd just assisted in Darian's murder.

The two men ran off immediately toward the burning buildings and the rest of the soldiers. The fighting was at its end, and the dead littered the streets, with survivors herded into a group. It was a strange sight for Greyson to behold, seeing his home burned to the ground. Soon Tara would have nothing left to suggest that it had once been a community rich with life.

Greyson could see several odd-looking men intermingled with the soldiers. There were no more than five or six of them, each wearing a black robe adorned with skulls. They were sinister in appearance, and he believed these men were somehow worse than the soldiers. Greyson sensed that they were behind the attack and that the soldiers were merely puppets used to carry out their evil deeds. The two men ran straight for one of these robed figures, and the man turned toward Matilda. He smiled and began approaching when he saw her, and the two soldiers ran off to gather her demanded supplies. Was Matilda in charge of all of them, even the strange-looking men?

His thoughts were interrupted by the low growl of Cerus's voice. "You reek of sex!" Greyson turned back toward the giant warrior to see that he now had Matilda by the shoulders, his massive spear stuck into the ground beside him. Greyson briefly thought of going for the weapon and skewering the man, but he also felt Cerus was baiting him to try just that.

Matilda didn't seem concerned that he had his hands on her or spoke in a threatening manner. Instead, she pointed to Greyson and said, "It was him. We spent the night together, and he satisfied me. He is a most excellent lover."

"What? This pathetic priest?" Cerus said, releasing her and grabbing his spear with a vicious yank that took a divot of grass with it.

She calmly stood in front of him, between him and Greyson, and slowly said, "Let me make this clear, Cerus. He is valuable to me, and I wish to keep him."

This turn of events gave Greyson a little hope that he might survive this horrible encounter. Cerus's gaze went from her to Greyson and back several times, his face contorted in rage, and the knuckles of his hand turned white as he clutched the handle of his great spear. Finally, seeing that Cerus would comply with Matilda's wishes and wanting to fight back any way he could after having witnessed the murder of his best friend, Greyson found the courage to say, "Yes, I pleasured her all night."

Matilda looked over her shoulder at him with a surprised look that quickly turned into a smile. Cerus could barely control himself, and

Greyson understood that the man was wounded to learn that Matilda had slept with him. "Eight times exactly … and once more this morning," Greyson said.

Matilda's eyes went wide—as did the smile on her face—and she stared at him in amazement. Greyson shrugged and smiled back. Cerus took a firm hand on her shoulder and turned her back to him. In the meantime, Garyn appeared and circled Greyson as if he were a shark stalking a defenseless seal. Greyson tried not to look at the strange man, but the evil stare bore a hole through him. The man she had referred to as Garyn simply walked around the trio, knowing that he shouldn't interrupt the conversation.

"You are my wife, and I forbid you to sleep with such a pathetic excuse of a man!" Cerus roared.

Suddenly Greyson's bravery dissipated like a cloud of smoke. "Wife!"

With reflexes as quick as a cat, Cerus was past Matilda and on Greyson too fast for his mind to register it. He suddenly regretted his words, understanding now that this man would have done more than gut him if Matilda weren't there to stop him. Cerus wrapped a giant hand around Greyson's throat and lifted him to his feet, and the grip was like steel. Greyson tried to pry the hand loose, using both of his, but to no avail. He was losing consciousness quickly, and his wounded head throbbed. But he refused to faint as he saw Darian's fresh corpse swinging gently from the branch behind Cerus's shoulder.

"I am Cerus the Grey, husband of Matilda and destroyer of men! You have disgraced me, and you will pay!" he spat in Greyson's face.

Matilda reached up and pried the fingers loose, and Greyson dropped to the ground, falling on his back. Again his head throbbed with the rush of blood pumping back to his brain. He moaned and held his wounded head, but Matilda was there to help him to a standing position. Greyson couldn't help but notice the strength in her small frame. He also couldn't help but take a peek through the sheer gown. He found her sexy and had sinful thoughts about her even as his life hung in the balance. Cerus didn't miss the glance he stole, making the man gnash his teeth.

"You are at a crossroads, Greyson Kavince," Matilda said, taking his head and gently turning it from Cerus to her. Their eyes met, and she then had his full attention. "You are a priest of a lesser god and should die for that blasphemy. However, I will give you hope, a chance to change your ways. You will have the opportunity to join us."

"Never!" Cerus yelled.

The anger Greyson saw on Matilda's face after Cerus's interruption frightened him. But of course there was a lot more to this woman than great sex. True, joining her would save his life, but what would be the repercussions?

"Don't contradict me, Cerus," she said. "You know the consequences of doing such a thing."

Greyson saw a hint of fear in the large man's eyes, which reminded him how little he knew about the tiny woman. His thoughts drifted again to the previous night and the time they'd shared. Then he recalled how she'd tried to keep him from leaving the barn just moments ago. Had she been trying to save him or just delaying his arrival to ensure Tara would fall? He watched on, lost in his thoughts, as she turned to the gathered soldiers, four in total now, as two returned with a lighted torch and a flask of oil to join the two already guarding him.

"Leave us, all of you!" Matilda said to the four men.

They took a quick look at Cerus, who made no move to contradict her, and they slowly left, leaving the four alone on the temple lawn. Garyn picked up the torch that the men had left on the ground near Greyson. Matilda likewise took the flask, removed the stopper, moved to Greyson, and looked deeply into his eyes. "This is the moment of truth, Greyson. Join us and become powerful—know eternity! Throw away your religious symbol and rebuke your god. It's the obvious choice, if you wish to live."

Greyson had no immediate response. He thought back to the caves again, to the zombie he had encountered, to the angel that had fed him, to the minotaur he had narrowly escaped. Most of all, he thought of the vision Plath had given him: the various women he would meet; the raven that dominated the picture; and, in the end, himself with demon horns. Greyson had felt Plath with him in that ordeal and felt that same presence now as Matilda asked him to deny the very god that centered his whole life.

"No," he said calmly, lowering his head and grasping his star symbol tightly.

Cerus moved to throttle the young priest, but Matilda stopped him with a wave of her hand. She took the flask, and Greyson thought she might douse him with it, but instead, she moved to Garyn and poured the thick liquid on his head, coating him with it. He didn't resist, only closed his eyes and relished the dousing.

"You see, Greyson, your god is weak. Take a look at the weaklings who hang from the trees! They lied to you! Plath is not the all-powerful god they told you he was. He is nothing compared to Marnelphion!"

"Marnelphion? I've never heard of this god," Greyson said, genuinely puzzled by the odd name.

"You will hear of him soon, my dear, for he is coming! On that day, I want you to be there by my side, witnessing the power of the ultimate god."

"A god of evil?"

"Evil or not, he is coming, and he will rule this world—all of it!" She approached him once more, leaving Garyn soaking in oil, holding a lit torch. Cerus took a step away from the fanatical priest, as if he expected something strange was about to transpire.

"Do you consider me evil?" Matilda asked Greyson. The look on her face was one of sincere concern. Perhaps she had never realized what evil was or that murdering a whole community was evil. The young priest shook his head and held his symbol before him.

"No, I don't. That's why you should join me! Together we will travel the world, and few will oppose us. You know we make a good team and should be together. So leave this warmongering fool and come with me."

"That's enough, Matilda!" Cerus yelled. "Let me gut him like all the other weaklings. He's even blasphemed against your god. Now hand him over!"

"Your god has no appeal to me," Matilda said. "If he was truly so powerful, how could he have let his flock die like this?" She waved her hand to the macabre trees. "He gave them no real power. This is power." She nodded toward Garyn.

The strange man's eyes went wide, and a smile crept across his face. He slowly held the torch up to his face, the flickering of the flame reflected in his crazy eyes. He brought the torch up to a cheek, and the oil smoked at first, then caught fire. It quickly spread and engulfed his entire head, and soon his whole body was burning. Greyson stepped back, awaiting the death screams that were sure to follow. The heat intensified, and all three had to take several steps away from the burning man. Yet there were no screams. The man burned, but he seemed unfazed by the flames.

He looked at Greyson and said, "Death to the nonbelievers!" He then turned and ran toward the temple, leaving flaming footprints in his wake. Greyson watched him go and understood that he would burn the temple to the ground. This fanatical fool was going to destroy the remnants of Tara. But instead of doing it with a torch, he would use his body and lose his life in the process of doing the dirty deed. A thought suddenly flashed in his mind—a talk that he'd had with Berro just a week before in his office.

"It is a scroll of returning," Berro had said.

"Returning?"

"Yes, once read … it will take me home."

"Only you?"

"Yes, or whoever reads it."

The scroll in Berro's office! That was his way out of this mess. Greyson had a chance to live, to survive this massacre. He had to reach that scroll somehow, but how could he, with Cerus blocking the way? His hopes diminished drastically as Garyn opened the door to the sanctuary and ran inside. Soon after, smoke billowed from a window on the ground floor.

Matilda came over to him and took his hand. "So what will it be? Marnelphion or Plath? Life or death?"

He held his symbol tight with one hand, feeling the power coursing through it, and squeezed her hand with the other one. A crash sounded from inside the temple, and a crazed laugh echoed from within it. Smoke billowed from several windows now as Greyson's hope slowly burned away. More important, the disgrace of his god was just too much for him to bear. Something inside him clicked, and the fear of death vanished. He was a disciple of Plath at that moment—he was a prodigy. He looked Matilda straight in the eye and very forcefully gave her an answer. "No. Plath is the only god for me. I will not join you."

The look on her face was one of hurt and rejection, and he thought for just a moment that she might consider joining him. However, the thought faded as she released his hand and turned away from him. "Very well. Have it your way, Greyson." She began to walk toward the smoldering homes where the soldiers were regathering. Cerus waited, not making a move as she walked. Finally, after many steps, she turned to look over her shoulder and gave Cerus specific instructions. Although Greyson fully expected to hear the words, they still stung him more than just a little: "String him up with the others."

Cerus moved quickly to fall on the helpless priest, but Greyson didn't notice. He was lost in communion with Plath, asking for the strength to defeat this monster and avenge his brothers' death. His holy symbol, the star of Plath, pulsed energy through his arm, and he unleashed it all at once. As it had been with the minotaur in the holy cave, his target was the eyes of his assailant. If Plath's light couldn't blind Cerus, then Greyson was indeed a dead man. He held the symbol up and concentrated all his energy on the large man's eyes.

There was a bright flash that lasted but a second, centered around Cerus's face. Greyson was moving then, not waiting to see whether the casting had any effect. He took a wide berth around the enraged warrior and proceeded with all speed toward the temple. Cerus blindly lunged at him, but Greyson was the faster and was already out of reach.

"Matilda!" Cerus yelled in frustration, rubbing and blinking his eyes to regain his vision. Matilda turned and saw Greyson moving with all speed toward the doomed temple. She smiled and shook her head once more, falling into her spell casting to defeat Greyson's magic. Cerus stood patiently, hearing her chant. His chest rose up and down as he breathed deeply, seemingly ready to explode with rage. Finally the spell took effect and her powerful magic quickly canceled Greyson's blinding light.

It took Cerus a few moments to regain his bearings after his vision returned. He found Matilda about forty yards in front of him, smiling. She pointed a tiny finger behind him, and he turned to see Greyson closing in on the temple door. He growled defiantly and lifted his colossal spear for a throw. The temple door was at least fifty yards away from where he stood, and the likelihood of a hit from this distance was minimal for most. Cerus wasn't like most warriors, though. His blood was that of Gorl, the god of war. No one could best him in battle, and his accuracy with a spear was uncanny even at fifty yards. He reared back with all his might and heaved the powerful weapon at the priest. His aim was true, and the spear traveled straight for Greyson's head.

As Greyson approached the temple, he could see flames licking the windows on the second floor now. The crazed priest had made it to that floor but was surely dead by now. Greyson glanced briefly up to the fourth floor, where this side of the building was made of glass, allowing the morning sun to bathe the room used for worship. The high priests' quarters and the scroll he desperately needed to find were on the back side of that floor.

He was at the door when a terrible sound broke his concentration. It was a sickening scream, and it came from behind him. It was awful; he couldn't even tell if it was from a human or an animal. Whatever it was, it was in pain—maybe in its death throes. He didn't want to look, but with one hand on the door handle, he did look over his shoulder in the direction of the awful noise. That's when he saw the spear flying straight for him. He managed to turn his body sideways, trying to make it as small as possible. The massive spear still hit him, but not directly, as it grazed his ribs, digging deep into his flesh and cutting him open. He screamed out and fell against the temple as the giant spear smashed through the front door, splintering it from its hinges.

Smoke billowed out of the broken door, and Greyson froze in fear and pain, holding his side, which was fast becoming wet with his blood. He looked from his blood-soaked hand to where he'd last seen Cerus. The giant man was standing in the same spot, having obviously thrown the massive spear from that great distance, and looked utterly enraged. The wail was still carried in the wind but was fast fading. He couldn't make out the source, but when Cerus looked up at Darian's corpse, Greyson could see that his friend's feet were jerking wildly. Then Cerus took out the wicked blade he had used to murder the priests and stabbed his friend again.

The kicking stopped, as did the wail, and it dawned on Greyson that his friend hadn't been dead. He'd saved his life by screaming that awful scream. Had he been alive with half his entrails lying on the ground?

Perhaps Plath had used his dying body to warn him of the attack? Either way, Darian had just saved his life, and he meant to make it count. Cerus was already running full speed toward the temple, which got Greyson moving quickly.

He dived through the broken door and was immediately overwhelmed by the smoke. He dropped as low as he could, but the searing pain in his side only allowed him to bend over so far. Tapestries and furniture alike were burning, and he saw one wall engulfed in flames. He made his way to the stairwell, which was beginning to burn. He remembered playing on those same steps as a child, and he realized then that he was the only one alive who could still call this temple his home. He fought hard against those memories as he made his way up the steps, choking as he did so.

The second floor wasn't as bad, but the smoke still rose toward the massive ceiling. The haze gave Greyson some cover, as he knew Cerus would soon be coming through the front door, but it also kept the air thick with smoke and made clean air a rarity at that point. The beautiful oaken stairwell ran around the center of the structure, which was fifty feet square. This opening ran to the roof, with that section of the ceiling being made of glass, allowing the sun to bathe the temple's stairwell at midday. Greyson wanted to get off the stairs as quickly as possible because he knew that Cerus would have a shot at him as long as he was on them. Given the seasoned warrior's aim, Greyson had little chance of dodging a second attack. However, luck was with him as he made the fourth-floor landing without having to dodge the wicked spear. He glanced back down the steps and saw Cerus just beginning the climb, spear in hand.

Cerus spotted Greyson and pointed an angry finger at him, screaming, "You're dead, priest! There's nowhere to run!"

Greyson didn't waste any time turning and fleeing down the hall. He made a right turn, which would take him to Berro's room, and that's when a glass vase shattered across his already wounded head. He dropped facedown to the floor, the pain too intense for him to do anything but cover his face and moan. He managed to roll on his back to see who or what had attacked him and found the crazed priest—he was alive! He was still burning, but flames consumed neither his robe nor his flesh. If he felt the bite of the fire, his demeanor showed no signs of it. He straddled Greyson, and the heat became unbearable for the young priest.

"How about a little fire?" the man said with glee, reaching down to grab at Greyson's face.

Though barely conscious, Greyson was still aware of the heat emanating from the living torch. He tried to scramble out from under him as the flaming hands neared his face, the man wildly staring at him from behind them. Greyson reached desperately across the floor, trying to find something to use as a weapon. He cut his hands on several pieces of the broken vase, and his bloody fingers finally closed around a more significant fragment. He swung with all his might at the grasping hands of fire, landing a solid strike, making the glass cut deeply into Greyson's palm. He loosened his grip, and the shard of glass went flying away, leaving him defenseless once more. He held his gashed palm to his chest, fighting the pain.

The attack surprised the burning priest, and he stood up straight. The delay gave Greyson a chance to crawl out from under his attacker. The look on the man's face was one of confusion as he held his left hand up to his face, turning it from side to side, examining the new wound. Only then did Greyson notice that only two fingers remained on that hand, the thumb and pinky. The other three fingers were now severed at the second knuckle. Greyson looked to the floor to find the three partial digits lying next to him. He was confused by how the shard had so easily removed those fingers, thwarting the attack. Then he remembered he was in the house of Plath. His god was with him! He was, after all, a prodigy.

Suddenly Garyn let out a horrific scream, eerily similar to Darian's. Greyson looked up to the burning priest to find the fire was now consuming the man. His robe was burning as well, engulfing the hallway in a foul smell. Then his skin started to bubble and melt, and his hair disappeared with a hiss. He ran wildly through the hall, crashing into the wall several times, still screaming that awful scream. Eventually he fell into a heap, silent and quite dead.

Greyson looked at the severed fingers lying next to him and realized one of them was still burning but not consumed by the flames. It was the one wearing a ring—magical, perhaps? One that resisted fire, by all accounts? Greyson used his boot to extinguish the fire and touched the metal band just barely to determine whether it was hot. It wasn't and was instead quite cool to the touch. He managed to remove it from the severed finger and stand on shaky legs. He tossed the finger onto the smoldering corpse and said, "Here. You dropped this."

The dizziness overwhelmed him as fresh blood poured from his forehead. The wound on his side was spilling too much blood as well—more than he expected from a grazing wound. He realized he was losing a lot of blood and considered casting a healing spell on himself. But the sight of Cerus running toward him, emerging from around the corner and hardly slowing, motivated him to find Berro's room instead. He turned and fled, unconsciously slipping the ring onto his left ring finger.

Soon he made it to Berro's room, and it was somehow unspoiled, to his relief. The scroll still sat atop the bookcase in the protective glass. All he needed to do was lock the door and skim the scroll. He shut the door behind him, but before he could latch it, it flew inward, throwing him to the floor. The madman known as Cerus stood before him now, larger than life, with the spear in hand. A giant muscular warrior with many kills under his belt, and Greyson knew he was doomed.

Cerus picked him up by the front of his shirt and swung him around, slamming him hard against the wall next to the door. The spear followed, thrusting into his left armpit and out the back of his shoulder with such force that the spear sunk into the thick wooden wall, impaling him. Bone cracked as the immense weapon shattered his shoulder. The pain was unlike anything Greyson had ever felt, and a bloodcurdling scream escaped his mouth. He fought to remain conscious, feeling his lifeblood soak the back of his shirt. He hung like a limp doll from the spear, pinned to the wall like some helpless insect. From his hip, Cerus drew his crude dagger—the very one he'd used to murder Greyson's family and friends.

"You bragged about being with my wife, arrogant boy. That was the last mistake you'll ever make!" Cerus said, waving the blade in his face.

Greyson moaned, finding himself in far too much pain to respond. His mind raced as he tried to think of what he could do. The wound to his shoulder would prove fatal if he didn't find healing, and Cerus was now going to torture him to death. Nothing could save him now, he realized as he glanced at the scroll on top of the bookcase, which seemed so close and yet so far away.

"I think I'll remove your manhood as punishment," Cerus said, undoing Greyson's pants. "Yes, I'll remove it before I remove the rest of your organs, one by one. You should've accepted your fate, weakling. You could already be swinging from a tree with your friends and enjoying the afterlife with whatever useless god you worship. Now you'll feel more pain before your death than you can imagine."

The room started to fill with smoke as the fire crept upward to the fourth floor. Greyson felt a bit of relief knowing that the evil warrior couldn't torture him too much longer without succumbing to the smoke himself. Greyson fished around in his right pocket, trying to find something to use as a weapon. Cerus then jerked his pants down, revealing his manhood, but not before Greyson's hand closed around the tiny tree charm Berro had given him.

An excellent idea crossed his mind at that point. He would honor Berro by activating the tree token! It wouldn't save his life, but it would celebrate Berro and Plath simultaneously. The older priest had carried the charm all his adult life but had never found a use for it. Perhaps this was the moment Plath had meant for it all along. It would be a perfect ending to Greyson's life and an honor to his adoptive father at the same time.

Cerus placed the blade at the base of Greyson's genitals and smiled. "Any last words before I remove your filthy member?"

Greyson whispered something. It wasn't audible, and he was surprised to find he had little strength left to say the word out loud. Cerus seemed pleased by this, and his smile widened. He leaned in close to him, cocking an ear. "You do have something to say? Do you want to beg for mercy? What is it, priest? Out with it!"

Summoning his energy, Greyson pronounced the word loud and clear: "Arbos!" He felt the token instantly grow warm in his hand and begin to enlarge.

"What?" Cerus asked, turning to look him in the face.

The tree grew quicker than Greyson could ever have imagined. He'd held the tree-shaped charm at its base, parallel to the ground, when he activated it, so it began to grow straight toward Cerus. The large man was surprised as a small trunk slipped past him toward the window. A small branch whacked the dagger from his hand, and it clattered to the floor, hidden by a sudden canopy of leaves. Cerus grabbed the spear's shaft just as a barrage of small limbs hit him repeatedly as the trunk grew to more than three feet in diameter. The tree crashed through the window, and the roots dug into the wall behind Greyson.

Greyson smiled as a tangle of leaves from a large branch smacked Cerus in the face. The man's surprised look, mixed with annoyance at the onslaught, was quite comical and made Greyson forget for just a moment that he was about to die. Cerus, his teeth gritted, held firmly to the spear. However, every time he moved from a tree branch's pounding, the spear moved with him, causing Greyson significant pain.

The tree was now nearly six feet in diameter and still growing. The roots busted out of the wall behind Greyson, strengthening their hold on the building. The temple groaned in protest as the fire, along with the tree's weight, threatened to take down the whole structure. Greyson could catch only glimpses of Cerus now as limbs beat the warrior mercilessly, one hitting his shin, bringing him to one knee. Leaves seemed to be everywhere, and the smell of the great tree was refreshing to Greyson compared to the smoke he'd been inhaling for some time now.

Cerus made one final leap toward Greyson in an attempt to gut the priest before the tree took down the building. He let out a war cry and lunged, only to meet a growing branch roughly three inches in diameter. It smacked him square in the face, crunching his nose, and the bramble of branches and leaves finally took the man from his feet and carried him quickly out the window. Cerus still held tightly to the spear and, in doing so, freed Greyson from the wall as the tree took the evil man and his wicked spear out the window. The pain once more was unbearable as Greyson slumped to the floor, trying desperately to remain conscious. Roots crisscrossed over him and continued plunging into every wall they could find, trying to gain a foundation for the giant tree to stand— only the tree was growing the wrong way and the multiplying roots did nothing to support it.

Greyson realized he might have just inadvertently saved Cerus from the death trap that the temple was quickly becoming. He managed to sit up against the wall, a pool of blood forming underneath him. He knew that he couldn't escape the root prison, and even if it were possible, he wouldn't be able to get very far. He sat back against the wall and said a small prayer to Plath. The building moaned in protest of the tree's weight. It had stopped growing, but the weight was too much for the building to bear. He tried to imagine what the temple looked like with a fifty-foot tree jutting out of the top floor, Cerus perhaps dangling from somewhere along its length. He let out a slight chuckle at that thought, leaned his head back against the wall, and waited for death. Finally he was at peace with what had transpired and was ready to meet his most wonderful god.

The floor would collapse soon, and he would plummet four stories to the fiery carnage found on the first floor. The fire probably wouldn't kill him, he thought as he looked at the ruby ring he now wore, but the fall surely would. The floor began to shake as the structure started to give. The root prison he found himself in dug downward about four inches, then caught on something that would delay the inevitable fall. Greyson realized that the tiny root cell would crush him against the floor, if the floor didn't give way first. At least he wouldn't die at the hands of the villain Cerus. He took great comfort at that thought and peeked down, satisfied that his genitals were also still attached.

The temple shuddered, and Greyson could hear windows shatter as the collapse began. He held on to the roots with his one good hand, preparing for the fall, and took a deep breath and waited. The bookcases fell across the large desk as the walls shook violently. Ironically, the scroll he'd come into this room to retrieve tumbled into the root tangle, the protective case shattering, raining fragments of broken glass on him. Once the shower of glass subsided, he opened his eyes to find the scroll lodged in the roots, just within reach. A final gift from Plath.

Greyson took the scroll with his right hand and feverishly unrolled it, pinning the other end beneath his leg. The floor moaned one last time in protest. Then he heard the walls splintering. He had only moments left as he started reading the scroll. Before he finished, the floor gave out, and he felt himself falling. He managed to hold his concentration and continue to cast the spell. He felt the release of energy as he completed it, then felt hurtled through space—not downward, but more of a horizontal feeling. He never hit the temple's bottom floor, as the magical scroll teleported him to a faraway place just as the impact occurred.

He felt as if he were being thrown a very long distance, maybe across the universe itself. The tree leaves became a green blur, and the smell of fresh bark and smoke faded away, replaced by new, clean air. The collapsing temple's rumbling diminished, replaced with silence, save for the happy chirping of a nearby bird. Greyson's sight slowly refocused, and he found himself in a bright clean room with a single large window that allowed in gentle rays of sunlight. He was still in a sitting position and still propped up against the wall of the small room. The door was next to him, the window directly across from it. A small, neatly made bed and a nightstand with a pitcher on it were the only furnishings. For the first time that morning, he felt peace; the chaos had finally subsided. He wondered if perhaps he was dead and this was the afterlife, but the severe pain in his shoulder and head convinced him that he was very much alive. The blood pooling around him also had him dismissing the notion.

He realized that he was coughing after gaining his bearings as his lungs worked to exhale the thick smoke that had nearly strangled him. His coughing fit drew the attention of a young woman, who peeked her head through the door. She might have been one of the most beautiful women he had ever seen, with golden hair cascading over her shoulders and the fairest face he could ever hope to see. He raised his one good hand and attempted a wave with a forced smile. The horror on her pretty face told him exactly how he must have appeared. He was vaguely aware then that his pants were around his ankles.

"Plath sent me," was all he could think to say before passing out.

She rushed toward him—whether to help or harm him, he would never know. Then, for the second time that morning, his world went black and he knew no more.

CHAPTER 9

ROYAL TREATMENT

FAR BACK IN THE CORNER OF THE MASSIVE LIBRARY'S CELLAR, Cassandra sat alone at a table piled with dusty old tomes. A lantern burned low, giving little light as shadows danced among the many shelves of books and stacks of old scrolls surrounding her. She studied an especially ancient scroll—one that showed Novafontera's old city before it had been cursed and covered in deadly gas. She searched for many answers to many questions.

Who was she? Was she even human? Who were her parents? Most important, who was the dark man who had invaded her dreams in her drug-induced stupor back at Oldorburg? Why could she see the same man in the painting at Victoria's tower and no one else could? What was the strange power she held over ravens, and why couldn't she maintain it, even when she concentrated on it? Too many questions!

She sat back in her seat and let the old scroll fall to the table and roll into the familiar shape it had remained for nearly a century in the dust-covered scroll tube in which she had found it. She closed her eyes and ran through the information she had gathered that day. She had learned more about the original New Order, who they were, and their accomplishments. She realized that the leader of that magnificent group, Spring Goodwright, was killed in battle long before he was the king of Novafontera. The old wizards reincarnated him as a half elf after his demise. He had been brought back from the dead by arcane magic, not the typical priestly magic most known for such miracles. Cassandra couldn't learn how they'd accomplished it, for nothing in all the tomes she'd perused had revealed the secret.

She was lost in her thoughts, trying to piece together the puzzle of her life, when she slowly realized the information she had gathered provided very little help. With a sigh, she vowed to continue her search the next day in this most beautiful library, which was far more significant than anything she had seen before. There were so many books and scrolls to browse that the process might take her years to accomplish. She vowed to obtain her answers, though. She had made a promise to her sister that she would become powerful and that no one would hurt them again. The start of that process would be to learn who she was. She needed to know what she was capable of before she could start to enhance her powers.

She opened her eyes and glared at the dying lamp. She thought of Kessi and Sera. Their time was growing short, just like the lamp that would soon burn out. They were in trouble; she could feel it. Something intangible in the air, some kind of sixth sense, told her that too much time had passed. She would be starting school the following day, having confirmed with Victoria her intentions to attend. She hoped it would keep her mind off things, as she had already been in Pelesea for more than two weeks. She could only imagine the tortures Ronnis D'Breeth was inflicting on her family even now. Her heart raced, and she panicked, sitting up straight in her chair and trying to catch her breath. Not for the first time since her quarantine, she had the urge to flee back to Oldorburg and complete the task she had started. Instead, she promised herself that if that monster hurt Kessi or Sera, she would kill him—and no one would be there to stop her next time.

~

Baxter had searched high and low for Cassandra that day with no success. The school was becoming busy as the students began populating the dormitory, preparing for the semester. Many of them were returning students, whom he knew, and invariably he found himself immersed in conversation whenever he crossed paths with them. He enjoyed his students, though, and was glad to see each of them again. All the while, he thought of Cassandra. She had not been in her room when he visited her that morning, and he had not seen her for nearly a week now. He had obeyed Victoria's wishes and stayed away from her, but he could no longer deny his heart; he had to speak with her.

He had learned that Kringus was leading a party out of the city at dawn to Oldorburg, and he wanted to tell Cassandra himself. He needed to ease her mind and wanted to be the one who brought such fantastic news to her. When he hadn't found her in her room or anywhere on the dormitory grounds, he had become worried. Where could she possibly be? Had she left school grounds or, worse, gone back to Oldorburg? How long had she been gone? All these questions raced through his mind, and none of them seemed like good options. He was falling in love with her, and although she was only half his age, there was no mistaking the feelings he had for her.

After spending most of the evening looking for Cassandra, he finally stumbled on one of his colleagues, a large fellow—in the waist, at least—named Cier Paldine. He had been tenured at the school almost as long as Baxter and was an excellent instructor. He got along well with the students and was a nice-enough fellow, in Baxter's opinion. However, the man would talk excessively and with hardly a break in the conversation. Today was no different as he stopped Baxter in the hall, arms loaded with empty beakers. Cier taught alchemy and knew more about potions and oils than any other wizard in a five-hundred-mile radius of Pelesea.

"My room is a mess!" the portly wizard exclaimed. "These beakers are filthy! Would you look at these!" he said, jutting his stomach out a little to present the armful of glass containers to him.

Baxter smiled and agreed that the classrooms needed cleaning when Cier started up once again.

"I hear," Cier said, "we have two very gifted students this year who accepted the free tuition that Lady Victoria so graciously awards each semester."

Baxter knew one of the students he referred to was Cassandra but knew nothing of a second one. He was about to probe for more information about the subject when the fellow continued.

"Can you believe that? Two in one semester? I must have my room straight if we have such honored students attending this year!"

Baxter decided it wasn't worth asking anything of the talkative man because he simply couldn't spare the time to discuss the issue with him. He was about to say his goodbyes and walk away when the man said something that finally caught his attention: "I hear one of them has spent the last three days in the library studying spells! She may be a handful for you this year, Baxter! I hope you've prepared for the likes of that one!"

Baxter smiled and clapped Cier on the shoulder, nearly making him drop his many beakers. Somehow he held on to them, talking the entire time, his voice crescendoing with each effort to right his cargo. He never did stop blabbering, and Baxter only smiled, which was his way of saying thanks and goodbye. The talkative wizard was still speaking as Baxter made his way down the hallway and to the library. Baxter's heart raced as the anticipation of seeing Cassandra again grew with each hurried step.

~

Kringus had his armor fitted in the royal armory, located on the castle's ground floor. It had been many months since he had donned his magnificent chain mail, and it had fit a little tight around the chest at that time. He wouldn't tolerate that on this excursion. He would leave in the morning to make the twenty-day trek to Oldorburg. The weather was turning cold as fall began to take hold of the land, and he wanted to get the trip over with before the first snow. However, that was not his primary concern about this mission; he was worried about what he might find in the small town and how the volatile Rho girl might react to any bad news.

"You look very handsome," Penelope whispered, breaking him from his train of thought.

He smiled and looked into the full-length mirror set on the wall nearby. "I do, don't I?" he said.

Brutus, his armorer, worked on a kink in the armor while Penelope stood nearby. Brutus marked the spots that needed mending and stood back to take a look.

"Do you agree, Brutus?" Kringus asked, striking a pensive pose.

"What? Your Majesty, I missed the question. My apologies."

"The queen paid me a compliment. She said I look dashing."

"Handsome," Penelope corrected him.

"Handsome, then! Do you agree?" Kringus asked.

The two men looked at each other sternly, Kringus with his long dark hair and many battle scars, dressed in his royal chain mail, and Brutus in his smithy apron, his large beard and larger arms emphasizing the fact that he could take a few hits and dish some out as well. Neither blinked or spoke. After a few moments, Kringus laughed, making Brutus double over immediately, sharing the king's joy. Penelope followed suit, and it would take several minutes for them to catch their breath and collect themselves. The doors to the armory opened then, startling the trio, and a castle guard entered.

"Excuse me, Your Majesties, but you have a visitor with urgent business," the guard announced, then stood aside for Alleah to enter.

The king and queen immediately knew something was wrong by the expression on the woman's face. She rarely came to the castle, usually only to attend the New Order meetings, and her arriving unannounced at that late hour spurred the royal couple's curiosity.

"Alleah, what is it?" Penelope asked before the woman could reach them.

"There is an intruder in the temple."

Kringus reached for his sword, which lay on a nearby table. "From Oldorburg?" he asked before he could catch himself.

Penelope turned to look at him curiously, reading his thoughts. The king cursed a little under his breath for losing his composure and then waited for the priestess to answer. Penelope slowly turned back toward Alleah, who was waiting patiently.

"I don't know, my lord," she replied, leaning to look past the queen and to answer his question.

Kringus nodded and was wise enough to say nothing more.

"He is injured and not a threat," Alleah said.

"What do you mean? How did he get into the temple?" Kringus asked, stepping up to stand beside the queen. He still held on to his sword and seemed ready to take action.

"We don't know. It looks like some form of teleportation, maybe. He is grievously wounded and clings to life."

Kringus rolled his eyes and then said to Brutus as he handed him the sword, "Help me out of the armor so you may begin the required adjustments."

Brutus nodded and began the process of removing the magnificent chain mail.

Penelope turned toward her husband. "What do you make of it, my dear?"

"I'm not sure. All I can say is that the intruder is your problem since I leave at dawn," Kringus said with a smirk.

Penelope shook her head and turned back to Alleah. "Have the priests not healed his wounds?"

"Yes, but there's one that won't stop bleeding."

"What have you learned of this stranger?"

"Not much since he continues to slip in and out of consciousness. We found a holy symbol on him of a passive god, so we think he is a priest and doesn't come with evil intentions."

"Who is the god?"

"Plath."

"Do we recognize that faction in the temple?"

"No, perhaps years ago, but we currently don't have a recognized group of worshippers for that god."

Penelope thought about the situation, very interested in how and why the man had come to Pelesea. "I'll visit him in the morning. Try your healing, Alleah, and I'll research a possible cure this night. Then, if things go well, we'll nurse this man back to health and find our answers."

"Yes, my lady. I'll stay with him this evening and look for you in the morning."

Alleah then gave a slight bow and left hurriedly from the room. Deep in thought and more than a little confused, Penelope turned slowly to look at her husband, who was now dressed only in the padding he wore underneath his chain mail. He noticed her looking his way and tried not to make eye contact. However, she continued her stare, making the strong king feel more and more uncomfortable.

"Don't look at me!" Kringus finally said. "He's your problem!"

Penelope smiled, enjoying the game she was playing with her husband. However, her mind did shift quickly back to the mysterious intruder. She didn't like the fact that he had so easily found his way into the city. She required answers, so she quickly kissed Kringus and excused herself. She knew one way to cure the man's wounds, and it sounded like time was of the essence.

~

Heinsvick walked into Oldorburg later that night, strolling into the small town as if he hadn't a care in the world. He was eyed suspiciously by the guards, and if they'd known just what an adversary he indeed was, they would never have let him enter their town without sounding the alarm. He headed to the small town center, where many shops were lit up with candles in their windows, signifying that they were open for business. It was cold outside, but Heinsvick hadn't felt temperature for centuries, so he felt none of the bite from the crisp night air. However, very few townsfolk were about, so it made him easy to follow, and being followed he was.

After allowing the two guards to trail him for a bit, he abruptly stopped and said, "Good evening, gentlemen. Am I breaking any laws?" knowing exactly why the men felt compelled to follow him, even if they did not.

Surprised by his sudden move, they became vigilant, and one even reached for the hilt of his sword. He caught himself before withdrawing the weapon but kept his hand nervously on the grip.

The other guard managed to answer, "Good evening to you, stranger. You've broken no laws; we're just wary of strangers in our town."

Heinsvick noticed that they kept their distance from him. He reasoned that they probably had no idea they were doing it and their intuition warned them that this stranger was quite dangerous.

"Especially one who walks into our town on a cold night such as this without supplies or even a coat to fight off the winter's chill," the other guard added.

Heinsvick looked down at his outdated clothing, realizing how out of place he indeed must have appeared to these two. He chuckled softly to himself for overlooking the obvious. Perhaps two centuries ago his clothing had been in style, but now he must have come across as foolish and eccentric to the two young guards. Also, the thin dress gave no protection from the cold, which made him look even more ridiculous. "You are correct, my good men. I have not sufficient clothing for this weather. That is why I have come—to stock up and perhaps stay a night or two."

The two guards looked at each other, unconvinced.

"Where have you come from?" the first guard eventually asked.

Heinsvick had to think quickly. He had wanted to sneak into the town, take what he needed, and leave without raising any suspicions. Unfortunately these guards were making that a difficult task already. He couldn't tell them the name of his true home, so he thought of the one town he knew was relatively close. It was a small town known for its less-than-desirable inhabitants. He didn't know if the town's reputation would help or hinder the situation, but he decided he would kill these two if it made things worse. "Please forgive my lack of manners. I am Heinsvick, and I hail from the town of Mecca-Loraine. Perhaps you've heard of it?"

The two men shared another look of concern, knowing what types of people the lawless town of Mecca-Loraine usually harbored. Heinsvick cupped his hands and blew into them, feigning an attempt to warm them. If the men had paid close enough attention, they would have noticed that his breath didn't produce a cloud into the cold air as theirs did.

"Well, if I have given you enough information, I think I'll purchase some items for my continued trip. You do not have to fear me, dear guardsmen. After all, I do not carry any weapons," Heinsvick said with a smile, holding his hands out to his sides. "But I do have money for supplies." He patted one of his pockets so that the coins jingled noisily.

The guards seemed to relax at his rationale.

"Bart has the best traveling gear," the first one said, nodding to a small shop just down the street called Beggar Bart's.

"Yes, and the best jerky!" the second guard added.

The two men shared a chuckle and waved him off, wishing him a pleasant stay. They seemed more at ease now, but he could feel their eyes boring into him as he walked away. He decided then that he would spend little time in the town. Instead, he would get his business over with and leave quickly in the night.

He made his way to the small supply shop, briefly noting the name scrawled over the door, Beggar Bart's, as he ducked inside. The shop had a few patrons, but once he entered, they quickly left. He watched them go, one by one, each as nervous as the last, just being around the vampire. Again, none of them knew why they felt the way they did; they just wanted to leave quickly, to be away from the strange man in the unusual clothing. At the store's counter, a large man stared at him nervously, which the vampire lord was slowly growing accustomed to. He assumed this was actually Bart, and if so, he would get his business over with quickly. He made his way to the shopkeeper, grabbing a backpack along the way and then laying it on the counter, followed by a small sack of coins. "Please fill this with things," he said.

"Things?" the man responded hoarsely.

"Yes, things for traveling—and some of your finest jerky," Heinsvick said with a smile, trying to make the man feel at ease.

The man took the backpack and came out from behind the counter. He opened the pack and began to stuff things into it—first a bedroll, then a tinderbox, then a lantern. Heinsvick watched him work but didn't follow. He wanted to be done with the nonsense as much as Beggar Bart did.

"So I have heard of the great wolf encounter that your town experienced some years ago," Heinsvick said.

Bart stopped and looked at him, and then his eyes went wide as if he suddenly remembered. "That's right, about a dozen years ago now," he said, glad to have something to discuss.

"How does the story go? I heard that a child thwarted a wolf attack."

"Yes, a strange little girl named Cassandra Rho was the source of that tale."

"Cassandra Rho? Does she live here still?"

Bart snorted out a laugh, unable to catch himself before doing so. He looked around to make sure no one was watching and whispered, "She's gone. She's wanted for attempted murder."

This news both shocked and infuriated Heinsvick. He was so close to catching his prey, so close to finding what very well may be the child of Kane. "What do you mean she's gone?"

"Well, they say she fled to Pelesea, but I don't believe that's certain."

Heinsvick knew where that grand city was since it was the closest neighbor Novafontera had and knew he would not so easily access the place as he had Oldorburg. "How long ago did she leave?"

"Not sure. Perhaps two weeks ago? The town's in an uproar over it."

Heinsvick thought of a way to find the wretched child quickly, but knowing the strength of Pelesea's military and the reputation of the vile city's king and queen, he didn't expect to walk into their front door and find her so easily. But if she had a family, he could speak to them perhaps. "Where is her family?" he reluctantly asked.

Bart made his way back to the counter with the backpack full of supplies, laid it back on top, and then grabbed a parchment and a quill and began writing out a bill of sale. "She has none that I know of. She grew up at the Oldorburg Orphanage, up on the hill." Bart motioned with a thumb in the direction of the orphanage.

"She's an orphan?"

"Yes, and she has a sister too. I don't think her sister is as creepy or mean as Cassandra, but they both grew up there."

"A sister? Where is she?"

"I don't know. Perhaps you can speak to Ronnis and find out."

"Who is Ronnis?"

"Ronnis D'Breeth is the administrator of the orphanage. He knows everything that goes on up there." After making his bill of sale, Bart read out the total: "Five gold, please."

Heinsvick picked up the loaded pack and nodded toward the sack that still lay on the counter.

The man emptied it, revealing ten gold coins. He picked one up and brought it to a nearby lantern, examining it. "Never seen this currency before," he said, still studying the coin.

"It is from a faraway land but is gold nonetheless."

Bart nodded, put five of the coins back into the sack, and moved it back toward the unusual patron.

Heinsvick shook his head and made his way to the door. "Keep the extra for a tip. You've been helpful."

"Thank you, sir," Bart said nervously. "Come back and see us!"

Heinsvick stopped with one hand on the door handle and turned back toward the man. "Perhaps I will," he said with a smile.

The man blanched and nodded.

"By the way, you said Cassandra Rho is wanted for murder. Tell me—who did she try to murder?"

"Ronnis D'Breeth."

"Interesting," Heinsvick said, his smile growing ever wider. He then opened the door and stepped out into the cold. The guards were gone now, and before he could walk even ten feet from the shop, he heard the door lock behind him. He smiled again and looked to his right. On the hill sat a large solitary building.

"The Oldorburg Orphanage, huh?" he muttered to himself.

Then he made his way straight there. *No time like the present to meet with an orphanage administrator*, he thought.

~

Baxter found Cassandra deep in the bowels of the library. He was lucky to locate her and probably would not have without the librarian's help, who happened to know exactly where the young woman had gone. He made his way down the dust-covered steps using Cassandra's lantern as a beacon to the back of the cellar, where the oldest tomes resided. The library's bottom floor contained many forgotten scrolls and parchments, and an abundance of dust and cobwebs showing just how little students read them.

There were four tables, empty, save for a couple of large volumes sitting on them, and dust covered. But in the far corner, behind several rows of large shelves, sat a smaller table loaded with books. Baxter circled the last one, his heart racing. Why was he so emotional over this girl? He was excited to see her and didn't know whether she would feel the same. That was one of the things he liked about her; she was unpredictable. He had come against Victoria's wishes, and he felt guilty about that. However, he just had to see her before classes began, plus he had news for her that she needed to hear.

She sat at the table with books and scrolls piled up around her, the one lantern slowly dying from lack of oil. She had her head low, looking over a scroll and reading quietly to herself. She was so immersed in her reading that she hadn't heard him come down the steps. He watched her for a moment, considering how young she was and just how beautiful he found her. His heart went out to her, understanding better than anyone just what pains she had suffered at the hands of Ronnis D'Breeth. He felt a little bad for her as well, having spent her day there in this dusty library instead of mingling with the other students. She was a loner and misunderstood by almost everyone. Baxter understood her, though, and wanted to learn more. The guilt washed over him as he again considered their age difference and the inappropriateness of his growing feelings.

"Well, you're a hard person to find!" he said cheerily.

Cassandra jumped and dropped her scroll, letting out a small yelp in the process. Baxter's smile faded as he realized he had frightened her.

"My apologizes; I've been looking all over for you."

She collected herself and held her hand to her heart. "You scared me!"

"I apologize. I didn't mean to—"

She waved his explanation away and smiled. "It's fine. I could use the company."

"May I join you, then?"

"If you can find a seat," she said, removing an armful of scrolls so that the table was less cluttered. Unfortunately she dropped them on the floor, creating an explosion of dust, which made her cough. She waved it away for several moments while Baxter took a seat and watched. He smiled on the inside, finding her youthful innocence endearing. She finally caught her breath and turned toward him, only to find a silly look on his face as he stared at her.

"What?" she asked, freezing in place to indicate that she was very aware of the way he was gawking at her.

"Nothing. I have a message!"

He hadn't wanted to blurt out the news so quickly. He had hoped to make some small talk first, but his nervousness got in the way. He wanted to verify that she was attending the school this fall and would be in his class tomorrow. Baxter had rehearsed what he would say when he spoke with her again, and this was not what he had planned.

"What is it? Does it concern my family?" she asked, sitting up straight in her chair, her blue eyes wide with excitement.

"Yes, Kringus is leaving in the morning to travel to Oldorburg!" he said, holding his hands out wide, awaiting her reaction to the joyous news.

Instead, she wrinkled up her tiny nose and yelled, "He hasn't left yet? I thought he would be on his way back by now!" She put her head in her hands and shook it, her long golden curls disturbing the tomes on the shelf behind her and stirring up more dust.

"But he plans on bringing them here so that you may be together," Baxter said.

"Don't you see?" she asked, sitting back in her chair, tears rimming her eyes now. "It's too late. Your king has waited too long."

"You can't know that. I'm sure he's arranged this as quickly as possible."

"I should have gone back for them," she said somberly.

Baxter looked down at his feet, trying to come up with some words of comfort. Deep down, he felt that the astute woman was right, but he didn't want to believe it. He wanted instead to make her feel better, to give her some hope. He looked up at her face, and the tears that ran down her cheeks made his heart race even faster. He hadn't meant to make her cry. He felt like a villain at that moment.

"Thank you for bringing me the news. I do appreciate you," Cassandra said, wiping her tears away, streaking her pretty face with dust.

He smiled and nodded. "You are most welcome."

There was a stretch of silence then that seemed to go on forever. As Cassandra looked absently at the scrolls on the table, neither said anything, and Baxter stared longingly at her. His thoughts were interrupted again when she spoke.

"You're doing it again," she said without looking at him, her unblinking eyes fixed on the table.

"Doing what?" he asked nervously.

"You're staring at me."

She then looked at him and sat up straight in her chair. He froze, not knowing what to do. He was twice her age but felt like a little schoolboy, wilting under her gaze. He had battled monsters with his powerful magic and had trained countless students. But in the presence of Cassandra Rho, he was an idiot, unable to think or act like an intelligent being.

"I'm sorry. I just … I haven't seen you for a while. I'm glad to be talking to you again," Baxter said. It was all he could think to say, but he was pretty sure she wasn't buying it. She looked into his eyes, and he swallowed hard, afraid he was giving away his true feelings. Finally he broke her gaze, looking around the small alcove nervously.

"So what are you doing down here?" she asked, eyeing him suspiciously.

Baxter could feel her trying to read his thoughts, and for a moment, he thought she actually might. However, she eventually broke her gaze and began collecting the scrolls, putting them back in their tubes.

"I've come to deliver the good news about your family. Also, I want to make sure you're attending class tomorrow." He looked around at the stacks of scrolls and other parchments. "What exactly are *you* doing down here?"

"I'm doing research, Baxter. By the way, what am I supposed to call you tomorrow in class? I very well can't call you Baxter, but I feel that we're too friendly for me to call you anything else."

"Well, I haven't thought of it," he said, "but I'm glad you've decided to attend the school!" He'd thought about her a lot. Actually, he thought about her all the time. Ever since he'd rescued her, he'd grown very fond of her. He thought of her attending his class and dreamed of their relationship somehow growing into something more, but he had not thought of how she would address him.

"If I weren't attending, I would have left days ago. So what do the other students call you?" Cassandra asked.

"Instructor or Instructor Baxter. Either will be fine."

"Very well, Instructor Baxter," she said with a smile.

She tried placing the scrolls on a shelf but dropped one, and it rolled to his feet. He picked it up for her and unrolled it on instinct. It was penned in an ancient dialect and appeared to be an accounting of the New Order. "What exactly are you researching?" he asked, lowering the scroll so he could see her face.

"I'm researching me," she said, holding her hand out for the scroll.

"Researching you? What do you mean?" he said, rolling up the scroll and handing it to her.

"I'm a freak, Baxter—I mean Instructor Baxter. I need to find out who I am."

He approached her and turned her around with a strong arm so he could look into her eyes. He wanted to embrace her, to comfort her. She was not a freak to him; she was perfect, in his eyes. She seemed surprised by his touch and turned on him with her eyes wide.

"You are you," he said sternly. "And that is something wonderful. Don't let anyone tell you differently, Cassandra Rho."

"I can control birds, I can cast spells without using components, and I can see magic floating in the air!" She took a step toward him, and he took a step backward. "I can see paintings move and images that even the greatest wizard of the city can't see! So what does it mean? Why can I do this? Who am I? That's what I want to know."

"And you think the New Order has the answers."

"Perhaps. I had a dream when I was under the effects of the poison back in Oldorburg. In that dream, I vividly recall a man—I refer to him as the dark man—summoning me to take a rod of power and something about a king."

"Wait, what?" he asked with a puzzled expression.

She took another step closer, and this time he stood his ground. They were face-to-face, and the low-burning lantern made the mood very intimate to him. His mind began to race with lustful thoughts. The flickering light that danced across her face made her stunning.

"The dark man–he's the same as the one in Victoria's tower. I assume she told you about the mural?" Cassandra asked, her voice low now as their eyes locked.

Baxter could only nod; he was overwhelmed by her being this close to him. He remembered the feel of her body when he had flown her on the magic carpet. She had leaned up against him, and Baxter had held her close, trying to keep her warm. That feeling returned to him now as he looked into her sparkling eyes. Baxter gulped loudly, giving away his nervousness. Once again, he felt powerless around her. It was like she was using his energy, as she had done back in Oldorburg when she had stolen his cantrip.

"You need to see Franklin. He's the history instructor. He might be able to shed some light on this dark man," he replied in his nervousness, trying to break the spell she had on him.

She nodded and backed away, grabbing the lantern. She sighed and looked around the dusty room. "I'll ask Instructor Franklin tomorrow after class. Thank you. Now I must be going."

He scolded himself on the inside then, realizing he'd taken away an opportunity to spend more time with her. He was acting like an idiot, and he realized then that his hands were sweaty. "I'll walk you back to your room," he said, nearly in a panic.

"Sure," was her curt reply.

As they made their way back up the library steps, out of the large building, and across the courtyard toward the dorms, he couldn't find the courage to speak. They passed many students. None of them seemed to recognize her, and she didn't acknowledge that they were even there. Most of them waved or spoke to Baxter, though, making him feel a little better. They eventually made it to her dorm room, and that nervousness washed over him once more, as if they were returning from a date and now was the time for that first kiss. Finally she stopped at the door and turned toward him, and his heart fluttered.

"Thank you for walking me back, Instructor Baxter," she said with a slight smirk.

He smiled back, truly happy to know this incredible young woman. "You are most welcome, Miss Rho. I look forward to seeing you in class tomorrow."

"Me too," she said and smiled.

She opened her door slightly, then paused, turning back to him once more. "Did you know that tomorrow is also my birthday?"

"Really?" he asked in surprise.

"Well, Kessi and I always celebrate that day as our birthday, but we were most likely born a day or two before that."

"So why celebrate tomorrow?"

"That was the day we came to Oldorburg on the front steps of the orphanage, the day our mother took us in."

"Yes, of course," he said and nodded.

"I'll be nineteen tomorrow—no longer a child, really," she said.

His heart skipped a beat, not knowing what she was getting at. He wanted to say something but was at a loss for words. So he stood there for the longest time, smiling—a smile that she returned. Then, finally, his mouth formed some words, and he blurted out, "Happy birthday!"

She smiled and hugged him unexpectedly. He held her tight, smelling her hair and trying to keep his composure. He could feel his heart thumping in his chest. She broke the embrace after a short while and gave him a peck on the cheek.

"See you around, Professor," she said with a wink, then quickly moved into her room and shut the door.

He didn't know how long he stood there afterward, but he felt his cheeks growing warm and his insides turning into a knot. His mind tried to register what had happened, as he wasn't sure whether what had just transpired indicated anything more than friendship. He reminded himself that Cassandra was so very young and had called him *grandpa* when they first met. When he finally snapped out of his thoughts and started down the hallway, he found Lady Victoria standing at the far end watching him, her hands crossed over her chest.

"Oh boy," he mumbled to himself, then straightened himself up and walked confidently toward her. He had some explaining to do but didn't care—he was in love!

~

Ronnis sat in his office all alone, save for a mostly empty bottle of brandy and a finely decorated black scabbard lying across his desk. It contained one of the most beautiful swords he had ever witnessed, its magnificent handle poking out of the end. He had wielded this powerful weapon years ago almost to his detriment and now considered doing just that once again.

His porcelain mask hung on a nearby hook as he absently picked his teeth through his scar. The biting wind blew outside and assaulted his window, making him feel even more alone. He had lost Sera, and Cassandra was unreachable now, having run off to the mighty city of Pelesea. All that he had left was his position of power and maybe Kessi. He was still fighting that battle with the merchant's guild, having demanded custody of the young woman, but the guild had taken her the same time they had arrested Sera and Quinn. They would probably detain her until they figured out what had happened to Cassandra. He felt truly alone, but more than that, he felt angry. The sword fed off his anger.

He poured himself another drink and gulped it down quickly, the warm liquid spreading through his gut. He studied the sword on his desk, the hilt black as night, designed to resemble the head of a snake eating its tail. The eyes, adorned with rubies, sparkled, reflecting the fire in the nearby hearth. The sheath was made of snakeskin and was also solid black. He dared not unsheathe the blade, but he knew from experience that it was blacker than death itself, forged from some unknown metal of extreme toughness. The weapon was pure evil, and he had traded someone for it years ago. It was called the Black Adder.

It was an intelligent, sentient blade, and he knew all too well the dangers of wielding it. He could faintly hear the sword's call once more as it sensed his desperate situation. He'd thought of wielding it ever since Cassandra had fled from him with Baxter, the wizard. He demanded justice for what the little witch had taken from him, and the sword could bring him that justice. He reached unconsciously toward the hilt, those little ruby eyes calling him. The time of the adder had come. However, before he touched the blade, there was a knock on the door. The sound startled him from his trance, and he withdrew his hand as if he were about to grasp a live snake. The knock came again, this time followed by the muffled sound of Prudence's voice. "Hello, Lord Ronnis. I have a special surprise for you!"

She sounded excited, and his first thought was that Agnew from the merchant's guild had come with news that he'd gained custody of Kessi Rho. The idea appealed to him very much. He would so enjoy playing with Cassandra's sister and making her pay for Cassandra's crimes! He would make Kessi suffer greatly. He couldn't think of another reason for Prudence to visit him at such a late hour.

He began to call to her, to invite her in, when a voice invaded his thoughts: "Beware who you invite into your room at such a late hour." He looked at the sword, recognizing the slithering, devilish voice from all those years ago. He stared at it for some time, not sure what to make of it and not sure how to handle the message he had just received from the powerful weapon.

"Ronnis? May we come in?"

Prudence's voice snapped him out of the spell. He shook his head and reached down beside the desk and hoisted the heavy blanket he kept there. He wrapped the sword and scabbard in it and quickly hid it under the desk within his reach. "Come in, Prudence!" he called after the sword was out of sight.

He stood at his desk, and Prudence entered, happy as a lark, followed by some tall and unusual stranger. The smile quickly faded from his face, and he absently grabbed the mask from behind him and put it on.

There was something unnatural about the man. His clothes were out of place and his complexion pale, and he simply gave Ronnis the shakes. He felt somehow protected behind the mask, as if he were hiding behind it.

"This is your old friend Heinsvick from Mecca-Loraine!" Prudence said excitedly. When Ronnis made no move to approach the new guest, and when neither of them said anything, Prudence motioned with her hands as if she were showing off some rare prize at an auction or a museum and exclaimed, "Ta-da!"

Ronnis felt like taking the sword and running it through her. She had always served him well, but this was a gross lapse in judgment, and he would scold her later about it. Who was this unusual visitor, and what did he want? Prudence didn't seem to know or even consider those questions; she just seemed happy to have brought the "old friends" together.

After a couple of uncomfortable moments, she finally moved toward the door and said, "Well, I guess I'll leave you two alone to get reacquainted!" Then, with one last smile, she left the room and shut the door behind her.

Heinsvick immediately locked it, then turned toward Ronnis. "Please do not be alarmed; the deception was well warranted. By morning, that simpleton won't even remember that I was here. Please be at ease, Ronnis D'Breeth," Heinsvick said and pointed toward Ronnis's chair.

Ronnis sat back down and slowly poured himself a drink. He felt for the wrapped sword with his right knee and took comfort in knowing it was so close. Heinsvick sat down opposite him, the same one Cassandra had sat in when he'd "negotiated" with Sera that fateful night all those years ago.

"I like your mask. It is very becoming," Heinsvick said with a smirk.

Ronnis nodded and held the bottle of brandy toward the stranger. "Brandy?"

Heinsvick shook his head and smiled. "Not right now. Perhaps later?"

If it was a joke, it was one that Ronnis didn't understand. The man gave him the creeps, and he wanted him out of his office. "So what is it that you need, Heinsvick from Mecca-Loraine?"

"Ah, quickly to the point. I like the way you operate, Lord Ronnis."

Ronnis nodded again, then removed the mask, placing it on the desk so that he could take a large gulp of brandy. Heinsvick watched and seemed to be amused by his deformity.

"Did the girl do that to you?" he asked, pointing to the hole in his cheek.

"What do you know of it?" Ronnis growled.

"Nothing more than what I have observed. I'm here for the girl—that much you should have assumed already. What she did or did not do to you is hearsay."

"What girl?" Ronnis asked, slowly pronouncing each syllable and clenching his fist tightly.

"Why, Cassandra Rho, of course."

Ronnis knew the answer before he'd even asked the question, but hearing that name made him sit back in his chair and reflect. Who was this man, and what did he want with Cassandra? He glanced at the adder leaning under his desk just a few feet away and thought about taking it up against this stranger who so boldly asked for his most coveted prize. "She's no longer up for adoption; I'm sorry to inform you," Ronnis answered, quickly reading the annoyance on Heinsvick's face. This one was going to be insistent, but Ronnis didn't care. Cassandra was his, and he would kill anyone who tried to stop him from possessing her.

"Where is she?" Heinsvick asked, leaning close, his eyes wide.

Ronnis suddenly became lost in those eyes, forgetting his anger and replacing it with a sense of calmness. Suddenly he wanted to help this man very much. He could too. He knew exactly how to retrieve the troublesome Cassandra Rho. The emotional waves assaulted him, rolling over him as the waves of an ocean might. He couldn't collect his thoughts. He considered Heinsvick a friend and slowly lost his hatred and fear of the man for reasons he couldn't explain.

Only the stubborn, vindictive side of Ronnis kept him from falling entirely under the vampire's spell. As he struggled to collect his thoughts, his right hand slowly reached under the table and grasped the hilt of the Black Adder underneath the blanket. It felt cold in his hand, almost slimy. He remembered that feeling, and he welcomed it. Suddenly the intrusive thoughts were gone and he could reason once more. He could feel the sword giving him incredible strength and easily defeating the vampire's charm.

Then came the mental intrusion from the sword: "The stranger is a vampire, you fool! We must disperse him from the building at once."

Ronnis knew that this man was dangerous, but a vampire? What did an undead creature want with Cassandra, and how much did he know about Ronnis? He suddenly felt terrified, even with the sword firmly in his grasp. "Go back to where you come from, Heinsvick. You will get no information from me!" Ronnis said, standing up, the blanket falling away to reveal the black sword that was now in his hand.

Seemingly confused, Heinsvick sat back in his chair. Ronnis had defeated whatever charming magic the vampire had just assaulted him with, and the Black Adder would protect him from further such attacks. Heinsvick glanced at the sword, and the look on his face told Ronnis that he knew the source of Ronnis's power. Hints of anger reflected on the vampire's face, and he seemed to struggle to control that anger. Eventually, his visage calmed, and he said, "Of course—how silly of me. You aren't as foolish as that repulsive woman you call Prudence. And considering the attack on your life, I'm sure your anger with Cassandra is well founded."

Ronnis nodded but took the compliment with a grain of salt. He kept the sword in his hand as he poured himself another drink, all the while staring hard at the unwelcome visitor. "She's no longer here. She fled to another city."

"So I've heard," Heinsvick said. "I have an idea that might work for both of us."

Ronnis sat back down and nodded. "I'm listening."

"I hear she has a sister. Is this true?"

Ronnis nodded.

"Is she available for adoption?" the vampire lord asked.

"No, she no longer lives here," was Ronnis's curt response.

"But you know where she is, don't you?"

Ronnis nodded again.

"Tell me where she is, and I will leave you be," Heinsvick said.

"How does that benefit me?" Ronnis asked with a snort.

"I won't kill you."

Ronnis stood up quickly and brandished the sword before him, feeling the power course through his arm. "Strike him down," the sword hissed in his mind. "Show him the power of the black blade!"

"Try it!" Ronnis said with a confident smile.

"I would kill you before you could even think to swing your powerful sword, my friend. You are overmatched here. Just give me what I need, and you'll never see me again."

Ronnis stared at the vampire, his knuckles turning white as he gripped his most potent weapon. Hateful thoughts filled his head, but the sword was intelligent and knew the enemy that sat before him. If there was a way to get rid of the troublesome vampire, the blade would gladly do it. And if that didn't work, the sword would gladly have Ronnis run it through the creature's back.

"She's being held in the jail by the merchant's guild," Ronnis finally said.

"Why?" Heinsvick asked with a puzzled expression.

"She's accused of helping her sister escape the city."

"She's going to be killed?"

Ronnis shrugged. "It wouldn't surprise me. I've tried to gain custody, but they have thus far refused my request."

"As they should. You aren't a neutral party here, and I imagine you have many tortures in store for the girl—that is, until you pluck Cassandra Rho from her hiding place. Am I correct?"

Ronnis laughed and sat back down, shaking his head. The vampire had guessed his plan exactly. However, at this moment, he didn't care. He just wanted to be left alone to work out the details of his scheme to recapture Cassandra. "So now that you know where she is, I demand that you leave my orphanage, vampire, and do not come back."

Heinsvick's shocked expression told Ronnis that he hadn't expected him to determine his true self—that Ronnis shouldn't have known he was a vampire. Ronnis smiled at the undead filth as Heinsvick processed that information. After a few moments, Heinsvick stood to leave, nodding. "Just one last thing, my dear man," he said, pausing to size Ronnis up one last time.

Ronnis met the vampire's stare, ready to strike the creature down if he made any threatening move. "Name it."

"The girl's name. What is it?"

Ronnis relaxed at the simple request. "Kessi. Her name is Kessi Rho."

Heinsvick nodded and smiled, then left quickly. Ronnis locked the door behind him and put his ear to it, hoping to hear no sound from the other side. Then, after a few quiet moments, he walked back toward his desk. After just a few strides, he stopped and held up the sword that had just saved his life. The unusual black blade glistened with the poison that perpetually covered it. Whether he desired it or not, the Black Adder was now his weapon once more.

~

Heinsvick found his way outside the orphanage in short order. The wind felt good to him as he stepped outside, leaving the stuffy and somewhat putrid den of the unusual man far behind. He made his way directly toward the jail and deviated from his course only briefly to retrieve his pack of supplies that he had tossed in an alley on his way to see Ronnis. The girl would need those supplies, he reasoned. He would at least try to keep her alive before he handed her over to Matilda.

He had easily formulated the plan during his discussion with Ronnis. First, if he couldn't have Cassandra Rho, he would take her sister. Then, he would brainwash the poor girl into thinking she indeed was Cassandra Rho. Finally, if the ruse worked, he would trade the girl for his beloved Emiline. As a bonus to the deception, hopefully, Matilda's sacrifice of the wrong sister would fail to summon the mighty demon lord Marnelphion. He would love to see the expression on the nasty priestess's face when her great summoning failed. At that point, she would know that Heinsvick had bested her. He chuckled at the thought of it, then found his pack buried in a snowdrift. He looked around to make sure no one was watching, then removed one essential item from the bag to keep for himself.

~

Kessi sat in her cell, which had been her home for the last ten days. Other than receiving three meals from the guards each day, she saw no one. When she inquired about the whereabouts of her mother, they gave her no straight answer. Sera hadn't visited her, and no one had given her information on her status or future. So she prayed to Adlesk almost constantly. One of the few items the guards allowed her to keep was her holy symbol, a small copper wire shaped into a tear that she wore around her neck. It had been a gift from her mother when she'd turned twelve.

She leaned back, resting her head against the cool bars of her cell, her thoughts suddenly centered on Cassandra. She missed her sister very much and wished more than anything she was there. Cassandra was always the protector of the two, the one who took charge. She would know what to do in such a hopeless situation. "Oh, sister, how I wish you were here! I'm glad you're not, though, and I hope you're safe. If it is Adlesk's will, we will see each other soon."

She kissed her holy symbol, closed her eyes, and said another prayer to her god. Then she thought she heard the front door to the jail open and shut, which brought her to her feet. She placed her hands on the bars and watched the door that led into the cells. It remained closed, as usual, and, she assumed, locked. The only times it had opened since she'd arrived was for the guards to bring her meals. Her heart raced as she thought that her mother had finally come to take her home. Then the two of them could leave the horrible town and find Cassandra, and they could all live happily ever after.

A smile found its way to her face then as she hoped against hope for just that possibility. But a sudden crash, followed by a muffled cry, made her smile melt away. She now had a bad feeling that someone had come not to rescue her but to kill her. She thought perhaps Ronnis had come, ready to take his vengeance on her since he couldn't harm Cassandra. She was the only prisoner there, and suddenly she wished there was someone else in the cells with her. She felt very alone then and grabbed her holy symbol absently in her hand and clenched it tightly.

"Dear Adlesk, give me the strength to resist this evil," she muttered. Her voice was shaky, the fear evident there. Suddenly smoke started to seep under the door. Her first thought was that there had been an accident and now the jail was on fire. She wanted to yell for help, but fear froze her voice. Her eyes widened as the small hallway filled with smoke. To her amazement, it started to gather in one place—seemed to grow tall, and take on the shape of a human. She realized that it was not smoke at all but some kind of gas.

She backed away from the bars, all the way back to the end of her cell. There were three solid walls to her cell, no windows, and the one wall facing the hallway was made of iron bars with a section of them cut into a hinged door. Her back was to the wall farthest from the hallway, and from her current vantage point, she could no longer see where the cloud of gas was gathering. She breathed fast, almost gasping, as she tried to remain calm. She could feel the evil in the hallway now, making it hard to maintain her composure.

Then there were footsteps. They came from the area of the hall that contained the gaseous cloud. Something had formed from that cloud! She had heard of such powers and guessed that whatever was coming toward her cell was not human. The steps grew louder and sounded as if they were from shoes—perhaps from a human. She didn't trust that thought, though, and assumed if it was a human, it must be a powerful wizard. Hope returned for just a moment as she considered the possibility that the wizard from Pelesea had come for her.

That hope faded fast when a tall pale man came into view. He stopped at the door to her cell and slowly turned to face her. He scared her, and she knew that he hadn't come to rescue her. She was pleased at that moment because the door remained locked. However, true terror overcame her when he melted into a gaseous cloud and seeped through the bars.

"Help! Somebody, help me!" she cried.

She ran to the bars once more and continued her screaming, hoping against hope that a hero would bust through the door and come and save her from this evil being. The gas started to re-form near her feet once it was inside her cell. She backed up to the far wall and gave up yelling. She knew she was doomed at that point, that no one would come.

The events of the last few weeks ran through her head. How had things come to this? First, Cassandra had attacked Ronnis, nearly killing him. Then, Kessi had saved the evil man, and she'd regretted it ever since. Then, Cassandra was injured and kept at the temple, vulnerable to whatever evil they practiced there. Finally, Baxter rescued her, or so Ronnis had declared, stating to the guild masters that the wizard had kidnapped her one night. Kessi hoped that story was true. Then, they pointed the finger at Sera and Quinn, Ronnis fabricating a tale that they had somehow assisted in freeing Cassandra and therefore were guilty of releasing a criminal. The guild had taken Sera and Quinn that awful morning and immediately brought Kessi to this cell, where she had remained uninformed and without hope. Now this. How had her happy life come to this?

"Kessi Rho?" the creature said, now fully formed and standing just a few feet in front of her.

She held her symbol toward him and summoned the courage to speak. "I am not afraid of you, a vile creature of darkness. My god rebukes you from this cell. In the name of Adlesk, be gone from this place!"

He laughed and moved toward her with a blinding speed that she did not expect. He covered her tiny hand and holy symbol with his large cold hand, closing over it entirely. "Dear child, that religious nonsense won't work on me. You are mine, and your god will not save you."

His breath was stale, somehow old, and he was cold to the touch. His hand slowly tightened, putting pressure on Kessi's hand and making the copper wire dig into her palm. She desperately tried to break the grip, using her other hand to pry his hand open. She could not, and she slowly fell to one knee.

"Please … stop," she finally gasped.

Surprisingly to her, the evil man did. He released her bruised hand, and she dug her small symbol out of her bleeding palm.

He grabbed her by her hair and quickly pulled her to her feet. "Be thankful, child, for I am freeing you from this cell."

She then felt her surroundings begin to spin. The walls blurred into a single whiteness, and she felt her feet leave the floor—or was the floor leaving her feet? She swooned and nearly lost consciousness as she suddenly felt as if she were falling. She wasn't aware of much in the few moments it lasted, but the one thing she realized was that the creature still held her tight and was very much in focus. Whatever was happening to her, whether good or bad, he was the one responsible for it.

~

The following day was crisp, the air very cool, but not a cloud in the sky. Kringus was fully armored in his refurbished chain mail and mounted on his warhorse. He was an imposing figure and gave the spectators something to cheer for as he assembled his small band at the front gates. Alongside him were the elven brothers Von and Lenore, both distinguished members of the New Order. Also along for the journey were four of the best cavaliers in the kingdom. Each rode on a massive warhorse, complete with heavy barding and an accompanying squire to carry weapons as needed.

So the troupe of eleven men formed up at the gates as a large gathering of the city folk had come to see them off. It was seldom that the king left the city, and that act would potentially cripple most cities. Not Pelesea, though, for Penelope had been queen for years before marrying Kringus. They had ruled together for the last ten years, but before that, the city had fared just fine with their lone monarch, and the city would be in capable hands without their king. Penelope was at the gate to see the party off.

"I guess word got out that you were leaving for a bit. The people are giving you quite the send-off," she said with a smile.

Kringus waved at the crowd to cheers and applause, then looked lovingly at his wife. Her elven features displayed prominently in the glow of the morning sun, especially her big green eyes. Their love was more profound than most, and Penelope could see it in his eyes. But something was bothering him—she could see it in his face. That's when he said, "This feels wrong, my queen."

"What do you mean?"

"I mean the purpose of this journey feels wrong. To go to such lengths just for a girl makes no sense to me."

Penelope shook her head. "You're doing the right thing. Trust me—you're living up to your reputation by helping an individual who needs you. The people love you for your courage, Kringus. Besides, you love the road and would rather be adventuring than sitting on the throne. You won't feel so bad about it once you're on your way. You know I speak the truth," she said and smiled.

He bent down so only she could hear his whispered reply. "I wish you were going with me."

She shook her head, her auburn locks flowing over her shoulders. "So we could spar?" she asked with a lewd smile.

"Every morning and every night, to be sure!" he exclaimed with a roaring laugh. "I shall not be gone long—a month and a half, at the most. We will return before winter sets in, my love."

Kringus blew his wife a kiss and waved once more to the gathering crowd, to more cheers. Knights lined the gate and saluted the group as they passed. Penelope watched, along with the rest of the gathered crowd, until they were out of sight, and then she turned and made her way directly toward the temple. Two guards followed closely behind, and she welcomed their protection, but everyone, including herself, knew she needed no such escort. The beautiful queen wore her slender sword on her hip, and Penelope was more than capable of handling herself if something happened. She was walking down the street of the best city in the world, and there was no threat there.

Children ran beside her, and people cheered, some giving her flowers as she passed. It was quite a parade, but she wasn't conscious of the events as they unfolded. Instead, her mind was on the intruder, as Alleah had called him. She wanted to make sure he wasn't a threat to the kingdom; then she could go back to the castle and do queenly things in peace until her husband returned. She had a gift for the man, if he were still alive—a rare item indeed and one that would probably save his life.

She was met at the temple steps by five high priests, who bowed before her. She bade them to stand and briefly discussed the temple's affairs before getting straight to the point. She had come to see the intruder, and she intended to see him right away. So they escorted her to the room, where Alleah and a younger girl were exiting when they arrived. The younger one was carrying bandages stained crimson with blood.

"How is he?" the queen asked.

Alleah bowed. Even though she and Penelope were both members of the New Order and excellent friends, she wanted to ensure she didn't show any disrespect in front of the older priests. Penelope nodded her appreciation and then waited for a reply.

"He's conscious but in a lot of pain. We're simply unable to stop the bleeding from his damaged shoulder."

Eldrick, the high priest of Censah, goddess of elements, and the one man who had the most influence over the temple of Pelesea, said, "Our cure spells have slowed the flow of blood and mended the broken bones in his shoulder but not cured the wound itself. It is simply beyond us. I've never seen anything like it, my queen."

"Where is he from, and how did he get here?" Penelope asked Eldrick.

"We've determined that he comes from a faraway place called Tara. It's a small community and not even identified on most of the maps we checked. It's on the wild continent of Varish, far across the seas."

"And how did he get here?"

"He claims to be a priest of Plath and used a scroll of returning from his old mentor. We haven't had Plath's followers here for many decades, so someone penned the scroll a very long time ago, if he speaks the truth.

"He said Tara was invaded by vicious men led by a powerful female priestess. He said all the priests of Tara are dead and he was the only one to survive. We found no weapons on the young man, only his holy symbol and a magical ring," the priest said.

"Did you have Victoria check the ring?"

"Yes, she has it now, but today starts a new semester for the school, and she's probably a little preoccupied. I'm sure she'll have it analyzed soon enough."

Penelope smiled and patted the older man on the shoulder. "Yes, I suppose you're right, Eldrick."

"My lady?" Alleah said.

"Yes, Alleah?" Penelope asked with a smile.

"Remember what I told the New Order about my sister followers of Sinnis who recently traveled through the city—the ones who warned of an assembling army of Gorl?"

"Yes, I do remember that. Why?"

"Well, this place, Tara, is very near to the rumored location of the Gorl army. I feel this is not a coincidence," Alleah said, her voice shaking.

Eldrick put up a hand to quiet the woman and chuckled softly. "I apologize, my queen, but Alleah takes the rumors of Gorl followers very seriously, and she may be jumping to conclusions here."

Penelope knew Alleah well, and the look on her face after Eldrick's comments told her that the young priestess believed there was a more significant issue. She would continue this conversation at a better time. She decided to direct the conversation back to the young man to perform the task she'd come to do. "May I see him?"

"Of course," Eldrick said, rummaging through the keys he wore on his hip.

Penelope moved Alleah to the side and said, "Take heart—I want to hear more about your concerns. Perhaps tomorrow morning at the castle?"

Alleah nodded, and Penelope could tell the proposal greatly relieved the young woman. The queen could tell that this was a meaningful conversation that would need to occur very soon.

"I need a basin of holy water—can you get that for me?" Penelope asked Alleah once Eldrick had unlocked the door but before they entered Greyson's room.

Alleah looked a little confused at the request. "Are you going to heal him?"

"I'm going to try, but I'm no priest, so I'm only hoping to help as much as possible."

Alleah nodded and called to a passing acolyte, "I need a basin of holy water, Itha. Be quick about it."

"Yes, my lady," the young girl answered with a bow, then hurried down a hallway to fetch the water.

They entered the room, and Greyson sat up, his arm in a sling and his gown stained with blood around his left shoulder. He was sweating profusely and was obviously in a great deal of pain. His eyes were closed, and his head leaned back against the headboard.

"He is but a child," Penelope said on first seeing the young man.

He half opened one of his eyes and tried to smile. "Don't let that fool you, beautiful lady. I'm well versed in many things."

Penelope's look was one of amusement, understanding the crude comment for what it was and knowing he had no idea to whom he was speaking.

"Young Greyson Kavince, may I introduce to you the lovely queen of Pelesea, Penelope Brahmore!" Eldrick said with an exaggerated wave of his hand.

Greyson's eyes flew open, and he took in his surroundings a little better. He was handsome for his young age but seemed only a child to

Penelope. He looked genuinely embarrassed by his crude words, and she tried to put his mind at ease with a friendly smile. He smiled back, but he looked her up and down as if undressing her with his eyes. She'd never seen one so young act so bold, and when he finally noticed her watching him, he only shrugged and smiled. He then noticed the knights who stood behind her and the gathering of priests, and his demeanor finally became serious. He then tried to sit up as best he could, grimacing from the pain, and wiped the sweat out of his eyes with his good hand.

"Apologies, my lady—I didn't know," he said.

Penelope smiled. "Greetings, Greyson from Tara. You have insulted no one here, and I want you to be at ease. I have come to see you since Alleah here told me your remarkable story," she said and waved a hand toward Alleah.

"Am I in trouble?" he asked, looking around nervously at the filled room.

"No, not yet, anyway," she answered with a comforting smile.

He seemed to relax then, although she could tell he was in a tremendous amount of pain. He studied her, enthralled, as if he had never met a queen before, and Penelope assumed that was most likely the case.

"Let's take a look at this wound, shall we?" Penelope said.

Alleah helped Greyson remove the sling, which seemed to cause much discomfort for the young man, and unbuttoned his nightshirt enough to move it down past the wounded arm. Penelope noticed the connection Greyson and Alleah shared and made a mental note of it. Then, to her surprise, she saw the young man look at Alleah the same way he'd just looked at her, undressing the priestess with his eyes and even chewing his bottom lip as she worked his nightshirt down. His gaze shifted to Penelope then, and he seemed to realize she was reading his thoughts. He smiled and shrugged once more. Penelope ignored his crude behavior but made a note of it as well.

"Forgive me, my queen, but I must ask once more: Can you offer healing that the high priests cannot?" Alleah asked.

Penelope examined the damaged arm, a concerned look on her face. "Well, I am no healer, but I am elven, which means I've seen many things over my lifetime. But I have to say I've never seen a wound like this."

Itha, the acolyte, entered the room at that time with a basin of holy water. Alleah instructed her to lay it on the bedside table. The young girl did as Alleah told her, then bowed and went on her way.

Alleah offered Penelope a sad look and said, "I know of something that can cause a wound such as this."

Penelope looked at her, seeing the fear and worry etched on the young woman's face.

"The spear of Gorl," Alleah said.

Penelope nodded, and Alleah refocused her attention on the wound, understanding Penelope respected her intuition. Penelope released Greyson's arm, gently returning it to its cradled position across the man's chest.

"Eldrick, do you or the other high priests have the ability to remove a curse?" the queen asked, turning to the five gathered priests.

"Remove a curse, my lady?" the old priest asked.

"Yes, this wound is as much of a curse as it is a tearing of the flesh. And, I feel this spell would provide needed assistance in healing this young man."

One of the old priests stepped up. "I can perform that spell, my queen."

She nodded and moved away from the bed so that the priest could gain access to the wound. He began softly chanting, forming the incantation of the spell that would hopefully heal the young man. As he did this, Penelope reached into a pouch and produced a large white feather. She walked to the holy water basin and placed the feather in the blessed liquid, where it floated. Alleah was soon beside her, and they watched the feather sail around the bowl and finally come to rest at the edge of it.

"A feather?" Alleah asked.

"An angel's feather," Penelope said, never taking her eyes off the water.

Alleah's eyes went wide. "How did you obtain such an item?"

Penelope smiled. "It doesn't matter. What matters is that I have it and it should be able to heal him."

The older priest backed away then and proclaimed the remove-curse spell a success. He turned back to the other priests, a proud look on his face. Eldrick even clapped him on the back for his excellent work. However, Greyson didn't look any better, and more blood ran down his side and pooled in the bed. Penelope was at his side once more. "There is a basin of healing water—the angels themselves have strengthened it! It is most potent, but you'll need to drink all of it for the effects to take hold of your wound. Do you understand?"

Greyson nodded, again staring lustfully into her eyes.

"Good," she said with a smile, then stood to leave. "Alleah, be sure he drinks all the water in that basin before noon today."

The young woman nodded and produced a flask, which she submerged in the liquid and filled up so Greyson could drink, careful not to disturb the precious feather.

"We will need to meet soon to discuss things," the queen said.

Alleah nodded and smiled.

As the queen walked toward the door and the escort of knights, she stopped and turned to Greyson. "Once you have healed, I wish to speak with you at the castle."

"Yes, my lady," Greyson said and nodded, then accepted the flask from Alleah and gulped down his first dose of healing liquid.

"Alleah, bring him to me tomorrow morning if the healing is successful. Then the three of us will discuss things over breakfast."

"I will, at the crack of dawn," Alleah said.

CHAPTER 10

LONELY BIRTHDAY

WHEN THE WORLD FINALLY STOPPED SPINNING, KESSI found herself in complete darkness. She couldn't see her hand in front of her face and could feel nothing but her feet touching the floor, if she was standing on such. She could still feel him, though—the evil presence of the creature that had brought her there. The coldness also assaulted her, the temperature suddenly plummeting. She found her small holy symbol, still around her neck, and grabbed it up in her wounded hand, praying like she never had before. She had been granted a few spells from Adlesk, and she began casting one of them, hoping to provide some light in the darkness. She needed to regain some measure of control, and even with the creature so very close, she had to try something. She held tightly to her holy symbol and began to chant softly, her eyes closed tight.

Almost immediately, she was struck hard on the side of her cheek. She fell sideways and hit her head hard against something solid, perhaps a stone wall. She lost all thought of the spell she had begun, her concentration broken with the impact. She hoped the creature wouldn't kill her, but she sensed an evil emanating from the being that promised just such a thing. Unfortunately, she lost consciousness before she could finish the thought.

She awakened some time later with a throbbing pain in her head and a swollen cheek. There was light and warmth as she discovered a fireplace beside her. She found herself in a small room with stone walls, the fireplace making light dance around her. Burning wood popped, and the smell of smoke overwhelmed her senses. There was a small table in the room, along with a single chair. She tried to stand, but the dizziness had her rethinking that decision, and she sat back down on the floor. She brought a hand to her head, feeling the matted blood from where she'd hit the wall. She felt for her holy symbol, and to her relief, she found that the small copper tear was still around her neck.

She moved gingerly to the nearest wall and propped herself up against it in a sitting position. That's when she saw the monster—he just seemed to appear from nowhere suddenly. He now stood near the fireplace, his face expressionless but still exuding evil more than anything she had encountered in her short life. Something about him frightened her tremendously.

"I have made you a fire for warmth and light," he said, extending a hand toward the fireplace. "The log is magical and will not burn out. There are supplies there." He gestured to a backpack in the far corner. "Inside, you will find some food. Not enough, but if you ration it, you will remain sustained. There are no doors here; I have long since had the lone exit sealed."

Kessi could see an old doorway behind the creature and the stones placed and mortared within it to close off the room. She saw no visible way out of the small prison other than the flue to the fireplace.

As if reading her thoughts, the creature said, "The flue is too small. Even a person of your small size couldn't hope to fit through it."

He smiled, and his canines became apparent to her. She paled at the sight, understanding finally what precisely this creature was: a vampire. She had read about such abominations but never dreamed she would one day see one, much less converse with it.

"What do you want of me?" she managed to squeak out.

"Oh, child, I want nothing more than your life," he said with a smile.

"What?" she asked, very much afraid now.

"Yes … your life … in exchange for your sister!" he said.

"Cassandra?"

"Yes, you will die so that she can live, and in the same selfless act, you will save humanity. You are quite a hero, young Kessi Rho. Stories will be told of you for years to come by the bards of Torlia!"

"Cassandra," she said quietly to herself.

"I will leave you now. Pray to your worthless god that nothing happens to me, or you will die in this room. I am the only one who knows you are here. Our training begins tomorrow night."

"Training?" she asked, but the creature was already blurring from existence, and if he'd heard her, he didn't respond. Soon he vanished from sight, leaving her alone in the small room.

Although she didn't like being in a sealed room, Kessi felt a great relief without the vile creature so close. And the vampire was an enemy she couldn't hope to defeat. Nevertheless, she managed to cast a cure spell on her wounded head and cheek, the pain quickly fading as the healing washed warmly over her. Once the healing energy coursed through her and the pain and dizziness subsided, she gathered the pack and emptied it on the table. There she found a lantern, some oil, a tinderbox, rope, a bedroll, a canteen, and a small pack of jerky.

She sighed. "Not much of a food selection." She thought about eating a bit of it then, realizing she was pretty hungry, but she thought better of it, remembering her captor's warning to ration the food. She decided to wait. She spread the bedroll near the fire and took the canteen. It was empty, so she said a small prayer to Adlesk and waved her hand over the top. Suddenly the canteen was full of pure water. She thanked her god silently for the ability to summon fresh water and took a large drink. She then settled in her bed for a night of most restless sleep. As she closed her eyes and tried to relax, a thought came to her, bringing tears to her eyes. She had a horrible feeling at that moment that she would never see her mother or sister again. "Good night, Cassandra. Happy birthday, my dear sister."

~

The first day of school proved to be a difficult one for Cassandra. She walked down the hall to her first class surrounded by many other students, but she couldn't have felt more alone. It was as if she were back in the orphanage all over again. Everyone was chatting excitedly, laughing and interacting, while she made her way silently down the hall, almost invisible to the other students. She'd never made friends with the kids at the orphanage, and she doubted that would change at this stage in her life. She hated the other students even though she knew nothing about them. They seemed not to have a care in the world and just enjoyed the moment. She, on the other hand, was worried sick about her family. Plus she had gone to bed feeling strange the night before, after the unusual interaction with Baxter. She had never had any interest in boys and considered them a nuisance more than anything else. However, Baxter was not a boy and was old enough to be her father. His behavior intrigued her.

"You must be the other me," came a cheery voice out of nowhere, breaking her contemplations.

She turned to see an exotic young woman walk up next to her, dressed in the finest clothing. She was gorgeous, by all standards, with olive skin, black hair, and bright blue eyes. She walked confidently and with a smile.

"Excuse me?" Cassandra said more hatefully than she'd intended.

"The other gifted student, I mean. You are Cassandra Rho, are you not?"

Cassandra stopped and looked at the girl, now very curious. "Yes, and who might you be?"

"I'm Cashmere Ruben. My parents own several merchant boats here in Pelesea. I have been blessed with a proper upbringing and plenty of wealth and have a knack for conjuring and controlling arcane magics. Some people say I was lucky to have been born with such privileges, but I call it destiny."

Cassandra rolled her eyes and began walking again. The young girl kept pace.

"So what do your parents do?"

"I don't know," was Cassandra's curt response.

The girl laughed. "So the competition begins already, huh? I knew that we would each strive to outdo the other, but you've begun a little early, haven't you?" She laughed again and walked away but turned to face Cassandra as she did, stepping backward in perfect balance. "By the way, my friends call me Cass. I guess that's just something else we have in common—our names!"

Cassandra stopped once again as Cass turned around and continued walking. Even her walk was graceful and beautiful, and Cassandra noticed more than one male student giving an appreciative glance at her backside as she walked by. It was safe to say that Cassandra hated the girl immediately.

After that strange encounter, she made her way quickly to class, where she found a seat near the front of the room. She didn't make eye contact with any of the other students but did take a few glances around when the opportunities arose. The students seemed to be mostly her age or older, and all were human, as far as she could tell. She'd never seen one, but she'd heard that elves made fine wizards, and she hoped she'd get a chance to see one. This particular class was about history, and she was very eager to learn about the New Order and perhaps gain some insight into her research.

An odd, thin man named Franklin Le'More instructed the class. He was about the same age as Baxter, she guessed, but wasn't nearly as interesting. Finally, after a few hours of a boring lecture, he dismissed the class. Cassandra approached the instructor as the other students were leaving the room.

"Excuse me, Instructor Le'More."

"Yes, young lady"—he shuffled through a small book on his desk and finally came up with her name—"Cassandra. How may I assist you?"

"I need to know more about the New Order."

"Yes, yes, we will cover that in week four."

"I'd rather pick your brain sooner rather than later concerning this subject. Instructor Baxter referred me to you, and I'd like to schedule a day where we can talk."

He smiled. "Very well. Come by my office after classes are through today, and we'll talk."

"I'll be there."

"Do you know its location?"

"Yes, near Baxter's—I mean Instructor Baxter's office. Correct?"

"Yes, that's correct."

The confused look on his face told her that he'd picked up on the slight error in Baxter's title. She would have to make sure she didn't make that mistake again, for her sake and Baxter's. She smiled and left in a hurry, only to find Cass standing out in the hallway with a smirk on her face.

"So … getting some extra help already, I see?"

"No, Cass, I just have some questions."

"I see," she replied with a knowing smile, making Cassandra feel very uncomfortable.

Cass walked beside Cassandra as she made her way to her next class. Neither said a word to the other, and Cassandra felt disquieted around the girl. She finally stopped and asked, "Why are you following me?"

Cass gave a derisive snort and pushed past her, right into the room in which Cassandra had been heading. Cass wasn't following her; she was going to class—the same one as Cassandra. Disappointment washed over her, especially since this was Baxter's class. Cassandra just stood there as other students filtered into the room. A tall, lanky young man passed her on her way in, and he turned and stared at her with a dumb look as he did. She felt like wiping it off his face with a perfectly placed burst of magical energy. The idiot sat next to Cass and started talking to her. Cassandra finally entered the room with a sigh and took a seat far away from Cass and the weird lackey sitting next to her. "Perfect couple," she muttered under her breath.

~

The lanky fellow, named Jabell, looked at Cass and, with an upraised thumb, pointed over his shoulder and said, "Is that her?"

"Yes," Cass replied, her arms crossed over her chest and a smirk on her face.

"Wow, she's not really what I expected."

"She's weird—almost rude. I tried to talk with her earlier. I introduced myself, but she was very standoffish. I think I intimidate her."

"Of course you do; you're prettier and far more powerful, I'm sure," Jabell said, complimenting her as he always seemed to be doing.

"May I tell you a secret?"

"Yes, of course, anything!" the young man said, leaning in close.

"I've seen her buttering up two instructors now, last night with Instructor Von Glord and now with Instructor Le'More. It seems to me that she's not beyond sleeping with the professors to get an edge."

"What?" Jabell said and burst out laughing.

Jabell's friend Leonard entered class then and approached them. He was a year older than Jabell and much better looking. Cass had quickly become friends with Jabell for the added benefit of staying close to Leonard.

"What's so funny?" he asked Jabell and took a seat beside his friend. Then he looked over at Cass and added, "Hi, Cass."

Cass smiled and waved back, showing him her perfect teeth as she did so. However, he took little notice of her, unlike all the other dim-witted boys who surrounded her. Jabell finally stopped laughing and looked at Cass for permission to spill the secret to Leonard. She smiled knowingly and nodded. That's how the rumor started that Cassandra Rho was sleeping with the professors.

~

Cassandra loved Baxter's class, and she was amazed at how well he ran it, finding a newfound admiration for her friend. He was very professional, and he made her feel important, and for the first time that day, she felt like she belonged. She loved that feeling, as it was one of the few times in her life that she had felt that way, which made her connection with Baxter even stronger. Even though Cass was in this class, being near Baxter made her feel safe and forget all about Cass and her idiot friend.

However, her last class was her favorite, a course on the study of magical items. Frederick Von Hueven instructed it and focused on identifying and creating magic items. Cassandra took a liking to it right away. She also enjoyed the instructor, who was younger than the others—and much better looking, in her opinion. Two unusual events occurred in his class that day that made her feel good. First, she was recognized for her unique talents, whereas in Oldorburg they'd jailed her for them. Second, she made a friend, whereas in Oldorburg she'd had none.

Instructor Von Hueven's classroom contained tapestries of mighty artifacts and potent magic items, with corresponding pictures of the wizards who had created them. Cassandra was mesmerized by the images, and she immediately tried to find the rod that had been in her vision with the dark man, but she had no luck. As she glanced over the tapestries, she was vaguely aware that Cass, who, unfortunately, was in this class with her, and the weird-looking boy, Jabell, were whispering to each other. They whispered while looking her way, then laughed, and

Cassandra caught them doing it several times during class. She couldn't help but feel they directed it toward her, making her feel self-conscious. It felt a lot like the orphanage all over again. She tried her best to ignore them and instead focus on the professor as he began his lecture.

"I am Instructor Von Hueven, and we will be working with magic items in this class! Magic items are the pride and joy of all wizards, and although this is an introductory class for you new students, you will be taking my advanced courses as you progress here at the school and will one day be able to create your very own magical items.

"Now, we have been lucky enough to have a sample item turned over to us from the queen herself. A stranger has come into our great city with a magic device that the queen asked Lady Victoria to identify, which she has already done.

"I know this is the first class, but I'm going to give you a chance to see what for many of you may be the first magic item you've laid eyes on before we hand it back over to the owner."

With that, the young professor held out his hand for the class and unclenched his fist. There in his palm was a ring with a large ruby setting. The students leaned in to see it, and the professor walked around the room so all could take in its perfect craftsmanship.

"You see," Instructor Von Hueven said, "wizards take an excruciating amount of time to make sure their final piece of work is perfect in every way. A good magic item can save your life and can make you a legend at the same time."

After he had made his way around the room so everyone had had a chance to see the magnificent item, the professor returned to the front of the room and held his palm out to keep the ring on display. "Now, can anyone tell me what they think the ring does?" he asked with a smile.

Cassandra focused on the ring and lost herself in its beauty. She let her eyes go out of focus just a bit, and the voice of her instructor faded. She heard someone, quite possibly Cass, say that she thought the ring was one of protection. The professor responded, but Cassandra couldn't hear his muffled words. It sounded like he agreed but wanted her to be more specific. Then Cassandra saw the flames as the ring appeared to burn. If it was in fact burning, Instructor Von Hueven didn't feel the heat.

"Fire," Cassandra said softly, almost to herself.

"What was that you said?" the instructor asked, turning toward her.

Her eyes remained unfocused and began to water. She dared not blink, hoping not to lose the strange vision of the flames engulfing the ring.

"What is your name, young lady?" Instructor Von Hueven asked, sterner this time.

That snapped her out of her trance as she blinked away the vision, then slowly brought her gaze to meet his. She couldn't respond right away and just stared at him, not knowing what to say. Then she heard Cass and the idiot Jabell giggle, inspiring her to speak loudly and clearly. "It is a ring of protection"—she turned toward Cass—"from fire."

"How did you know?" he asked in amazement.

Cass's smile faded with the realization that Cassandra had correctly determined the actual function of the ring.

"It burns with fire energy," Cassandra said.

"Well, you have quite a gift, Miss—you still didn't give me your name."

"Cassandra Rho," she replied.

"Miss Cassandra Rho. Excellent observation, young lady! Behold a ring of fire protection, class!" he exclaimed, holding the ring with his index finger and thumb.

Some of the students clapped, which made her feel good, and the instructor's praise made her feel special. Finally she managed to look over at Cass, who rolled her eyes, and Jabell, who sat there with his big mouth hanging open.

Once class was over, a small pale-complected girl approached her. She wore dark makeup around her eyes and several piercings in her ears, as well as one small loop on the side of her nose. Cassandra found her to be beautiful.

"I'm Binta Mulay. I liked how you showed up that bigmouth Cass," she said, offering her hand to shake.

"I'm—"

"Cassandra Rho," Binta said and smiled.

Cassandra smiled back and shook hands with the friendly girl. It had been an eventful day, mixed with good and bad happenings. In the end, Cassandra liked her classes and the instructors and was excited about her new friend. However, she had been greatly distracted, with thoughts of Kessi and Sera heavy on her mind—especially of Kessi, who shared a birthday with her that very day.

Binta walked with her down to Instructor Le'More's office, and they talked about the school and their backgrounds. Cassandra found it easy to talk to the girl and discovered that Binta had even fewer friends than she did. They had a lot in common, which was unusual for Cassandra indeed. As they parted ways, Cassandra found she missed her company almost immediately. She felt a strange closeness to the girl and was excited about the possibility of being her friend. She watched her walk away, and Binta even turned once more and waved. Cassandra returned the wave and smiled.

"Hello, Cassandra," came a voice from up the hall, making her jump.

She looked up to see Baxter standing in the doorway of his office with a smile on his face. "Hello, Instructor Baxter. Why do you insist on startling me each time we meet?" she said and smiled.

"You impressed Frederick today, you know. You're making quite a first impression!"

She smiled and nodded. "It was a good day. Thanks for making me feel like I was a real student."

"But you are—don't doubt yourself. I foresee great things for you."

"Ah, Miss Rho, I have been expecting you," came Instructor Le'More's voice from the neighboring office. Soon after, his head poked out into the hall, and he waved her in.

"Goodbye, Instructor Baxter," she said and waved, smiling privately at him.

"Until tomorrow, Miss Rho!" he called after her.

Franklin ushered her into his office, and the door shut behind her. Baxter leaned against the doorframe for a very long time, eventually letting out an audible sigh and ducking back into his office as if he were a lovestruck boy.

Franklin Le'More's office contained bookcases from wall to wall, and many tomes and parchments filled those bookcases, some spilling out onto the floor in neat stacks. "Please sit down, Miss Rho," he said, extending a hand to an empty chair at his desk.

She obliged and took in the magnificent sight of the unique office.

"I have just the thing you need," he said, his back to her and his attention fully on a particular bookcase. It took him many moments to finally retrieve a hefty tome from the top shelf. "Ah, here it is!" he exclaimed happily before blowing the dust from its cover. He took a seat behind the desk and laid the extensive work on it, between Cassandra and himself. "What do you know of the original New Order, young lady?"

"Not much, just that they ruled the city of Novafontera almost seven hundred years ago and fought and defeated the demon lord Marnelphion."

"Well, that's partially true, but there's much more to the New Order than that."

"Yes, that's why I've come to you for answers. There's a dark man in particular I want to—"

"Read this tome, young lady, and then we will speak," Franklin said.

"I've read many books on the New Order at the library, and—"

"You have not read this one."

She became aggravated at his continued interruptions, but then he said something interesting: "This book was scribed years ago, at the height of the New Order's power. It comes directly from the journal of Leo, one of two powerful wizards—"

"Who were members of the New Order," she said, enjoying the chance to interrupt him for a change.

He smiled and nodded. "Read this book. Then come see me again with your questions."

She agreed and quickly gathered the giant tome before walking straight to her dorm room. She laid it on her desk, made herself a light meal, and soaked in a long bath. She thought of delving deep into the book that very night, but it had been a long day, and she was tired. As she settled down for the night, she remembered her and her sister's birthday. On this day the previous year, she and Kessi had celebrated their special day together, and Sera had fixed them something delicious to eat as a birthday meal. It dawned on her that she had never been apart from her sister on their birthday until today. She missed her family so much that her heart ached. She walked to the window and looked out on the dark city, realizing yet again that the unfamiliar place would be so much more enjoyable if her family were there to experience it with her. She hadn't the energy to begin reading the large book. Her thoughts were heavy with more important things. "Happy birthday, sister. I hope to see you again soon," she said with tears in her eyes. Then she quickly climbed into bed and softly cried herself to sleep.

~

As Cassandra experienced her first day of classes at the magnificent school for wizards, Greyson Kavince, his shoulder now mended, found himself walking to the castle with Alleah Mansuell. His shoulder still throbbed, but the bleeding had stopped, and the pain had greatly diminished. He wore the injured arm in a sling, which Alleah warned might be a necessity for the foreseeable future. That didn't bother him so much now that the pain had abated. He had been fearful for his life, not knowing whether he would survive the wound, so the sling seemed a minor inconvenience to him.

So he finally got the chance to leave his room and see some of the grand city. The air was crisp that morning, but the sights were breathtaking. He had never been to such a large city, and there was a lot for him to take in. According to Alleah, one place that would be of significant interest to him was the magnificent school of magic, where the new semester had just begun. He found the school's architecture captivating.

Alleah had to remind him that he had witnessed only a small piece of the city, and he in turn asked her to show him around once he felt up to exploring the city in its entirety. She agreed as their friendship continued to blossom.

Once Greyson and Alleah arrived at the castle, two guardsmen escorted them to the appointed chamber where Penelope desired to meet. The large room was the same that the New Order had used a few days earlier, and food adorned the table once more. The smell made Greyson's stomach rumble immediately, and he eagerly took a seat as servants prepared a plate to his liking. There were meats and cheeses and bread and fruit, and he had no problem loading his plate. Alleah sat across from him and took a much smaller sample. He started eating once the vessel was in front of him, but as he took a large bite of bread, he noticed Alleah smiling and shaking her head.

"What?" he asked, several crumbs dropping from his overstuffed mouth.

"Not before the queen arrives, Greyson."

"Oh, right."

With that, he spat the mouthful onto his plate and wiped his mouth. His lack of manners and his simple innocence gave Alleah the giggles, and soon she was near crying, laughing so hard. Thankfully, Penelope entered before things got too far out of hand.

"Welcome Greyson, and my dearest friend, Alleah," said the queen, dressed in a beautiful green gown that matched her eyes—Greyson noticed right away. She wore her crown, indicating that this meeting was official business of the kingdom, and the new friends suddenly felt very cured of the giggles. Alleah rose, and Greyson followed suit.

"Your Majesty, you are a sight worthy of a queen," Greyson said, and his mouth hung open as he watched her gracefully glide across the room and take her seat at the head of the table.

"Why, thank you, Greyson, and you're looking much better this morning," she replied.

Alleah took her seat, and Greyson, wide eyed, didn't pick up on that fact right away and remained standing. "Thanks to you," he said, still mesmerized by the beautiful elf.

"Please sit, Greyson," Penelope said, waving her hand at him as servants prepared her plate.

His face turned red as he realized he was still standing, and he quickly took his seat, glancing up long enough to see Alleah smiling at his discomfort. They began eating and said nothing for the first few minutes. Greyson tried to pace himself, realizing he didn't understand the etiquette required to share a queen's meal. He tried to follow Alleah's lead.

"So you're feeling better this morning, and it looks as though the angel feather has saved your life," Penelope finally said.

"Yes, your feather has very much saved this man's life—I agree with that," Alleah said.

"I don't want the credit, Alleah. You know that. I'm just glad to see that it worked," she said and smiled.

"Regardless of whether you want the credit, dear lady, you have saved my life. So I at this moment pledge my allegiance to you and this wonderful city," Greyson said.

Penelope smiled and sat back from her plate. "That is appreciated, Greyson, and I will hold you to that allegiance if the time comes. But for now, we must determine who you are, why you are here, and how you even got here. There are many questions I hope you can shed some light on for us. Also, Alleah here has some theories about what happened to your home. Are you ready to discuss these things?"

"I owe you my life, dear queen. I will answer all the questions you may have," Greyson said.

"Very well. We have heard your tale of how you got here. You read a scroll by an old priest named Berro, high priest of Plath, correct?"

"Yes, my lady."

"Pelesea's priests have determined that there was indeed a thriving faction of Plath here at one time. Therefore we believe your story and don't take your entrance into our city as one of trespass or malice."

"Thank you, my queen," Greyson said.

"That faction is long gone, I'm afraid. However, we will welcome it here once more if you so desire."

"I would like that. Plath demands that I travel and experience many new things, but I would be glad to start a following of Plath here before I move on," Greyson said.

"Well, Alleah can help make that happen, and the other high priests have assured me that they will assist you in getting your church started once more.

"Now, Alleah"—Penelope turned her attention toward the young woman—"you are suspicious of the attack on Tara and who might be behind it."

"Yes, I feel that after what Greyson has told me and what I've heard from my sisters—"

"You have sisters?" Greyson exclaimed, excited by the news.

"Not biologically, Greyson, but in faith," Alleah said.

"Oh, right," he mumbled, turning his attention back to his breakfast, more than a bit disappointed.

"Tara's assailants were very much following the creed of Gorl: the destruction of the priests; captives, probably used as slaves; and their choice of weapons, all spears," Alleah said excitedly.

Greyson looked up from his food, watching her retell the horror he'd lived through just a few days earlier. The sight of Berro, Darian, and the others swinging from the trees would weigh on him for the rest of his life. Alleah continued and even asked him a question, but he couldn't hear her, his mind on the trees.

"Greyson?" Penelope asked sternly.

"Yes, sorry," he said, suddenly not feeling well.

"Alleah believes that the spear you were struck by is the actual spear of Gorl. Do you believe this could be the case? Do you feel that the wielder was a god or a demigod capable of using such a weapon?"

He looked over at Alleah, whose bright blue eyes waited for his answer, and he knew she wanted him to confirm her theory, but he couldn't be sure she was correct. He slowly shook his head. "It's hard to say. I've never met a god, or demigod, to my knowledge. But the man I faced was evil—as were they all. However ..." He thought of Matilda.

"Please continue, Greyson. Today's meeting is an opportunity for the three of us to consider what transpires halfway around the world and if it will have a direct effect on Pelesea," Penelope said.

"Yes, of course—my apologies. Well, from what little Alleah has told me about the worshippers of Gorl, they have no true priests. The warriors, hateful and warmongering, are the true worshippers. If this is true, then these men might not be worshippers of Gorl at all."

Alleah looked disappointed but seemed very curious about his reasoning. He hadn't mentioned Matilda at all partly because he had powerful feelings for her and wanted to protect her and partly because she was not the one who'd tried to kill him. Now, though, it made sense that he told of her part in the massacre.

"A priestess led them."

"What?" Alleah gasped.

"Yes, and she followed some demon lord and didn't worship a god at all," Greyson said.

"What was the name of this demon lord?" Penelope asked, her interest now piqued as well.

His forehead creased up as he tried to recall the exact name. Matilda's image had burned in his brain on that sunny but cold morning in front of the temple. She'd doused that crazy priest with oil and helped light him on fire. Her words were stuck in his mind then: "Plath is not the all-powerful god they told you he was. He is nothing compared to Marnelphion!" How could the small woman so perfectly matched with him as a lover be so evil and heartless?

"Greyson?" Penelope asked, again shaking him from his thoughts.

He looked up to realize he had been daydreaming once again as both women waited attentively for his response. "Marnelphion. The demon's name is Marnelphion," he finally said.

A small gasp escaped Penelope's mouth, and Alleah's face showed one of pure panic as she stole a glance with the queen.

"What?" Greyson asked, now puzzled by the significance.

"Are you sure that was the name of the demon she worshipped? Think carefully, because this is important," Penelope said rather sternly.

"I'm sure, my lady. What does that mean?" he asked.

"It means that the situation is graver than we expected." Penelope leaned back in her chair. "And my husband and most of the New Order are away. However, we will meet again once they return," she said, and Alleah nodded. "Greyson, I must insist you meet with the New Order at that time; we may require more details from you."

"Yes, of course, I'm glad to."

The rest of their time together was quiet as a dark cloud seemed to hover over them. Greyson slowly realized during that meal that Plath had saved him for a reason. He was alive so that he could warn them of the pending doom. From his days as a youth, the young man knew that he had a special connection with his god, and he vowed then not to disappoint him or the two women who had saved his life. He would die for them.

~

Matilda and Cerus rested easily in the natural pool in their quarters, having just made love. Cerus wore a satisfied grin as he rested against the side of the small and relatively warm pool wall. His massive arms lined the top of it on either side of him, stretching wide, while Matilda, equally pleased, rested a few feet away in a similar state of bliss. They had just returned from the Tara and Attins massacres, with slaves and goods in tow. It had been a successful endeavor, despite Cerus's broken nose at the hands of Greyson Kavince.

Attins had been ransacked and abandoned, an eerie landmark to remind those viewing it of things to come. After that successful excursion to inventory their supplies and stock the dungeons with their new slaves, they had immediately made their way back home. The women and children were housed separately from the men as potential sacrifices for the unholy offering. The few men they kept alive would expand the underground caves and fortify the stronghold's defenses. These slaves would most likely work themselves to death long before the great summoning.

Matilda lazily opened her eyes, taking in the sight of her muscular husband. He was always so proud after their lovemaking. She was submissive to him, especially after cheating on him, which stoked his ego and gave him the illusion of control. Unfortunately she'd hurt him this time, mentally and physically, as Greyson Kavince had not only cuckolded him but broken his nose as well. Now that he was sexually satisfied, she would take the opportunity to push a subject he hated. She silently called for Emiline, who had been hiding in the shadows this entire time, watching their lovemaking as Matilda had instructed her.

Cerus's eyes were black and swollen, and his nose wore a small bandage. His ego had suffered the most bruising, and he had vowed to destroy any priest of Plath he ever came across from that day forward. Matilda had done well to stroke that ego, but truthfully, she was greatly disappointed in losing the most incredible lover she had ever had, in Greyson. She watched as Emiline slowly undressed, then hesitated briefly, before gently sliding into the pool beside her.

"I want us back on the offense as quickly as possible, Matilda. My scouts have spotted our next target, a small community to the west," Cerus said with a confident smile, his head tilted back and his eyes still closed.

"In time. We mustn't overexert ourselves. We still have several years before the great summoning," Matilda said while coaxing Emiline closer to her.

"Ah yes, the great summoning," he grumbled, still too relaxed to even open his eyes.

"Then, my husband, you will have all the warmongering you could ever want!" she said coyly.

That brought a bigger smile to his face, and Matilda knew he wouldn't tolerate a delay in their subsequent invasion, regardless of how it affected the summoning.

Just then, his warrior instincts seemed to detect a presence. In a flash, he grabbed his dagger, which he had laid near the pool's edge, within easy reach. His eyes went wide, and he took in the surroundings, quickly spotting the intruder sitting next to Matilda in the shallow pool. His anger only seemed to escalate when he saw the vampire. Then, after realizing what was transpiring, he relaxed and said, "Why must you bring your plaything into this room?"

"She is part of us," Matilda said. "She makes us stronger, and I want her to enjoy her new home." She turned to Emiline. "Are you happy?"

"Happy?" Emiline responded, giving her a puzzled look.

"Yes, are you glad to be here, with Cerus and me?"

"You, yes," she said and turned a hateful glare toward the giant man.

"Cerus, put down your dagger and make her feel welcomed."

"I would rather destroy the filthy thing!" Cerus roared but tossed the weapon out of the way.

"You must learn respect, my husband," Matilda said. She motioned for Emiline to join them, and the vampire reluctantly did so.

Matilda could destroy the vampire with but a thought, and Emiline knew it. Matilda knew she would obey her without question, even though the creature genuinely hated Cerus. Also, her husband would not stand against her because of the continued promises of war and domination Matilda offered him. However, neither could refuse her, and that was something she intended to take advantage of fully. Once Emiline was standing next to them, she took Cerus's hand and placed it on Emiline's naked breast. The look on his face was priceless, a mix of fear and disgust. Emiline accepted the touch but looked just as disgusted. The two truly were beginning to hate each other.

"How does that feel, my husband?"

"Like a cold, dead fish," he replied, malice dripping from his words.

"Do you enjoy his touch, Emiline?" Matilda asked the vampire, ignoring her husband's insult.

"Enjoy?" Emiline said, sounding confused.

"Kiss her," Matilda said to Cerus.

His face didn't change expression, but that was only because of the trained warrior within him, Matilda knew. She could see the inner turmoil her request was causing. Matilda watched as he removed his hand from Emiline's breast and moved closer to their new pet. The vampire was beautiful, and Matilda knew he would have found her attractive if undeath hadn't cursed her. He put his arms around her, and she reciprocated hesitantly. She was a lifeless thing, and Matilda knew she felt cold and dead. Matilda looked on excitedly as they kissed gently. A small peck on the lips at first, their eyes never leaving the other. Emiline tightened her grip on his forearms as he grabbed two handfuls of hair. Matilda could not tell if her husband was forceful because of his lust or anger but assumed his hate was driving him. He tightened his grip and forced Emiline back into a kiss. This one was more passionate as the warrior kissed her deeply. Matilda, satisfied that she had initiated the final stage of her plan to introduce the vampire into their lovemaking, slid to the other side of the small pool to allow nature to take over.

She noticed Emiline's knuckles whiten as her small hands dug deep into Cerus's colossal biceps. He in turn had two giant fists of her hair and was turning her head roughly to manipulate his kisses, which seemed to invade her mouth with savagery equal to that of his invasion of Tara the previous day. He suddenly pulled back, and she could see the hate in his eyes; his mouth was bleeding, and Matilda could only suspect that Emiline had bitten his tongue. There was a slight pause as they looked at each other with disgust, and then it was Emiline's turn to attack Cerus with her kissing, obviously having become more aroused now with the presence of blood. Matilda leaned back against the pool's wall and enjoyed the show. That's when she felt the mental intrusion: "Matilda, I have news."

She let herself fall into the mental connection. She knew it was the brand and, more precisely, Heinsvick. She could still see the physical struggle that Cerus and Emiline shared, but her mind no longer registered it. She fell within herself and reached out to Heinsvick: "I am here, faithful one. What news do you bring me?"

"First, how is Emiline?" the vampire lord said.

"She's safe," Matilda answered and smiled to herself, focusing once more on the kiss that the two potential lovers shared.

"I long to see her, and I have news that will complete our arrangement."

Matilda stood up in the pool, and her eyes were wild, darting back and forth, as she tried to take in the information. "What did you say?"

"I may have the child of Kane!"

"How sure are you?" Matilda asked, on the verge of screaming. She stepped out of the pool and wrapped herself in a towel. Cerus and Emiline broke their embrace immediately, and Emiline gave Cerus a sour look as she followed Matilda out of the pool.

"I'm positive. A female named Cassandra Rho, and her virginity is intact. When can we meet?"

"Immediately! Meet me at the docks of Racip!"

"On Varish? It will take me nearly a month to reach the port," Heinsvick said, lying. Although he could teleport Kessi there in the blink of an eye, he needed time to brainwash the woman and didn't want Matilda to know of that particular trick.

"In one month, then. We'll meet at the docks of Racip. Bring the girl. Do not be late. Soon you'll have your precious Emiline back, my faithful servant!"

Matilda couldn't believe her luck, having thought the hunt would be nearly impossible to complete and the chance of succeeding minimal. But now, if Heinsvick had indeed come through for her, her dream would become a reality.

"I will be there," came Heinsvick's curt response, and then the connection faded.

Matilda turned toward Cerus, who rose to his feet, a concerned look on his face. "What is it?" he asked.

"Heinsvick! He has potentially found the child of Kane!" Matilda replied, nearing hysteria.

"Heinsvick?" came a small voice behind her.

She turned to see Emiline standing there, nude and dripping with water. Matilda removed the towel she had wrapped herself in and draped it over the vampire, immediately understanding her error in mentioning the vampire lord. In her delight at the sudden news, Matilda had forgotten just how fragile Emiline's ego still was.

"Yes, it was Heinsvick, my dear," Matilda said, her face suddenly somber.

"He is coming for me?" the innocent girl asked, her eyes hopeful.

Matilda shook her head with a disappointed sigh and said, "No, my dear. He has decided to let you stay with us. He doesn't want you anymore."

Emiline looked on the verge of tears, and her bottom lip quivered. "He doesn't … want me?"

Matilda shook her head and then hugged the vampire, who fought to stifle her tears. Matilda held her tight, trying to comfort the creature. "There, there. Cerus and I will let you live with us. You'll be happy here—I promise."

Matilda broke the embrace and held the vampire out at arm's length and stroked the side of her cheek, where fresh tears ran. Emiline kept her gaze to the floor and sniffed back her tears as best she could. Cerus was now climbing out of the pool, his hatred for the creature plastered all over his face. Her husband hated Emiline, but Matilda knew she was slowly winning over the naive vampire with her lies.

"Come, my dear. Let me take you back to your room. I'll give you a nice meal, and you'll feel better in the morning. Your life will be very fulfilling here. I love you, and Cerus will, too, if you start treating him better. Understand?"

Emiline nodded but kept her head hung, emotionally defeated. Matilda threw on her robe and walked the vampire to her quarters. She remained calm during the trip to the lower part of the caves where Emiline resided, but on the inside, she was busting, too excited about the news Heinsvick had shared. She couldn't wait to tell Cerus the conversation's details and make plans to pick up her prize sacrifice.

Emiline's cell was large and fully furnished. Her casket was in a dark corner, but the rest of the room was plush with pillows and other furnishings. Matilda sent a guard to find a healthy slave from the pool of new arrivals, one who would make an excellent meal for Emiline. The nervous guard bowed and left immediately to hand select the vampire's meal.

While they waited, Matilda sat with her and gently stroked her hair. She eyed the back of the cell, which had recently been modified with another row of bars, cutting off a section of the freshly excavated cave. The effect essentially created another small prison cell at the back of the vampire's cell and was accessible only by walking through Emiline's luxurious room. It wasn't large yet, only about ten feet in circumference, and the slaves would be brought in to work on it while Emiline slept each day. It would quickly become more significant with the slave labor and hold special prisoners for the great sacrifice.

"Do you know what that new edition is for?" Matilda asked, nodding toward the back of the cell.

Emiline looked where Matilda pointed, still gently crying but now curious about the new construction. She cocked her head in her usual manner and tried to understand the new set of bars with a tiny door hinged in the center. Matilda watched her, ever amazed at the lifelike characteristics and mannerisms the creature displayed. Emiline got up and walked over to the new bars. When she saw the girl in the new cell, she gasped and looked back at Matilda, her eyes wide with wonder. "A friend?"

"Yes, in a way," Matilda said, wanting her to get past this business with Heinsvick. Finally, Matilda walked over to her and pointed to the unconscious girl. "She is a special hostage, and others will soon be joining her."

"Hostage?"

"Yes, special and important. I'm giving you the task of guarding the girl and anyone else I put in that cell. Do you understand?"

Emiline nodded but didn't take her eyes away from the sleeping girl. "Is she … like me?"

"A vampire?" Matilda asked.

"Yes."

"No, you are very special to us, Emiline. Do you understand that? You are our only vampire," Matilda said, hoping to make her feel special but knowing she wanted a companion of her kind. "It is important you let no one near these special hostages. Do you understand?"

"Yes, they are special … like me."

"That's correct," Matilda said with a smile and then looked back into the new cell.

There lay the girl named Sabrina who they had captured in Attins. Matilda had thought her a potential candidate for the spawn of Kane when she had first seen her in the white dress. Garyn had grabbed her and stripped her of her clothing, the very dress Matilda used to seduce Greyson that same night. Matilda had decided to add the new cell section and put all hopefuls down there with Emiline. Cerus's men wouldn't dare come near the vampire, so Matilda knew the virginity of those captives would stay intact. It was probably the safest place to keep them other than directly in her room.

The sound of approaching guards broke the silence, and both turned to see a terrified slave, one of the young men from Attins, being dragged toward the cell. He was near hysterics already, but when he saw Emiline, he started struggling and screaming. The commotion woke Sabrina, who let out a yelp and crawled to the back of her cell.

"Bring him in, gentlemen," Matilda said.

The guards opened the cell, then pushed the man roughly into it, slamming the door behind him. He turned immediately and started banging on the bars with his hands. The man was terrified. He looked over his shoulder at Emiline, and his eyes were as large as saucers. "Please let me out!" he said to the guards.

One leveled his spear toward the man, a smile on his face. He poked it in through the bars, and the slave had to fall away to avoid it. Emiline was on the man with sudden speed, using one arm to grab him by the throat and lift him from the ground. The man kicked and smacked at Emiline's hand, trying to break the grip.

"You can't come near here—she is special!" Emiline hissed, pointing to the girl in the far cell. The man only struggled more, gasping for air. Finally, Emiline brought him close to her face, where she showed him her fangs. "And I am special!"

Matilda watched with glee as the young man slowly suffocated. The vampire was genuinely loyal to her, having embraced the task of protecting the young virgin. The two guards also witnessed the display and looked on with amazement and terror. The word would spread among Cerus's men of the ever-watchful vampire, which Matilda knew would keep these captives safe.

"I must go now," Matilda said to Emiline, who tossed the dead slave to the ground. "You have done well, my dear. I task you with the duty of protecting the virgin and any others I put in that cell—understand?"

"Protect them," Emiline said with a nod.

"Good. Now feed on this one. He's young and healthy—his blood should taste delicious, I would imagine."

Emiline's pupils dilated, and she looked at the dead slave with a hunger in her eyes.

As Matilda exited the cell, she could hear Emiline pounce on the fresh corpse and start feeding, the strong sucking sound of her bite cutting through the air. The young virgin screamed and began to cry, terrified at witnessing the unnatural act. Her discomfort brought a new smile to the face of the powerful priestess. She quickened her pace; she suddenly wanted to make love to her husband again.

~

Kessi found sleep hard to come by that first night in her tiny prison. The magical fire kept the room warm, and the air somehow remained clean, even with the burning log. It was the thought of her predicament that was the culprit of her restlessness. The vampire had taken her so she could serve as a sacrifice in place of her sister. None of it made any sense to her, and she prayed for the strength to confront the creature the next time she saw him. She needed to understand what his plans for her entailed.

There was no sense of time in that small room, as she found little sleep and couldn't determine day or night. She knew only that he would return as the sun went down. At some point during her restless sleep, she got up and sat at the desk, eating a bit of jerky and drinking the pure water that her god had provided. She prayed hard after her small meal and asked for the strength she would so desperately need to confront the vampire. When she finally fell asleep at the table, her dreams were unpleasant and vivid. And it took her a while to understand that the fear she felt was real, not a part of her imagination.

She awakened with a start to find the vampire standing over her, watching her sleep. She yelped and nearly fell over in the chair at the sudden appearance of the creature. He found her distress humorous, and that made her angry. She used that anger to focus on her god and the few powers he had granted her. She would use everything at her disposal to make a stand.

"It's time for your training, child," he said comfortingly.

"No!" she said defiantly, standing up and backing away from the table.

"What did you say, foolish girl?"

"I said no!" she yelled, trying to steady herself.

"You are brave beyond your years, girl, and just as stupid. But I have ways of making you cooperate," he said.

"I will fight you, even if I die trying!"

"You are in no position—"

Kessi was scared and mad and refused to listen. "I *am* in the position, vampire! You will tell me what this is about, or I will not cooperate!"

Her sudden defiance shocked Heinsvick as he took a step back from the girl. This outburst was unexpected but mostly annoying to the old vampire. "I can destroy you, little girl!"

Kessi backed into the corner as the vampire came closer. She held up her holy symbol and began to pray. Heinsvick grabbed her by the throat and lifted her off the ground, and she kept her eyes closed, knowing the charming effects vampires possessed.

"Look into my eyes," he said.

"No!" she yelled, squinting her eyes tighter.

"Your sister's life hangs in the balance, you fool!"

His grip tightened around her throat, and she gasped for air.

"I will … cooperate … but … I need to know—"

"You want to know how you will save Cassandra?" he said through gritted teeth, his face inches from hers.

She could no longer find breath or speak, so she nodded as best she could. She was near the point of passing out when she felt herself flying across the room. She landed near the fire, the wind was knocked out of her with the impact. Again she gasped for breath, her throat already bruising from the vampire's firm grip, as he calmly made his way over to her. "Time for your training," he said once again.

Kessi looked around and grabbed the burning log from the fireplace and flung it at him. It burned her hand for just a moment, but she released it quickly, so the pain was minimal. The agile vampire easily dodged it before it smacked against the far wall and fell to the floor. Using the log as a distraction, she quickly got to her feet and ran to the table. She grabbed the flask of lantern oil and slung the contents in his direction. Her aim was true, and soon his face, neck, and chest were coated in thick oil. She dived toward the burning log, which now lay on the ground beside her.

"You come near me, and I'll throw this in your face, vampire! I will not miss this time," she said, her teeth now gritted with determination.

Heinsvick stopped and laughed. "You are a resourceful one, now, aren't you? I like that in a female. If circumstances were different, I would make you one of my brides."

"Aren't I the lucky one?" she said and smiled.

"I should kill you, but that would delay my plans, and I have no more patience to continue dealing with Matilda," Heinsvick said. "First, we must end your threat—don't you think?"

He pointed a finger toward the log, and it rose from the ground in response and telekinetically followed his pointing finger back into the fireplace. Then he turned back toward Kessi, who was coughing from the smoke gathering in the room. "Next time, I will let you suffocate!" he said, and the way he looked at her left little doubt in her mind that he would do just that. "Now sit up here at the table if you want to hear the truth of your sister. I will tell the story once, and then we *will* begin your training. Do you agree to these terms, daring but foolish girl?"

She got to her feet and nodded, waving the dispersing smoke from the air. She climbed back into the single chair at the table while Heinsvick stood over her. They stared at each other for a long while, and Kessi felt her nerves faltering. She said a silent prayer to keep up her strength against the fierce creature. He had easily unarmed her, the clever trick quickly spoiled, and yet was willing to give her the explanation she demanded.

"So?" he finally asked.

"So … tell me your name first."

"Heinsvick, the vampire lord of Novafontera."

The city's name struck Kessi as one she recognized from her studies at the orphanage.

"Where are we?" she asked.

"In the bowels of Novafontera."

"What does this have to do with my sister?"

Heinsvick growled in frustration but eventually told her the story of Matilda coming to Novafontera and kidnapping Emiline and how he believed Cassandra was Kane's child from his visit with the werewolves. He also explained his theory that if Kessi took Cassandra's place at the altar, it might spoil the summoning.

"So how am I supposed to save Cassandra, much less humanity?" Kessi asked, genuinely puzzled.

"I can make you believe you are Cassandra."

"So you'll brainwash me, then?"

Heinsvick nodded.

"If the subject is willing, the brainwashing becomes more real, so you have granted me my questions, then?"

"You are wise beyond your years, Kessi Rho. I regret that you have to die," he said and nodded.

The impact of that statement reminded her of her predicament, and despair washed over her once more. She was willing to die for Cassandra and possibly thwart the great summoning, which benefited humanity, and Heinsvick, she noted. His plan seemed reasonable, but it would require her death. Was she strong enough to give that? If it meant saving her sister, then she indeed hoped so. "What if you take me to my sister and we three take a stand against Matilda?" she asked, hoping against hope that she could find a way to spare her own life.

He shook his head. "No, I won't stand against that one; she has too much of a hold on me. All I want is Emiline back, and then my family and I will go into hiding, someplace the nasty priestess can't find us. A human's lifetime is not so long, and we will hide until she passes from this world."

Kessi lowered her gaze to the table, a solemn look on her face. The vampire had been truthful with her, she believed, and she would hold up her end of the bargain. She would take her sister's place, but her heart was heavy in knowing she would never see Cassandra again.

"Ready for your training?" Heinsvick asked.

She nodded and looked up at him. "Yes."

"Good. Let's begin."

The vampire lord fell over her, and she let him into her mind. She found comfort in knowing she was saving her sister and quite possibly the world. She gave herself entirely to his charming effects and soon became lost in his bloodshot eyes.

CHAPTER 11

HEINSVICK REVEALED

FIVE DAYS LATER, THE ROYAL TROUPE FROM PELESEA FOUND themselves at the gates of Novafontera's cursed ancient city. The horses whinnied nervously as Kringus and his men looked on, always mesmerized by the sight of the poisonous gas spilling over the top edge of the city wall.

"It looks the same as the last time we were here," Lenore said, struggling to control his steed.

"Yes, and yet the horses sense something. I don't remember them being this anxious the last time we traveled this way," Kringus said.

"Perhaps there's something to the ranger's suspicions of a change in the city," Lenore said with a frown.

"Did you ever doubt my evaluation of the cursed place, dear elf?" came Daro's voice from behind them. They all turned to see the ranger, Daro, stepping out of the woods with Arrin at his side. "Please do bring the poor horses away from the place so that they may relax," Daro said.

Kringus dismounted and handed the reins of his steed to one of the squires. Then he approached the two men and clasped hands with them as the rest of the men similarly dismounted.

"There is a cave not fifty yards from here that can provide shelter for all of us, and the horses may be tethered and fed there," Daro said, motioning with a hand in the direction from which he and Arrin had just come.

The rest of the group handed their steeds over to the care of the squires. Then they took them safely away from the cursed city and toward Daro's cave.

"So have you noticed any changes since your return here a few days ago?" Kringus asked Daro, with Von and Lenore flanking him and the cavaliers creating a protective perimeter.

"None other than the nervous behavior that the animals display," Daro said.

Kringus nodded with a thoughtful look on his face.

"We have found one interesting thing, my king," Arrin said.

All turned to regard Arrin, who nodded to Daro, who returned the nod and added, "Yes, we should probably show you this phenomenon."

The group followed the two around the eastern side of the city. As they walked along the great wall, an uneasy feeling settled on all of them, as if the place were alive and watching them. As they made their way along the old wall, they noticed no apparent weaknesses in it. Even after being deserted for centuries, it seemed the city was still quite fortified. They also noticed that the poisonous gas seemed to dissipate as it reached the top of the wall, never leaving the city's perimeter. The chilly wind cut across the top of the wall, but even that couldn't disrupt the gas's range.

After walking several hundred yards, Daro stopped and pointed to a place at the wall's base where smoke slowly rose. "There, Kringus. Do you see it?"

Kringus nodded. "Yes, but what is it?"

"It is not part of the curse but something different, I feel," Daro said.

"It's an exhaust," Lenore flatly stated.

"Smoke exhaust from a fire," Von said.

"I agree," Daro said. "Come—let me show you."

The group made their way to the source and discovered a slight flue jutting out of the wall. Kringus knelt to examine it and agreed with the elven brothers that it indeed was an exhaust. "So someone or, more likely, something has a fire burning within the castle?" Kringus asked.

"That's what we've determined," Daro said.

"Also, there's this, Kringus," Arrin said, now standing a few dozen feet away from the flue. There an old rusted metal grate with no discernible door was located at the wall's base. It rested in the ground about a foot lower than the wall.

"A drainage system?" Kringus asked Arrin as he approached.

"Most likely," Arrin said. "However, it appears unused for a very long time, possibly before the curse ever took hold of this place."

"Interesting," Kringus said. "We'll need to investigate this at some point. Especially if there's some activity within the bowels of the city." Kringus rose and asked Daro, "Who or what do you think is within these walls?"

"There can only be two possibilities, in my opinion. It would have to be a creature in an undead state or quite possibly a demon. Both would be immune to the gas."

"That seems unlikely. Why would either have a fire burning within a hearth?" Kringus asked, shaking his head.

"They wouldn't," Daro said with a shrug. "However, if it is a creature that requires heat, then it is certainly not undead or demonic and is living under the city. Perhaps the curse of Marnelphion doesn't reach the bowels of the place."

Kringus clapped the ranger on the shoulder. "You may be onto something there, old friend. It might be safe to enter the city through this grate and avoid the poison. That opens up possibilities for us, and we need to determine what exactly has taken up residence underneath the city, if that is the case."

"These drainage grates exist at about fifty-yard intervals along the wall, and none seem recently used. We can use horses to open one of them if you wish, my lord," Arrin said.

Kringus thought for a moment, weighing the options to investigate the drainage systems or carry on to Oldorburg. Then, after several moments of consideration, he shook his head and said, "Perhaps soon, but not now. I must complete this diplomatic mission—and quickly. We'll discuss this again upon our return. In the meantime, Daro, just keep a watch on the place."

"Of course," Daro said with a bow.

"Arrin, I'll need your assistance on this trip to Oldorburg. I have a bad feeling about the place and could use your sword," Kringus said, turning to his captain.

"As you wish, my lord."

"It's nearly nightfall. Let's go back to the cave and share a meal. You can all be on your way in the morning when the horses are rested," Daro said.

And so the group made their way to the small cave where Daro had a fire burning low, and soon everyone was resting comfortably, albeit a little cramped, sharing a meal. The horses were tethered outside and were now far enough away from Novafontera to be at ease. The first signs of the coming winter were evident outside the cave as light snow began to blow in the cutting wind. Soon the darkness overtook the woods, and the world became silent, eerily so. The elven brothers stood next to Kringus at the cave's mouth, looking into the darkness of the night, while the squires attended the horses.

"Tomorrow, we will ride at full speed to Oldorburg. I want this trip over with as quickly as possible," Kringus said quietly.

"You have a bad feeling about this trip?" Lenore asked.

"Yes. Although I feel the cause is just, I don't feel that they will welcome us, especially if we try to remove Cassandra's family."

"Therefore you've asked Arrin to join us?" Von asked.

"Yes, we will need the assistance, just in case negotiations don't go well."

"Will your negotiations include your sword?" Lenore asked, turning to the king with raised eyebrows.

Kringus turned to face his friend and, with a nod of his head, said, "If need be."

~

At the other end of the flue was the small room where Kessi had lived for the last week, undergoing her transformation into Cassandra. She sat quietly in the room, her eyes closed, fully opening her mind up to Heinsvick's suggestions. In her mind, she could hear his voice reminding her of who she was. She was Cassandra Rho, the virgin daughter of Kane, the lich god. Kessi tried to absorb the information and believe it as reality. She had to do this for her sister, and it was exhausting. She tried to grasp the vampire's suggestions—she'd been trying for days now—but it just wasn't working as planned. The vampire delved deep into her consciousness, stripping away her memories and replacing them with Cassandra's. Still she knew her true self, and Heinsvick grew agitated.

Early in the process, she had told Heinsvick Cassandra's life story, including as many little details as she could remember. Then the vampire lord had spent several days asking her those details so he could replant them back into her mind as her own. The process was slow and painful to poor Kessi, and she had spent the last three days trying to absorb the suggestions. It was an arduous process, and her head was pounding from the effects.

"Kessi Rho. Come to me," the request echoed in her head from Heinsvick nonetheless.

She was confused by the simple demand, unsure if the voice addressed her or her sister. She tried clearing the jumbled memories to answer him, but all she succeeded in doing was recalling things from her past that she wasn't sure were true. The voice was persistent, though, beckoning her to come back from her dreamlike trance.

"Kessi Rho. Come back to me."

She couldn't resist and started her climb from the subconscious. The whirl of thoughts and memories bombarded her. She saw two little girls in her mind; one was her, but she couldn't remember which one. The memories were sad primarily because she knew one of the girls was in trouble. She tried to climb out of the stupor, to open her eyes, but they were heavy, so cumbersome. She saw a wolf, her dead mother, her sister—or maybe it was herself—using a powerful magic spell to kill someone. Then she saw the teardrop symbol of her god, Adlesk.

She opened her eyes, and the vampire was there. His pale face was close to hers, and he stared intently into her eyes, studying her face.

"Who are you?" he asked sternly.

"What?" she asked, trying to blink away the swirl of jumbled memories.

"What is your name?"

"Kessi. Why?"

The vampire was fast and powerful, and his hand struck her in the face before her mind could register the action. He hit her with enough force to topple her over in her chair. She hit the floor hard, but before her groggy mind could comprehend any of it, she was off the floor again—the vampire pulling her up by the hair and pushing her hard against the wall.

"You doom us all, foolish girl!" he yelled in her face.

A mixture of fear and anger washed over her at being treated so violently by the volatile creature. After spending the last few days together, they had made a bit of a connection, but his violent nature continued to get the best of him. He had hit her on more than one occasion over that time, and she could not allow that to continue.

"Don't touch me again," she managed to squeak out, summoning all her courage to do so.

He brought his face closer to hers with a snarl, showing those long canine teeth, still pinning her against the wall. Her heart raced, and her courage faltered, but she did not back down.

"What did you say, little girl?"

"I said let me go and don't touch me again, or the deal is off," she said and backhanded him across the face.

He didn't budge, and if the hit had harmed him at all, he didn't acknowledge it. Kessi's hand stung as if she had swatted a tree, and she yelped in pain, holding her wounded hand to her chest. He did release her at that point, and she crumpled to the floor.

"So you wish to die?" he asked, but there was no anger in his tone.

She looked at him through tear-filled eyes but didn't change her resolve. "I'm already dead. We can work together, or you can kill me now, but there's only one way you're getting your Emiline back."

Her response seemed to startle him, and he backed away, giving her some space. She managed to stand and stagger over to the chair, sitting it back up and taking a seat once more. She held a hand to her now-swelling cheek, having experienced the sensation more than a few times over the last few days. First, she felt weak and dizzy, and now it felt as if she had a broken hand. "I can't do this anymore," she whispered.

Heinsvick snarled and bristled at her response. "So you desire death today, then, child?"

"No, but I haven't eaten well since you brought me here, and you've caged me in this small room for days. Now you've taken my supplies, including my canteen, so I haven't drunk anything in days, and my food ran out long ago!"

"You wish for me to give back your supplies so you may douse me once again with oil with the intent to destroy me. Do you think me some fool?"

"Yes, if you let me die from starvation," Kessi said with a shrug.

"Would a change of scenery help the process for you?" he asked suspiciously.

"Yes, it would. I have no reason to escape. I want my sister to live. Try to remember what it's like to be hungry and thirsty. I'm sure if there was a better environment to do this in, and at least some food and water, it would be easier for me to succeed."

He thought for a moment, and she could see him processing the information. However, she didn't feel her demand unreasonable, and after a few moments, the vampire said, "I will take you somewhere, but a place of my choosing."

"Agreed," was her meek response.

The vampire then faded from existence, leaving her alone once again in the small room. She laid her head down on the cold table and quickly fell asleep, feeling overwhelmed by dealing with such a powerful adversary. As she drifted to sleep, she tried to picture her sister's face, but all she saw was her own.

~

Heinsvick sat on his throne in Novafontera, his brides surrounding him, stroking his legs, happy that he was back. He had been gone for more than a week, but little did they know he'd been beneath the castle for most of that time, trying to manipulate Kessi's memories. Allustria sat the closest to him, the oldest bride now that Junet was just a pile of ash on the floor. Her remains were still there, Heinsvick unable to bring himself to remove her. He didn't want to lose more brides to the nasty priestess. He would soon have Emiline back and destroy Matilda for what she had done to him. He hoped that the deception with Kessi would be a success and she would thwart Matilda's summoning. He smiled at the thought of it.

"We missed you, my husband!" Allustria said, caressing his leg.

He looked down into her beautiful blue eyes and stroked her hair. "And I missed you as well, my love. But unfortunately I must be leaving again for a few more weeks."

Her face turned into a pout, and she lowered her head. He gently lifted her chin back up so she could look him in the eyes, and as he did, he remembered the day he had transformed her. She had fought more than the others, and he had gone into a frenzy as her heart pounded in her chest while she struggled to live. In the end, he had feasted and feasted well! He had spared her life that day, and they had enjoyed several centuries together now. He truly loved her and cherished their many years together, but as he gazed at her, he realized the love he had for all his other brides combined did not compare to his passion for Emiline.

He ran his hand through her hair and grabbed hold hard, tilting her head back slowly. The rage welled up inside him. He wanted his Emiline back! He considered snapping her neck, but his love for Allustria was real, and he managed to refrain. He smiled and loosened his grip. "You are in charge until I return. Leave the castle only to find food. When I arrive, we will feast and celebrate the return of Emiline. Do you understand, my love?"

She nodded and smiled, and he released her hair. She laid her head on his leg and continued stroking it. He understood the dangerous test ahead of him. If the lie that was Kessi Rho failed and Matilda found out he was trying to deceive her, he would indeed be putting himself and Emiline in danger. He understood at that moment that he might not ever sit on his throne or see his beloved brides again. "You must protect the family. They look up to you now in my absence. Therefore, if I do not return within twenty moons, you must take the family out of Novafontera and back to the caves we lived in before coming here. Do you remember where that is?"

"Yes, master," she said and then turned to look him in the eyes. "We need you. I am not strong enough."

He stroked her hair lovingly, agreeing with her but not wanting to say it out loud. His family would likely be doomed if he failed. He made love to Allustria and as many of his other thirteen brides as possible that night, knowing he may never see them again. All his hopes hinged on the likes of a teenage girl. The lie would be successful only if Kessi truly believed she was Cassandra Rho. If she couldn't do that and be convincing, all was lost. He would have to prepare spells to battle Matilda if things took a wrong turn and the lie failed. He would need the most potent magic in his repertoire if it came to that.

~

The next night, Heinsvick and Kessi roamed around the deserted elven village that Logan and his pack had destroyed. The place was very far to the south of Oldorburg, and Kessi had no idea how far from home she was. Although Novafontera was experiencing autumn, the elven village was moderately comfortable, with the hints of the colder weather yet to come. The trees were in bloom, and the birds and bees were thick among them. Evidence of the carnage that had played out a few weeks earlier was still there; bloodstained leaves on bushes and pools of dried blood on the grass were visible. As Heinsvick had suspected, Logan had not taken much of the food stores from the place. Gathering the elves' foodstuffs served no purpose for the werewolf clan, and the underground storage bunker remained undisturbed.

"What happened here?" Kessi asked as she wandered through the deserted village.

"It is none of your concern, child. All you need to know is that you are far from home and there's no escape if you decide to flee from me. You may eat what you find in the stores, and the river is close so that you may drink. I will lock us in the cellar during the day."

"You still think I'll try to escape?" Kessi asked.

"I don't know you, girl, or your merit," Heinsvick said.

"I'm willing to do this, to save my sister," she said, shaking her head. "I do it for Cassandra."

"Whatever your cause, I have no faith in you to stay put during the process," Heinsvick said.

Kessi didn't respond, only shook her head in defeat. The moon was full, giving her enough light to rummage through the storeroom, find supplies to start a fire, and gather kindling for the firepit. She was striking the flint and steel, trying to produce a spark, without much success. She had never properly learned how to build a fire, so she quickly became frustrated with it. Heinsvick only watched from a distance, amused at the spectacle. Finally giving up hope, she sat down on the ground and threw the flint and steel down beside her.

Heinsvick found the poor girl to be quite pathetic at that point but also understood her frustration. He had little patience for the living and shared no empathy for them. However, he was not an evil creature, despite his undead state. He calmly and silently walked up to her and watched her pout. After some time, she looked up at him, her pretty eyes expressing her frustration. "I am tired, hungry, and thirsty, and I can't even build this stupid fire," she said, near to crying. "Please. I am so hungry … I need to eat."

He knelt and could see the tears streaming down her face then, glistening in the moonlight. He vaguely remembered what hunger felt like and found some sympathy for her. He sighed, resigning to help her; she would need her energy to endure the brainwashing he had planned for her. He reached a hand out to the kindling and produced a flame that shot from his fingertips. The flame quickly ignited the kindling, and Kessi, surprised by the move, promptly manipulated the small fire to take to the larger logs. Soon there was a roaring fire.

"Thank you," she said, wiping her tears and standing to face him.

He wanted nothing more than to feed on her, to turn her into a creature of the night. She was beautiful and would fit in well as one of his brides, and if the situation were different, that transformation would have already occurred. Instead, mixed with emotions, he responded, "Eat. You will need your strength," and then walked into the woods and out of sight.

Kessi watched him go, then quickly prepared a stew that Sera had taught her to make. Soon she had eaten her fill and had drifted to sleep near the fire. Heinsvick watched her sleep, having stayed very close to the camp. His departure was nothing more than a test to see whether she would run once he had left, but perhaps he wasn't giving her enough credit. Maybe she was loyal to the cause. He would find out shortly because dawn was approaching and he would have to find cover for the day. He would have to put his trust in the girl. She was different and somehow trustworthy, even with the knowledge that she would die. Suffice it to say, he was impressed with the young girl, and a piece of him regretted that he would have to turn her over to Matilda.

~

Allustria made her way back into the throne room, where the remainder of her family dwelled. She felt alone and terrified, but she knew that she would have to take a leadership role if the family was to survive. Heinsvick had always been there to take care of them, and now he was gone. She loved her husband, her creator, and she would take that leadership role in his absence as he had requested of her. For her own sake and the sake of her family, she would learn to lead until he returned. She had left the city on her own and found them a meal. A small one, but it was a human, and she could not resist the urge to feed on it. She entered the throne room, where the others lay around lazily. She made sure to avoid the remains of Junet, giving the pile of ash a wide berth.

"I have spotted an easy kill for us this night," she said.

Tabitha, one of the newer brides, looked at her with wide eyes. "A feast?"

"Perhaps for a few of us—those of you brave enough to leave the protective walls of the city," Allustria answered.

Several gasped, and some crawled behind the throne.

"But he said for us to stay in the walls until his return!" Tabitha said.

"Yes, but he also said that I am to lead you if he fails to return. Our hunt is merely an exercise to see how powerful we truly are without him! Who will come with me?"

Tabitha looked around at the others, most of them hiding their faces and some whimpering. Then, her eyes wide with excitement and bloodlust overwhelming her senses, she finally said, "I'll go."

"You play a dangerous game, Allustria," came a voice from behind Tabitha.

Malgema gently moved Tabitha to the side and walked up to stand before Allustria. She was tall for a female and very intimidating to the other brides. Even Allustria had a hard time standing up to her. Malgema was always jealous of the other brides, especially Emiline, who she knew was Heinsvick's favorite.

"I play no game, Malgema; I am in charge. Heinsvick said so," Allustria said.

"It will not please him if you expose us to the outside world," Malgema said as she circled her.

Allustria didn't try to follow her and simply stood, facing the throne, where the others could see her expressionless face. "Yes, but it's only one human. Homeless. No one will miss him."

"You've been outside the wall!" Malgema said, moving fast to stand before her once again.

"Of course. I went scouting for food, and I found some. I have done well finding us sustenance. Now, would you like to come with Tabitha and me or stay here and miss out on the fun?" Allustria said.

Malgema thought about that for a moment, tapping a finger on her lips. "Hmm. It seems that I have nothing to lose since you're the one who will provoke his wrath if this goes badly."

"Is that a yes, then?"

"Yes," Malgema said.

The three vampires left the city of Novafontera soon after in search of the lone human.

~

Daro sat by the fire as the chilly fall night set in. Kringus and the rest had left early that morning to continue on their way to Oldorburg. The ranger picked up on Kringus's uneasiness about the trip, even going so far as to relieve Arrin of his watch over Novafontera. Daro kind of missed the companionship of the young captain, though he would never admit it openly. Daro lived alone and enjoyed that aspect of his life, never needing or wanting other people around. However, he and Arrin had made a good team for the few days they were together, sharing the night watch and other duties.

He slowly ate one of the coneys he'd killed that day as the other one roasted on the spit at the mouth of the cave. He had to admit he felt a bit alone now with the group having left him, especially given his uneasiness being this close to the city. Someone or something was underneath the city; that much was clear. Something stirred in Novafontera. Even Arrin had felt it for the few days he had stayed with him. Daro could feel it now, the dark of night making the feeling more pronounced.

He stopped chewing, and his hands went to the hilts of his twin swords. He stared in the direction of the city, his eyes searching for movement in the darkness. The city wall would be barely visible from his vantage point if it were daylight. The fact that the city was there but invisible in the night made him much more anxious. He concentrated on the sounds of the woods, and it was deathly quiet. All he could hear was the crackling of the fire and the occasional sizzle of juice dripping from his meal. He did feel a presence but saw nothing.

The feeling passed soon enough, and his eyes never picked up an intruder. He relaxed once more and began to eat again. It would be a long night, and he would have to build a defense around the cave entrance if he were to get any sleep.

A movement to his left caught his eye, and he slowly turned to see a great gray wolf standing at the edge of the camp. He stared at the creature and continued to eat his meal slowly. The wolf was only twenty yards from him and had sneaked up on the vigilant ranger quickly enough. They stared at each other for several moments as Daro ate his food and the wolf licked its chops. It eventually issued a long, low growl.

"Hey, no need to get upset, Gray—you know I'll share!" Daro finally said. The wolf came into the camp and sat next to the ranger. "The only thing I ask is, next time, let me know you're coming, and I'll save you a rare one. You know how long it takes to skin and cook these things?" the ranger said, patting his old friend on the side.

He soon took the other coney off the spit and eased it to the ground in front of the wolf. "Remember—let it cool first. You know what happened last time, right?"

The wolf growled in response.

Daro laughed at the wolf he had rescued from a hunter's trap when it was but a pup. He had named him Gray, and the wolf had stayed in the area, never moving very far from the ranger. However, he had not shown up since Arrin had moved in, and Daro was happy to see the return of his friend, especially while camping this close to the cursed city.

"Again, if you had let me know you were joining me for dinner, I wouldn't have cooked yours," Daro said with a smile.

Gray was no longer listening to him. His ears had gone flat, and his teeth were now visible behind curled lips, and a real growl issued forth from the wolf. He was staring hard into the woods, toward the city, in the same place Daro had just sensed a presence.

"What is it, old friend?" Daro asked, moving up to stand beside Gray.

He didn't see anything but could feel that presence again, something unnatural in the woods. "Great," he muttered to himself. "Demon or undead?"

Neither option sounded promising, but one thing was for sure: he would defend his woods from any such abomination. "Well, I guess we'll do battle this night, my friend—something we have not done in quite a long time," Daro said, unsheathing his two swords and taking a few steps away from the fire.

He stood, swords crossed at his knees, a smile on his face. "Come on out, whoever you are. We know you're there. We don't take kindly to trespassers in these woods!" he yelled. "Right, Gray?" he whispered over his shoulder to his friend. There was no return growl, so Daro looked over his shoulder and asked, "Right?"

He turned just in time to see the wolf pick up his dinner, turn, and trot off into the woods. Daro watched in amazement as the wolf abandoned him. Then he turned fully toward the direction Gray had run off in and yelled, "Thanks for the support! I know you have pups to attend to now, but no one abandons a friend! Not cool, Gray!" Then he muttered to himself, "I can't believe it," and turned back around.

A small woman now stood a mere forty yards away, just in the radius of light generated by the campfire. She was young, maybe in her twenties. She was pale, but whether it was from cold or fear, he couldn't tell. Dressed in a white nightgown and barefoot, she was lovely. However, something in his mind said that what he saw was not an accurate indication of what stood before him.

"Please help me, good sir," the woman said in an accent he couldn't identify.

"Well, as much as I like a beautiful woman, especially with a fine accent, I have a feeling I'm the one who needs help here."

"Explain," she said, a puzzled look on her face.

"Well, you're out here in the cold wearing a gown similar to the one my great-great-grandmother probably wore. You are not afraid. I have a feeling you are not what you seem."

The woman seemed hurt and stood with her hands on her hips. "Not true! I am a damsel in distress. Can you not see that?"

"I don't know about that, but I do like your accent. Tell me—did you live in Novafontera during the time of the New Order?" he asked bluntly, secretly enjoying the confusion of the bewildered woman.

"No, I have only lived there since—" She stopped, realizing her error.

Daro smiled and shrugged, understanding that whatever it was that stood before him, it wasn't human.

"No fair! You tricked me!"

"It's a shame, too, because under different circumstances I would have loved to see what lies beneath your granny gown," Daro said, taking a few steps toward the woman and raising his swords.

The woman looked genuinely wounded at the remark, holding her gown out at the sides and studying it. Finally, she slowly raised her head, her visage reflecting a snarl, with sharp canines visible. "I died in this gown, fool," she spat.

"And so you shall once more, my lady," Daro said with a bow.

At the last possible moment, he saw another figure lunge at him from his right. He ducked and rolled but still got clipped by the second vampire on his right shoulder. The hit wasn't substantial, but the cold touch of the creature seeped deep into his bones. He completed his roll and stood once more, now facing two of them. He noticed that the new woman was just as beautiful as the first.

"I must admit—your master has good taste in ladies," he said, trying to shake the effects of the minor hit.

"You know nothing of Heinsvick, stupid man!" the first one said.

The second vampire turned to the smaller one and yelled, "Silence, you fool! Don't give him information!"

"He's as good as dead, so why does it matter?" she answered, coming up to stand beside the second one.

"Well, there are two of you, but I seem to have a sword for each one. Perhaps I'm not exactly as good as dead," Daro said with a smirk. Both vampires just smiled at him, so he eased his battle stance a little. "What?" he asked.

The smaller one giggled like a small child, and it dawned on him what was so funny. "Another one of your friends is behind me, right?" he asked.

Before they could answer, a commotion from the woods to the left of the camp distracted all three as Gray charged into battle and took on the third vampire, who had been creeping up silently behind Daro and was now only about twenty feet from him. As they engaged, both combatants snarling and showing vicious fangs, Daro turned his attention back to the two in front of him. He ran at them, swords ready, and said, "The odds are now even, and once I finish destroying you vampire filth, I will have a few words with Heinsvick!"

The vampires showed no fear and met him head-on in battle. He was the quicker of the three and decided to focus his efforts on one opponent. He dodged the smaller one's vicious charge by again going into a roll and coming up on one knee close to the larger one. His blades were fast, and his skill level with a sword was legendary in Pelesea and neighboring communities. His aim was true, and he expected to feel the steel blades slip into the flesh of his target. But he knew that he had erred, seeing the vampire flash past his weapons before they could find their mark.

He looked up at her for an instant before she backhanded him hard across the face. It was the most brutal hit he had ever taken, and he flew backward and landed in the dirt at the smaller one's feet. The impact dislodged both swords, and he lay on his back, unarmed, swooning from the vicious hit. He could vaguely hear Gray doing battle with the third vampire, and his heart ached in knowing that the creatures would slaughter his dear friend if he failed to destroy the two he faced. It barely registered in his mind that the more petite vampire had thrown herself on him, ready to rip his throat out.

She was much stronger than the petite damsel she betrayed, and she would have easily killed him if he hadn't been quick enough to remove the two daggers from his boots. She had impaled herself on them when she attacked and now looked at him with a shocked expression. Soon that turned to pain as blood trickled from her mouth and fell on his face.

"Gross!" he said and moved her off him. He felt terrible for her because he knew the wounds were fatal and she was no longer a threat. "Sorry," he said, then quickly gained his feet to face the second vampire, who suddenly stopped her approach.

He was shaky on his feet, the hits he had taken doing more damage to him than he had realized. In that moment of weakness, time seemed to freeze for the ranger as the remaining vampire decided whether she would attack him. She hesitated slightly, and then there was a shriek from behind him as Gray tore two fingers off the third vampire's hand. She held her hand up, blood gushing from the gristly wound.

The sharp pain in her hand was enough for Malgema, as she ran screaming back toward Novafontera, "Heinsvick! Heinsvick, help us!"

Allustria watched her go, and when she turned around to face the ranger, the snarling wolf was beside him, blood thick on its muzzle.

"So what will it be? Care to join your little sister here?" Daro said, extending a blade toward Tabitha's still form. "Or would you care to lose a few fingers to my friend?" he added, nodding toward Gray.

Allustria looked to Tabitha and wanted nothing more to do with this one. She looked into his eyes and hissed, then hissed once more at the nasty wolf, and fled back the way she had come. Soon she was scaling the great wall that would take her back into the protective confines of Novafontera. Sure, she'd have to hear Malgema complain about the incident and Tabitha's death, but she was relieved to be back home. Heinsvick's words rang in her ears—his demanding that she leave with the rest of the family if anything should happen to him. She hoped he would be home soon. She knew now that she was simply not strong enough to lead them.

After he was confident the vampires had retreated, Daro gently turned the vampire over as Gray showed his teeth at her, sensing that she was still a threat. Her eyes were wide and unblinking, and her mouth continued to move slightly, with no words coming forth. Her hands held her chest where the dagger wounds now saturated her gown with blood. She rolled her eyes toward him as tears welled up in them, and he felt pity for her.

She then tried to speak. "Hein … Heins …" That was all she could get out before she expired.

Daro relaxed and sat down hard next to her. The two hits he'd taken had hurt him, and he needed rest. He smiled weakly at Gray, who was now more relaxed, confirming the vampire's destruction.

"Thanks for saving my life. I shouldn't have doubted you."

If the wolf understood the words, he didn't show it; he simply got up, walked to the fire, and lay beside it. Daro knew there were no more creatures in the area because of the wolf's relaxed demeanor. He looked at the beautiful vampire once more, knowing she had probably been just an innocent young girl in her former life. Now she was dead to his blades, and he felt guilty. He had a lot to tell Kringus upon his return and silently hoped that the trip would be quick. The information he had concerning Novafontera was now rather urgent.

Then the vampire began to turn insubstantial. Daro jumped to his feet, nearly falling from numbness in his arms and legs, which he could only surmise was due to the vampire attacks. He brought his two daggers up. Gray lifted his head for only a moment to observe the commotion, then laid it back down, making Daro relax a little.

Daro had no real experience with vampires, so he didn't fully understand what was going on with its body. Within a few moments, her entire corpse had turned into a greenish cloud of gas and started drifting back toward Novafontera. He had no idea if the creature was indeed dead or if it was alive and trying to find its way home. Either way, he had no way of stopping it, so he just watched as it disappeared into the night.

Soon after, he packed his things and traveled deeper into the woods to his home, a cottage far away from Novafontera. Gray eagerly traveled with him part of the way before leaving to rejoin his family. Daro knew he would see the wolf again soon but was disappointed in his departure. Somehow he no longer felt safe in his woods, and he thought for the first time that he was entirely too close to the ghost city of Novafontera.

~

Heinsvick awakened with a start. Light seeped into the elven cellar where he slept. It was minimal but enough to make him nervous. The trapdoor remained shut, and he had magically locked it for good measure, so there was little chance anyone could open it as he slept. He had decided to leave Kessi outside the cellar to show that he trusted her to some degree. And so he had made a place to sleep in the food cellar of the elven camp, the nasty vegetables attacking his senses and creating a nearly intolerable condition. He missed his coffin, the one place he could sleep comfortably. It would be a long two weeks there as he picked apart Kessi's strong mind.

Now he had been startled from his light sleep, hearing male voices and perhaps a horse. He cautiously moved from the dark corner to stand as close as he could underneath the trapdoor. Light filtered in, so he couldn't get very close, but he could hear more now as there seemed to be at least two male voices, probably human, conversing with Kessi.

"… your husband now?" one asked.

"Hunting, but he should be back soon," he heard Kessi say.

"Well, perhaps we should keep you company until he returns," a second voice said.

"Yes, that's what we'll do. Whatever attacked the elvish camp could still be in the area. You'll need our protection," the first voice said.

Both men shared a laugh, and he could hear them unpacking their horses, assuming that was indeed what they were riding. The animals were nervous, probably sensing Heinsvick's presence. "Why are the horses so jittery?" one of the men asked.

"Because the creatures are still about—the ones that killed the elves," Kessi said, trying to discourage the men from unpacking.

They moved away from the cellar doors then, and Heinsvick couldn't hear what they were saying after that, only mumbling. He could determine that two new guests were above, and he didn't like how they were forcing themselves on Kessi. He could only imagine their intentions, and if they wanted to rape and kill her, he usually wouldn't stand in their way. However, he needed the girl, and it would probably be best if her virginity remained intact, to add credibility to the lie.

He had probed deep into her mind over the last week and now knew most of her secrets. The one thing he was sure of was that she was indeed a virgin. He would have liked to remedy the condition, but bringing his Emiline home was more important, and so he had left her be. But if these two vagabonds had rape in mind, he would have to stop them somehow. From what he could tell, the sun was bright, and the day was still in its early-morning hours. Who were these men, and why were they wandering around this deep in the woods? The questions didn't sit well with him. Kessi was in trouble, he believed, but she would have to fend for herself until nightfall. He just hoped it wouldn't be too late by then.

~

Kessi watched the men suspiciously as they unsaddled their horses. Both wore dirty clothes and carried no weapons that she could see. Their steeds were almost as skinny and dirty as their riders. Something seemed out of place to her, and she didn't trust them. She tried to look busy, stirring the fire, and she frantically tried to think of a way to get the men to leave. Without Heinsvick, she felt vulnerable. She wished her sister were there. She could count on Cassandra to protect her—or was it the other way around? She couldn't remember. She pondered that for a few moments, absently stirring the smoldering firepit.

"Are you daft, girl?" one of the men asked.

She then realized that the men were standing on either side of her. She looked at each and noticed that they wore the same lewd expression. A wave of fear overwhelmed her, and she looked around for the best path to flee into the woods. She knew at that point that the men were up to no good.

The first man spoke again, and her suspicions were confirmed. "Looks like she's ignoring me, Bart. I might have to teach her some manners."

"Yeah, boss, she hasn't even offered us food or water … or a kiss," Bart said.

She stood, and both men took a step closer. She could smell their body odor, as well as alcohol on their breath. She was more frightened at that moment than she had ever been in her short life, even more than when Heinsvick had entered her cell back in Oldorburg. She had to think of something quick, and the only hope she had was Heinsvick.

"My husband found food and drink in the cellar," she exclaimed, pointing to Heinsvick's current resting spot.

The two men looked at each other and smiled.

"Are you thinking what I'm thinking, Bart?" the first one asked, ignoring her comment.

"I sure am, boss."

Suddenly, both men lunged at her, each grabbing an arm. She was too quick for the one named Bart and slipped out of his grip. The other man held her tight, though, and pulled her close to him. She fought to break free, but the wiry man was much stronger than he looked. His grip on her arm tightened, and she slapped at his face with her good arm, again trying to break free. She had to get to the cellar!

She began to scream to Heinsvick, when something hard hit her in the stomach, knocking the wind out of her. She couldn't breathe for a moment, and her knees buckled. She certainly couldn't call out to the vampire, then, and how could he help anyway with it being full daylight?

She understood that not-Bart had slugged her in the stomach while she was smacking and clawing at his face, and now she was on her knees, his grip still painfully tight on her arm. As she struggled to catch her breath, the man named Bart grabbed her other arm once more. He twisted it painfully behind her back, making her cry out. He pushed her face down on the ground and soon had her other arm behind her. He put his knee into the small of her back and pressed his weight fully on her. She couldn't breathe, and she couldn't move. Soon she felt him binding her hands. Once they had her arms tied with some twine, they turned her over and similarly bound her ankles together.

Once they were done, not-Bart said, "That should hold her. Watch her while I check the cellar."

"Sure thing, boss!" Bart said with a wicked smile on his face.

As she was on her back now, he lay down next to her, looking up at the bright morning sky. "You and I are going to get very acquainted, missy. So you might as well get used to that idea!"

With that, he grabbed her by the hair and kissed her hard. It was her first kiss, and she didn't enjoy this strange man's tongue invading her mouth. She struggled to turn her head, but he held her firmly by her hair with one hand while the other began to move down the front of her shirt.

She had to do something, so she did the only thing she could think of and bit his tongue hard. He screamed in her mouth, and she could taste his blood. Finally he released her and sat up, holding his mouth, a stupid look on his face. He moved his hand from his mouth and looked dumbly at the blood there.

"You stupid whore, you bit me!" he said through gritted teeth.

He stood and spat the blood from his mouth and took his belt off. He began wrapping the leather strap around his right hand, covering his knuckles. "I'm going to teach you a lesson now," he said and straddled Kessi.

"Your boss might not like that!" she said desperately, looking over to see the cellar doors open and the other man nowhere to be found. The doors were open! Heinsvick had locked them magically—he'd told her so. How had the buffoon opened the doors if they were locked unless Heinsvick allowed it?

"He told me to do whatever I want with you, just as long as I don't mess up that pretty little face. You see, we have to have you looking your best for the slave market, but that doesn't mean we can't defile you in places that aren't visible. And that's what we intend to do. But first, you will learn to be submissive, and this belt should do a fine job in minimizing the bruises on your face."

He sat hard on her stomach, pinning her to the ground with his weight. He pounded his right hand into the palm of his left with a big grin on his face, the belt making loud smacking sounds with each hit. She couldn't defend herself, so she just closed her eyes and hoped beyond hope that Heinsvick could save her.

~

The man called "boss" opened the cellar doors quickly enough, and the morning light fell on a rack of elvish wine. He happily climbed down the ladder to take a closer look. To his delight, the shelf contained at least a hundred bottles! A smile spread across his face as he gently took one and tried to read the elvish writing. He gave up quickly but kept the bottle, thinking to give the girl a good dose of it so she would be easier to handle. Next, he turned to survey the food stores, hoping there would be some dried meat and not all dainty elvish fruits and berries. His heart skipped a beat when he turned to see a pale man standing just a few feet away, emerging from the darkness.

"Sorry, mister, your wife said you weren't here. She …" he began before the vampire's gaze fell over him.

"Do not speak; just look into my eyes. I have a special task for you that is most urgent," Heinsvick said.

He dropped the bottle, and it bounced away on the dirt floor, his mind lost in those terrible yet amazing eyes. "Yes, master," was all he could think to say.

~

Kessi had her eyes closed tightly, waiting for the first strike from Bart. She then heard the other man's voice calmly say, "No."

She opened her eyes, and the so-called boss was there, staying the other man's hand. He had a weird look in his eyes, but his visage was one of calmness.

"But you said we could rough her up a little!" Bart said.

"No. Get off of the girl," the man said, looking off in the distance as if in a trance.

"You all right, boss?" Bart asked, standing up.

Boss bent down and gently helped Kessi stand. He took out a rusty knife, and Kessi's eyes went wide. However, instead of using the blade on her, he cut the twine that bound her ankles and hands. She began to run off, but he quickly grabbed her by the arm and shook his head. "No, you must come to the cellar," he said, looking through her more than at her.

"Ah, you found us a spot to have us some fun, then. I like it, boss, I like it!" Bart said, putting his belt back on as he followed the other two to the cellar.

Soon Heinsvick had both men under his control, and they both stood guard outside the cellar doors with instructions to kill anyone who tried to enter. Kessi was in the cellar with him now, and his magical lock had been reestablished on the doors.

Kessi sat on the ground at his feet, visibly shaken by the ordeal, but held her tears. She no longer felt afraid around the dangerous vampire, knowing now that he cared for her enough to protect her. She knew it was because he needed her, but she still felt a bond with him after the encounter. "You saved my life," she finally said, not looking at him but staring at the sliver of light on the dirt floor from a crack in the doors.

"Only to use you as bait, child. Do not confuse the effort with me caring for you, Kessi Rho."

"What did you call me?" she asked, her voice rising a little as she stood to face him. Heinsvick stood there with a puzzled expression mixed with a bit of hopefulness. "Answer me, Heinsvick! Why did you call me by my dead sister's name?" She stopped and shook her head. "Wait, what did you call me?" she asked, suddenly unsure of herself.

"I called you by your name, Kessi Rho," he said as a test.

"Oh, I thought you said … something else," she said and rubbed her temples.

"This is good, Kessi! You've shown the first signs of believing you are Cassandra. We will begin your training again tonight. Now get some rest."

"All this is doing is jumbling my thoughts. I'm afraid I won't be convincing once I meet this priestess you speak of."

"You are open to my suggestions, and my most powerful brainwashing spells are beginning to affect you. Therefore you must open your mind further if you wish to succeed and save your sister," he said.

"I can do nothing more. I'm open and willing. But now, with the ordeal this morning, my mind is a mess," Kessi said, her voice cracking at the thought of the two men and how close she'd come to being hurt badly.

"You are far from your home, child. Unfortunately rape is a common occurrence in this part of the world. You must not be distracted by such trivial things."

"Trivial?" she cried. "Trivial to you, maybe, mister vampire lord, but not to me. I haven't died before, and I find it frightening." She regretted saying those words even before they had left her mouth. She looked at Heinsvick's face but could see little of it in the dark. "I'm sorry. I didn't mean—"

"I know what you meant, and I understand your remark is out of frustration. But get some sleep; you need the rest. I will watch over you, and you will be quite safe from those goons. But I do need you rested, so sleep."

"It's hard … I mean, it's daylight. I don't sleep during the day, usually."

"Try," was his curt response.

"Will you lie down with me?" she asked after a few moments of uncomfortable silence.

"Why?"

"I don't know. I guess I feel protected with you around, especially with those two so close," she said.

"You have nothing more to fear from them."

Tears began to roll down her cheeks. "Listen. I'm trying to do what you want, and—"

"Silence!" he demanded before the crying could start.

He found a spot in the dirt and spread a tarp for them. He then lay down and offered his hand for her to join him. It was an awkward situation for both, she was emotionally spent from the encounter that morning and he did not particularly want to cuddle with the living. Finally, after a moment of hesitation, she took his hand and lay down next to him. Although she wasn't very tired, she felt somehow safe next to him, and soon she found sleep.

Although Kessi slept, Heinsvick did not. He hadn't cuddled the living for centuries, and her warmth was foreign to him. The smell of her blood and the beating of her heart made it impossible for him to rest. The few times he did dose off that day, she would awaken him by snuggling up or simply breathing. The interaction was strange, but he did it for her. Soon enough, he would have his Emiline back, and this nonsense would come to an end. He sniffed her hair and hugged her tighter, the thought suddenly not sitting well.

~

Before Kessi arose that night, Bart and his boss were floating facedown in the river beside the deserted elven settlement. Heinsvick had fed well, and the two fools were well downstream before Kessi stirred. Also, he had released the frail horses, and they had fled in fear. Terrified of him, they were miles away by the time Kessi rose.

She emerged from the cellar more rested than expected and looked around cautiously for Heinsvick. The moon was out and lit the camp, but she didn't see him. She sensed he was nearby, though, so she made her way to the firepit and tried once more to start a fire. Finally she was successful with the flint and steel after a few failed attempts, and soon the fire was roaring. She began to prepare another stew as Heinsvick approached the fire. She jumped at first but was relieved to see him.

"Heinsvick! I'm glad it is you. Where are Bart and not-Bart?" she asked.

"I have taken care of them. I will have a powerful suggestion for you so that encounter will not hamper your thoughts again."

She sighed and worked on making her stew. She didn't look at him when she asked the question because she already knew the answer. "You killed them, didn't you?"

"Of course."

After a long hesitation, and after she had her stew on the fire, she asked, "Normally you would have killed me too, right?"

"Long ago," he said and nodded.

"Do you no longer feel compassion since … well … in the state you're in?" she asked.

"Would you prefer that I kept them alive so that they may have their way with you?"

"No, of course not, but you could have let them go," she said.

He shrugged. "Tonight, we begin the toughest part of the brainwashing. Eat well—you'll need your strength."

"I feel prepared but skeptical."

"Do not be. You must focus and open your mind," Heinsvick said.

"I have focused, and all you've accomplished is making my mind a mess. I can't sort my thoughts, especially those of Cassandra."

They sat in silence for a while as she gathered a bowl and poured herself some stew. He just watched her, not threateningly, as before, but almost longingly. She was confused by the change in demeanor but thankful he no longer struck her. Perhaps they did share a bond; she felt it after sleeping next to him the previous day.

"Why were you able to charm those men immediately yet the process has been difficult for me even though I'm willing?" she asked.

"The charming effect of a vampire lord is potent, and the additional effects of my spells should easily have you brainwashed into thinking you are Cassandra. However, I have concluded that you are special because your strong mind is more powerful than a normal human's. Furthermore, it is resistant to most of my powers, which is rare indeed. The charming effects I possess easily overwhelm the weak minded, but those of superior intellect are a bit of a challenge."

"You have my word; I will try to cooperate. However, I know time runs short for us to accomplish this."

"Yes, I trust that you are willing to accept my suggestions and hypnosis. But that is not the issue. Your mind, which seems greater than most mere humans', is too strong for me to complete the transformation. So all we can do is keep trying."

They sat in silence for a bit longer, and then, as she finished her meal, he stood. He looked up to the stars, deep in thought.

"What is it?" Kessi asked.

"Nothing. I only know of one thing that could ensure the transformation—something powerful enough that even your strong will could not resist," he said.

"That's great news!" she exclaimed, jumping to her feet. "What is it?"

He looked at her with a frown and shook his head. "It is nothing to be excited about because it is something you would not desire."

Kessi looked dejected and stared at her feet. "Well, tell me anyway. Perhaps there's a way to compromise." She looked him in the eye, and he seemed impressed with her resilience. Then she took a step closer and said, "Tell me—what is your idea?"

"The one thing that would help me have more power over your mind and make my suggestions more effective is if I drink your blood."

She took a step back, her fear of the vampire renewed. She caught herself right away, realizing that he could have bitten her a long time ago and there would have been nothing she could have done about it. After a few moments, she said, "Won't I become a vampire and ruin the deception we have in store for Matilda?"

He turned to look at her and smiled. "Yes … if I drink for too long. The process would then turn you into one of my brides."

"But you'll know when to stop? I mean, you'll stop before that happens?"

He looked at her doubtfully, almost lustfully, as the scenario seemed to play out in his head.

Then, finally, she summoned the courage to ask, "Why do you look at me as those two fools did yesterday?"

"Because I desire you, Kessi Rho. I want more than anything to feed upon you," he said, perfectly calm, walking toward her now with a crazed look.

She started walking backward, but she bumped into a large tree and just stood there, her arms giving the large trunk a reverse hug. Her eyes went wide with fear at realizing that Heinsvick could do as he wished with her. "But you must not! If you have any hope of getting Emiline back, you mustn't do this."

The mention of his love's name had the vampire lord stopping and shaking his head. And when he looked back at her, his expression was once again regular, the wild look gone.

"You scared me," Kessi whispered after a few moments.

"I scared myself, girl."

"I have an idea," she said with a smile, pulling herself from the tree, walking past him and toward the fire.

~

Later that night, as the moon reached its zenith in the sky, Kessi sat on a log next to the fire, poking a stick into it. Heinsvick sat next to her and stared into the fire as if meditating.

"So after a count to five hundred," he said, still looking into the fire, "you will end it if I have not?"

"Yes."

"I may not want it to end—I may not be able to stop."

She pulled his face toward her, and he seemed changed, eager, and ready to pounce on his prey. She was scared, by all accounts, but she was strong and courageous at the moment. "You will remember me. You will stop—do not doubt," Kessi said softly.

His pupils dilated, and he looked hungrily at her. She took a deep breath and tried to relax. He looked into her eyes, trying to charm and hold her, but she looked away into the fire before it could take hold.

He grabbed her by the arm and began to kiss it, softly at first. She did not resist, and soon his gentleness was replaced with aggressive nibbles. They did not tear her skin, but they stung like little bees assaulting her. She grimaced a bit but did not pull away. His bites turned to licks as his eyes somehow became wilder and more animal-like. She was rethinking the wisdom of this course of action when he suddenly bit down hard on her tiny wrist.

The pain was excruciating at first, and Kessi cried out as his teeth sank deep into her. Still, she did not resist as he began to suck her lifeblood. The power of that act surprised her as she felt her life force being devoured by the vampire ever so slowly. Finally the pain subsided enough to where she barely felt the puncture wounds; instead, she focused on that strange feeling of him draining her blood.

She almost forgot to count and practically submitted fully to his feeding. She managed to stay focused on the fire and began her count. It took a very long time to reach five hundred, and she nearly passed out several times. Once she got to the magic number and realized he had no intentions of stopping, she called out to him. But he didn't answer, seemingly lost in the ecstasy of the feeding.

She barely had the strength to pull the stick from the fire and gently place it on his arm just as they had planned. That's when the wild vampire broke off the feeding and stood with a blur of motion. To Kessi's surprise, he now held the stick and stood before her. His eyes were wild, and her blood saturated his mouth and chin. "How dare you!" he said, throwing the stick into the fire.

"Heinsvick, it's me, Kessi!" she said but had little energy to reason with him, the loss of blood taking a toll on her. She felt very faint.

"You are mine," he said, advancing on her once again.

"Remember!" she shouted, presenting an item before him.

Once he gazed at it, the wildness left his eyes, and he remembered. "Kessi?" he whispered.

With a slight smile, she passed out, toppling backward. The dexterous vampire was there, though, quick enough to catch her well before she hit the ground. He cradled her in his arms and took the item from her hand, holding it up to the fire. "Oh, Kessi," he whispered once again, looking admiringly at the unconscious girl.

He tossed away the small piece of tarp she had torn from their makeshift bed and picked her up quickly. He took her back to that same bed for her to rest a bit. She had stopped him, which was good, but he could not stay. The temptation that was Kessi Rho was too much for the vampire lord, so he magically sealed the cellar door, keeping her safe inside, and then changed into the form of a giant bat and flew away. He hunted that night and fed well, not returning until he was bloated and no longer interested in feeding on her.

CHAPTER 12

MAKING FRIENDS

CASSANDRA WATCHED THE SNOW GENTLY FALL OUTSIDE HER dorm window. It had covered the ground already and looked peaceful and quiet. But to Cassandra, it reminded her of the orphanage—too much so. She put her hand on the cold glass, feeling helpless and, in a way, very hopeless that she would reunite with her family. It had been three long weeks since Kringus had left the city, and still no word. She knew in her heart that they had waited too long. Kessi and Sera were probably already dead. She tried to steady her breathing, but she was fogging up the window with it.

"You all right?" Binta asked from behind her.

Cassandra turned from the window and slowly moved her hand from it. Binta sat on Cassandra's bed, her scrolls and notes from their magic-item class strewn across it. Binta had become a big part of her life the last few weeks as they had grown very close very quickly. Cassandra didn't associate with any of the other students, but she felt a kinship with Binta. They had studied in Cassandra's room almost every night since school had started.

"No, not at all," she replied and smiled.

Binta closed the book she was reading and came over to stand by her at the window. She looked outside at the snow. Cassandra watched her and was glad they had become friends. They had a lot in common and had quickly bonded. They thought so much alike that each could almost guess what the other was thinking. She had previously shared that bond with Kessi, so it was a welcome feeling for her and one she needed at that trying time.

"Your family?" Binta asked, still looking out the window.

"Yes," Cassandra said, studying her friend's face.

Cassandra found Binta's look unique and beautiful. Her odd way of dressing and her many piercings intrigued her, especially her nose ring, which was secretly Cassandra's favorite. No one else noticed how pretty she was, and Cassandra figured it was because of her piercings and makeup. She simply looked different, which probably scared people, but it appealed to Cassandra very much. The fact that Binta didn't make friends easily reminded her of herself. Cassandra turned her attention to the events outside the window, seeing the miniature people walking downtown, fighting with the snow like tiny ants.

"They should be at Oldorburg by now, you know," Binta said.

"They should have been there a month ago. Kringus waited too long," Cassandra said.

"Agreed," Binta said, showing once again that she thought the same way Cassandra did. "What is she like?"

"Who?" Cassandra asked.

"Your sister. What is she like?" Binta said, turning toward her friend.

Cassandra smiled. "She's pretty and kind. She's a fledgling priest—or at least wants to be. Her god of choice is Adlesk, the god of mercy. He has granted her healing powers, and I've seen her use them on our mother. She helps everyone she can, from other orphans, the sick, and the needy. She cares about people; you could say she's the complete opposite of me."

Binta smiled. "You care about some people, right?"

"Some."

"Like Instructor Baxter?"

"What?" Cassandra asked, her eyes going wide.

"I see the way the two of you act around each other. You like him," Binta said.

"He's old … way too old for that! But he's a good friend, I admit," Cassandra said.

Both girls turned back toward the window, and they watched the snow fall in silence.

Finally, Binta said, "I've slept with him."

"What! Who?" Cassandra said, grabbing Binta by the shoulder and turning her to face her once more.

A smile spread across Binta's face as she shook an accusing finger at her. "You do like him, don't you?" she asked.

"I … I think it's weird that you would sleep with Baxter—that's all," Cassandra said, a blush spreading across her cheeks.

"Your face is flush, and your nostrils are flaring," Binta said, still with a big smile on her face.

Cassandra then became aware of just how flustered she was. She moved a hand to her cheek and felt the warmth there. She relaxed her nostrils so they would no longer flare and pushed her hair behind her ear with one hand, trying to find some kind of composure.

"Don't worry, Cassandra. I didn't sleep with him," Binta said soothingly.

"Then why did you say that?

"To see how much you care for him, and trust me—it's a lot!" Binta said.

"The information just caught me off guard. That's all," Cassandra said.

Binta stepped closer, still wearing a genuine smile, and took Cassandra by the shoulders. "We all have secrets, Cassandra. Don't be ashamed if you like him. You can tell me anything, you know. We are pretty close friends now, after all."

Cassandra looked into those dark eyes and found nothing but compassion. She trusted her new friend and believed what she was saying. However, she didn't understand this line of questioning. "Why are you so convinced all of a sudden that I like instructor Baxter?" she asked curiously.

Binta's smile faded, and she released her friend's shoulders. She turned back toward the window to again watch the snow. Cassandra could tell something was on her mind.

"Tell me," Cassandra said rather forcefully, stepping in front of the window to dominate Binta's view.

Binta didn't say anything immediately, so Cassandra gently put a hand on her shoulder and turned her back around to face her. "You just told me that I could tell you anything. The same applies to me. So why are you asking me these strange questions about Baxter?"

"Well, I heard a rumor today," Binta said, looking into Cassandra's eyes.

"A rumor? About Baxter?"

"Yes, Instructor Baxter and …" Binta paused. Her dark eyes darted back and forth between the window and Cassandra's face as if she were both nervous and looking for some sign that her friend knew what she was about to say.

"Spit it out, Binta!" Cassandra said a little louder than she'd meant to.

"Very well!" Binta said, taking a small step away from her. "I heard that you're sleeping with him!"

"What! Who said such a thing?"

"That idiot Jabell!" Binta said, recalling how the boy had casually thrown that information out there like it was secondhand knowledge.

Both girls fell silent. Cassandra felt as if someone had just slapped her. Her eyes scanned the floor as she tried to find some reasoning behind the lie.

Finally Binta stepped back toward her and gently lifted Cassandra's chin so that they were looking eye to eye once more. Binta evidently saw the pain there, not just from the rumor but from a lifetime of mistreatment, because her eyes watered. "I thought you should hear it from me first," she whispered.

Cassandra nodded, tears welling in her eyes, as well, and at a loss for words.

Binta stepped closer. "I'm so sorry this hurt you, but it's only a rumor. Jabell is jealous that you have someone in your life who makes you happy. You must ignore this lie and rise above it."

Cassandra looked into her friend's eyes and became lost there. Binta was so beautiful to her at that moment, for she cared when most others would not have. Binta was aware of Cassandra's pain and seemed to empathize with her. At that moment, Cassandra thought there was not a more beautiful person in the world.

"I didn't sleep with him," Cassandra whispered, still fighting back the urge to bawl.

"I believe you," Binta whispered, stroking Cassandra's hair.

"You do?" Cassandra asked, her voice barely audible.

"Of course. You are my friend, and I trust your word. Even if you had slept with him, I wouldn't think less of you. I didn't mean for my words to hurt you; I didn't want you to hear the rumor from someone else."

Binta moved even closer, and now the girls were only about a foot apart. Cassandra had never had anyone invade her personal space so, except for her sister. Her heart fluttered as she looked at Binta's beautiful face so close to her own. Time seemed to stop for both of them, a special connection forming their genuine feelings for each other.

Binta slowly moved her hands to either side of Cassandra's face, holding her head steady. "You know, we all have secrets, and friends shouldn't keep secrets from each other," Binta whispered, her breath warm on Cassandra's face as she moved even closer.

"What secrets?" Cassandra asked, barely aware she was even speaking.

"I love being with you … you are very special to me, even though we haven't known each other long," Binta said softly.

Cassandra watched as her friend moved slowly closer to her, their lips just inches apart. She couldn't speak or move. She could faintly smell Binta's perfume, and it was intoxicating. Her heart skipped a beat as their lips touched for just a moment. Then Binta moved a step back and removed her hands from Cassandra's face, waiting for her response.

"I … I am not a lesbian," Cassandra said.

"Neither am I," Binta said, then moved in again.

This time she kissed her harder and embraced her passionately, pulling Cassandra tight against her. Cassandra didn't resist and even kissed her back. It ended as quickly as it had begun, and Binta pulled away to measure her friend's reaction. Cassandra didn't fully understand this turn of events and just stood there dumbfounded. Binta smiled lovingly at her.

"That was nice," Binta whispered, her cheeks becoming flushed.

"Yes," Cassandra replied softly.

Still showing that loving smile, Binta moved her hands up and began to play with Cassandra's hair. Cassandra stood there, frozen and unable to move. Binta grabbed two fistfuls of her locks and initiated another kiss, this time very passionately, kissing her fiercely. Cassandra kissed her back just as forcefully, having never kissed anyone before, especially another woman, yet feeling it was perfectly natural. It was a magical moment for Cassandra, and it had a fantastic effect on her as a wave of electricity washed over every bit of her body. She tingled everywhere, and her heart thumped so hard in her chest she could hear it!

When Binta finally broke off the kiss and Cassandra opened her eyes, Binta said, "Remember: not all secrets are bad, Cassandra."

Cassandra stood there mesmerized, unsure of what to do next. Binta held her gaze as she walked back to the bed and gathered her books and scrolls. Cassandra decided then that she was the most beautiful girl she had ever met.

"It's late; I must retire to my room. I'll see you in class tomorrow?" Binta asked nervously. She hugged her books to her chest and waited.

Cassandra finally smiled, her first genuine smile in some time. That made Binta smile with relief, and she moved quickly back over to Cassandra and hugged her. Then she left, closing the door gently behind her. Cassandra stood in place for many minutes, absorbing what had just transpired. That night, instead of having the usual restless sleep, filled with nightmares concerning the fate of her family, she dreamed of Binta. And it was a most erotic dream.

~

The same evening that Binta and Cassandra shared their special moment, Victoria met with Baxter in his office. It was an unusual meeting because the semester was only a few weeks old now and Victoria usually didn't ask for progress updates this early. Those meetings were also generally held in her tower, not at the school itself. Baxter didn't mind, though; it would allow him to brag about Cassandra and how well she was doing. "So you preferred to meet in my office this evening?" he asked innocently enough.

"Yes, I wanted to mingle with the students and get a sense of the general attitude of the student body," Victoria said as she sat patiently in his office, waiting for him to sort the various papers for her to review.

He felt her watching him intently, studying his actions, and he soon understood the true meaning of her visit. He went about his business as if her being there were perfectly normal and hoped that would keep her from broaching the subject. "Yes, here we are, Victoria. I feel you will be most pleased with the progress—"

"Baxter!"

"I'm in trouble, aren't I?" he muttered as he sat back in his chair.

"No—well, maybe."

"Why? Have I not followed protocol?"

"You know why, and as one of your best friends, I expect you to start being truthful with me," she said, a fire growing in her eyes.

They had been friends for many years, and he was one of the school's original professors when Victoria had taken over operations. They had been through a lot together, and they knew each other well. He knew that she was usually levelheaded, but she could also be a fiery redhead when angered. He knew that she was on the verge of losing her temper—he just wasn't sure why. All he knew was that he didn't want to be on the receiving end of her wrath. "Yes, I suppose I do," he said in defeat. "This is about Cassandra, isn't it?"

"Yes, this is about Miss Rho and what activities you may or may not have been sharing!" Victoria said.

"Wait, what activities? I assure you I have been nothing but professional!"

"I know you care for her, and I'm happy for you. I only wish that you would fall for someone your age. I simply can't have you involved with one of my students."

"Look—I can't help how I feel. I told you that my feelings are growing strong for the young woman. I know it's wrong, but I'm not doing this intentionally!" Baxter said, tossing a book of grades on the desk.

"Are you sleeping with her, Baxter?"

"What? Of course not! Why would you ask such a thing?"

"Because there is a rumor going around the school that you are," Victoria said calmly, her words hitting him hard.

"Why is this rumor going around the school when I have done no such thing?" he asked.

"I was hoping you could tell me."

He shook his head. "I have no idea, but I assure you—I have done nothing physical with her. To my knowledge, she doesn't know how I truly feel."

Victoria nodded. "I believe you, but we must put a stop to this rumor."

Just then, there was a knock on the door.

"Come in," Baxter said, more than a little irritated at the interruption.

A young student poked her head in and said, "Excuse me, Instructor Baxter, but Lady Victoria has a visitor."

"Thank you, young lady. Please tell me your name," Victoria answered.

"My name is Annabel, second-year student," she said, opening the door enough to give a slight curtsy.

"It is a pleasure to meet you, Miss Annabel. Now tell me—is the visitor here on business, or is the visit personal in nature?" Victoria asked.

"I think you'll want to see him; he carries the queen's seal," Annabel said.

Baxter and Victoria shared a brief but concerned glance, and then Victoria smiled at the young girl and said, "Please show him in."

Annabel curtsied once more, then opened the door fully to allow the young man into the room. He was young, probably in his late teens, and very handsome. His smile had a certain charm, and the confidence with which the young man carried himself was beyond his years. His left arm was in a sling, and he wore priestly robes.

"This is Greyson Kavince, my lady," Annabel said, then hurriedly left and shut the door behind her. However, Baxter noticed the young girl stare longingly at the young man as she left.

"Greyson Kavince, it's nice to meet you finally. The queen has told me much about you and your recent exploits," Victoria said, standing to shake his hand.

Greyson, being a natural charmer, instead took her hand and tilted it to kiss the back of her knuckles. "You are just as lovely as I've heard people tell, and your beautiful red hair reminds me very much of our comely queen," he said with a smile.

Victoria glanced at Baxter with a slight grin, and Baxter could only roll his eyes at the charming young stranger.

"I am Baxter Von Glord, one of the instructors of this great school. Please sit down," the professor said, motioning to an empty chair.

"Hello, Baxter. I will politely decline your invitation to sit, for I only need a moment of your time. That is, of course, unless Lady Victoria would like to spend some time getting to know me."

Victoria's eyes widened. "I think not, Greyson I—"

"I'm worldlier than the typical eighteen-year-old. So I can show you some things that you've probably never seen before," Greyson said with a wink.

For the first time, Baxter saw Victoria turn flush and fail to find her words. He watched this young, slightly arrogant kid come into his office and completely subdue the mightiest wizard in the city. Baxter couldn't even speak to Cassandra without tripping over his words. Who was this kid?

"I … think we should … maybe stick to your business at hand," Victoria finally said, shaking her head and looking at the parchment he carried.

"Oh, this? Of course," Greyson said with a sigh. "However, the alternatives are far more interesting, beautiful Victoria."

Again Victoria was speechless, and her face became nearly as red as her hair. Finally, she held out her hand, and Greyson handed over the scroll. Once she verified that the seal was indeed Penelope's, Victoria broke it and unrolled the parchment. After reading it, she moved to Baxter's desk and asked for a quill and ink, which he quickly produced. Baxter watched her graceful movements with the quill and noticed Greyson looking down her shirt as she bent over her work. Baxter looked on in amazement, and after the young man saw him, he smiled and shrugged at Baxter, then continued his indecent viewing. *Who is this young man?* Baxter wondered.

Then Victoria caught him stealing a peek, but he hardly seemed to care, and he gave her a lewd smile instead of diverting his gaze when she looked up. She sat up and handed him the scroll and said, "Professor Von Hueven, two doors down, has your ring. Give him this scroll, and he will hand it over."

She didn't release the parchment right away, and Baxter looked on as the two shared a brief moment. She smiled nervously and licked the end of her finger. Greyson smiled, perhaps thinking the gesture sexual, but then Victoria put her finger on the scroll, and it glowed, leaving a new seal with a crimson *V* next to the queen's broken seal. She released the scroll.

"Thank you. I hope we will meet again soon. I have many stories and experiences to share," Greyson said.

"Yes, perhaps. Thanks for the use of the ring; it is a fine magic item," she said, blushing.

He smiled and left, closing the door gently behind him. Victoria stared at the door for many moments, seemingly in a daze. Finally, Baxter broke her train of thought by loudly clearing his throat to get her attention. She turned to regard him, and he wore an accusing look.

"What?" she asked, focusing back on her surroundings.

"I thought you said I shouldn't fall for one so young as Cassandra Rho," he said, crossing his arms over his chest. "Does the same set of rules not apply to you?"

It was Victoria's turn to be scrutinized with regard to her feelings. Baxter tried to be stern but could not. After all, Victoria was a good friend. So, instead, he shook his head and sat down, wondering once more who that young man was who had so easily made Victoria blush.

~

The following day, Cassandra awakened with a smile on her face, and her first thought was of Binta. What exactly had happened the night before? She wasn't sure—it had all happened so quickly—but she was sure of one thing: she had liked it and wouldn't mind if it happened again. She was very nervous about the coming day and seeing Binta again, but it was a good kind of nervousness, one that made her a bit giddy, which was a feeling she could grow to like. She prepared herself for class and took extra time fixing her hair and ensuring her clothes fit nicely. She wanted to look suitable for her friend. For the first time in her life, she cared about how she looked.

As she walked down the school hall, lost in thought, she never noticed Baxter until he was beside her. "Miss Rho," he called as he caught up to her.

"Instructor Baxter!" she said and smiled.

"Well, someone's in a fine mood this morning!"

"I'm always in a good mood—haven't you noticed?"

"Well … no, I haven't," he said with a chuckle. "I need to speak to you, Cassandra."

"I'm on my way to class—"

"I know. This will just take a moment," he said, motioning to a side hallway where no students roamed.

She sighed, shook her head, and walked past him to the hallway he desired. She heard him sniff in her perfume as she passed, and she became a little embarrassed. Perhaps she had done too much primping this morning. She panicked at the thought of it. Did she stink? Did she have on too much perfume or makeup? A million thoughts ran through her mind, and all she could focus on was how Binta would react to seeing her or even smelling her. Then, as she pondered it, she noticed Baxter just staring at her with that dumb look again. She had no patience for that now. "Well, out with it—you're going to make me late!"

She hadn't meant to yell at him, and it seemed to make him even more nervous. She realized then that he was indeed having a hard time spitting out what he needed to say.

Eventually he found his voice. "Cassandra, there's a rumor going around the school …"

"Yes, yes, we're sleeping together, right?"

Her matter-of-fact attitude rocked him back on his heels. "Why, yes, that is exactly—"

"I know about this. I think the idiot Jabell made it up," she said, looking over Baxter's shoulder to the crowd of students moving down the hall.

She saw Binta and smiled, waving a hand nervously. Baxter turned to see Binta waving from a distance, walking with the flow of students perpendicular to the hall in which he and Cassandra now stood. "Binta?" he whispered, then turned back to Cassandra.

Cassandra barely registered the fact that Baxter was there. Her heart pounded in her chest, and she felt warm all over. What was wrong? She felt almost sick at the moment and just continued to wave until her friend was out of sight.

"So you and Miss Mulay seem to be very happy this morning," Baxter said as Binta disappeared around a corner.

"What? Yes, I'm sorry, but I'm distracted this morning. Unfortunately I'm also late for class, so I must be going," she said rather giddily.

He put a hand on her shoulder as she tried to walk away and turned her gently around.

"What?" she asked, looking down at his hand on her shoulder.

He realized then what he was doing and quickly released her. "Sorry, but I wanted to let you know that Lady Victoria has demanded that I address this rumor."

"And?"

"And I'm going to address it with each class, even yours. I just wanted you to be aware of it before I did it."

There was a pause as Cassandra studied his face, her eyes darting back and forth. She finally smiled and said, "Thank you, Baxter." She hugged him before running off to her first class. She had no time to address the rumor, and quite frankly, it was the last thing on her mind at the moment. Instead, Binta filled her thoughts, and only Binta mattered to her right then. If she hadn't been so distracted, she might have noticed that dumb look again on Baxter's face as he watched her walk away. Or, more specifically, the lustful way he watched her backside as she hurried to class.

Cassandra excitedly made her way to her first class. She couldn't wait to see Binta again, but she would have to wait for her last course of the day because that was the only one they shared. She gazed out the window and watched the sunrise in a dreamy state of mind.

"Miss Rho?" Instructor Le'More said.

"Yes, sir?" she asked with a jump.

"I hope I didn't startle you; you seem to be a million miles away," the professor chuckled, now standing next to her desk.

"No, I'm fine. Did you need something?"

"No, no, I just want to know how the tome is coming. Have you finished the work yet?"

"No, I have not. It has many pages, and some of the writing is hard to understand," Cassandra said. It was true, but she had spent most of her time with Binta over the last three weeks instead of reading as she had initially planned.

"Very well. I'm here if you have any questions," he said with a smile.

"Yes, of course. Thank you," was all Cassandra could think to say as he walked to his desk to begin his lecture.

She heard little of what he discussed that morning, her mind quickly slipping back to Binta. How could this have happened? It was terrific and frightening at the same time. Cassandra knew two things: she loved Binta as a friend, but she was not a lesbian. All she knew was that she longed to see her friend again, and whatever happened when she did would be natural. She would not stop it.

Her second class was with Baxter, and dread washed over her as she neared the room. She wished Binta was in this class with her; she could use her support, as she now felt very much alone, especially with Cass in attendance. If she had been paying more attention, she would have noticed some of the smirks and sideways glances students gave her as they left his first class. But instead, she quietly walked inside and took her seat. She didn't make eye contact with Baxter, but she could feel him watch her as she entered.

As the students settled in, Baxter started his speech. "Hello, students. Before we begin our lecture today, I want to address something that I became aware of yesterday. There seems to be a nasty and untrue rumor floating around the university concerning Miss Cassandra Rho and me." When he said her name, she slid lower into her seat and glanced around quickly. So many eyes were on her. It felt like the orphanage all over again.

"I want to state for the record that whatever you may have heard about Miss Rho and myself is not true. We are friends for sure, but nothing more. I'm not sure how this ugly rumor began, but it would be nice if the perpetrator reiterated my words."

She heard Cass stifle a laugh and glanced over at her. She was whispering to one of Jabell's friends, and both looked her way. The boy then smiled and nodded. Cassandra simmered, knowing that either Jabell or Cass had probably started the rumor in the first place and were now getting a good laugh at her expense. She honestly didn't like Cass, but she swallowed her pride and let the laughter roll off her back.

After class, she quickly made her way to the alchemy lab to get away not only from Cass but from all the staring eyes that watched her go. Unfortunately, she felt like Baxter's announcement had done nothing more than draw attention to the issue. It had been a long day for Cassandra, and it was all leading up to her class with instructor Von Hueven. That class was the only one she had with Binta, and she had eagerly awaited it all day. Her stomach full of butterflies, she paused at the door to straighten her clothes and pull her hair behind her ears. No one had ever made her feel this way, especially not another girl.

She entered the classroom and saw her friend immediately. Binta was seated at her desk and looked especially attractive. She waved and smiled, and Cassandra smiled back. She put her books on her desk and then walked over to Binta's, near the back of the classroom. Cassandra still felt like all eyes were on her, but she didn't care, not with Binta there. "Hello," she said meekly, trying to keep her voice down so no one could hear.

"Hi, Cassandra."

An awkward silence followed, and Cassandra shifted from foot to foot.

"Do you feel all right?" Binta asked. "I heard Instructor Baxter's speech about the rumor."

"Yes, everyone's heard it by now," Cassandra sighed.

"It was probably for the best … you know, get it out in the open," Binta said encouragingly.

Needing to change the subject, Cassandra blurted out, "Want to come to my room to study tonight?"

"Oh … well … um, tonight is bad for me."

The words hit Cassandra like a ton of bricks, knocking the air out of her. She had no idea what to say or do. She had waited for this moment all day and looked forward to some alone time with her friend. She needed to see what would happen when they were alone again. Had it been just a one-time kiss that they would never share again, or was it the beginning of something extraordinary? Binta's response was not what she had expected, not after the previous night's passionate embrace. Her pained expression betrayed her thoughts.

"I'm sorry—I have plans tonight," Binta said. "Tomorrow night for sure, though?"

"Uh, yes … sure … whatever," Cassandra said, playing off the rejection as no big deal.

"I have business in the city. I'll be out late, but I want to study with you." Binta leaned a little closer so that only Cassandra could hear and whispered, "I *really* want to study with you."

The smile on Binta's face was sincere, and it made Cassandra feel a little better, but she was still in a state of shock. Cassandra felt so disappointed, and suddenly her stomach was in knots. The vague explanation of why Binta couldn't make it that night didn't sit well with her. She nodded and flashed a smile, then turned and made her way to her desk. It was the longest walk of her life.

As she sat down, Cass, a few seats over, leaned over Jabell's desk and said, "Tough day, huh, Cassandra?"

Jabell and his good-looking friend Leonard both laughed, and Jabell added, "Yeah, had her sex life broadcast to the whole school, then got rejected by her girlfriend."

All three shared a good laugh then at her expense. She felt so humiliated and sank deep into her seat, tears welling in her eyes. Did they know somehow about the kiss, or was Jabell just trying to make fun of the situation, perhaps start another rumor? It was by far the longest class ever.

When it was finally over, Cassandra picked up her things and left quickly. She didn't want to speak to anyone, not even Binta. She especially didn't want to be taunted by Cass and her stupid friends. As she made her way quickly down the hall, she heard Binta call her name. She turned to see the girl running toward her.

"I'm so sorry about that," Binta said once she'd caught up.

Cassandra simply turned and kept up her speedy pace toward the door. Binta had to walk that much faster just to keep up with her.

"It's not your fault; you have plans," Cassandra said. "No big deal."

Once they were outside, where their voices wouldn't carry and others wouldn't hear them, Binta grabbed her by the arm and stopped her. "Listen, Cassandra," Binta said, her breath visible in the cold air. "This thing just came up."

"Oh yeah, what came up after you left my room last night? Do you recall that we shared something special—something that I had until now treasured?" Cassandra asked. "Or did it not mean as much to you?"

"It meant everything to me—I promise! But I ran into a boy last night after I left your room. He asked me to dinner tonight in the city."

Cassandra had the wind knocked out of her for the second time that day, hearing the words she would never have expected. "A boy?"

"Yes. Remember—I said I wasn't a lesbian."

"Yes, and you also kissed me last night! That is very conflicting information, Binta!"

Binta took Cassandra's hand and squeezed it. "Yes, I know. I am just as confused as you, but I can tell you one thing: last night meant the world to me, and I want to come to your room tomorrow night. I like being with you."

They shared another moment there in the cold, gazing into each other's eyes, holding hands. They knew not what the future would hold for them, but it was evident that the kiss they had shared had meant a lot to both of them. That's when they heard Jabell making kissing sounds behind them. They both turned to see him and Cass walking by toward the dorms. Jabell had his mouth twisted into a pucker and kept making those stupid sounds. Cass smiled and waved in mock friendship. Many other students made the trek to the dorms, and some laughed at the mockery.

They immediately let go of each other's hands until the gang of students had passed. Cassandra's face was fiery red when she, at last, looked back toward Binta. "I hate those two, and I will teach them a lesson if they keep it up!" she said through gritted teeth.

"Those two? They're idiots. Ignore them," Binta said.

They shared a brief laugh, then headed toward the dorms, the cold weather getting to both of them. Once inside, Binta hugged her and said, "I will tell you everything tomorrow night."

Cassandra nodded meekly.

Binta then smiled that beautiful smile and turned to head for her room.

"Wait!" Cassandra said.

Binta turned back and waited.

"Who is this boy?"

"Just some boy from the city. He was here last night, visiting the school," Binta said.

"A student wizard?" Cassandra asked.

"No, I don't think so. He lives in the temple and is an acolyte or maybe even a priest."

Cassandra frowned, particularly because Binta's face lit up when she spoke of him.

"What's his name?" Cassandra said, a little more than jealous.

"Greyson Kavince," Binta said excitedly. She then smiled and turned to leave once more, a spring in her step. She called over her shoulder, "Enjoy your studies tonight. I'll catch up to you tomorrow."

Cassandra watched until Binta was out of sight, then turned to walk toward her room. "Greyson Kavince, huh? Sounds like a troublemaker," she whispered to herself.

That evening after her meal, Cassandra kept a watchful eye out the window. The wind howled against the pane as the cold fall evening set in. She watched intently until she finally saw Binta leave the dorms. Her heart skipped a beat when she saw her hurrying on her way as if she couldn't wait to see this Greyson Kavince. She told herself it didn't matter, that they had only shared one kiss and it didn't mean as much as Cassandra had first thought. Binta would share her story about Greyson tomorrow night, and the two friends would carry on as if nothing had happened. She would be fine with that, but tonight she felt very alone with the realization that the kiss had been the first and last time the two girls would share a special moment.

Thoughts of her family started to drift into Cassandra's mind once more. She hadn't thought of them all day, and that had been the first time since her arrival that she hadn't. She felt guilty about that, even more so since it was due to her kissing some girl. She vowed it wouldn't happen again; Kessi and Sera were her priorities until they were reunited.

She sighed as Binta left her field of vision and melded into the city streets. Soon her friend would be with Greyson and perhaps be kissing him just as passionately as she had kissed her. Perhaps more than that would happen. The thought had her panic stricken, and she needed something to occupy her mind. She spied the tome that instructor Le'More had given her, and she picked it off her desk. She had read very little of it, but that would change tonight.

She perused the pages, absorbed the information, and learned of the olden days of the New Order. She kept an eye out for information concerning the dark man; the key to her vision was unlocking who he was. There was no trace of the dark man, but she did find an old law that

Novafontera once had in effect. It was referred to as "wizard's privilege" and allowed a wizard to challenge another wizard to a magic duel if one had publicly offended the other. It was perfectly legal, and as long as the challenger proclaimed it as wizard's privilege, it would go unpunished, even if death resulted from the duel.

"Wizard's privilege," she whispered, closing the massive tome. She turned in shortly after with many thoughts in her mind. Was Binta kissing Greyson? Was her family safe? Why was it taking Kringus so long to get back? How easy would it be to defeat Cass in a duel of wizard's privilege? Too many things were on her mind, and it took her a very long time to fall asleep.

~

The next day dragged by for Cassandra, and her thoughts were dark, primarily focused on her sister. She had not seen Binta, but a little piece of her looked forward to spending some time with her after classes. Things would sort out, and perhaps she could determine whether the kiss meant that little to her friend. Either way, she was mentally prepared for anything.

She made it to her last class uneventfully, aside from Baxter having asked how she'd felt after his announcement the day before. She had assured him that she was fine and didn't feel like talking about it much, so she kept the conversation brief. She entered the last class, again with her heart racing just a little at the thought of seeing Binta. She was disappointed once again when she saw her friend's empty desk. Cassandra moved slowly to her seat, wondering where Binta could be. Had she attended her classes today? Had this Greyson fellow hurt her? Many questions floated through her mind at that moment. Thoughts of Binta entwined with him filled her head, making her want to shout in frustration.

"Looks like your girlfriend is as much of a whore as you are," Cass said.

Cassandra took her seat and turned to face her foe. Jabell and Leonard sat there with stupid grins on their faces. She could feel her face growing warm with rage. She wanted to lash out at all three of them, to strike them down as she had done to Ronnis. But instead, she gripped the edge of her desk so tight that her knuckles whitened. She wanted to remain in good standing with the king, hoping against hope that she would be reunited with her family and start a new life in Pelesea. That's the only thing that kept her from attacking Cass then and there.

"Don't talk about things you don't understand, ignorant girl," Cassandra said.

"What, things like you sleeping with the instructors or that your little friend is whoring around with the priests?" Cass said.

"Yeah, you miss your little girlfriend, don't you?" Jabell said.

"I'd much rather date a girl like Binta than an idiot like yourself, Jabell," she said calmly. Then, as instructor Von Hueven began his lecture, she added in a lower whisper, "I'm at the end of my rope with you two. Push me some more, and you'll be sorry."

"Miss Rho?" Instructor Von Hueven said.

Grimacing still from her exchange with Cass and Jabell, she turned in her seat to regard him.

"Please turn to the front—the class has begun," he said with a smile.

Cassandra smiled and did as instructed, but she fumed as her three tormentors continued to make remarks under their breath to irritate her. Their bullying tactics worked, as she became more enraged as the class continued. Where was Binta? She felt so alone without her friend. As class dragged along, she finally decided enough was enough. She thought of her readings the night before and how the wizard's privilege was legal in Novafontera. She wondered whether it was legal in Pelesea as well.

When class was over, she waited in her seat for the three to leave. Cass smiled at her as she left, digging at her one last time. Cassandra gave them a bit of a head start, then followed them. The usual stream of students made their way out of the university building and toward the dorms. The afternoon was warmer than the day before, and the sun was bright in the sky. She wanted to challenge Cass openly, where there would be witnesses. If she could adequately challenge the girl, then perhaps the rules of wizard's privilege would apply. All she knew was that she could no longer take the bullying from Cass, not with all that she had on her mind concerning her family and Binta. It had to end now.

"Cass!" she shouted loud enough for the crowd of students to hear.

Cass stopped and turned around, shaking her head when she saw that it was Cassandra. She walked up to stand before her, followed by Jabell. Leonard didn't approach but stood where he was to watch the confrontation. Many other students stopped to watch as well.

"What do you want?" Cass asked, folding her arms across her chest.

"I want to end this game you're playing," Cassandra said.

"I don't play games, little girl; I simply don't tolerate snotty little orphans."

Cassandra fumed some more. What had she ever done to this girl to deserve this much provoking? Why did it seem that people put her down or caused her grief every step of the way? At that moment, she was furious. At that moment, she lost control.

"I formally proclaim wizard's privilege!"

"What are you talking about?"

"Under the old laws of Novafontera, wizards could challenge each other to demonstrate their power."

"So?" Cass said with a shrug.

"So I'm challenging you. A display in front of the student body that will prove who is the greatest student of magic between the two of us," Cassandra said, gesturing to the gathered students.

That sent Cass back on her heels a bit, and she suddenly didn't look so confident.

"You're making this up, aren't you?" Cass said, trying to gain some measure of control.

"Does it matter? Either you accept the challenge, or all the students will know that you accept defeat. What would Mommy and Daddy think if you weren't the number one student at school?" Cassandra said.

Now it was Cass's turn to become angry as more and more students gathered around the two.

"Take her up on it, Cass! You are better than she is!" Jabell said.

"Shut up, Jabell. Everyone knows that, right?" she asked, looking around at the gathering mass.

No one spoke, and some even shook their heads, which was Cassandra's pleasant and unexpected surprise. Cass looked back at her, her eyes wide in disbelief but also filled with anger. Cassandra only smiled and waited.

"Yes, I'll do it! Once I defeat you, there will be no doubt left that I am the best student, that I will become the better wizard, and that you are far inferior to me!" Cass said. "What are the rules of this stupid wizard's privilege?"

"The rules are that the contest is between the two wizards only, and no one can interfere, even if it results in the death of one of them. Furthermore, there must be at least ten witnesses. The two involved can set a time and place for the duel. The results are final."

"So when I emerge victoriously, you will bow down before me and acknowledge that I am your superior?" Cass said and grinned.

"We'll see."

"It sounds like there are no real rules to this challenge and even death is perfectly acceptable?" Cass asked.

"Yes, that is my understanding," Cassandra said. "So we have the challenge offered and accepted," Cassandra said loud enough for all those observing to hear. "Now all we need is a time and place," she added, turning back to Cass. "How about tomorrow morning at sunrise, in the garden at the back of the dorms?"

"How about now so your girlfriend can watch you lose?" Cass said, shifting her gaze to look over Cassandra's shoulder.

Cassandra turned to see Binta rushing up toward the gathering. She noticed Binta was making her way up the walk that led from the city proper and wearing the same clothes she'd had on the night before. Was her friend just now returning home? Her heart raced as she watched her quickly make her way toward the group.

"Cassandra!" Binta yelled out, trying to move through the multitude of people.

"Oh, Cassandra?" came Cass's voice from behind her.

She realized then that Cass had used Binta merely as a distraction and that one mistake would cost her dearly. As she turned back to face her opponent, she saw her already in the middle of spell casting. Cassandra didn't need to cast her spells and could easily outduel her opponent if they simultaneously started their spells. However, Cass had gained an unfair advantage by distracting her.

"No!" Cassandra screamed just as the blue dart left Cass's fingertips.

She had never defended against such a spell, the same biting ball of energy that she had used to nearly kill Ronnis. She knew the damage it could do, and she also knew it probably wouldn't miss. All she could do was brace for the impact. It slammed into her midsection a moment later, and the force sent her flying to the ground, landing on her back. The pain was unbearable as it burned her skin and dug deep into her as an arrow might. She cried out, holding her midriff.

The crowd took a step back in realization that the challenge was happening now and that things would get ugly quickly. Even though the semester had only begun three weeks prior, the entire freshman class knew of the rivalry between these two young women and had fully expected something like this would eventually occur. Binta was still trying to get through the crowd when Cassandra yelled out, but she heard her scream and knew it was her friend. She pushed people out of the way as fast as possible, but it was slow moving.

Cass turned toward Jabell and said, "Make sure that one does not interfere," motioning toward the parting sea of students, where Binta was fast approaching.

Jabell nodded and moved off to intercept her. Cassandra had gotten up to a sitting position at that point, holding her torn abdomen and wincing in pain. She saw that Cass had produced more components and began to cast another spell. Rage washed over her.

"Cheating bitch!" Cassandra cried and returned the attack with a similar dart of green energy. She smiled as it slammed into Cass's chest. She knew this would have a two-pronged effect: first, it would severely injure the girl, and second, it would disrupt the spell she was beginning to cast. Cass didn't scream out, to Cassandra's surprise, and didn't even flinch as the energy bit into her. To make matters worse, she continued to cast her spell. Cassandra noticed a medallion around her neck that seemed to glow with green energy as if it had absorbed her magic. "Impossible," Cassandra whispered, wide eyed.

She could hear some of the students gasp and heard Binta scream her name as she made her way out of the gathering of students. However, she couldn't focus on her friend at that moment, as Cass blew a handful of sand at her, sending it sprinkling all over like golden rain. Again there were more astonished gasps from the other students. Cassandra didn't know what to make of the spell, but it didn't hurt at all.

"Go to sleep, little Cassandra Rho," Cass said.

She tried to get up, but the pain shot through her midsection, and she sat back down hard. Then, to her amazement, she did get tired—exhausted—and suddenly Cass's suggestion that she sleep seemed like a very, very good idea. She slowly lay down on the ground, trying unsuccessfully to keep her eyes open. She vaguely heard Binta scream her name again, but she sounded like she was miles away now. She drifted off.

"And there you have it, folks—the fastest wizard's duel ever!" Cass said, extending her hand to her fallen enemy, who was now sleeping soundly.

"Cassandra!" Binta screamed again as Jabell struggled to block her way.

"Shut her up!" Cass yelled.

Jabell held Binta out at arm's length, then slugged her hard in the stomach. All the air went out of her, and her knees buckled. She fell to the ground holding her stomach and gasping for breath. She curled into a fetal position and noticed Cassandra lying motionless just a few feet away. Jabell kicked her in the stomach very hard, and Binta almost threw up. Waves of nauseating pain washed over her, and she almost blacked out. Still, out of either fear or shock, the other students didn't move to assist either of them.

"No interference—your girlfriend said so!" Jabell yelled at Binta.

Cass dragged Cassandra over to a small tree and sat her against it, facing it. Cassandra moaned at the apparent discomfort from the awkward position and the nasty wound on her abdomen. However, Cass's powerful spell kept her from waking up. Cass took the long blue ribbon holding her ponytail and shook her long hair down. She then walked to the other side of the tree, took Cassandra's hand, and tied the ribbon tightly around her wrist. She then tied the other end of the ribbon to the other wrist so that Cassandra was bound to the tree in a hugging position. Cass made her way back to Cassandra and took a small knife from her boot. Several students took a step back, and a few even ran off, probably to inform the instructors.

"Everyone should note that I easily defeated my opponent today, and without a scratch to show for it. I will also note that if she had somehow won, she probably would have killed me," Cass said, turning the small knife over in her hand. "Well, I have every right to do the same thing, but I'm not a vicious, nasty person like Cassandra Rho. I choose the higher road!"

With that, she knelt beside Cassandra and put the knife to her neck. Binta reached a hand toward her friend, fearing that she was witnessing her murder. She spit up blood and went into a coughing fit. Some students covered their eyes, and several yelled, "No!" as the knife dug in. There was a collective sigh of relief when Cass began to cut the back of Cassandra's collar and not the girl herself. She sawed through Cassandra's shirt, and once she had that split, she made a slit down the back of it, exposing her back. She took her hands and ripped it a little farther, revealing as much skin as possible.

Cass then stood and put the knife away. "So poor Cassandra was sorely overmatched today and is not worthy of challenging me at anything, much less a wizard's duel. I will now make sure that she admits as much." She knelt back down and slapped Cassandra's cheeks hard. "Wake up, loser. Your humiliation has only just begun."

Cassandra's eyes fluttered open. She could barely keep them open, so Cass continued smacking her face until she knew her surroundings. Finally Cass forced Cassandra's head to the side so she faced the crowd of people. Cassandra tried to blink away the sleep, and that's when she saw Binta lying on the ground a mere twenty feet from her, holding her stomach and coughing up blood. Again Cassandra tried desperately to shake the sleep without much success.

Cassandra could see Cass smirk at her as she tried to shake the effects of the powerful spell. Then, as her vision became more focused, she noticed Cass loosen and remove a slender belt that cinched her dress at the waist. The evil girl then walked up beside her and held it threateningly like a whip.

"And now we will hear from the loser," Cass said to the gathered students. "Cassandra Rho, is it true that I have defeated you and I am far superior?"

Cassandra refused to answer, so Cass struck her hard across the back with the belt. The pain shocked her more than she'd expected as the tough leather bit into her tender back. She screamed out in pain as Cass laughed.

Cassandra noticed Binta had managed to sit up and then tried to stand while holding her side. Of course she had to help her friend; she was responsible for Binta's pain. She was relieved to see two other students come over and help her up, even asking whether she was all right. But then Jabell was there, shoving them away and backhanding Binta hard across the cheek. She couldn't defend the attack and took the hit square on the side of her face, which knocked her back to the ground, where she lay motionless.

"Leave her alone!" Cassandra screamed, only then realizing that her hands were bound around the tree. She wanted to cast a spell to wound or even kill Jabell, but she couldn't move her hands properly even to summon the energy.

Cass repeated her question three more times, asking Cassandra to admit her defeat and acknowledge Cass as her superior. Again Cassandra refused to respond and continued to struggle to free her hands. Binta needed her! She knew Cass would eventually lose patience with her stubborn refusal to answer, but she didn't care about her safety at the moment.

Then, as expected, Cass struck her repeatedly with the belt, each strike sending waves of pain through Cassandra's torn stomach. Cass placed the strikes perfectly, continuing to attack her sensitive back in the same spot each time. After four or five of these, Cassandra was in so much pain that she began to cry. Unfortunately her tears only made Cass hit her harder. Cassandra eventually felt the blood running down her back and knew she was in trouble.

She focused everything on Binta, who continued to lie on the ground, not moving. Finally Jabell made his way over to witness Cass's vicious attack, leaving Binta alone. As he cheered Cass on, several students went to Binta, which gave Cassandra some relief.

Suddenly the whipping stopped, and Cass bent down, grabbing a handful of Cassandra's hair. "It looks like your girlfriend can't help you," Cass whispered in her ear. "So tell everyone who the better wizard is," Cass said, waving an arm to the gathered students. She pulled Cassandra's hair and forced her to look at her classmates.

She saw all their faces. Most wore smirks, but some seemed shocked or even saddened by the display. It was the orphanage again; some liked seeing her lose, and others thought she was a freak. She could only sob in response. Then, when she didn't answer, Cass hit her hard with the belt in rapid succession, delivering a half dozen blows before Cassandra finally had to give in and scream, "You are!"

Cass stopped the beating and bent down once more to whisper in Cassandra's ear, "You are pathetic. Don't ever challenge me at anything again. The next time you do, I will kill you for it." She then stood as Cassandra openly wept. But instead of ending the torture and humiliation, Cass unleashed yet another flurry of strikes on Cassandra's wounded back. Lash after lash rained down, splattering blood all around, and Cassandra neared passing out. All she could do was scream and cry, overwhelmed by the immense pain. Then, after at least a dozen vicious strikes, it was finally over. Cassandra barely clung to consciousness as Cass and Jabell walked away laughing. Cassandra turned her head to watch them as best she could, tears blurring her vision. Several other students joined them as they went, patting Cass on the back and applauding her powerful display of domination.

The remaining students stood watching in shock. Some were assisting Binta, who was regaining consciousness. Cassandra felt such a wave of relief at the sight of her friend stirring that she temporarily forgot about the immense pain that racked her entire body. None of the students approached her, leaving her sitting awkwardly, still tied to the tree. She didn't care—she knew Binta was now safe, and that was all that mattered. She closed her eyes as her tears continued to fall, her humiliation complete. To make matters worse, Cassandra could hear the beginning words of the nursery rhyme Cass sang as she walked triumphantly away: "Little Cassandra Rho, tromping through the forest, being way too loud and bringing the wolves upon us."

~

Annabel had left the fight scene quickly and made her way to Instructor Von Glord's office. She burst in without knocking—something none of Baxter's students ever did. Her sudden entrance startled him, as he was in the middle of fixing a special drink he partook of every day after his final class.

"Instructor Von Glord!"

He dropped his glass at the sudden intrusion, and it shattered on the floor. "What, girl?" he asked in frustration.

"Come quickly … to the front lawn," she said between gasps of air, winded from having run there.

Baxter looked out the window and saw the gathered mass but couldn't make out any details. "What is it?"

"Cass and Cassandra … wizard's privilege!"

"Wizard's what?" he asked. "Cass and Cassandra?"

"Yes, come quickly … she's going to kill her!"

That got him moving, and he was soon running off with the young girl. When they arrived, Baxter found no sign of Cass and her band of friends, but Cassandra and Binta were in dire need of medical attention. Baxter's heart raced as he took in Cassandra's condition.

"Run, Annabel … to the temple … bring healers! Quickly, girl!"

The girl ran off at once. He only hoped she would be quick enough.

CHAPTER 13

The Evil of Oldorburg

KRINGUS AND HIS TROUPE FINALLY ARRIVED AT THE SMALL town of Oldorburg as the first autumn snow began to fall. It had taken them just over three weeks to reach their destination, and they were anxious to get their business over with and get back home before the weather worsened. They were a sight to behold for the guardsmen of the small town. Kringus rode his magnificent steed, which fit the giant man's physical stature and personality, with Arrin and the elven brothers flanking him. The elves shared a horse now, as Arrin had borrowed Lenore's when they left Daro's woods, and each of those elven horses were adorned with bells that lightly jingled with each step. The four cavaliers, Erik, Marcus, Franklin, and Jimmon, followed. The warhorses were decked in plate barding similar to that of their riders. The final row consisted of the four squires, all equally imposing fighters on their own.

This amazing group of soldiers quickly gained the town guard's attention. Several guardsmen greeted them cheerily. "Good evening to you," one said. "We rarely see such a magnificent band of warriors in our humble town. May we inquire as to what your business may be with Oldorburg?"

"We have come a long way to meet with the leader of your fair town. I am Kringus, King of Pelesea, and these are my most trusted men who have accompanied me," Kringus said as he dismounted his horse.

Arrin similarly dismounted, as did the elven brothers, but the cavaliers remained on their steeds, ready for any possible trouble.

The squires quickly took the reins of the dismounted horses, perfectly coordinated, as if they had practiced the routine hundreds of times, which of course they had. Finally Kringus approached the guards, extending his hand in a friendly greeting toward the one who had spoken, and the guard happily shook it.

"We are honored to have you in our town, Kringus of Pelesea! I am Max, captain of the guard. If you'd like to find lodging and then come to the sheriff's office, I will make sure you find an audience with the guild leaders."

Kringus nodded and said, "We appreciate your hospitality, Max. We will find our lodging and be at the sheriff's office within the hour."

"Might I recommend the Mighty Oak Inn, the first building after the mercantile on the left? William, the proprietor, will take good care of you. However, the accommodations may not meet the expectations of a king such as yourself."

"The accommodations will be fine, for we have spent the last three weeks in the wilderness. A bed of any type will be an improvement," Kringus said.

Max smiled, and he and several of the guardsmen made their way to the sheriff's office. Kringus and Arrin watched them go, and Von and Lenore joined them.

"Seems like a friendly town," Arrin said.

"Too friendly," Kringus stated flatly. "Von and Lenore, keep your eyes open. This feels wrong to me."

Lenore nodded. "I believe we should be vigilant."

~

Max quickly headed to the sheriff's office, which still had no sheriff, but finding the sheriff was not his mission. A crucial meeting was currently in a back room between the guild members and several high priests. He had some important news to deliver to them.

Buster Agnew, leader of the merchant's guild, was heading up the meeting and had come to power in the last few weeks. He wasn't particularly fond of being in his current position, but in the end, it had been a direct effect of his dismissing Sheriff Quinn. The guild had taken over since Buster had made that mistake, but he held no real power over the town. Instead, he had become a puppet for Barktuck Misol and the other priests. The guild leaders had discovered that Lord Ronnis and Barktuck were in cahoots shortly after the sheriff's dismissal. Still, they did not fix the error by reinstating Quinn and instead continued acting in Barktuck's best interests. Mostly out of fear.

Once Cassandra Rho had escaped, and following her sister's disappearance, things had gone from bad to worse, and the whole thing was just spinning out of control. Ronnis D'Breeth had surfaced more and more at these meetings, and the temple was trying to recognize the orphanage as an interested party in the legal affairs concerning the Rho girls. Things had spiraled out of control quickly, and Buster found himself in a very uncomfortable position.

"The temple's share of the taxes comes to fifty-six gold pieces this month, Barktuck," he said, sliding a small sack of gold to the priest, who was sitting to his right.

Barktuck smiled and put the small sack into a pocket of his robe without even acknowledging the contribution. His actions held an air of entitlement, as if his temple deserved the gold and he would take it whether the guild freely offered it or not.

"Now," Buster said, "as far as appointing a new sheriff—"

Barktuck put his hand up. "There's no need to rush the appointment, my friend. We have plenty of time to find an adequate replacement for that idiot Quinn."

"But we should have a sheriff; it's in the town's bylaws," Buster said.

"Besides, the townsfolk like you, Buster, and trust the merchant's guild to lead them through this difficult time," Barktuck said, ignoring Buster's argument altogether.

Buster nodded, conceding to Barktuck's will. Barktuck spoke on for a bit, addressing the need to increase taxes for repairs to the temple and many other things that benefited the priests and the orphanage. Buster's attention lasted as long as it took to notice the swinging bodies on the gallows across the street. Their blood stained Buster's hands, and although he had done nothing to enforce or enact that punishment, the guild was responsible for the deaths of two townsfolk who were innocent of any crimes.

Buster had had no choice but to carry out the punishment, even though he had greatly opposed the idea. The temple, backed by Barktuck, had demanded swift retribution, even threatening Buster's family if he didn't comply. When he acquiesced to protect his family, he had inadvertently joined this league of conspirators. Now there was no backing out.

Suddenly, a knock on the door interrupted Barktuck's directives.

"Enter," Buster said, glad for the talk to be cut short.

The door opened with an urgency that silenced all at the table as they turned to look at the new arrivals. Max and two other soldiers were there, grim looks on all three faces.

Buster stood and asked, "What is it, Max?"

"We have guests in the town asking to see the sheriff."

"Is it an urgent matter?" Buster asked.

"I would assume so. One proclaims to be the king of Pelesea!"

Buster sat back down in his chair as his legs lost all strength, and he turned to Barktuck, the color draining from his face. Barktuck just shook his head and fixed him with a stern look that had him sinking farther in his seat. The gaze didn't last long, but it was enough of a warning to Buster that things needed to be handled delicately for the sake of his family.

"Did you inform the king that there is no longer a sheriff in place?" Barktuck asked casually.

Max looked at Buster, not understanding why the old priest questioned him instead of Buster.

Buster nodded as if permitting him to answer.

"No, we did not. We wanted to seek out the advice from the guild before doing so," the captain replied, then glanced in the direction of Buster, who seemed lost in thought.

"Excellent thinking, Max. We now know why you are the lead guardsman of the town," Barktuck said with a smile.

Max gave a slight nod and asked, "What shall we do? He's coming to the sheriff's office within the hour."

Barktuck sat back, and his smile became even larger somehow. "Let them come. How many are in the group?"

"We counted twelve men. They all appear to be warriors, no wizards," Max said.

"That's good because, as we know, magic is illegal here, correct?" Barktuck asked.

Max nodded. "So what shall we do?"

"We shall welcome our guests, of course," Barktuck said. After a brief pause, he added, "If there are a dozen of them, gather enough guards to neutralize any threat they might present."

Max nodded once more and then looked to Buster for confirmation.

Buster slowly raised his eyes to look him in the face and gave him his silent assurance.

The young captain then took the two guards and exited the room, shutting the door behind him. There was a brief moment of silence before Buster turned to Barktuck and asked, "Should we remove the bodies from the gallows?"

Barktuck, showing no sense of panic or urgency, shook his head. "No, leave them. If this so-called king from Pelesea is here concerning Cassandra Rho, which he certainly is, we must stand our ground and show him how we punish those who break our laws. We might be a small town compared to his grand city, but he has no authority here. You remember that when you're dealing with this group, guild master—understood?"

"Of course," Buster answered. "So I am to meet with him?"

"You are the leader of the merchant guild, are you not? You now serve in the capacity of the sheriff and therefore will meet with our distinguished guests. You will meet with this man and get to the bottom of this most unusual visit. You know what to say and how to act, and if things get out of control, do not hesitate to use force to help him see things our way," Barktuck said.

The priest then leaned in closer and added, "And most important of all, make sure you properly ask for the return of Cassandra Rho. That should be a nonnegotiable demand of yours. We want her sister as well; I am almost certain that both of the little witches are hiding in Pelesea."

Buster grimly dismissed the meeting and asked the guild members to return to the same room in a few hours so he could debrief them on the meeting with the king. They agreed and hurried on their way, anxious to be far away from the building, sensing that the meeting could prove disastrous. The four priests followed, Barktuck leading them arrogantly and confidently to the temple. Buster was soon left alone—more alone than at any other time in his entire life.

~

Kringus looked out the inn's window from the second floor, Lenore standing beside him. Both were scanning the town's layout, especially the sheriff's office, which they could see across the street about fifty yards from their location. The sun was beginning to set, and the guards were lighting the lanterns around the town. They seemed a little nervous, and it didn't take Kringus long to determine that something was amiss.

"Seems like things are normal," Kringus finally said. "Perhaps a little too normal for my liking."

Lenore nodded. "Yes, and those archers on the roof of the sheriff's office and the building across the street indicate that things are not as they appear."

"Agreed," Kringus said solemnly. "Arrin, inform Franklin and the other cavaliers to be vigilant. We will go to this meeting fully armored and equipped."

"Of course," Arrin replied and quickly left the room to inform the cavaliers of the new developments.

A few minutes later, Kringus and the other seven hardy warriors moved toward the sheriff's office. The squires remained with the horses to ride quickly to Pelesea if trouble ensued during the meeting. Kringus wore his buckler on his forearm, which had a red background with angel wings of Pelesea proudly displayed on it. He had seen many battles with that buckler and wore it now in anticipation of what trouble they might find behind those doors. Dented in many places and with paint flaking away, it symbolized the freedom Pelesea represented. But more important, it was his calling card. When he wore it, it meant he expected to use it. For many of his enemies, it was the last thing they saw on the battlefield before death.

As they made their way to the small building, Von and Lenore counted a total of ten archers on the rooftops now. It was dusk, so visibility was becoming an issue, and neither was sure whether the count was accurate, but there were at least ten.

"Franklin, you and the other knights stay outside. Be prepared," Kringus said as they made a perimeter around the sheriff's office.

Each warrior stood at a different corner and within sight of one another, as their training had taught them. Their plate mail armor was extra padded this evening to protect them from the growing cold, the snow already an inch deep. Once they were in place, Franklin gave the signal to Kringus, who nodded and began to open the door.

Arrin stopped him by grabbing his arm. "Kringus, look," he said solemnly, nodding toward the other side of the street.

Kringus and the elves turned to see a set of gallows near the town center for all to witness. Hanging from them were two bodies, gently swaying in the slight breeze, the falling snow giving them a surreal appearance. Kringus moved swiftly toward the gallows, a new sense of urgency in his step. He was followed closely by Von, Lenore, and Arrin. The cavaliers drew their swords but held their positions at the ready. As the group approached the bodies, they sensed many eyes on them, not just from the archers but also from the townsfolk. Few were on the street, sensing something profound was about to occur. Kringus stood at the gallows' base then and could tell that one was a female, the other male. Moreover, they reeked of decay, even in the cold temperatures, which meant they had been hanging for some time.

"They have been there a while," Arrin said.

"Cassandra's sister?" Lenore asked.

"Too old. Perhaps Cassandra's mother, though," Kringus said, shaking his head.

"And the male?" Von asked.

"I'm not sure, but we need to find out," Kringus said, moving once again toward the sheriff's office. Once there, he signaled to the cavaliers to be ready for trouble, and then he entered the building. Arrin, Von, and Lenore quickly followed their king. They found Max standing behind the sheriff's desk inside the office, with six other guardsmen in the room. A man sitting behind the desk smiled as they entered. Kringus noticed a wooden door behind and to the left of the desk and a steel door on the room's left wall that led to the cells.

"Good evening, distinguished guests from Pelesea. My name is Buster Agnew, and I am the leader of the merchant's guild," the nervous man said.

"I am Kringus Brahmore, King of Pelesea, as you must know. We seek the sheriff."

"Unfortunately, we have no sheriff at this time. However, the guild holds temporary powers to enforce the town's laws."

Kringus shared a concerned glance with Lenore. "To hang people?" he asked bluntly.

The man smiled even more nervously and said, "Yes, but not without the approval of the temple."

"Are you not taking the credit for their execution, guild master?"

"The only credit I take is trying to enforce the rules of this fair town until a new sheriff is elected. Until then, I rely on the council of the temple and the other guild members before carrying out any sentence as severe as a hanging," Buster said.

A bead of sweat rolled down Buster's forehead, and Kringus understood that the man was probably more of a puppet than an official. He knew at that point that he would have to deal with the priests for answers.

"May I ask their names?" Kringus said calmly, trying to take control of his boiling emotions.

The nervous official made eye contact with Max, who only returned the gaze knowingly and seemed just as anxious.

"Of course," Buster said. "The man was our former sheriff, and his name was Quinn. The lady was an orphanage worker by the name of Sera."

"Sera Rho?" Kringus asked as calmly as possible.

"No, her surname was Jasmine … but she was the surrogate mother of the Rho sisters, if that's what you're referring to."

Anger boiled within Kringus as he understood that they had traveled so far to retrieve nothing more than corpses. He wanted to draw his weapon and lash out at the ignorant weakling behind the desk. The knowledge that this man, although not innocent, was not the real culprit of this tragedy only added to his frustration. He set his jaw and asked, "What were their crimes?"

"You should already know the answer to that," Buster said, which did not sit well with Kringus.

"What is the meaning of that statement? If I knew, I wouldn't ask," Kringus said, narrowing his eyes.

Max took a step toward the king, prompting several other guards to do the same. Kringus ignored them, focusing his gaze solely on Buster. Arrin took a couple of steps to stand between Max and Kringus, even going so far as to face the guard captain directly. He placed a hand on the hilt of his sword and winked at the young guard. Max didn't move, but the tension in the room was rising. Buster could sense this and tried again to regain some control. "I simply mean that your trip here concerns Cassandra Rho, who has taken refuge in your fair kingdom. Is that correct?"

Kringus only looked at him with a blank expression, his scarred neck flexing.

"Furthermore, if that is the reason you have come, then you understand you're harboring a criminal, and we would like her returned to us," Buster said.

"So you may hang her too?" Kringus asked. "A child to join the unhappy family of corpses? I'll ask once more—what were their crimes?"

Buster slumped his shoulders a bit in resignation and said, "They were both charged with assisting in Cassandra's escape, then later her sister's escape."

"And what evidence did you have that was so convincing that it cost them their lives, might I ask?"

"You, of all people, must understand that I must enforce the laws of this town."

"What evidence did you have to convict them?" Kringus asked again, on the verge of losing his temper.

"Lord Ronnis declared that he saw Sera and Quinn both fleeing the scene on the night Cassandra fled to your city with the wizard. He also claims to have seen them the night before Kessi disappeared, snooping around the sheriff's office!"

That was all Kringus needed to hear. As soon as the words left Buster's mouth, Kringus hurled himself over the desk and punched the small man in the mouth, sending him flying against the wall. Before Buster could slump to the floor, Kringus was there, holding him up with one arm by the front of his shirt, his other arm already holding his sword at the throat of the closest guard. Arrin simultaneously drew his weapon and pointed it similarly to Max, who raised his hands in the air. The elves drew their bows and notched arrows in the blur of an eye. They drew a bead on the remaining four guards, moving their aim from one to the next, daring one of them to move. The four guards were stunned and raised their hands, following Max's lead.

"Lord Kringus," Buster began, "I beg you—"

"Silence, you worm!" Kringus yelled in his face. "You took the word of the person charging Cassandra for her crimes—a person whose immediate concerns are to punish anyone he sees fit for his losses? Are you some kind of fool?"

Buster's lip was torn open from the punch, and warm blood ran down his chin. He appeared to be on the verge of crying, and his legs seemed shaky. He had both of his hands on Kringus's large forearm, trying to gain some kind of balance, and he tried to find the words to ease the large man's wrath, but all he could do was stammer something incoherent. Then, finally, Kringus released him, his wrath quenched, as he understood that this man had no real power and was just a pawn of Lord Ronnis. Kringus's fight was with that man, not the frightened bureaucrat who stood before him. "I have come for the family of Cassandra Rho. Are you telling me that her mother is dead and her sister is missing?"

Buster leaned against the wall, trying to hold himself up. All he could do was nod. Kringus put away his weapon, sheathing it in one quick motion. Arrin followed suit, and the elven brothers likewise lowered their bows. Kringus walked around the desk, staring each guardsman in the face as he passed. None made a move to intercept him, and few found the courage even to look him in the eye. Once he reached the vicinity of his friends, he turned to regard Buster once more.

"You should be ashamed of what has transpired here. The blood of the innocent is on your hands," Kringus said, pointing out the window toward the hanging bodies. "I am taking the bodies with me, and if you or any of your men try to stop me, we will defend ourselves with deadly force. Make no mistake about it: if your men make any aggressive moves toward me or any of my allies before we leave this wretched town, you will feel the full force of Pelesea's army in retribution. Am I clear, guild master?"

Buster's eyes revealed the fear and the pain in his heart. He nodded his understanding.

"Good," Kringus said. He began to leave but stopped and added, "As of this moment, I pardon the charges against Cassandra Rho. But if I catch you, Lord Ronnis, or any other fool trying to find her in my city, your punishment will be swift and severe."

With that, Kringus, Arrin, and the elven brothers exited the sheriff's office. Once all were outside, Arrin signaled to Franklin and the cavaliers to gather as Kringus gave specific and hurried instructions.

"Arrin, you and I will cut the bodies down while Lenore and Von keep us covered," Kringus said. "The squires need to bring all the horses to us so that we can make a quick exit."

Two cavaliers dispersed at once to retrieve the squires and the horses from the stables. The rest of the group made their way to the gallows.

"The snow is growing thicker. It's not safe to travel in this," Arrin said.

"So you'd rather stay in this town with the murderous government?" Kringus asked, not slowing his pace.

"Of course not, but perhaps we should make haste toward the closest settlement," Arrin said.

"Yes, my thoughts exactly," Kringus said. "It's going in the wrong direction, but we could reach Mecca-Loraine in four or five days, depending on the weather. We could wait out the storm there, and since it's a coastal city, we could find passage to Pelesea on a ship."

"Then let's be done with this evil place and be on our way."

The two climbed the stairs to the gallows and gently cut the bodies down. The cavaliers, Franklin and Jimmon, helped ease them to the ground so they wouldn't fall. All the while, the always-alert elves noticed the guards were advancing from the sheriff's office and more than a few dozen archers lined the rooftops now.

"They sorely outnumber us, brother," Von said.

"Should we inform Kringus that we may not be able to fight our way out of this if they decide to attack?" Lenore asked.

"Would it alter his actions to know this?" Von asked.

Both elves stood straight and thought for a moment. Then they shook their heads at once.

"No," Lenore finally said.

"Then we say nothing," Von said grimly.

Both seasoned warriors knew they were in a fix then, but they were fiercely loyal to Kringus and would fight to the death with him. And both knew that they would soon get the chance.

~

A few hours before Kringus and his men had arrived at Oldorburg, a lone figure had entered the town. The guards had barely noticed him as he quietly made his way to the orphanage. He was a member of the Brotherhood of Fire, a distinguished monastery located in Mecca-Loraine. The brothers there were carofex, a race of humanlike creatures who mastered the element of flame. Furthermore, they had the reputation of being deadly fighters, with or without weapons. They were masters of hand-to-hand fighting and dangerous to all who opposed them. Above all else, they were mercenaries for hire, and a certain carofex had answered the call of Oldorburg. The carofex were considered mysterious and dangerous, and only the most desperate people hired them when dirty work required attention, as long as the price was right, of course.

Boz was a younger carofex, having seen only two and a half decades of life, and he possessed the monastery's typical characteristics: a shaved head, a red robe, and a giant flame tattoo on his back. Even at his young age, he was one of the finest physical specimens the monastery had to offer. Unfortunately, he was also one of the most dangerous and unpredictable carofex, killing several people who had hired him. As of yet, he had never failed a mission and demanded a high price because of it—one that Ronnis D'Breeth was willing to pay.

The carofex, summoned by none other than Ronnis, now stood in the lord's chambers at the orphanage. He dressed in a thin robe, a hood drawn and covering most of his face. He kept his head lowered so that only his mouth and chin were visible from the hood. Ronnis sat at his desk, sipping his brandy, studying the strange carofex. He knew the reputation of the carofex well, having lived part of his life in Mecca-Loraine, and had heard great things about this particular one.

Various parchments and scrolls lined the desk, and Boz studied them intently. Ronnis waited patiently as the young man read and reread each scroll that Ronnis had prepared for him. The man liked to know his targets well and was in the process of memorizing every detail Ronnis had given him concerning Cassandra Rho. He absorbed the information on the scrolls, documenting the ravens-and-wolves incident, Cassandra's history at the orphanage, her arrest, her escape, and so on. Ronnis had commissioned artists to draw renditions of the young woman that came out near perfect. The carofex had been at his work for almost an hour and had made not a sound. He stood at the end of Ronnis's desk, having not even shifted his weight once in the time he had been there.

Ronnis waved his hand at the empty chairs at his desk, which were on either side of the young man. "Do you wish to sit, Boz?" he asked for at least the third time.

The carofex slowly shook his head and said, "I do not desire that."

Ronnis smiled and took another sip of his favorite drink. "As you wish. As you can see, I have provided—"

"Where is the sister?" Boz asked, never looking up from his scrolls.

"What?"

"Kessi Rho. Where is the girl?" Boz asked.

"Gone."

For the first time that long evening, the lord had gotten a word out of the rigid man. The carofex looked up from the notes, and Ronnis could see the cold blue eyes burning deep within the hood, the dancing flames of the hearth reflected there.

"Gone?" the carofex asked.

"She was locked up at the jail until a vampire came to this very room asking about Cassandra," Ronnis said with a smile.

"A vampire?"

"Yes, and his questioning eventually led to Kessi Rho. I told him where he could find her, and the next morning, she was gone without a trace. Unfortunately, both guards on duty that night did not survive, so no one has any information on Kessi's disappearance other than what I just gave you."

Boz stared hard at him from within the robe, studying Ronnis's face, his eyes slowly focusing on the wound, the hole in his cheek that none other than Cassandra Rho had given him. The carofex prepared to speak, perhaps to ask more specifics about the wound, but Ronnis continued.

"I have all the confidence in the world that you will succeed, Boz, and my swift payment is evidence to that very fact," he said, opening a desk drawer and taking out three small sacks.

He opened one and poured it on the table, spilling out many tiny rubies and sapphires. He tossed the other two onto the desk. "Gems worth five thousand gold in each bag, as we agreed. When you complete the task, I will have another fifteen thousand gold's worth of diamonds for you."

Boz quickly placed the unopened sacks in his robe, and in one quick motion, he had the spilled bag filled once more and in his robe with the other two. Ronnis knew that the payment didn't matter to the strange and mysterious carofex; instead, he did what he did for the challenge. He had never failed a mission, so Ronnis had heard, and had never turned down an opportunity—the exact two reasons Ronnis had sent for this one in particular.

Boz once again took his place behind the desk's chairs and folded his hands in front of him. "Do you have the antidote I require?"

"Of course," Ronnis said, reaching into a separate drawer to pull out a small vial. The carofex had asked for an antidote to the strong poison the priests of Meshlor used. So Ronnis had asked his good friend Barktuck for a vial, which he quickly produced. The carofex added the vial to the pockets of his robe.

"Why the antidote?" Ronnis asked.

"Why not?" Boz replied curtly.

"Just seems strange you would ask for an antidote to a poison used by my colleagues."

"I've learned to trust no one."

The two stared at each other for several moments, and Ronnis even considered drawing the Black Adder, which now hung from his hip. Then, before either could say anything, there came a knock on the door.

The muffled sound of Prudence's voice sounded through the oak door with a bit of urgency. "My lord, you must let me in! I have urgent news!"

"Do come in, Prudence!" Ronnis said, somewhat annoyed at the interruption.

The portly woman opened the door, her face dotted with red and her hair disheveled. She noticed the strange carofex right away, which kept her from speaking and fully entering the room. "I'm sorry, my lord," she said, standing at the threshold, never taking her eyes off Boz.

"What is it, Prudence? We are busy!" Ronnis roared, smacking his hand on the table.

That broke her trance, and she said, almost in a panic, "My lord, please forgive me, but there is a situation brewing in the town proper!" She pointed to his west-facing window and scampered to it. "Look for yourself! A king from a faraway land has come to claim the bodies of Sera and Quinn!"

Ronnis rushed over to the window and wiped the fog from it. It was difficult to see from this far away, especially with the snow coming down and the night sky offering very little light. Nevertheless, he could vaguely make out men rummaging around the gallows and the town guard slowly forming a semicircle around the area. "Who is our guest of honor?" Ronnis asked.

"Kringus by name. Lord of Pela-something," she said, her face scrunching up as she tried to recall the city's name.

"Pelesea?" Ronnis said.

"That's it! Pelesea!" she said, nodding eagerly.

Ronnis glanced at Boz, who merely nodded and then made his way to the window. Prudence let out a little shriek and moved out of the carofex's way as he passed her. Ronnis calmly took a step back, letting Boz view the unfolding spectacle.

"My apologies, my lord, but the strange man …" Prudence began, pointing at Boz and taking a step back toward the door. The carofex still unnerved the woman, and rightfully so.

Soon Boz had the window open, and the cold air blew into the room with a good amount of snow.

Prudence quickly left, closing the door behind her and leaving Ronnis alone with the carofex once more.

"What are you thinking?" Ronnis asked.

"I think we are blessed this evening," was all the cryptic carofex said. "I will deliver your prey when winter is at its coldest."

"I will anxiously await your return in Mecca-Loraine, carofex. Now, tell me, how—"

Before Ronnis could complete the question, the carofex jumped up on the window ledge and crouched in perfect balance. He studied his surroundings quickly, observing the potential issue forming far below at the gallows and noticing the archers along the building tops on both sides of the street.

"What are you doing?" Ronnis asked from behind him.

Boz turned and smiled and with a nod of his head whispered, "In three months, we will meet again at Mecca-Loraine. Bring the diamonds." With that, he fell forward, over the ledge, and to his apparent death from the five-story-high window.

Ronnis was so surprised that it took him several moments to react. However, he eventually found his wits and moved to the open window. He expected to see the broken form of the carofex on the ground below, but there was no sign of him and no markings or footprints in the fresh snow to indicate he had landed or walked away from the jump. Ronnis slowly shook his head and closed the window. He knew the many skills that the carofex possessed, and there was no doubt in his mind that the young man lived, even after that fall. He sat back at his desk and poured another drink, then played with the hole in his cheek, deep in thought.

There was a long silence before his sword, the Black Adder, reached out to him telepathically from its sheath: "The carofex lives, and we should leave this town. It has become unsafe."

Ronnis agreed with the sword; the sooner they reached Mecca-Loraine, the better life would be. With the visit from the vampire a few weeks earlier, followed by the disappearance of Kessi, and now a king from a foreign land coming to claim the body of Cassandra's surrogate mother, things were getting out of control. It wouldn't take long for someone to start pointing fingers at him, like the fool Buster. He sipped his drink and looked around the quiet room. He had called this place home for the last twenty years, but now it was time for him to go. He had preparations to make for Cassandra Rho.

~

Erik and Marcus had trained under Kringus personally and were two of the most prominent cavaliers of Pelesea. They had broken from the leading group and hastened toward the stables to fetch the squires and horses. None of the men from Oldorburg followed, and it took all their willpower not to turn back and fight beside their king. It went against all their training to leave a potential conflict, but they were following orders. They would soon be mounted on their excellent steeds and rushing back to their king, which kept them going forward to the stables. The guards didn't follow but instead focused their attention on Kringus and the others gathered at the gallows.

"We should be there now, swords ready to defend Kringus!" Erik shouted to his fellow knight.

"Agreed! Let us find Calvin and the other squires and make haste! I shall find comfort in holding my lance once again!" Marcus replied.

Both nodded eagerly and continued their trek toward the stables. They noticed that few townsfolk were about and even saw a few faces peering from the small shops that lined the stone street, watching in fear. The sight was unsettling and confirmed their suspicions that something was amiss in the wicked town. They finally reached the stables to find it deserted of people and livestock, including the squires and horses. They looked at each other knowingly and drew their swords. That's when they heard laughter coming from behind the stables. They quickly made their way toward the sound, their hearts heavy at what they might find.

They found an odd man standing beside a pile of weapons and armor—those of their squires. Then they saw the four squires—their assistants in battle and personal friends—each bound to a support pole of the stables. Each man's hands were tied behind him, a rope drawn tight around his neck, holding his head in place. One of the squires was foaming at the mouth, his eyes rolled back in his head, gurgling sounds escaping his parched lips. The other three shared the same blank and horrific expression; their eyes were wide and lifeless. They were already dead.

"Morris!" Erik yelled, his eyes wide in disbelief. Morris was Erik's squire and, more important, a good friend. The cavalier-squire relationship in Pelesea was more profound than most, with the men becoming the best of friends, the cavaliers knowing that their lives depended on the squires in times of battle. Morris had spent many nights at Erik's home as a guest of honor after a perfect performance on the battlefield or just because their friendship ran that deep. Now Erik's heart ached at the sight of his friend dying. The crazed man had poisoned him, and there was probably nothing he could do to save him. The other squires had already met that fate.

The strange man, noticing the arrival of the two warriors, laughed even louder. He was dressed only in a dark robe and wore a heavy necklace around his neck, depicting a holy symbol in the shape of a broken halo. He held a bottle of dark liquid in one hand and carried a whip rolled up on his belt.

"Priest! Use caution!" Marcus said to his friend.

The two cavaliers moved to flank the man, who took a large quaff of the dark liquid and said, "They were not worthy! Meshlor rejects the interlopers from Pelesea!" pointing to the squires, including Morris's convulsing form.

"Cut them down, Erik! I'll take care of this fool!" Marcus said, rushing in at the strange man, sword high and ready to strike.

A volley of crossbow bolts, fired from the shadows of the stables, assaulted him before he ever reached the crazed priest. As the bolts engulfed him, he lost sight of his target but could hear his hysterical laughter grow all the louder.

~

"Kringus of Pelesea! You are sorely outnumbered here!" Buster called from behind the line of guardsmen as they approached the gallows. "I have archers on the roofs, and they are awaiting my command. And, unfortunately, we cannot allow you to take the bodies of these criminals."

Kringus stepped up to Lenore and whispered, "Move the bodies under the gallows, and you and Von focus on the archers. Give us some cover."

Having heard the command, Lenore nodded, and Von was already moving Sera's body gently under the gallows platform. Lenore quickly followed, doing the same for Quinn.

"Spread out, warriors of Pelesea, and follow my lead!" Kringus said to the other men who stood beside him.

They quickly moved into position, with Franklin and Jimmon, the fearless cavaliers, moving to each end of the line. Arrin stayed closest to Kringus, and when everyone was in position, they formed a line with about twenty yards separating each man. Franklin was to Kringus's left and Arrin on his right, with Jimmon at Arrin's right.

Kringus pulled his sword, and the guardsmen stopped their approach. The other three men pulled their swords, ready to die for their king. They were about twenty-five yards from the line of guardsmen, who shifted uncomfortably but didn't draw their swords. The archers on the building tops had their crossbows nervously at the ready. Von readied his bow, drawing a bead on the first archer on the building to the group's left. Lenore did the same to the first archer on the building to the right. No one moved, and the only sound was the whistling of the wind. Buster and Max whispered back and forth, and although none of the allies could hear what was said, Buster became more agitated as the seconds passed.

Kringus finally spoke. "Guild master, and interim leader of Oldorburg, I ask that you choose your next actions carefully. What you do next could provoke a war between our two communities. Therefore, I *am* taking these bodies. If anyone decides to stand in my way, it will be considered an act of war against Pelesea!"

Buster tried to speak over the wind, but his voice cracked, showing Kringus that his heart wasn't really in this conflict. He cleared his throat and began again, stepping up in front of the guardsmen. "You are right, king of Pelesea. What I do next affects so many." He looked around at the young guards, who wanted no part in this conflict, as well as the nervous archers on the roof.

"I do not want a war with your fair city," he said, "but you have to understand what is at stake for us here. We follow our laws, and if those laws are not fair, we will change them. For now, though, we will enforce them."

Kringus made no move and didn't respond. Instead, he glared at the struggling leader, understanding that he was not an evil man but a spineless one who carried out the temple's commands and possibly those of the other guild members.

Buster said, "Of course, I must also demand that you return Cassandra and Kessi Rho to us for the same reason. They have broken our laws, and we must try them accordingly."

"Silence, you worm!" Kringus finally yelled, the veins of his muscular neck protruding, the rage showing on his face. "You speak of laws and justice, but you know they are wrong! You know that what you have done here to these two people is wrong and that the Rho girls will receive the same treatment, if not worse! How many innocent people will die before you change the laws of this godforsaken town?"

Buster shook his head and ran his fingers through his hair, soaked from the amount of snow accumulated there. "You have to understand: I have no choice," he whispered to Kringus.

"We all have choices, guild master," Kringus said.

"Please … I have a family," Buster said, nearing tears once more.

There was suddenly a sharp cracking sound in the air, and something struck Buster. He screamed and fell to his knees, his hands covering his face. A figure appeared beside him then, an older man dressed in priestly robes, carrying a scourge in one hand and wearing a smirk on his face. Buster moved his hands from his face, and blood covered them; five long streaks of red now adorned his shocked face. He tried to ask why, but his mouth couldn't form the words. The fresh wounds quickly began to bubble with pus, and Buster's face contorted into a desperate scream. But instead of words, a gurgling sound escaped his mouth, and he fell back in the snow, holding his throat and thrashing in the throes of death.

"I always said that if you want to do something correctly, do it yourself," the old priest said with a smile.

Kringus took a step toward him, but the priest raised his hand to signal the archers, a crazed look in his eyes. "And now you will face the wrath of Meshlor for your foolish actions, king of Pelesea! For I am Barktuck Misol, high priest of Meshlor and your executioner!"

Kringus's attention was diverted from the priest to Buster's dying form, now rolling and gagging in the snow, foam forming at his mouth. Max, the lead guardsman, knelt by him, trying to comfort the man, but soon stood in defeat, understanding him beyond help. It registered briefly in Kringus's mind that the death of the guild master was something the young guardsman accepted as if it were commonplace. He realized then just how dangerous and evil the priests of this small town indeed were.

"Fire!" Barktuck screamed, quickly lowering his arm to signal to the archers.

Soon, Kringus and the warriors from Pelesea found themselves blanketed in a volley of crossbow bolts, similar to what Erik and Marcus had encountered at the stables just moments before.

~

Erik lost sight of his fellow cavalier as he had to dodge the bolts flying from the stables in a killing wave. He heard the bolts hit Marcus's armor, ringing out in the night air, and listened to his friend grunt with the impact, indicating that some bolts had found their mark.

"Noooo!" he screamed in frustration, knowing that his friend would probably die because of the sneak attack. So instead of assisting the dying squire, he diverted his course and crashed through the stable's door. There he found four archers attempting to reload their crossbows. They looked up at once as he stumbled over the breaking boards of the door. "Cowards," he whispered and moved in, sword at the ready.

Marcus couldn't hope to dodge the bolts as they washed over him, so he didn't try. Instead, he raised his shield to protect his face and let his fine armor block the rest. Two bolts bounced off the thick armor, but two found creases, sticking him hard in his right hip and left knee. The extra padding probably saved his life as the one in his hip didn't dig in too deep. However, the one in his knee shattered his kneecap and brought him to his knees. He dropped his shield and planted his hands in the snow as the pain washed over him.

He vaguely heard Erik entering the stables and confronting the attackers, and he hoped that his friend could distract the crossbowmen because he was completely vulnerable. Then he noticed the strange priest, chanting and casting some kind of spell. He had placed the vial of liquid gently in the snow and was now waving his fingers menacingly his way. Marcus could feel waves of energy wash over him as the spell reached fruition. He sat up simultaneously, trying to prepare himself for whatever witchcraft the priest was throwing at him. Finally, he sat back on his haunches, his knee screaming in pain.

The waves intensified, and all his muscles tensed in unison as if they would no longer follow his command. He recognized the spell for what it was and quickly fought it off, having trained to defend against such paralyzing magics. He held perfectly still, though, wanting to bait the vile man to come close enough to strike. Unfortunately, he was wounded and would not do well fighting someone who could attack him from a distance with spells.

The wild man looked at him, eyes wide, believing that the spell had worked and that his prey was now helpless. Marcus remained perfectly still, and a smile grew on the strange priest's face, which slowly developed into hysterical laughter. He grabbed the bottle of poison, took another gulp from it, and danced around the wounded cavalier. He eventually came up and knelt in front of him. Marcus could smell alcohol on his breath in addition to whatever poison was in the bottle.

"And now we see if Meshlor accepts your life offering," he said, lifting the visor of Marcus's helm and raising the bottle to his mouth.

Before the priest could get the liquid anywhere near him, Marcus struck with the speed of a cat, taking his sword and plunging it deep into the evil man's belly. The wild priest's eyes widened even farther as the shock and pain sunk in. He tried to smile, but he couldn't quite summon the strength to do so. A look of confusion crossed his face as blood began to trickle from his mouth, and he dropped the vial of poison into the snow.

Marcus leaned in and said, "Your god's magic does not affect the righteous. Therefore I take your life in partial payment for the evil you have done here. May your god have mercy on your soul and accept you into whatever hell awaits you."

The priest slid off his sword and fell dead beside him, the snow turning bright red as blood pooled around him. Marcus fell back to alleviate the pressure on his wounded knee, which was now throbbing with pain. He could hear the battle taking place in the stables and wished to join his friend in combat. No more bolts came at him, so the cavalier took that as a sign that Erik was winning the fight. He took a deep breath and pulled the bolt from his side. He swooned at the pain, grimaced through it, took a deep breath, and reached for the one in his knee. That one would be much more difficult to extract.

Unable to assist his friend, Erik focused on the men in front of him instead. He noticed that the four were part of the town guard, recognizing some of them as those who'd greeted them when they'd first arrived. None seemed old enough to be true warriors, much less able to stand against a highly trained cavalier in combat. Nevertheless, Erik moved in swiftly toward the closest one, wanting to gain an advantage before they could reload their bows.

The young guard raised his crossbow in defense, and Erik's finely made broadsword sliced through it, destroying the weapon, then scored a deep cut across the man's forearm. He screamed out and retracted his arm, tucking it close to his side. Before he could recover enough to draw his sword, Erik swung hard with his shield, hitting the man square in the face. The young guard fell in a heap at Erik's feet. The cavalier paid no more attention to the wounded guard and turned to square off against the remaining three. Two of them had dropped their bows and now held swords; the third had taken a step back, still reloading his crossbow. The two with swords looked nervously at each other and didn't close in on the cavalier. The third quickly had another bolt loaded and leveled the weapon at Erik.

Erik straightened his pose and lowered the point of his sword. Then he raised the visor on his helm and said, "The three of you have acted evilly and without honor, and the king would imprison you for such cowardly deeds in Pelesea. But unfortunately I haven't the time to bring you to justice, and I offer you each the opportunity to surrender and repent your actions. However, if you proceed with your attack, I will be forced to defend myself, and I will do so to the best of my ability—that I promise. So what will it be?"

The three men stood their ground and looked nervously back and forth. Erik had little time for indecisiveness because his friends were in peril, so he took a small step forward. The man with the crossbow fired with an unsteady hand at Erik's first move. Erik partially deflected the bolt with his shield. It ricocheted into his breastplate, but the shield had slowed the bolt enough, and it bounced harmlessly aside.

Erik lowered his visor quickly and charged. The guard with the bow turned and fled while the other two tried to stand their ground, but their stance was unsteady at best, and their defense routine was uncoordinated and sloppy. Erik quickly pressed his attack against the one on his right while keeping the other one at bay with his shield. Then, with a quick spin of his sword, he dislodged the guard's sword and had it flying far to the other side of the stable. The man looked at him briefly, his eyes wide in horror, and then turned and fled.

Erik squared off against the remaining guard, who stood frozen in place, unsure of his next step. Erik helped him in his decision-making process by saying, "Flee, you coward, or taste the blade of righteousness!"

The guard turned and fled, following the path of his friends. Erik turned and made his way quickly back toward Marcus, only to find his friend lying on his back next to the priest, the snow surrounding them red with fresh blood.

"Marcus!" he yelled as he removed his helm and knelt beside his wounded friend.

Marcus waved him back and raised his visor. "Save Morris. I'm fine."

Erik, trained to trust his fellow cavaliers, gently patted Marcus's breastplate and ran off to the squires who remained tied to the stable posts. He approached his good friend Morris first. The man's eyes were wide open, and he stared up at the night sky. Foam continued to form at the corners of his mouth, but he was gone—no light left in his pain-filled eyes.

"I'm sorry, my dear friend," Erik whispered, his voice near breaking.

He then drew a knife and cut the rope that ran deeply across Morris's throat. Next, he severed the ropes that bound his hands and the thicker bindings wrapped around his chest. Finally, he caught the weight of his friend as Morris's lifeless body fell from his restraints. Erik gently lowered him to the cold ground and closed his eyes with a swipe of his fingers.

He wanted to break down and cry or even take out his frustrations on more guards. At the moment, though, he knew Kringus needed him. So he left his friend there in the snow with a heavy heart and similarly cut down the other squires. However, the dark task was interrupted by a commotion from the other end of town. It sounded like a battle had broken out, and Erik knew his time was limited.

Marcus sat up but couldn't stand. He knew that time was of the essence and called to Erik, "Go! Ride to the aid of our king—do not delay!"

"Where are the horses?" Erik asked, looking around for some sign that the steeds were not dead.

"I know where your horses are," a young man announced, moving from the shadows of the stables and into the light.

Erik drew his sword quickly and pointed it toward the boy. "Who are you?"

"I am Stephan, the stable boy. Your horses are near," he said, pointing to a large building across the street.

Erik quickly sheathed his sword and said, "Lead the way."

The young man nodded and turned to lead him to their steeds. All were found unharmed, and the two quickly gathered them, with Erik mounting his fearless warhorse and having Stephan free the others.

"Will they not run off?" the stable boy asked.

"No, they are well trained. They will follow my horse … all but that one," Erik said and pointed to another large warhorse.

"Surely that magnificent steed is trained!" Stephan exclaimed.

"Of course he is, but he's Marcus's horse. Please lead him to my injured friend and help him mount it."

"Yes. As you wish," Stephan said.

By the time they arrived back at the stables, the fighting at the other end of town had broken out in full, the clanging of metal and screams of agony echoing through the calm, snowy night. Marcus was now standing, stubbornly fighting away the waves of pain caused by the bolt still lodged in his knee. He whistled, and his steed broke away from Stephan and ran to him. Marcus somehow mounted his horse without assistance, grimacing away the excruciating pain.

"Let us ride, Erik. Our king needs us!" he said.

"No, my friend. You must leave the city with our dead comrades," Erik said, motioning for Stephan to take two of the riding horses.

"I will fight for my king, same as you!" Marcus said.

"No, you can't. Your task lies elsewhere," Erik said, pointing to his friend's knee, which was bleeding profusely, dripping blood in the snow.

Marcus understood his friend's logic but couldn't leave Kringus; it was against the knightly code that the cavaliers swore. He began to argue once more, but Erik raised a hand and shook his head.

"Take our friends a mile south of here and wait," Erik said. "Then, if we don't come within the hour, make haste home and inform the queen we have a new enemy."

Stephan managed to hoist one of the squires onto a horse and began moving the next one into place so he could do the same with it. He could drape two bodies over each of the riding horses.

The sight of their friends' lifeless forms was heartbreaking to both cavaliers, but there was work to do, and their mourning would have to wait.

"Thank you, Stephan. Pelesea owes you," Erik said as he guided his horse beside Marcus.

Marcus looked back in the direction of the battle as Erik joined him. The street was thick with falling snow, and they couldn't make out the battle, but they knew their king was there, on the far side of town.

"I should go to them," Marcus said.

"No," Erik replied defiantly, his stern visage leaving no room for discussion.

Marcus nodded. "You are correct, and I don't mean to doubt your wisdom, my friend. However, my sword is with my king; I shouldn't be running from a battle."

"You are not running but are simply doing your part. At this time, that means taking our dead friends out of this hellhole and awaiting our arrival. The next time, after we get you mended, you will be in battle again, beside Kringus. Don't doubt your worth in this."

Marcus stood still for a very long time, looking into the falling snow, knowing his king was just a few hundred yards away, possibly fighting for his life. It was the hardest thing for him to turn back to his friend, and it took all his willpower to do so. "Go then. Help Kringus. I will be waiting for you," the proud cavalier finally said.

Erik smiled, lowered his visor, and spurred his great steed into action, the remaining horses following. Marcus watched them go until they were out of sight, the heavy snow quickly swallowing them. After that, he just stared toward the town proper, listening to the battle and trying to focus on the task at hand. Finally, after some struggling, Stephan had the bodies draped over the two horses and gave Marcus the lead rope.

"Good luck, sir knight," the young man said and half bowed.

Marcus smiled briefly, nodded, turned his steed toward the town gate, and led the horses away as Stephan watched. Soon he was on the road to Mecca-Loraine carrying the bodies of their dear friends. He just hoped there wouldn't be more bodies by the time he reunited with his king.

~

More than two dozen crossbow bolts showered Kringus and his men from the rooftops. The bowmen flanked the group and had the perfect angle to rain their bolts from up high. So they quickly began to reload after the first volley, wanting to fire at least once more before the intruders joined in melee with the town's guards.

Kringus didn't try to dodge many of the bolts. He deflected one with his well-worn buckler but caught another one in his forearm that penetrated his chain mail and lodged deep in his arm. He grimaced away the pain and waded into battle. Arrin took the worst of the attack, with several bolts penetrating his chain mail as well. One drove deep into his left shoulder, and another buried itself into his right hip. He, too, growled away the pain and proceeded to close in on the ranks of guardsmen. Franklin and Jimmon fared much better with their armor deflecting any bolts that got past their shields. Von and Lenore took cover under the gallows and, after the initial wave, came out firing their bows, one at each group of bowmen.

Barktuck approached Max and said, "Capture the king; we can trade his life for the Rho girls. Kill the others."

Barktuck didn't wait for a response but started barking orders to the priests forming behind the guards' row. Max looked down at Buster's lifeless form and understood just how much the priests of Meshlor had a hold on the town. He watched Barktuck organize the attack that would soon come from the gathered priests. There were a dozen of them, and they spread out in a straight line behind the guards who were tentatively moving toward the invaders.

Max's men purposefully delayed their advance, allowing the archers another shot. Not nearly as many bolts rained down with the second volley, and very few came from the right flank at all. Von picked off the first bowman on the left to show himself, placing a well-timed arrow in the man's chest before he could fire. His second arrow missed the target, but it still foiled the attack as the bowman dodged the missile. On the other side, a man stood straight up, and Lenore picked him off immediately, noticing briefly before the arrow hit that the man wasn't even facing the street but was looking more to the roof behind him. A second man stood, then a third, but none fired from that side, as they all seemed to be preoccupied with a commotion coming from behind them. Lenore didn't have time to consider the good fortune and instead dropped another attacker with a second arrow.

With the second volley primarily ineffective and not scoring any hits, the guards of Oldorburg charged into battle, outnumbering their wounded foes three to one. Unprepared for Kringus's countercharge because his focus was on the priests, Max was caught off guard as the king attacked. He noticed the enraged king at the last moment and sidestepped a mighty swing. Two guards who rushed in to help defend the young captain saved his life, taking the full brunt of Kringus's wrath so that Max could draw his sword.

The brute force and precision of Kringus's strikes had the first man off-balance and driven to one knee. Kringus quickly smashed him in the face with his buckler, knocking the man backward and making him lose consciousness before he hit the ground. The second man would have been dead as Kringus slashed across with his massive sword, but Max had recovered and helped parry the attack by then, although the strike nearly dislodged his weapon.

Kringus was confident he could easily win this skirmish and then focus on the priests, who would be the biggest threat. As if on cue, he felt waves of energy roll over him as the priests unleashed their magic. He recognized the magic as one to slow and hold him. He knew if he fell to that spell, it would mean certain doom, so he fought through the waves, growling away the effects. Max and the remaining guard squared off with him, spreading out to flank him. He wanted to reach out to Max and convince him of the priests' evil ways but decided to let his sword speak for him.

Von and Lenore concentrated their attacks on the bowmen on the left roof, as no new attacks came from the right. They saw one bowman fall to his death from the right-side building, and whatever chaos was disrupting the bowmen, it made the elves' job less demanding, by allowing them to focus their attacks to the left. The archers proved no match for the elves and were soon overwhelmed and fleeing from the rooftop.

"Von, Lenore, the priests!" Kringus yelled over the melee.

They took up their bows once more and opened fire on the priests casting their spells.

Barktuck witnessed the failure of the paralyzing spells all the priests had cast in unison, and then he heard the galloping of many horses coming from behind him. He turned and could see a hazy form of one horseman through the snow, along with many riderless horses coming toward them. So he began casting one of his most potent spells, summoning a thick wall of vines with large razor-sharp thorns just in front of the horseman.

As he completed his casting, the rider ran headlong into the vines, unable to stop his momentum. He came through the barrier cut in many places, his horse gravely wounded. The cavalier managed to land on his feet as his horse fell to the ground. His armor was still intact but heavily damaged from the barrage, and the man was wounded and staggering. His horse snorted a few times, then lay very still. A smile widened across the old priest's face, but it didn't last long.

The swoosh of arrows and the thudding sound of them hitting a nearby priest had him turning to see one of his dear friends fall back into the snow with two arrows protruding from his chest. Barktuck turned to see the elves now focusing their attacks on the priests. He quickly glanced to the rooftops, saw no bowmen there, and understood that it was time to leave. He summoned the power of his magical ring to turn himself invisible once again, then quickly made his way toward the orphanage to hide. He stepped over his fallen friend and promptly left the battlefield.

Von and Lenore quickly picked off the priests with their bows, and the others seemed to have the melee in hand, having defeated most of the guardsmen by now. They witnessed the brutality of the wall of vines and saw a cavalier run headlong into that death trap. They looked at each other knowingly, understanding that the knight was seriously wounded. Then they noticed more activity from the rooftop to the right as a man wearing a robe stood precariously on the lip, holding one of the bowmen over the edge by his collar, his feet kicking in the air. The robed man dropped the bowmen to his death, then stood perfectly still, watching his victim fall. Lenore raised his bow to shoot, and the man just stood there, hood drawn, not moving. Lenore hesitated, not wanting to release the arrow until they knew more about the killer. It appeared as if the strange man may have interrupted the archers and saved the lives of his friends. Lenore watched as the man jumped, his robe flying behind him and slowing his descent. Von continued to pick off the priests with his bow, not noticing the hooded man, and the priests were now in full retreat.

"Von, Lenore, help Arrin!" Franklin yelled as he fought off two attackers.

Lenore turned toward Arrin to find him frozen in place and with a priest approaching him with a wicked scourge in hand. The man reared back to strike at him, and the whip dripped with poison. Arrin couldn't move, and Lenore could only watch as the attack came—he couldn't reach him in time.

Andre, the same priest who had impersonated Ronnis D'Breeth on that fateful night Cassandra had escaped Oldorburg, now stood alone against one of the elite warriors of Pelesea. He saw the open to attack and didn't hesitate. His scourge came back, and Arrin eyed him not with fear but with a knowing look that he would die. Andre was vaguely aware of the other priests falling dead all around him, picked off one at a time by the elven arrows. Nevertheless, he focused on his attack; for the glory of Meshlor, he was going to get his kill. Andre struck out at Arrin, the scourge ripping open his face and the poison quickly doing its work. He didn't feel the first arrow hit him in the chest just as his weapon ripped Arrin's cheek. Andre was driven back with the next two arrows, though, and he lost all strength in his arms, dropping his small whip.

He fell to his knees and looked down at his chest, three arrows protruding there. He looked back up at his target and smiled as he saw the telltale foam begin to form around Arrin's mouth. Andre would get his kill, and Meshlor would be pleased. As he died, he yelled for Barktuck, his mentor. Little did the young man know that Barktuck had already fled the battlefield, leaving his fellow priests there to die. Regardless, Andre died with a smile on his face, ready to meet Meshlor in the afterlife.

Kringus saw the attack on Arrin and used his anger to lead with his weapon, slashing hard against the two guardsmen, trying to reach the priests. Few matched his skill with a sword; even Max had little chance to defend against him. So Kringus used his strength to bat the captain's sword to the side, then hooked the other man's sword and dislodged his weapon with a flip of his wrist. Off-balance slightly from the move, the guard fell to one knee, where Kringus placed his sword at his throat.

Kringus turned to the captain and yelled, "Yield!" He watched as Max struggled with the decision. Then, finally, Kringus looked around and said, "Yield! This battle is over—take a look around you!"

Max did just that, realizing that many of his men lay dead or wounded all around him. The futility of continuing the conflict seemed to sink in then. He nodded to Kringus and sheathed his sword. "Yield, guardsmen of Oldorburg! Yield!" the young captain called.

Kringus did the same and assisted his opponent back to a standing position. Before the man could register the gesture, Kringus was gone, moving swiftly to his friend and the captain of his army. Arrin's paralysis ended before Kringus could reach him, and he fell to the ground beside the dead priest. He convulsed and foamed at the mouth, the potent poison doing its efficient work. Kringus reached him first, followed by Von and Lenore. The king knelt and cradled him in his arms, trying to comfort his dying friend.

"Arrin, I'm sorry! I'm here, my friend. Fight the poison!"

Arrin's eyes rolled into his head, and he gurgled something unintelligible. The deep cuts on his face from the attack now oozed pus.

His good friend was dying, and the king was helpless to stop it. He looked up, misty eyed, and now Franklin and Jimmon stood on either side of him. Max and some of his men had begun to gather as well.

"The priests use a strong poison; he hasn't much time," Max said.

"Do they have an antidote?" Kringus asked, nodding toward the dead priest.

Lenore knelt and quickly checked the body. He soon stood and slowly shook his head. Kringus looked down at his friend, blood now joining the foam at the corners of Arrin's mouth. Frustration and anger mounted inside the king. He was responsible for his men, and he never expected to lose one in a small town like this, especially not a dear friend and fellow member of the New Order.

"Can no one help him?" he yelled out in frustration.

"I can," came a calm reply from behind Lenore.

Everyone turned to see a robed man, his hood drawn so that only his mouth and chin were visible. In his hand, he held a small vial between his thumb and forefinger for all to see. Lenore recognized him immediately as the man from the roof who had assisted in the skirmish.

"Antidote," he proclaimed and tossed the vial to Kringus, who caught it and looked at him doubtfully for a moment.

"This man assisted us with the bowmen during the battle," Lenore said.

That was all the confirmation Kringus needed to trust in the stranger. He pulled the stopper off with his teeth and quickly poured the liquid down the throat of his friend, who involuntarily swallowed. They all watched and waited for what seemed like many minutes. Finally, Arrin slipped into unconsciousness, his breathing shallow but unlabored. His body was untensed, and he seemed to no longer be in pain. Kringus gently laid him down on the ground, and Lenore removed his cape and covered him.

Kringus now stood and faced the mysterious man who had offered the antidote. "We are in your debt, stranger."

The man slowly nodded once but didn't offer a reply.

"Is he going to live?" came a question from behind Kringus.

Everyone turned to see Erik, with his visor raised, his face bloodied and bruised, his armor cut in many places, and blood dripping from those cuts, staining the pure white snow. Kringus understood then that the chivalrous code the cavaliers followed was the only thing keeping him up. The wounded knight limped over to where Arrin lay and gingerly knelt next to him but lost balance and fell onto his back.

Kringus was there by his side immediately. "Rest easy, my friend. The fight is over."

Erik nodded slightly and seemed to relax then, resting his head on the ground.

Kringus knew that the cavalier's wounds were severe, but he also knew Arrin was in much more danger. The magical vines disappeared then, seeming to sink back into the ground.

Kringus dealt with many emotions at that point, anger being at the top of the list. He saw the riderless horses approaching now that the vines were gone and knew their time was ending in this town. Yet he still couldn't believe they had suffered so much at the hands of the evil priests. He turned to Max, gritting his teeth. He pointed at the young man and said, "Blood now stains your hands, son. And if either of my other friends perish, this town will face retribution greater than anything you can imagine!"

Max looked at Arrin and Erik and knew the king was not exaggerating.

"Forgive me, my king, but there are currently seven bodies this wretched town must answer for," Erik added, his breathing labored.

"Explain," Kringus said, suddenly feeling very ill.

"The woman, the sheriff, the squires, and a horse. They killed my horse," he said, the pain of that fact evident in his cracking voice.

Kringus turned back to Max. "Seven bodies, and whether they were human or equine, I assure you they were friends to these men. This town will pay for these deaths, and I will be back—that I promise. How we exact punishment on this town will be based on what I find when I return."

"I understand. We do not side with the priests of Meshlor," Max said, pointing a thumb to the surrounding men, who nodded.

"Then now is the time to strike! Go to the temple and flush out the rest of this disease! End the evil of Oldorburg once and for all. They have used some of their powers this evening; they are vulnerable," Kringus said.

"Will you assist us?" Max asked.

Kringus took a step toward the man, gritting his teeth once more. "No, I will not risk losing more men in this town. This town is your home, and this is surely your problem. The day I return and find any of the godforsaken priests still here, I will raze every building, and Oldorburg will be nothing but a pockmark on the land!"

Max nodded and began organizing his men. Kringus gently eased Arrin on his horse's front; Jimmon offered his horse to Erik, who somehow managed to mount it, ready for the road. The elves and cavaliers climbed onto the rest of the steeds as Max offered the party a fresh horse to replace the one they had lost.

Kringus looked at the robed man, who still stood motionless where he had first appeared. He brought his horse up to him and said, "We ride to Mecca-Loraine, stranger. Before I go, I would like to know to whom we are indebted. What is your name, and why did you help us?"

The man looked up and lowered his hood, revealing his shaved head. "I am Boz of the Brotherhood of Fire, a monastery of Mecca-Lorraine."

"Convenient," the king replied.

The carofex nodded and added, "I am here visiting, arriving this very night. The carofex from Mecca-Loraine travel here often to gain knowledge of the goings-on of their neighbors. I am also hopelessly linked to the Cassandra Rho legacy."

The mention of Cassandra's name held Kringus's attention as he tried to extract the bolt from his forearm. He was in excruciating pain now that the adrenaline was slowing down a bit, and he felt the vicious wound immensely. "Ironically, I think I need a priest," he said, staring at Andre's corpse. "So, Boz from Mecca-Loraine, how are you linked to Cassandra Rho?"

"My brothers and sisters of the temple sent me here to collect data on the girl, to see if the tale of the ravens is true. But, to my dismay, I just found out that she no longer resides here, so my mission is at an end."

"There are other priests—good priests who can heal you and your men," Max said, interrupting their conversation.

Kringus turned to face the man and the twenty gathered guardsmen. The young men had been collecting their dead and wounded, and a few goodly priests were healing those who might live.

Kringus nodded and said, "We are leaving before the priests of Meshlor return. As long as they and the fiend Ronnis D'Breeth are in this town, it is not safe for anyone. Tell the goodly priests we will pay them to administer healing now."

Max nodded and went to relay the message. Kringus turned to find Boz standing next to his horse. Slightly startled, the vigilant king made a mental note of how easily the man had approached him without a sound.

Boz held up his hands in response and said, "I am a carofex and know much about the human anatomy. Therefore I can help you extract the bolt in a way that will cause you less pain and not tear more tissue in the process. Moreover, I can do this much more proficiently than those priests."

Kringus looked over at Lenore, sitting on his horse, and the elf nodded. Kringus then nodded for Boz to proceed, holding out his torn arm.

"Put your arm in the same position it was in when the wound occurred," Boz said.

Kringus tried to do precisely that. Boz took the man's arm and felt around the wound. He adjusted the angle a couple of times until he thought he had it where it should be to lessen the pain upon removal.

"This may hurt just a—" Boz began but then jerked the bolt out of the arm with one swift move before he finished.

Kringus grimaced from the intense pain, but it only lasted for a moment. Then blood poured from the wound, and Boz stepped back.

"Now you are ready for the priests," the young carofex said.

The priests enacted powerful healing spells on Kringus, Arrin, and Erik, enough so that they could ride to Mecca-Loraine. Arrin did not awaken, but his breathing became steadier, so Kringus was satisfied that they could now travel.

"I would like to learn more about you, Boz, especially how you fit in all of this with Cassandra Rho. Also, we could use a guide to Mecca-Loraine. Care to join our little band?" Kringus said.

Boz walked over to the horse that carried Sera's body and stroked her hair. "This is the real reason I am here, to study the girl and her family. I will see to it that this woman's body finds a proper resting place. So I will accept your offer to mutual satisfaction, I am sure."

Kringus turned to Max. "One more horse for our new ally, then?"

"Of course." The captain motioned for one of his men to gather another steed and then turned back to the king. "I wish you the best of luck, Kringus of Pelesea, and I apologize for your treatment by the priests. This turn of events has opened my eyes to the betrayal of the temple, and I assure you we will eradicate the vermin this very night!"

"You are taking the right steps, young captain. Accomplish this feat and proclaim yourself the new sheriff. The people will follow you; they need a leader," Kringus said.

Max looked around at the gathered townsfolk, who had ventured out from hiding now that the fighting had stopped. They assisted the priests with the wounded men, but none of them approached the fallen priests of Meshlor. Max could easily do what Kringus had just suggested; the townsfolk would support him. Kringus knew that the young guard would see it through.

"Until we meet again, king of Pelesea," Max said, offering his hand.

Kringus clasped it and nodded. "I assure you we will meet again. Good luck this night. May victory be yours."

With that, Max and his men left to invade the temple of Meshlor. Kringus and his men exited the town while the fighting broke out there, meeting Marcus at the designated area a mile out of town. After breaking the sad news of the injuries to Arrin and Erik and the death of one steed, the party made haste toward Mecca-Loraine. However, their new ally and guide, Boz, quickly had them turning toward a small farming village only five miles south of Oldorburg. There, he promised, they would find food, rest, and medicine until the weather cleared. Kringus agreed to Boz's suggestion. He looked forward to learning more of this new ally they had conveniently found.

A few hours after Kringus and his men had left Oldorburg, Ronnis D'Breeth and Barktuck Misol sneaked out of the town unseen. The fighting in the temple of Meshlor had served as a distraction, and they set their sights on Mecca-Loraine. But they were unaware that the troupe from Pelesea was heading in that same direction.

Epilogue

Six days after the battle at Oldorburg, Ronnis sat in an oversized chair in Barktuck's quarters inside the significant stronghold on Mecca-Loraine's southern side. The place housed priests and other high-profile officials of the port town. He swirled his brandy absently in his glass, his thoughts not on the moment at hand.

Barktuck opened a bottle of the best wine the stronghold had to offer. He had far better bottles in his stash in Oldorburg, but there hadn't been time to gather them in their rush to flee the town. The drink was tolerable and he poured himself a healthy glass of it while sniffing the cork. Ronnis paid no attention to his friend, his mind centered only on Cassandra.

Barktuck put the cork on the counter and made his way to stand in front of Ronnis. "To new endeavors," he said, raising his glass in a toast.

That broke Ronnis's thoughts, and he shifted his eyes to meet Barktuck's. The priest smiled and raised his glass, and then he motioned for Ronnis to follow suit when he didn't return the toast. Ronnis sighed and half-heartedly toasted with his friend. He then downed the entire glass in one gulp.

Barktuck gulped down a healthy portion of his glass as well, then moved to the bottle to refresh it. "You know, we will do well here, my friend. The temple has set us up nicely, and we will enjoy the greatest comforts the town has to offer."

"We?" Ronnis asked, sitting up in the chair.

"Yes, we are a team—"

Ronnis threw his glass against the wall. "You have been given another chance at life!"

Barktuck tried to calm his friend, but Ronnis put his hand in the air when he tried to speak, cutting him short. "I have nothing now! I lost my position of power at the orphanage—which was quite lucrative, I might add—as well as the most beautiful lover I have ever known, and had to flee my home, leaving all my possessions behind! I'm like a newborn babe, with no wealth and no stature."

Ronnis sat back in the chair once more, then put his hand to the hole in his face. "That brat took everything from me, including my looks," he whispered, and Barktuck nodded solemnly.

"The carofex will find her, and she will soon be in your possession once more," the priest said.

Ronnis licked his lips and thought of all the delicious things he would do to Cassandra once she was back in his grasp. Finally, after several moments of silence, a tear rolled down his cheek, and he turned his gaze once more to meet his friend's. "I will have my revenge … That I promise you, Barktuck."

"I do not doubt your words, Ronnis, and I will do everything I can to make sure it happens. After all, she turned my world upside down as well. I have lost much because of that spoiled brat!"

Ronnis sat back and smiled at the thought of it while Barktuck fixed him a new glass of brandy. Barktuck then proposed the same toast, and Ronnis eagerly drank to it, seeming to feel much better about things. Next, he focused on all the vile things he intended to do to Cassandra Rho, which made him feel very content.

~

Kringus watched as the local healer of Farmer's Stop, a small farming community just south of Oldorburg, applied the healing salve to the cloth and placed it on Arrin's forehead. They were in a small home belonging to a kind and elderly couple named Quentin and Ella, where Arrin remained unconscious. His fever had spiked, and the old healer had done everything to bring it down.

He rose from his work and looked at Kringus. "Mighty powerful poison in this one. Might be that he doesn't make it through the night, especially if he can't shake this fever."

Von and Lenore flanked their king, who nodded his gratitude to the older man. "I appreciate your efforts, and I'm sure you're doing everything you can to help him," Kringus said.

"Yup, the next thing might be a dip in the ice if the salve doesn't help."

Kringus nodded grimly as the man shook hands with Quentin and Ella and said his goodbyes. The couple engaged in some small talk with the healer as he gathered his instruments and potions. Kringus tuned them out and walked over to the bed where his dear friend and the captain of Pelesea's army fought for his life. Kringus had lost four men already, and although Erik was on the mend, it would be many days before the knight would be fit to travel. He knew he would have to leave the small community long before that to find proper healing—he couldn't let Arrin die.

He couldn't help but wonder what Arrin's fate might have been had their strange new carofex ally not shown up with an antidote. There was no doubt in his mind that Boz had saved Arrin from certain death, and had given him a chance to live. He was indebted to the carofex, especially if Arrin pulled through this.

As if reading his thoughts, Lenore said, "Kringus, you must see this."

Kringus turned to find Von and Lenore flanking the one window in the room. Lenore motioned with his head for him to look outside. Puzzled, he made his way over to the elven brothers and peered out into the falling snow. The king saw Boz, shoeless and naked from the waist up, standing perfectly still in the falling snow. He had his eyes closed, and he grasped his forearms horizontally, elbows out. His right foot rested comfortably on his left knee, creating a four shape with his legs. He meditated, but that wasn't what the three friends found unusual about the scene.

As the snow fell in large flakes, blanketing the world outside, not one bit touched the carofex, and a ring of grass and mud circled him as the snow quickly melted in his immediate vicinity. They could see the falling snow melting in the air before it even touched him, hissing in protest. Kringus shared a concerned look with the elves. Their new ally was mysterious indeed.

~

Binta awakened with a start and immediately felt the pain rack her side. She grimaced as her hand instinctively went to the area where Jabell had kicked her. She was sore and now wore a tight bandage around her midsection. She looked around the room, at the tapestries, religious tomes, and holy symbols decorating the place, and understood she was in the temple.

There was a wide window in the small room, but the curtains were pulled, dimming the light that trickled in. There was a chair near the window, where Greyson Kavince was fast asleep. That made her try to sit up all the more and look presentable. After all, they had made love the night before Cassandra's conflict with Cass. Greyson was an excellent lover, and he had spared nothing during that encounter—the two had an immediate sexual chemistry. She chewed her lower lip and watched him sleep, lost in thought. She sat up but quickly discovered that was an unwise move as her ribs screamed at her. She yelled and froze, grimacing away the pain. When she opened her eyes, Greyson was there, helping her into a sitting position against the headboard. Once she was comfortable, he sat on the edge of her small bed and rubbed his sleepy eyes.

"How do you feel?" he asked.

"Terrible."

They shared a laugh, and he looked lovingly at her, reaching a hand up and tucking her hair behind her ear. She locked eyes with him, falling into his gaze as he leaned in and gently kissed her forehead. He pulled back with a warm smile and said, "You have a few broken ribs—nothing major. A day in bed and a little more healing is all that you require."

Binta smiled. "That's good news, but I'm not concerned with myself. How is Cassandra?"

Greyson stood and said, "Baxter, the school instructor who brought you and Cassandra to the temple, just visited you not more than an hour ago. He had just come from her room and informed me that she is sleeping soundly."

"So she'll be fine? Is she hurt?" Binta asked, more than a bit of panic in her voice.

Greyson gave her a knowing look and smiled lewdly. "According to the instructor, she is fine and will recover fully. He also said that the priestess attending her was amazed that her wounds weren't more serious. She seems to have come away from this conflict with very few injuries."

"That's good. I want to see her!"

Greyson sat back down on her bed, shaking his head. "I'm a priest—remember? Unfortunately you aren't strong enough to walk right now. Perhaps tomorrow or the next day. In the meantime, tell me about your relationship with Cassandra Rho."

"We're friends—"

"No. Tell me your true feelings for her."

"There's not much to tell," she said and swallowed hard.

"Yes, there is, and we have all the time in the world to talk about it." He moved in and kissed her lightly on the lips.

Her resistance melted away, and she kissed him back. They spent the rest of the evening and most of the night discussing Cassandra Rho.